GOLDEN GIRLS ON THE RUN

JUDY LEIGH

Boldwood

First published in Great Britain in 2025 by Boldwood Books Ltd.

Cover Design by JD Smith Design Ltd

Cover Images: Shutterstock

Interior Images: Boldwood Books

A CIP catalogue record for this book is available from the British Library.

Paperback ISBN 978-1-78513-261-2

Large Print ISBN 978-1-78513-262-9

Hardback ISBN 978-1-78513-260-5

Trade Paperback ISBN 978-1-80656-130-8

Ebook ISBN 978-1-78513-263-6

Kindle ISBN 978-1-78513-264-3

Audio CD ISBN 978-1-78513-255-1

MP3 CD ISBN 978-1-78513-256-8

Digital audio download ISBN 978-1-78513-258-2

This book is printed on certified sustainable paper. Boldwood Books is dedicated to putting sustainability at the heart of our business. For more information please visit https://www.boldwoodbooks.com/about-us/sustainability/

Boldwood Books Ltd, 23 Bowerdean Street, London, SW6 3TN

www.boldwoodbooks.com

For my own Mammy

In the cookies of life, friends are the chocolate chips.

— SALMAN RUSHDIE

NOTE FROM THE AUTHOR

Dear reader,

If you've already read The Vintage Village Bake Off, *thank you.*

You'll have met Robert Parkin and his sisters, Hattie and Bunty, who live in Millbrook and Ballycotton, fictitious towns in Devon and Ireland respectively. Robert is, you'll remember, a talented and much-admired baker. Hattie has recently moved to Devon to live near him.

You'll soon meet Sadie, who is the mother of Sean, Bunty's husband. And Bronagh, who's the sister of Sadie's deceased husband, Alfie. They are both widows who live next door to each other in Ballycotton.

In the previous novel, Sean and Bunty have at last come to terms with the long-ago infant death of their only child, Daniel, and returned together to Ireland.

You'll meet two of Sadie's other grown children, Niall and Nora, and their spouses.

You'll also meet the wonderful Rory, Sadie's grandson.

(Sadly, you won't meet Bronagh's only daughter, Kathleen, who is a nun.)

I hope you'll enjoy the characters, old and new, and their journey.

Best wishes,

Judy x

The O'Connor and Parkin Family Tree

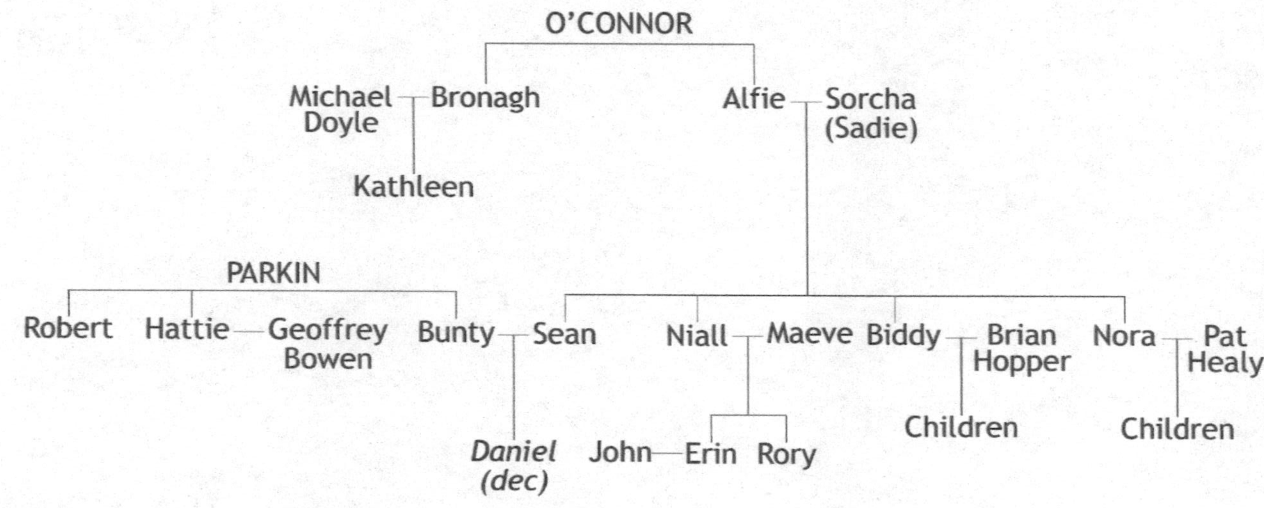

PROLOGUE

The pale morning sun streamed through the window. Robert Parkin was lying on the sofa in the conservatory, eyes closed, listening to Bach's *Goldberg Variations*. His cat, Isaac Mewton, was stretched across his chest, purring, with one eye open. The music rose and lilted, and Robert breathed out calmly. He was almost asleep when there was a knock at the front door.

Tressy's voice came from the kitchen. 'Can you get that, my lover? I'm just taking the key lime pie out of the freezer.'

Robert, long and lean and septuagenarian, blinked hard and sat up. He took a moment to remind himself that he was in his home in Devon, with his beloved Tressy, and they'd planned a trip to Cornwall to see some of Tressy's friends. They were leaving in an hour.

'Hattie?' he called out, then he remembered that his sister was in Oxfordshire. Her house had sold. She was collecting the last of her things and putting her piano into storage. She'd be back in a day or two.

The knock came again, a little more persistent.

'I'm coming,' Robert said, but in fact he was still standing in the conservatory listening to Bach. It was an effort, but he propelled himself forward through the hall, towards the door and tugged it open. A blast of cold winter air hit him in the face and he was suddenly wide awake.

'Hello, Angie.'

Angie Pollock was wearing a tightly belted coat and scarlet lipstick. Leather knee boots. She leaned seductively against the door jamb.

'Robert, I need your help badly,' she purred. 'I made a sponge cake and it didn't rise. I wondered if you could advise me.'

'Did you leave the oven open? Or overbake it?'

'I've no idea.' Angie fluttered her eyelashes. 'I really need one of your recipes.' She shivered dramatically. 'Can I come in?'

'Well, Tressy and I are off to Cornwall,' Robert said, not knowing whether to invite Angie in or not. She could be persistent. And she wouldn't want to leave until she'd tried his baked goods.

'When are you leaving? Are you staying there for Christmas?'

'No, we'll be back in Millbrook soon. You remember, I'm doing a talk on icing cakes in The Pig and Pickle.'

'So, why are you going to Cornwall?'

'Tressy's Cornish. We're catching up with some of her old friends. She used to run a teashop in Padstow and they've taken it over. They're New Agers, and Tressy's made them an avocado key lime pie.'

'Oh, I wouldn't like that.' Angie pulled an unimpressed face. 'But then I'm not Tressy, am I?'

Tressy appeared at the door, just beneath Robert's arm. 'Key lime pie's very nice with avocados. And a ginger biscuity base.' She beamed. 'Hello, Angie.'

'Hello, Tressy.' Angie's voice was less than enthusiastic. 'I need to see Robert. I need his help with my sponge. It wouldn't rise.'

'Well, I'm afraid I'm taking him away for a few days, maid, so you'll have to manage. But I'm sure he'll be able to help when we get back.' Tressy's grin broadened. 'And we'll see you in December's meeting in The Pig and Pickle.'

'Oh.' Angie looked disappointed. 'When exactly are you back from Cornwall?'

'We haven't decided. Next Thursday, maybe. We'll see how we get on.' Tressy tugged Robert's arm. 'We'd better get a move on.'

'Yes, yes.' Robert paused. Tressy's face always reminded him of an apple: round, sweet, beautiful. He couldn't help how she made him feel.

'So, who's looking after all the animals while you're away?' Angie wanted to make conversation, to stay as long as possible.

'Francis,' Robert said. 'It helps to have the vicar on side. And Eric said he'd look in on the chickens. And Colin. And Barry will pop in.'

'That's half the village,' Angie said.

Tressy pressed her arm kindly. 'When we're back, come round and I'll give you my recipe for Cornish Hevva Cake.'

'That doesn't sound very inviting.' Angie made an unimpressed face. 'I prefer Robert's fluffy sponge.'

There was a moment's uncomfortable silence.

'Well, we'd better get off.' Robert shifted his feet awkwardly.

'Right.' Angie didn't move.

Tressy gave her a smile. 'Then it'll be Christmas and we'll have a drinks party here. You're always welcome, Angie.'

'Oh. Thanks, Tressy.' Angie finally seemed ready to leave. She fluttered her fingers in the air. 'Have a lovely time, then, Robert.'

'I will,' Robert said.

He and Tressy stood in the hall and he closed the door with a clunk. Tressy gave a mischievous smile. 'Grab the cases, Robert – let's make a dash for it.'

'Why?' Robert looked confused.

'I just saw Susan Joyce coming down the road, marching with intent.' Tressy winked. 'She'll be wanting some jam for her scones. If she comes in, she'll stay for an hour.'

'Oh, my goodness, it never ends.' Robert let out a long breath. 'Yes, let's go to Cornwall.'

Tressy kissed his lips. 'I can't wait. Just me and you. Cornish pasties. Scones, done the right way, cream on top.'

'The cream goes on first.' Robert kissed her back. 'It's the only thing we disagree on.'

Tressy rolled her eyes. They'd been together such a short time, after last summer's bake off. But they'd never argued once. 'Only a few weeks to Christmas. We'll be busy when we get back.'

'Then let's enjoy these few days,' Robert was thinking of brisk early morning walks on Padstow beach, lingering over coffee at breakfast.

'Next year, we should go up to Bunty's,' Tressy said.

'I haven't been to Ireland in a long time.' Robert smiled. 'I bet they're having fun in Ballycotton, Bunty and Sean and their big family.'

'Then we should definitely go,' Tressy said. 'Mind you, I bet it's cold there this time of year.'

'It must be,' Robert said.

There was a thump on the door. Robert looked suddenly nervous. 'It's Susan. Can you talk to her?'

Tressy took his hand. 'We'll give her a pot of jam and have a quick tittle-tattle. Then you and me'll take ourselves off to Cornwall.' Tressy stood on tiptoe and brushed his lips lightly with hers. 'We both need a break, Robert.'

1

BALLYCOTTON, COUNTY CLARE, IRELAND

'It's Baltic this morning, Sadie.' A gravelly voice that belonged in a horror movie screeched from the other side of the fence.

'It's Baltic every morning in Ballycotton,' Sadie O'Connor said grimly as she pegged a pair of knickers on the line. She changed her mind. 'They'll be solid with frost within the hour. I'll put them on the rack in the bathroom. Fancy a cup of tea?'

'Let's have a quick half in The Hole in the Wall instead. Ryan'll have a roaring fire going, and it's not raining, which is unusual for a Saturday.' Bronagh Doyle poked her head above the wooden fence. She presented a happy face that wrinkled like a walnut. Her usually wild hair was a mixture of purple and natural silver, now pulled back in a knot, and she blinked through gold-rimmed glasses. 'So come on, Sadie – let's wet our whistles in The Hole.'

'Ah, you've talked me into it.' Sadie put her hands on her hips. She was taller than Bronagh, broader and two years older, but Bronagh had always been the bad influence. Sadie smiled, filled as ever with affection for her best friend and sister-in-law.

'If I stay here, I'll only feel sorry for myself. Let's get ourselves some mother's ruin.'

'I was ruined long ago,' Bronagh cackled. 'I'll meet you at the front door.'

Five minutes later, Sadie and Bronagh stood side by side in coats and headscarves at number eleven and number thirteen Kildare Avenue. They'd lived there all their married lives, since Sadie had married Bronagh's brother, Alfie, and Bronagh had married Michael Doyle. God rest them both.

Bronagh threaded an arm through Sadie's. 'Here we come – Ballycotton's answer to Thelma and Louise.'

'I hope not.' Sadie was appalled. 'Didn't they kill someone?'

'Well, Cagney and Lacey, then.'

'They were sleuths. I'm not getting into any trouble.'

'Well, French and Saunders.'

'Comediennes. That's us.' Sadie felt pleased. 'Good friends, up for a bit of craic.'

'And they're good-looking,' Bronagh added. 'I'll be Saunders.'

'All right.' Sadie paused, thinking. 'Wasn't the French one the vicar of somewhere?'

'I think so,' Bronagh said. 'She acts the maggot, doesn't she – always up for shenanigans? That's us. I was thinking – Ryan does stew and soda bread on a Saturday. Will we stop for lunch?'

'And make an afternoon of it?' Sadie said. 'Sean and Bunty might be in – Sean's always good for a round.'

'We can buy our own.'

'I know, but Niall loves to treat us. That's two drinks and a plate of stew.'

'Indeed – what's the point in having children if they don't treat you? I often regret that Michael and I only had the one child, and Kathleen's dedicated her life to the Lord, so she'll not be standing us lunch in the pub.' Bronagh hugged Sadie's arm against the wind. 'Ah, but we need something to keep the cold out.'

'The stew?'

'The drink.'

They turned the corner where The Hole in the Wall came into view, an old brick building with welcoming lights twinkling in the windows. Sadie pointed towards the cars in order to work out which of her children were in the pub. The car park always told a story. Sean's Peugeot 406 estate stood next to his brother Niall's Range Rover and Niall's son Rory's gleaming red Ferrari. Nora and Pat were too busy to drive down today, but the family would all catch up tomorrow for Sunday lunch. Biddy and Bryan were away with their sons in Tossa de Mar.

Sadie was delighted. Her heart expanded with love for her children every day. 'Sean's here.'

'Sean and Bunty are good as gold,' Bronagh agreed fondly. 'Niall will put his hand in his pocket too. He made money on the houses he bought and sold in Dublin, but family comes first, always. Rory's his da's boy – look at that fancy motor he's bought himself. He makes money hand over fist. He's a sweet young man though – no airs and graces on him.'

They approached the Ferrari, and Sadie paused to admire the gleaming paintwork. As ever, she was bursting with pride for her grandson. 'It's a babe magnet, this car. The whole family has a key to it in their pocket. Everyone likes Rory.'

'Especially the ladies. Rory should settle down.' Bronagh frowned. 'Is he still going out with that Aoife wan? The one with the short skirts and the false eyelashes?'

'I think they split up. She wanted a ring on her finger and Rory's only twenty-six He likes to play the field.' Sadie always felt protective where Rory was concerned. 'He's got a good heart though. I always say he's just like my Alfie. Handsome. And generous to a fault.'

'Alfie was one of the best.' Bronagh agreed. 'My Michael was a darling too. Except when he had a glass of port at Christmas.'

'That's the truth. It was never a good thing to let Michael near the port.' Sadie smiled as she remembered. Talking of the past always made her feel sentimental, a bit tearful. 'Remember the time he fell into the acrylic Christmas tree and almost knocked it into the fire?'

'And the time he drew a pair of glasses on the TV screen during Prime Minister's Question Time. Disrespectful.' Bronagh covered a smirk. 'But it was the drink. Michael and port should never have been in the same room. He was all right on the Guinness though.' She put a finger to the corner of her eye. 'Ten years, my Michael's been gone.'

'And a year later, I lost Alfie.' Sadie sighed as she pushed open the door to The Hole in the Wall, immediately exposing the pair to the heat from the log fire and the strong smell of beer. She visibly pulled herself together. 'Ah, well, will I get the first one in?'

'I'll have a half,' Bronagh began, but a man with pale curls beneath a squashy cap waved from the bar and called over to them.

'I'll get them, Mammy. How are you, Auntie Bronagh?'

'I'm grand, Sean,' the two women said together, settling themselves at a table, placing their handbags in front of them like shields.

A few moments later, a dark-haired woman plonked two half-pints in front of them. 'Here you are.'

'Thanks, Bunty.' Sadie reached for her drink. 'How are your family over in England?'

'They're well,' Bunty said. 'Sean's ordered you both the stew.'

'Ah, he's a good man,' Bronagh murmured, her mouth full of stout.

Sadie watched her daughter-in-law walk back to Sean at the bar and kiss his cheek. They spoke together quietly, their eyes locked. Bunty and Sean looked happier together than they had in a long while. The sight of them so close together now cheered her. 'The trip Sean and Bunty took to the Canaries did them good.'

'It'd do me good too,' Bronagh grunted, her lips to her glass.

'Their marriage wasn't quite right, not since little Danny.'

'That must be getting on for fifty years ago.' Bronagh made wide eyes. Time flew past. 'No, things took a big turn for the worse when she took off to Devon in the summer. I think she had a short fling with a plumber. Sean said he was an eejit. But it turned out all right, once Sean got there. They're all mad, the English.'

'Since Sean brought her back, they seem more settled. I like Bunty.' Sadie's eyes moved to the couple next to them: a tall man with pale curls and his wife, whose face held an expression of distaste. She said, 'I'm not so sure what's wrong with Niall's wife these days. She looks miserable, poor soul.'

'Perhaps Maeve needs more fun.'

'She's a good mammy to Erin and Rory. But Niall doesn't seem to notice her. He's always working – oh, look, there's Rory.'

'That's a smart suit he's got, Sadie.'

'And another new girlfriend – look at the big hair. And the sprayed-on trousers. But Rory's handsome.' Sadie couldn't look at him nowadays without seeing Alfie O'Connor.

'I don't suppose he's with her for the conversation.' Bronagh waved fingers and called, 'What's the story, Rory?'

A good-looking man walked across, wearing a smart suit and a pale shirt. He had a gold earring beneath a floss of dark curls, and a cheeky face. 'How are my favourite ladies? Gorgeous as ever.'

'Don't act the maggot.' Bronagh patted her purple hair, flushing pink from the flattery.

'You're looking good tonight,' Sadie said, lifting her glass, all interest. 'Who's the new squeeze?'

'She's called Lola, Grandmammy. We're here on a quick visit,' Rory said. 'I met her in Dublin two weeks ago. She's staying with me for the weekend but we popped over for the afternoon. She's a nice girl.'

'I bet she is.' Sadie raised an eyebrow.

'And she's staying at that luxury bachelor pad of yours?' Bronagh asked.

'She has a flat in Clondalkin with another girl, but my place is more central.'

'Does she do the cooking?' Sadie wanted to know.

'We order food in.'

'She doesn't look like she cooks – look at those fingernails.' Bronagh was unimpressed. 'Is she *the* one?'

'Ah, no, it's early days,' Rory said hesitantly.

'Lola's a fancy name.' Sadie was fishing for more information.

'It's not really Lola at all: it's Lorraine but she doesn't like it.' Rory glanced across the bar. 'Can I get you both drinks?'

'Why not?' Sadie looked at her half-full glass. 'You're not drinking and driving? I saw the car outside.'

'Ryan does a good NA lager. And the Guinness zero's not bad.'

'No alcohol, Rory?' Bronagh pulled a disapproving face. 'What's the point of it?'

'He's brought his car.' Sadie elbowed her gently. 'How's tricks at work?'

'Just grand.' Rory ran a casual hand through his curls. 'I'm back to Dublin later this week to sort out a few deals.'

'Does Lola work for you?' Sadie leaned forward.

'No, she's a model.'

'What does she model?' Bronagh was eyeing Lola across the bar. 'Is she one of those centrefold women who doesn't wear anything at all?'

'I've no idea.' Rory seemed completely oblivious. 'Will you have half a pint or a pint?'

'A half's grand,' Bronagh said. 'Besides, Sean's getting us stew.'

'Coming up.' Rory strolled back to the bar. Sadie watched, eyes narrowed, as Lola clung to his arm.

Ryan, the landlord, with pale red hair, brought a tray over, almost balancing it on his belly. The steaming dishes were filled with meat, gravy and chunky vegetables. Sadie closed her eyes, inhaled and said, 'It smells lovely.'

'Enjoy,' Ryan said. Bronagh patted his arm.

'We can't let you and the missus retire, Ryan. The Hole'd be nothing without your stew.'

'I'm glad you think so.' Ryan glanced at Sadie. 'Your boy has just been grumbling about my puddings.'

'Sean?'

'Niall. He said my sticky toffee pudding plays havoc with his fillings. And we only ever do sticky toffee.'

'I didn't know Niall had fillings,' Bronagh said. 'Doesn't he have all the implants?'

'Just a couple,' Sadie said. 'The ones at the front he knocked out that Christmas Eve.'

'Niall has a point, though,' Bronagh agreed. 'You should do a brownie with ice cream.'

'Or apple cake,' Sadie suggested. It had been one of Alfie's favourites.

'Or change the pudding every week,' Bronagh said.

Ryan scratched his head. 'It's only me and Emma here.'

'We were saying,' Sean called over from the bar, 'you should bake some of the cakes Bunty's brother makes.'

'So you want me to bake cakes as well?' Ryan was aghast. 'Sweets, puddings, cakes. They'd all go down a storm. But I've no time.'

'That's a shame.' Sean brought his half-pint from the bar, sat down and cradled it on his knee. 'How's your stew, Mammy?'

'Grand, thanks, Sean.'

'My brother could advise you.' Bunty plonked herself down next to Sean. 'Robert's an amazing baker.'

'It's made him a sex symbol in England, Ryan. I'm just saying.' Niall O'Connor sat on the other side of Sadie and Bronagh. His wife, Maeve, joined him, her leather jeans swishing.

'We don't have many sex symbols here,' she said pointedly.

Niall didn't seem to hear. 'Bunty's brother, Robert, was on the TV with his baking.'

Bunty agreed. 'They'd sell like hotcakes.'

'Something different from the usual might be nice,' Bronagh said.

'It would.' Maeve's expression showed that she wasn't talking about desserts.

'Alfie always loved my fruit cake.' Sadie felt the familiar pang of loss.

'I make Irish apple cake,' Bronagh said. 'Put custard on it and it's a pudding.'

'I loved the soda bread with chocolate in it, Mammy. Best thing I ever had,' Niall gushed and Maeve's face reddened.

'Maybe we could make biscuits?' Ryan was still loitering. 'We could do biscuits on a weekday, maybe.'

'Well.' Bunty beamed. 'Why don't we have a little mini bake off here, just for charity, for the fun of it? Like Robert did in Devon. You could pick the recipe you like best, Ryan. It wouldn't really matter if you made one here or not. It would be a blast. For charity.' She looked pleased with herself.

'Bake off?' Maeve looked disgusted. 'Whatever for?'

'Because everybody likes cakes and puddings,' Bunty said.

'An entry fee would raise money for charity.' Sean put his hand gently over Bunty's. 'The Lullaby Trust, for instance.'

'Oh, yes.' Bunty squeezed his fingers. 'Let's have it a week next Saturday and give the other half of the proceeds to the kiddies' Christmas presents fund in Ballycotton.'

'All right.' Ryan straightened. 'A week next Saturday it is. Shall I do posters?'

'Brilliant. We'll fill the bar with treats, and you and Emma can be judges, Ryan,' Niall said.

'I might pick someone else.' Ryan scratched his head. 'I've no sweet tooth at all.'

Niall seemed to notice Maeve. 'What will you bake, love?'

'Me?' Maeve looked shocked. 'I don't make cakes. Or puddings. I buy them from the shop.'

'Maeve runs a tidy home.' Sadie was acutely aware of her discomfort. 'And you're a great mammy, Maeve. You and Erin are so close. And Rory thinks the world of you.'

'Rory's the best son anyone could have.' Maeve's face clouded despite the compliment. 'But Erin's always travelling. I miss her.' She clutched her glass. 'They say a daughter is a friend for life, but Erin has the wanderlust. It's one holiday after the other.'

'Our Biddy's away too, in Spain. She's staying all through

December.' Sadie felt sorry for Maeve. 'I miss them when they're away.'

Maeve's face was sad. 'Niall's never home. Erin and Rory keep me sane.'

'Don't let it get you down.' Bronagh patted Maeve's knee. 'My Kathleen's with the Dominican Sisters at Siena Convent in Drogheda. She's been there for so long I've forgotten what she looks like.' She wiped a tear from her eye. 'Oh, well.' She took a swig from her glass and returned to the stew. 'You can't have everything. And I was named to be sad.'

'What do you mean?' Maeve said, horrified.

'Sadie's real name is Sorcha; it means bright and shining, whereas Bronagh is from the Irish Gaelic word *brón* meaning—' she skewered a piece of potato '—*sorrow*.'

Everyone was quiet for a moment, then Sean said, 'A mini bake off will cheer us all up.'

'A week next Saturday?' Bunty added.

'Can you invite your sex-symbol brother up?' Maeve asked hopefully. 'He could be judge.'

Bunty said, 'Robert has chickens and goats to look after.'

'Leave it to us, Ryan.' Niall clapped his hands. 'We'll run the first Hole in the Wall Bake Off, all proceeds to the kiddies' charities and The Lullaby Trust. We'll charge a tenner to enter.'

'You're on,' Ryan said. 'How many cakes and puddings do you think we can line up on the bar?'

'I'll bake something,' Rory said cheerily, a bottle of ale in one hand, the other holding an unimpressed Lola's. 'I'll chuck a donation in too.'

'I'll spread the word around Ballycotton,' Sean added.

'I'll bung something at the oven,' Bronagh promised.

'I might enter.' Maeve set her mouth determinedly. 'I'd love to show Niall that I'm not hopeless in the kitchen.'

'I'd take some convincing,' Niall joked and Maeve shot him an evil look.

'That's fab,' Bunty said. 'Cakes and puddings and money for charity.' She turned to Sean and kissed his cheek.

'I love a challenge.' Sadie winked in Bronagh's direction. 'So – what treats shall we serve up?'

2

It was half past seven, pitch dark already, one glimmering street light illuminating the two houses, number eleven and thirteen Kildare Avenue. Sadie and Bronagh emerged through their front doors at the same time, Sadie cradling an old biscuit tin as if it were a sleeping baby. She whispered as if she might wake it. 'I've made a Death by Chocolate cake.'

Bronagh, wrapped warmly in her headscarf and coat, said, 'I made a pineapple upside-down pudding.'

Sadie looked at her with surprise. 'Do you like those things?'

'No, they're disgusting, but I had a tin of pineapple rings in the larder and I thought I'd better use them up.'

'Rory's baked a polenta cake, whatever that is when it's at home. But it's grand he can bake.' Sadie felt herself puffed with pride as she tucked one arm through Bronagh's, the biscuit tin beneath the other. The air was chilly and she shivered. 'Bunty's made limoncello scones and Sean's made an egg custard, all from her brother's recipes.'

'Mine's rubbish.' Bronagh pushed forward into the raw wind and stared up at the star-filled sky. 'It's a cold one tonight.'

'Niall says Maeve's made something top secret, but it includes chocolate and Guinness. She thinks it'll impress him.'

'She won't.' Bronagh frowned as a gust of wind almost blew her headscarf off. 'Is Maeve showing off?'

'I think she's lonely.'

'It's because Niall doesn't make her feel like a sexy woman any more,' Bronagh said.

'You've been reading the romance books again.' Sadie grinned. 'Niall only thinks about work. And the horses, cars, a good whiskey and a day out fishing with the boys. Poor Maeve.'

'She has plenty of money but she lacks the attention of a good man. You and I were the complete opposite.' Bronagh was quiet for a moment. Sadie knew what she was thinking: she missed Michael badly. Alfie's death had left her devastated too. Thank goodness they still had each other. Bronagh continued, 'Ah, romance books take you to a place where you feel happy and bathed in the soft light of love, even if it's someone else's. I might lend Maeve a few books. It would cheer her up. I think she'd like *Sense and Sensuous* – or *Falling, Falling, Fallen*.'

'Are they saucy?' Sadie lowered her voice.

'Ah, they are, very saucy.'

'I'll borrow them first perhaps.' Sadie narrowed her eyes to stare at the car park ahead, where the fog had descended and lights glimmered like rising sulphur gas. 'The car park's full. There's a good turn-out.'

Bronagh was suddenly anxious. 'Do you think I made a mistake? Doing the pineapple upside-down cake?'

'No, it'll be grand. Anyway, if Bunty's baking her brother's prize-winning scones, we don't need to worry about a winner's speech.' Sadie winked. 'We'll just have a drink or two, scoff a few slices and go home.'

'Right.' Bronagh noticed the gleaming Ferrari. 'Look, Rory's here.'

Sadie hesitated outside the door, listening. There was a cacophony of voices inside, people cheering. Someone was playing a tune on a banjo, a bodhrán. She felt a moment of anxiety. 'That's the "Clare Jig." So Deirdre Quinn's here. There's bound to be trouble.'

'Deirdre's a great musician.'

'Oh, she is but—' Sadie lowered her voice as they walked inside the pub. The Hole was packed, heaving; there were cakes and desserts displayed on every surface. At the far end of the bar, a woman in a tangerine dress was playing the banjo, a man next to her beating a bodhrán. Sadie's mouth was close to Bronagh's ear. 'Deirdre was born on the seventh Monday after Easter, Whit Monday.'

'That's a fatal time,' Bronagh agreed. 'My mother used to say that if someone born on that day bumps into you, you'll never recover. Bad luck follows her around like a ghost.'

Sadie shivered as she stood clutching her tin, watching Deirdre play 'Skibbereen'. Her fingers were going nineteen to the dozen.

Bronagh said, 'She's keen tonight.'

'She is.' Sadie stared around the bar. 'But look at all the people. And all the puddings.'

'Will I put the upside-down pudding in a bin?' Bronagh asked nervously. 'There's a jam sponge, a trifle, a tiramisu and an Arctic roll melting all over the place. They make mine look rubbish.'

'No, it'll be fine.' Sadie tugged Bronagh towards the bar and yelled, 'Hello, Ryan. Hello, Emma.'

Emma Kennedy, a small woman with large glasses, didn't

look up from pulling pints. 'I put your stouts on the bar. Niall got them in.' She blew through her bottom lip and her fringe lifted on the puff of air. 'It's heaving in here tonight. And warm. My hot flushes are hell.'

'I remember the menopause,' Bronagh said with a shudder. 'You should go to bed and leave Ryan to it.'

'I wish,' Emma said apologetically. 'No, I'll battle through. That's what I do. Anyway, we're getting the cakes and puds judged early doors.'

Sadie was surprised. 'I thought you'd wait until last orders.'

'Deirdre Quinn's here,' Emma said to the filling glass. 'That's bad luck. Ryan and I thought the judging would happen early and then she'd go home with twenty pounds and a slice of cake for her troubles.' She began to fill another glass. 'I like Deirdre, but misfortune follows her...'

'Like a ghost.' Sadie and Bronagh shared a nervous look. They picked up their glasses. 'Thanks, Emma. *Sláinte.*'

Sadie squinted around short-sightedly; someone was waving to her across the bar. It was her daughter Nora, in head-to-toe denim, with her husband Pat, a smiling man, balding with a thin ponytail that extended beyond his shoulders. His face was round as the sun. Nora held up her hand and mimed a drink.

Sadie held up her full glass and winced; the noise was intense, people raising their voices over Deirdre's jangling banjo. Next to Nora, Sean was leaning on the bar, his arm around Bunty, and Rory was in deep discussion with Niall and Maeve while Lola looked bored. Sadie gripped Bronagh's arm.

'Let's join the others.'

As she pushed through the crowd, greeting everyone as she progressed slowly forward, she felt something hard crunching beneath her foot. As she took a step forward a short, square-shaped man in a heavy jacket yelped in pain. Sadie turned, horrified. 'I'm sorry, Partlan.'

'My corns!' Partlan Brown growled, his face red. 'I'm in agony.'

'It must be all the hours on the beat.' Sadie felt sorry for him. He never looked happy.

Partlan gazed at the biscuit tin. 'And I've been asked, as Ballycotton's guard, to be the judge tonight.'

'Your cake has no chance now, Sadie.' Bronagh pretended to look troubled. 'I don't suppose you're partial to pineapple puddings either, Partlan?'

'I thought Emma and Ryan were judging.' Sadie was puzzled.

'They're far too busy. No, they gave that job to me. And I have to say, Mrs Doyle, as I'm not open to bribery.'

'As if we would,' Bronagh said, mock horrified. 'But Sadie's done a lovely Death by Chocolate.'

'I'm not sure I like the name.' Partlan gazed towards Deirdre, who was playing. 'I think there's enough tempting fate tonight with Deirdre here.'

'She can't help her birthday,' Sadie retorted, always quick to take the side of someone who couldn't defend themselves. 'Anyway, it's not about winning, it's about charity. And I'm sorry about squashing your toes, Partlan. I'd leave the clumpy boots at home but it's so cold outside.' She gripped Bronagh's arm and tugged her away through the crowd. She was still worried about having injured a member of the gardai. 'I didn't mean to step on him. But he's always had it in for the O'Connors.'

Bronagh snorted. 'Forget him. Let's sup our stout and put our bakes on the end of the bar. Did you bring the recipe with your name on?'

'I did.' Sadie was gazing with admiration at the impressive

spread. 'Look at Rory's lemon polenta cake. That looks melt-in-the-mouth.'

'People have gone to so much trouble: meringues, Eton mess.' Bronagh was drooling. 'And I hear someone made a gin-and-tonic tart. I might help myself to a bit of that after Partlan's done judging.'

'But look at that one on the shiny blue plate – it's Maeve's.' Sadie was impressed. 'Fudgy Guinness chocolate cake with Irish buttercream. It's bound to win.'

Bronagh was amazed. 'It looks very professional.'

There was a loud family whoop and they were suddenly hugged on all sides. 'Hello, Mammy,' came from Sean and Nora.

'How are you doing, Auntie Bronagh?' from everyone.

'What's the story, Grandmammy?' from Rory, with a kiss.

Sadie and Bronagh beamed. 'We're fine.'

Niall kissed the top of Sadie's head. 'Are you ready for a refill, Mammy?'

Bunty took their tins. 'I'll put these on the bar.'

Maeve was preening like a peacock. 'Put them next to mine, Bunty. Don't you think my Guinness cake stands out?'

'You can just throw mine in the bin, Bunty,' Bronagh called mischievously. 'It's embarrassing.'

Pat wrapped an arm around her. 'I'll eat it, Auntie Bronagh. I love pineapple pudding.'

'So do I,' Nora agreed. 'Pat makes a lovely pina colada; we like those.'

'I like the look of your chocolate cake, Mammy,' Sean said loyally. 'It's bound to win. Or Bunty's scones.'

'My brother's recipe.' Bunty's voice was full of pride. 'Robert and Tressy love baking.'

'Is she the Cornish lady?' Nora asked.

'She is.' Sadie nodded. 'They met at the bake off last summer. The scones brought them together.'

'We should go to Cornwall, Rory,' Lola said loudly. 'How long would it take to drive there?'

'We might do it in a day or two.' Rory looked at Bunty for assurance. 'You can fly from Shannon in a few hours though.'

'You could take the ferry from Dublin to Holyhead and then drive,' Bunty said. 'Robert would put you up in Devon, I'm sure, and you could go on from there.'

'That sounds like heaven.' Bronagh hadn't had a holiday in years.

'It might be lovely, just the two of us,' Lola began, but Nora waved a finger to quieten her.

'Shh, now; the judging's starting.'

A bell rang and Sadie leaned forward excitedly. Ryan boomed from the other end of the bar. 'Thank you all for coming. We have fifty-three cakes and puddings that will now be judged by Partlan Brown, who has kindly offered to pick the winner.'

Partlan squeezed in between Sadie and Bronagh, and Bronagh whispered, 'Will you sample them all? You won't be able to budge afterwards.'

'I'll only try the ones that look nice,' Partlan said officiously. 'I can't eat fifty-three, so I'll sample ten. The eyes judge first, and if they pass the Partlan test, I'll try a small mouthful.'

The crowd closed in. Sadie felt a push in her back and when she turned, she saw the face of Deirdre Quinn.

'Sorry, it was my banjo bumped you,' Deirdre mumbled apologetically.

Partlan coughed, all self-important, and set about the process of judging, pointing to a certain cake, which Ryan passed across the bar dutifully. Partlan picked it up, peered at it and sniffed it.

'I wouldn't eat that now he's stuck his nose in it,' Bronagh commented loudly.

Partlan ignored her. The crowd was compressed, everyone leaning over each other for a better view. Bunty could be heard whispering, 'That's mine,' as Partlan lifted a cream-filled scone and took a bite.

'Very nice,' Partlan said, as if he knew everything about scones. 'Perfect texture and lightness.'

'Robert's recipe,' Sean said proudly. 'He's my brother-in-law.'

Partlan walked along the bar, sampling cake after cake after pudding while everyone watched tensely. He picked up a meringue and was helping himself to a creamy mouthful. 'Italian meringue – with buttercream, I think. Madagascan vanilla.'

Bronagh made a disapproving face: Partlan was making it up. He pushed the pineapple upside-down cake to one side as if it were offensive and reached for a slice of a rich, dark cake.

Maeve caught her breath. 'My fudgy Guinness chocolate cake with Irish buttercream.'

Partlan took a bite. 'Mmm. Mmm.' He rolled his eyes in ecstasy and took another bite. 'Heaven. A mouthful of magic.' He pushed another large spoonful into his mouth. 'I declare this one the winner.'

'I've won!' Maeve exclaimed with joy.

'He didn't even taste mine.' Sadie's face crumpled with disappointment. But she wasn't surprised.

'Or mine. Right. It's going in the bin.' Bronagh lifted up her pineapple pudding and dropped it in a wastepaper bin with a thud. 'It was rubbish anyway.'

She was about to turn away. 'Wait a minute.' Bronagh delved into the bin and snatched up a crumpled box indignantly. Her hands were covered with sticky bits of cake. 'Look. It says here,

"Doughty's Delights, Ballycotton". And look – there's the price. Twenty euros.'

'What is it?' Sadie asked.

'A ripped-up empty box. From Doughty's. It says "Chocolate Guinness cake. To be collected. Maeve O'Connor."' Bronagh raised her voice. 'Maeve's cheated.'

'I did not.' Maeve was furious, her cheeks red. Sadie immediately understood her embarrassment and felt sorry for her. She'd wanted to impress Niall.

'It's a bought cake, from Doughty's. They're the best in town. Jim Doughty's my cousin; he's a baker.' Deirdre's voice came from behind and she lurched towards the cake for a better look.

'Let me see that box.' Partlan threw an arm towards Bronagh. 'And give me the cake. Let's see if it fits.'

'Like Cinderella's shoe,' Sadie whispered, fascinated. The crowd leaned in as one to examine the battered box.

'Right. I've got it. Here you are.' Bronagh tried to pass it to Sadie to pass to Partlan, just as he was holding out the cake towards her to try it for size in the box. Sadie inserted the cake a bit too enthusiastically.

She wasn't sure what happened next: it was too quick, too confusing. Deirdre pushed the banjo hard against her arm. The crowd surged. Perhaps someone else knocked into her. She didn't know how, but the cake, squashed inside its box, was propelled from her grasp and flew upwards, out of control. Partlan must have moved forward at the wrong time. Sadie took a deep breath of shock as she saw his face plunge into the cake, and as it fell away there was a brown sticky mess stuck to him through which two eyes peered.

Bronagh extended a finger and took a creamy bit that hadn't touched his skin, shoving it into her mouth quickly. 'It tastes good.'

The crowd stepped back. Partlan faced Bronagh and Sadie, cake and all. 'You did that deliberately.'

'We did not,' Bronagh said hotly.

'You've assaulted a member of the gardai.'

'Well, we never meant to,' Sadie began.

Partlan was hopping mad. 'Assaulting an officer's a criminal offence.'

'Don't be silly, Partlan,' Bronagh said nervously.

'It was an accident,' Sadie interrupted, siding with Bronagh as she had done since they were children. It was second nature now.

Partlan blinked cake from his eyes. 'You're both as bad as each other, Sadie O'Connor.'

'Hang on a minute.' Sean's voice came from the bar. 'Mammy and Auntie Bronagh didn't mean anything by it.'

'It's a deliberate attempt to interfere with my judging, damaging the property of another competitor.' A piece of cake dripped from Partlan's nose. The crowd roared.

Someone called out, 'I'm liking the cakey make-up, Partlan. Is it pancake?'

'Ha ha, shut your cakehole, Partlan,' someone else guffawed. A chorus of insults followed.

'That's the icing on the cake.'

'Feeling crummy, Partlan?'

'I heard of taking the biscuit, but Partlan took the whole cake.'

'Right, that's enough.' Partlan was furious now. He wiped his face with his fingers, revealing glowing cheeks. 'Someone will have to pay for this.'

'And it was twenty euros, that cake,' Bronagh said with a grin. She grabbed Sadie's hand and whispered, 'We should run for it.'

Sadie looked around, her heart bumping with alarm. She

was reminded of Bronagh's playground japes years ago and the trouble that always followed her around. Sadie had always got in trouble too, defending her. 'What?'

'Run – come on.' Bronagh clutched her friend's arm and they scuttled through the crowd, out of the door into the cold, damp air of the car park.

Bronagh pointed to the Ferrari. 'Let's get going.'

'What?' Sadie felt her heartbeat pound even more. She had the horrible feeling that Bronagh was going to do something she shouldn't. Again.

'I have one of Rory's keys in my handbag.'

'What?' Sadie repeated.

'We'll run for it.'

'In the car?'

'Just for a few hours.' Bronagh put her hands on her hips. 'Until the heat dies down.'

'Heat?' Sadie panted. She watched as Bronagh opened the Ferrari door. 'I can see ice on my breath.'

'Get in,' Bronagh was already scrambling into the driving seat, fastening the seat belt.

Sadie clambered in apprehensively. She'd seen that determined look on Bronagh's face so many times before and every time, it scared her. 'Where are we going?'

'Anywhere.'

'But it's Rory's car.'

'He won't mind. It's just until Partlan calms down. He wants to make a holy show of us.'

'Shouldn't we just face up to him?'

'Partlan? That jumped-up little eejit? He's definitely not putting me in a cold cell.' Bronagh started the engine. 'Let's go, Sadie. You never know, we might even have some fun.'

'Fun?' Sadie doubted it.

'We deserve a little trip away.' Bronagh's eyes sparkled. 'Let's drive back to Kildare Avenue, pack a case and get the hell out of town.'

'A case?' Sadie was staring, dumbfounded. 'Have you lost the plot?'

'It's a grand idea. Come on.' Bronagh revved the engine, a smile spreading on her face. 'It's time for an adventure, Sadie. We're off, with Partlan in hot pursuit. Didn't I tell you we were just like Thelma and Louise?'

3

Sadie rushed out of her house nervously, clutching her handbag and an ancient overnight case stuffed with pyjamas, a toothbrush and a change of clothes. Bronagh's bigger and fatter case was installed already. She was ready to go, revving the engine of the Ferrari; she'd already stuck a notice to Sadie's front door with Blu-Tack. Sadie peered at it, reading aloud. '"Dear Rory, We took the car. It's only till Partlan calms down. We'll bring it back safely tomorrow."' She turned to Bronagh, confused. 'Are you serious?'

'What else can we do?'

'We'll tell Partlan not to get his knickers in a twist.'

'They are already twisted right up his—' Bronagh hissed, her breath mist on the air. 'Get in.'

'Where will we go?' Sadie was terrified. When Bronagh made her mind up it was impossible to change it.

'We'll find a nice pub. I have my credit card.'

Sadie was dithering out of fear. 'This is a Ferrari though. It goes like the wind. When did you last drive?'

'My licence is still good. I got rid of the Fiat last year when it failed its NCT.' Bronagh took Sadie's case from her hands and heaved it into the car. 'And my eyesight's pretty good with the glasses on. My optician told me that when I last had my eyes tested.'

'Oh, yes – I came with you. You have great vision. I can't drive it. My licence expired and I'd be scared to drive that thing anyway.'

'Right.'

'But shouldn't we stay and face the music?' The idea terrified Sadie, but it was better than the alternative. 'Sean will sort it out. Or Niall can get Partlan a whiskey.'

'He'd love to bang two old ladies up in the slammer,' Bronagh said and the twinkle in her eye was visible beneath the street lights. Sadie felt faint at the thought.

'But we can reason with him.'

'We're talking about Partlan here.' Bronagh waved Sadie towards the car. 'Besides, we'll stop in a lovely country pub. My treat.'

'But...' Sadie was unconvinced. She heard a shout from the end of Kildare Avenue. A little man was running along, flapping his arms. There was a crowd following him. She glanced both ways and her heart missed a beat.

'Jaysus, it's Partlan, come to arrest us,' Bronagh gasped. 'Get in.'

Sadie didn't wait to be told again. She leaped in as fast as she could, slamming the door. 'Drive, Bronagh.'

'Like the clappers.' Bronagh revved the engine again and they were off. She pointed a finger and hooted, 'Up yours, Partlan.'

Sadie stared wide-eyed at her friend as they screeched around the corner. 'Was that wise?'

'He'll calm down. By tomorrow he'll be blaming it on Deirdre Quinn's birthday. And by that time we...' Bronagh changed gear and the Ferrari lurched like a kangaroo. 'We'll be miles away, drinking whiskey and smoking cigarettes with very bad men.'

'But we don't smoke.' Sadie tugged her headscarf tighter against the night air. Bronagh wasn't listening. They hurtled through a set of green lights and onwards into the darkness. As Bronagh accelerated, Sadie put a hand to her head. She felt dizzy and sick with fear. 'This car sounds like an aeroplane. They'll hear us coming for miles.'

'But they won't catch us, will they?' Bronagh winked. 'Come on, let's live it up a bit.'

* * *

Partlan Brown squinted at Sadie's front door and folded his arms. 'They've gone.'

Sean, Bunty, Nora, Pat, Niall and Maeve peered over his shoulder to read the note. Rory, always concerned for his grandmother's well-being, pushed to the front, pulled it down from the door, Blu-Tack and all, and said, 'Ah, well, they'll bring the car back tomorrow.' He turned to Niall, completely untroubled. 'Can I borrow the Audi for a bit, Da?'

'Of course you can,' Niall said.

'They've stolen your car, Rory.' Lola was astonished. 'Aren't you furious?'

'You could make an official complaint,' Partlan urged.

'Why would I want to do that? Grandmammy and Great-Auntie Bronagh are family. We O'Connors share everything.' Rory shrugged. 'I'll get it back soon enough. It's only a car.'

Lola was horrified. 'It's a Ferrari.'

'It's just a car though,' Rory said. Lola clearly didn't understand his family. His grandmother's actions made him smile. 'I don't mind at all.'

'It's not the car that worries me; the baking competition was declared null and void,' Maeve whined. 'And I was the winner.'

'No you weren't,' a chorus of voices replied cheerily.

'Doughty's make good cakes though,' Niall seemed unaware that Maeve's cheeks glowed with shame.

'Don't worry, Maeve. Emma and Ryan said the good causes won.' Sean was delighted. 'It's about the charity, not the bakes. Everyone's in there now eating enough pudding to get them through next year.'

'We can run the competition again,' Bunty agreed.

'And Deirdre's in The Hole, playing "Wild Rover" and scoffing meringue like no tomorrow. Everyone's happy,' Pat said.

'No one cares about the Doughty's cake,' Bunty said kindly, wrapping an arm around Maeve, who hunched her shoulders.

'I shouldn't have brought it in the box but I wanted to keep it looking nice,' Maeve protested.

'You're all missing the point.' Nora folded her arms. 'Mammy and Auntie Bronagh have run away.' She turned to Partlan. 'That's harassment of two old ladies, and it's your fault. What are you going to do about it?'

'Me?' Partlan was amazed. 'I wouldn't have laid a hand on them.'

'You threatened to arrest them,' Pat reminded him.

'I didn't mean it,' Partlan stammered.

'But they're helpless pensioners,' Niall said.

'Helpless? Those two?' Partlan's brow clouded. 'They'll be back tomorrow, won't they? And I'll buy them a half-pint and we'll forget it.'

'And what if they don't come back?' Sean asked. 'What if they have an accident in that car? You'd be responsible, Partlan.'

Partlan scratched his head. 'Should I alert the gardai in

County Clare, ask them to look out for two old ladies in a Ferrari?'

'No way.' Rory was finding the whole thing too funny. 'Can you imagine that chase, with Great-Auntie Bronagh at the wheel thinking she's Lewis Hamilton? It doesn't bear thinking about. Leave them till they're ready.'

'We should go back to the pub. Get a drink in, and have some cake,' Sean said.

'Can't you ring them and tell them to come home?' Lola asked.

'What an idea.' Niall chuckled. 'Mammy, with a mobile phone? I bought her one once. She won't use it.'

'Can Bronagh drive?' Bunty looked concerned.

'Oh, she's fine,' Niall said, 'She's driven the Ferrari before too. She liked it better than her old Fiat, that's for sure.'

'They can borrow it. The Ferrari will outrun everything else on the road anyway,' Rory said confidently. 'They'll be back tomorrow; it's Sunday.'

'Yes, it's Sunday,' Sean said, as if that were the answer to everything. 'They'll be fine.'

'Dandy,' Niall agreed.

'I feel depressed,' Maeve groaned. 'Everyone knows I cheated.'

'Ah, don't worry,' Sean reassured her. 'It's only a cake.'

Partlan looked worried enough for them both. 'If anything happens to those poor old ladies, it's down to me.'

'Poor old ladies?' Nora laughed once. 'I'd like to see anyone messing with Auntie Bronagh and Mammy. They won't take any prisoners.'

'Let's go back to The Hole,' Niall suggested.

'I'll buy you a whiskey, Partlan. In fact, I'll get everyone one,' Rory said, with the hope that everyone would calm down and let it blow over. He preferred peace to arguments. He wrapped an arm around Lola. 'And we'll all stick some money in the charity box.'

Niall added, 'And I'll get you a Mojito, Maeve. Cocktails always cheer you up.'

'Not tonight, they won't.' Maeve was still thinking about the Guinness cake.

'Right.' Partlan looked a bit happier.

'Maeve?' Niall wrapped an arm around his wife. 'Will we go?'

'All right.' Maeve still looked miserable.

'We need to keep this Baltic cold out somehow,' Sean agreed. 'I'll call round first thing tomorrow and get Mammy some breakfast. She'll be starving when she gets home.'

* * *

'I'm starving,' Sadie said as they drove up the M18, the engine making its distinctive throaty roar. Her stomach growled to prove her point. 'What time is it?'

'Nine o'clock. I'm famished too. We should have eaten properly earlier on.' Bronagh overtook a small yellow car and noticed how the driver stared at the Ferrari with envy. 'This car's a cracker.'

'So will we stop somewhere for a bite?' Sadie was more concerned about the gnawing in her stomach and the increasing ache between her eyes. 'We can get our heads down.'

'We will, we will,' Bronagh said. 'Just as soon as we turn onto the M6.'

'Where will we go?' Sadie wriggled in the seat. She'd imagined that an expensive car would be more comfortable. She wished she'd brought a cushion. 'Aren't you stiff as a board?'

'I am. I just thought we'd get as far as Dublin. Rory says it takes him two and a half hours to get there from home.'

'Two and a half hours? Why would we go to Dublin?' Sadie asked.

'I haven't been since you and I went with Michael and Alfie twelve years ago.' Bronagh stared through the windscreen. 'It brings back memories.'

Sadie closed her eyes for a moment, recalling the wonderful times they'd had as a foursome. It filled her with regret, even now. 'But it'll be bedtime when we get there. Everywhere will be closed.'

'Nothing closes in Dublin. We'll find a bar, a B & B.'

'It's bedtime now.' Sadie tried to move her legs. They ached badly and her toes were numb.

'Right, I'll pull off somewhere when we get to the M6. Paddy's House in Cappataggle is good. Niall and Maeve stay there sometimes.'

'Can we get there soon?'

'Another ten minutes, twenty maybe. Thirty tops.'

'My arthritis is killing me.' Sadie stretched her limbs and made a pained face. 'Make it ten, Bronagh.'

'All right.' Bronagh's foot hit the accelerator and the car took off with a guttural growl like a rocket.

Sadie caught her breath in fear. 'It's a good job there's not much traffic about. What speed are we doing?'

'Cruising.'

'What speed?'

'A hundred and sixty.'

'Miles an hour?'

'Kilometres – don't worry. This car purrs like a kitten.'

'Slow down. The speed limit's one hundred and twenty.'

'That slow?' Bronagh eased back. 'Killjoys.'

'The law's meant to keep people safe from reckless drivers.' Sadie wriggled again. 'I need to go.'

'Go where?'

'To pee.'

'Of course.' Bronagh noticed a passing sign. 'We're about to hit the M6.'

'Hit?' Sadie closed her eyes. 'How long?'

'Five minutes or so. We'll be at Cappataggle,' Bronagh said. 'We'll get twin beds, some fish and chips and a pint of stout. We'll be grand.'

'I hope so.' Sadie didn't believe her. 'I wish I'd brought cushions...'

'We'll buy some tomorrow,' Bronagh said.

'Tomorrow? Aren't we going home?'

'When we're halfway to Dublin?' Bronagh turned her head for a moment. 'Dublin, Sadie. Let's have some fun.'

'But Rory needs his car for work.'

'Ah, Niall has cars,' Bronagh said. 'And Rory'll understand. We'll give him his car back next weekend.'

'Next weekend? But I thought we'd go home.'

'Why would we do that when we can let off some steam in Dublin?'

'But Sean will worry, and Nora and Niall.'

'We'll send them a card.'

'We will.' Sadie wasn't sure.

'Let's live it up,' Bronagh said. 'We're a long time in the wooden box.'

'We are,' Sadie agreed half-heartedly. 'Well, right. Dublin it is. I suppose if we send three cards, one each to Sean and Niall and Nora, they'll all know where we are and they won't worry.'

'Exactly.' Bronagh overtook a lorry. 'Did you see how that

fella in the cab up there looked at us? I haven't been looked at like that in a long time.'

'He was looking at the car.'

'Ah, but we're in it,' Bronagh replied.

Sadie puzzled over her reply for a moment. 'Was that the sign to Cappataggle we just passed?'

'It was.' Bronagh peered over the wheel. 'I'll come off at the next exit and we'll find a place to stop.'

'Please.'

'You still need the jacks?'

'I do, badly.'

'Right.' Bronagh blinked into the blackness as she slid past two more cars. 'Next stop, Gortaderry.'

'It can't come soon enough.' Sadie groaned. 'I'm desperate.'

'Just imagine a nice soft bed – duck-down-filled pillows and duvet.'

'I am.'

'And crispy fish and chips, a cool half of Guinness.'

'Mmm.'

'And we'll have a nice power shower in our room.' Bronagh's eyes twinkled with mischief. 'All that hot water, drip, drip, drip.'

'Stop, stop.' Sadie winced. 'It has to be now. Come off the motorway, Bronagh. Find us somewhere to stop, a hedge, a field, a puddle. Anywhere. This is an emergency.'

4

It was past ten when Bronagh drove into the car park of Finn's Bar. Sadie was feeling relieved in more ways than one, having stopped to stretch her legs and to answer nature's call near a five-barred gate in Banefield. Now she was weary and hungry. They clambered out of the Ferrari and Bronagh was fiddling with the key.

'How do I lock this thing?'

'Does it have the central locking?'

'What do I do to central-lock it?'

'Try putting the key in the keyhole in the door.' Sadie paused. 'Or it might have a remote thingy.'

Bronagh pushed the key in, turned it and the door clicked. 'It works just like normal. I thought you could lock all cars nowadays by saying abracadabra.'

'I don't know.' Sadie was confused; technology made her head buzz like annoying flies. Besides, she and Alfie had always lived without all that palaver. She wasn't about to change now. 'It's all too modern.'

'This Ferrari locks with a key.' Bronagh grabbed her handbag and adjusted her headscarf. 'Will we go in?'

'We will.' Sadie took her arm. 'Let's get a comfy room and a drink and some food. We can plan what we'll do tomorrow.' They approached the door. Music came from inside. Lights glowed a warm welcome. 'I just want to sit down in the warm and rest my aching legs. My ankles are like balloons.'

Bronagh helped a tired Sadie to the bar. The pub was busy; there was a restaurant area off to one side, a red carpet, wooden tables with white cloths. Bronagh waved at a young barman in a crisp green shirt. She thought he looked about twelve years old, but he had a light moustache. 'Could we get some food?'

'No, I'm sorry.' The young man glanced at her fleetingly. 'The kitchen's closed.'

'Closed?' Bronagh was horrified. 'Can't you just open it?'

'Chef goes home at ten.' The bartender wiped glasses, uninterested.

'Does he have any chippers left?' Bronagh asked desperately. 'We're half starved.'

'We've come a long way.' Sadie was so weary she thought she might burst into tears.

'Our Ferrari's outside,' Bronagh added cockily. 'And we need a room for the night.'

The young man looked dumbfounded. 'We've no vacancies.'

'What? None at all?' Bronagh took a step back, pretending to be outraged. 'No food. No beds? What kind of pub is this?'

'A busy one.' The bartender's face was expressionless. 'Hang on. I'll go out the back and see what I can do.'

He walked off somewhere. Bronagh turned to Sadie, appalled. 'Is he going to give us a sleeping bag?'

'I'd sleep anywhere right now.' Sadie was dead on her feet. 'I need food or I'll pass out.'

Bronagh's eyes scanned the bar. 'They've peanuts, popcorn. Meanies, Keogh's salt and vinegar crisps.'

'Guinness is food. I'll have a pint.' Sadie slumped against the bar, her head on her arms, exhausted. The young man was back.

'So, I can get you a plate of chippers – we can heat them up.'

'You're a little lifesaver,' Bronagh breathed out with relief. 'Right, we'll have the chippers, two pints of black stuff and two whiskeys.'

'What about a bed?' Sadie was ready to beg. 'Surely there's something?'

'The manager says you'll have to sleep in your car. It's the best we can do.'

'In the car park?' Bronagh stared at him. 'We'll freeze to death.'

'It's best to book online in future.' The young man began to pour a pint of stout into a glass.

'We don't do booking on the line,' Bronagh said. 'How will we sleep in the car?'

'I can get you a couple of pillows? A duvet?'

'We'll die.' Sadie imagined it and was horrified. 'We're in our eighties.'

'But we look good on it,' Bronagh added.

'It's December, for goodness' sake,' Sadie said desperately. 'Can we just sleep in the bar?' She looked around. 'We'll be two frozen skeletons tomorrow morning.'

The young man placed two pints of stout on the bar. 'Wait there.'

Sadie and Bronagh exchanged glances. Then they reached out at the same time. There was a deep supping sound. Bronagh said, 'If we die of the hypothermia, we'll make sure we have some liquid refreshment first.'

Sadie eyed her worriedly. 'Alcohol makes your body temperature drop.'

'It won't matter if we're dead, will it?' Bronagh said.

The bartender came back with chips, and little dishes of ketchup. He said, 'Good news. There's a single room on the first floor. We usually keep boxes in there, stock and stuff, but the manager says she'll make you a bed up.'

'A single bed?' Bronagh teased. 'Where will you sleep, Sadie?'

'I'm older than you. So you'll have to sleep on the floor.' Sadie grinned, a moustache of stout on her top lip.

'We'll top and tail.' Bronagh reached for a chip and dunked it in ketchup. 'Ah, we'll be grand.' She eyed the bartender. 'Thanks. You've saved our lives, young fella. By the way—' she reached into her handbag for her purse '—don't forget the whiskies. And can you look in the kitchen to see if there's any pudding left over? I could murder some apple pie.'

***

It was midnight. Sadie huddled beneath a duvet in a tiny room that smelled of mildew. It certainly needed airing. Bronagh's icy feet were in her face and she pushed them away. At least she wasn't hungry and the toilet next door worked, although it smelled of bleach. She pulled the duvet over her ears and hung on tight as Bronagh tugged it sharply. Bronagh's voice came from the darkness. 'The apple pie was nice.'

'It was.'

'And the young one behind the bar, Dylan, he was a good lad.'

'He was.'

'I ate too much.'

'I know.'

'We only had a couple of drinks.'

'It was enough, Bronagh.'

'But we'll have a lovely time in Dublin. We can see the sights and dine out.'

Sadie let Bronagh's words hang in the air for a moment. 'I'm all of an ache. Do you think we should go home?'

'Not at all.' Bronagh's laugh was filled with mischief. 'Let Partlan sweat. He'll be having kittens.'

'Right. It'll be fun.'

'It will.' Bronagh wriggled her feet again in Sadie's face. 'We deserve to pamper ourselves. We should learn to practise self-care.'

'What's that when it's at home?'

'Well...' Bronagh rolled over, taking the duvet with her. Sadie hauled it back. 'Ordinary women are told that we don't have much value in the world. We're marginalised; we don't believe we deserve anything special.'

'I suppose that's true of all women, isn't it?' Sadie said. 'Remember Princess Di?'

'And some men feel like that too,' Bronagh said. 'Like they're not important in the scheme of things. So we have to practise self-care and tell ourselves that we're worth it.'

'Worth what?'

Bronagh frowned. 'It. Whatever *it* is.'

'Everyone should practise self-care, then.' Sadie was thoughtful for a moment. 'Do you think you don't deserve anything special, Bronagh?'

'I never had much when I was a kid, I suppose. That's where it starts. We were brought up to be grateful for scraps. You know that, Sadie. We O'Connors were poor in the fifties. Your family too, the Walkers.'

'I remember eating bread and dripping,' Sadie said. 'Mind

you, it was proper bread with a good crust on it; my mammy made it. Not like this chewy spongy stuff you get now, full of preservatives.'

'But we made do in those days: we didn't expect much. Second-hand clothes. Darned socks. And at the end of the week, just before Da was paid, we'd eat scrag-end stew with carrots and turnips.'

'And porridge for breakfast. Or bread and jam,' Sadie murmured in the darkness. The memories were still clear pictures in her mind. Happy times. The best times.

'Mammy used to cycle up to Patrick Street to get a bit of thin bacon and potatoes. It was all weighed on heavy scales and tipped into a paper bag. We had no supermarkets.'

'And my mammy used to scrub the front doorstep so the neighbours would think we were decent,' Sadie remembered fondly.

'No wonder we have low self-esteem.' Bronagh sighed.

'I never knew you felt like that. You always seem so sure of yourself.'

'It's my face, Sadie. That's what lets me down.' Bronagh's voice was sad.

'What's wrong with your face?'

'It's like a horse's.'

'It is not. You've a pretty face, Bronagh.' Sadie felt the rising desire to protect her best friend.

'No, it's too long. I always wanted a nice round face like yours. Alfie always said you had the sweetest angel face.'

'Maybe I did, back in the old days. Now it's wrinkled.'

'No, it's still sweet. You've kind eyes. And the nicest smile.'

'So have you,' Sadie insisted. 'Michael Doyle always looked so proud with you on his arm. Alfie used to say to me, "My sister looks a right feek tonight. All the fellas are ogling her."'

'He never told me that. He called me skinny and pulled my hair.'

'When you were kids,' Sadie said, reminiscing. 'We were all scrappers together at Ballycotton Primary, all ages, stuck in the same stinky classroom.'

'Good days, though.' Bronagh chuckled quietly. 'We've been lucky, Sadie. At least we had Alfie and Michael, but now they're gone.'

'God rest them.' Sadie wiped away a single tear that had drizzled down her cheek.

'We still have each other.'

'We do.'

'Are your Bunty's family in England rich?' Bronagh asked.

'I don't know.' Sadie was drifting off.

'I mean, her brother has hens and goats.'

'A smallholding by the seaside.'

'It sounds lovely. Bunty's a nice girl.'

'She is.' Sadie was quiet for a minute. 'After they lost little Danny, it was hard. They look out for each other now.'

'We all look out for each other, Sadie.'

'That's what families do.'

'So we'll make the most of it tomorrow,' Bronagh said firmly. 'We're taking ourselves off to Dublin in the babe magnet.'

'What babe magnet?'

'The Ferrari.'

'But why would we need a babe magnet?' Sadie asked. 'We don't want to attract babes.'

'Especially not ones like Rory's Lola, who thinks a Ferrari is some kind of fashion accessory, like a big red handbag.'

'I expect she's only looking out for herself, like the rest of us are,' Sadie said kindly.

'What's the opposite of babe magnet? What do we call a car

that women drive that magnetises the men? Hunk magnet? Stud charmer?'

'I don't know,' Sadie admitted. 'There's no word for one.'

'Fox catcher? Dish dazzler?' Bronagh tried again. 'Adonis bait?'

'No, Bronagh, definitely not.'

'We'll have to *be* the babes in the babe magnet.'

'Why would we do that?' Sadie asked. 'I've had my fill of attracting men.'

'Why? You look good.'

'Well, I don't feel good. My legs ache, Bronagh. My back kills. The arthritis has flared. I need my meds. I overdid it today.'

'We'll check into a swanky place in Dublin,' Bronagh soothed. 'Put the Ferrari in the car park. And if the men fly at us like iron filings, well, we'll just have to live with it.'

Sadie yawned in the dark. 'It's time for sleep. I'm exhausted. Goodnight, Bronagh.'

'Goodnight, Sadie.'

'Sleep well.'

'You too. Make sure the bedbugs don't bite.'

'Do you think there are bedbugs?'

'No – go to sleep.'

'Night, Bronagh.'

The sound of Bronagh snorting drifted on the air. She was already asleep. Sadie closed her eyes and felt tiredness tug her away.

5

Sadie and Bronagh made their way to the car park after a full Irish breakfast with soda bread. Dylan, the young barman with the light moustache, came to the door to watch them clamber into the Ferrari and wave them off.

'See, the car *is* a hunk magnet,' Bronagh said delightedly.

'He's only a little boy, and besides—' Sadie shook her head; Bronagh was incorrigible, '—I'm surprised the car's still here. What if someone had stolen it?'

'Like we did?' Bronagh was feeling chirpy this morning. 'Come on, Sadie. We can be in Dublin for lunch.'

'I couldn't eat another thing.'

'But the bars'll be open and there's music.'

'We ought to find somewhere to stay first. Dublin can be expensive.'

'I've got money.'

'Made of it, are we now?'

'Michael made sure I'd be all right.' Bronagh winked. 'Alfie left you comfortable. And I can't take it with me and Kathleen won't want any of it because she's with the Dominican sisters in Drogheda.'

'Don't you miss her, Bronagh?'

'Kathleen? Every day.' Bronagh sighed as she hurled herself and her luggage into the Ferrari. 'The sweetest little girl, she was. I always knew she'd have the calling.' She seemed to pull herself together. 'Your four are just like my own kids. Sean and Niall, Nora and Biddy, although Biddy's always gadding off.'

'They'll be in Tossa de Mar until after Christmas.' Sadie tugged her seat belt. She missed Biddy every day. They sat in silence, both reminiscing.

'Christmas is coming. Perhaps we can do some shopping in Dublin.' Bronagh started the engine, enjoying the now-familiar rumble. 'And the lights will be on. It'll be festive.'

'Maybe we'll see Santa Claus,' Sadie teased, trying to lift the moment's melancholy.

'We can sit on his knee and tell him what we want for Christmas.'

'Ah, but have you been good all year, Bronagh?' Sadie joked.

'I've no plans to be good.' Bronagh accelerated and the Ferrari roared out of the car park. 'I can't wait – shopping, lunch, a nice hotel. What about a spa?'

'We can visit the medieval crypt at Christ Church.' Sadie liked the airy buildings, the old architecture. They gave her both a sense of the past and a sense of hope.

'Crypt?' Bronagh pointed the car towards the M6. 'No way. Let's go to see Kilmainham Gaol. It's full of gory stories.'

Sadie had a dreamy look. 'I want to go to the Famine Sculptures. They're so moving. And Molly Malone's statue.'

'We could visit the Jameson Distillery, in Bow Street.'

'The Spire of Dublin's 120 metres high.'

'Let's go to The Irish Rock 'n' Roll Museum Experience,'

Bronagh said. 'We'll pretend we're Bono's aunties and get in for free.'

'Let's find a nice hotel, will we?' Sadie was thinking of her aching legs. 'I don't want to be stuck in a single bed again.'

'You won't be, trust me,' Bronagh boasted. 'It's a beautiful day, look. The skies are blue. It's all going to be such great fun.'

They roared onto the M6, overtaking two lorries. Sadie looked round nervously for a Garda car or an officer holding a laser gun. She shouted, 'Stick to the limit, Bronagh.'

'I will.' Bronagh leaned forward excitedly, revving the engine like Penelope Pitstop. 'We should be in Dublin in an hour and a half. Oh, Sadie, I can hardly wait.'

* * *

The skies were grey and it was drizzling by the time they reached Dublin. Bronagh had to drive slowly, stopping and starting at traffic lights, allowing other cars the right of way, while the windscreen wipers sloshed as she stared at the road signs.

'We need a hotel with parking,' Bronagh said firmly. 'It's not easy to park in Dublin and leaving a Ferrari in a back street mightn't be wise.'

'Rory has a nice little bachelor flat in the city.' Sadie imagined the masculine lines, the comfort. 'It's a shame we didn't ask him if we could have his key for that too.'

Bronagh shot her a sideways glance to see if she was joking. She wasn't.

'What about the Citi Hotel? Niall's stayed there. He says there's parking just a few minutes away, in Fleet Street – it's down here, I think. Just beyond Dame Street.'

'How do you know?'

'Instinct.' Bronagh tapped her nose. 'Michael and I loved Dublin. You know it was our second home.'

'I know you stayed with his cousin sometimes. Didn't he have family in the north of the city, in Ballymun?'

'He did.' Bronagh took a left turn. 'It's not far now.' She turned a corner and braked, catching her breath, pausing to look up at a beautiful three-storey white nineteenth-century building. 'That's lovely. Look.'

'It's too swanky.'

'Trust me, Sadie. I've enough money.'

'Are you sure?'

'Sure I'm sure.' Bronagh indicated the hotel. 'Take your bag and go on in. Act like you're a film star. I'll park our chariot in Fleet Street and join you in a minute.'

'What will I do?' Sadie knew too well what happened when Bronagh took over. Things got out of control.

'Have a cocktail. Ask about the availability of twin rooms. Tell them at the desk that you're Cillian Murphy's granny.'

Sadie clambered out nervously, her handbag and battered old case in her hand, and stood in the rain. Being with Bronagh always led to some mischief or other. It would all end badly. She watched her roar away and grinned. It would be what it would be, but it'd be fun. There was never a dull moment with Bronagh.

She hurried through the grand entrance.

* * *

The Citi had a mahogany reception desk with glossy paper in the register and an antique phone. Bronagh didn't bat an eye when she heard the price of the rooms. Smooth as silk, she said, 'We'll book just the one night to start with,' and handed over her card.

They were given the keys to a twin room on the first floor. Sadie walked in and glanced around, a bit disappointed. It was not as big as she'd hoped; the walls were beige and there was an abstract picture in a huge gilt frame. Chocolate-coloured velvet drapes with gold tassels hung over double windows, framing the shops and a tall building outside. It was tidy and neat, and smelled fresh. The oak wardrobe and wooden table were spotlessly polished and there was a flat-screen TV on the wall. Sadie inspected the en suite: small, tasteful, a bath, grey tiles and a silver mirror. She turned to Bronagh. 'Well, here we are.'

'What will we do now?' Bronagh asked.

'Maybe I'll have a little lie-down.' Sadie's legs and back ached from the journey.

'So, what does this brochure say?' Bronagh picked up a hotel leaflet and read, '"Linking the Georgian, Cultural and Medieval areas with its own distinct feel and nightlife atmosphere within sight of historic Trinity College, and a stone's throw from luxury shopping on Grafton Street, the Citi is your gateway..."' She paused. 'What's it saying about the nightlife? Ah. Here. "The bars with live music will make sure that your nights are every bit as much fun as your days." That's good news, isn't it?'

'Grand.' Sadie sprawled on one of the beds. There was a gold-coloured cushion behind her head and she pushed it away, closing her eyes, luxuriating.

Bronagh was still reading. '"...all rooms feature tea- and coffee-making facilities for your convenience... each room is equipped with a multi-channel television." Well, we won't be needing the TV. We'll be out enjoying ourselves. Shopping first, then dinner. I thought we'd find a little bistro somewhere.'

'We'll send postcards to tell everyone where we are,' Sadie fretted as she tried to make herself comfortable.

'I'll make us that tea.' Bronagh bustled about, filling the kettle in the bathroom. 'I love the grey tiles in here. I might get some like it at home.' She reappeared. 'Will you have a tea or a coffee? Oh, here's a chamomile. But you don't want that, Sadie, it'll send you off to sleep. I might have a bath. Just to relax me after the long drive. Then we'll hit the shops. What do you say? A new dress and some shoes – maybe a proper winter coat. After all, it's only money. Here's your tea.'

She turned round. Sadie was curled on the bed, eyes closed, snuffling.

Bronagh put the cups down. 'Well, bless your heart, Sadie O'Connor, you're out for the count. You won't be needing the chamomile, that's for sure. Right. I'll have a long soak. You clearly need your beauty sleep. Then we'll paint the town red.'

* * *

The skies over Dublin were dark but the city was breathing with a life of its own. Laughter and music pumped from bars, people thronged the streets, as Bronagh clutched Sadie's arm. Sadie wore her best floral dress beneath her warm coat and Bronagh had brought her glad rags, a black sparkly dress and red shoes. They hugged each other for warmth: the rain had stopped but a cold wind was funnelling down the road. Sadie said, 'I feel all the better for a sleep. Travelling exhausts me nowadays.'

'Well, you're on holiday,' Bronagh assured her. 'We'll go shopping tomorrow.'

'In Dublin?' Sadie was horrified.

'Who counts pennies nowadays? After all, if we get stuck, we have Niall. He'll bail us out.'

They paused outside a bar, painted bright red. Violin music thrummed inside, a hearty voice singing something about the girls not leaving the boys alone. Bronagh's eyes twinkled mischievously. 'This is our cue.'

'Right,' Sadie agreed as they walked in. She caught her breath: the place was a fairy grotto, adorned with lanterns of all colours from the ceiling downwards. Behind the bar, more lights twinkled.

'We've died and gone to heaven.' Bronagh gasped.

There was a small stage, a man playing the violin, a woman strumming a guitar. They finished their song to deafening applause – the bar was already heaving – and launched into 'The Irish Rover'. Bronagh grabbed Sadie's wrist, tugged her towards the bar and waved a finger. 'Two pints of the black stuff, bartender.'

A woman wearing a black T-shirt sporting the bar's logo lifted two glasses. 'Coming up.' She allowed the stout to fill, the dark potion swirling. 'Are youse on holiday?'

'We are.' Bronagh leaned on the bar like Calamity Jane. 'We came up in the Ferrari.'

'You're kidding me.'

'No, it's my grandson's,' Sadie explained. 'He lends it to us.'

'And where are you staying in Dublin?'

'The Citi.' Bronagh waved a hand as if she were there every week. 'Home from home.'

'So youse are both out on the town for the craic.' The woman placed the pints on the counter.

'We are.' Bronagh flourished her card. 'What time are you open till?'

'Late. The music goes on past midnight. Are you here for a session?'

'We certainly are.' Bronagh was delighted. 'I can still drink any man under the table.'

Sadie raised an eyebrow: Bronagh had that gleam in her eyes. 'Bronagh, let's just take things slowly.'

'I won't make a holy show of myself.' Bronagh put her glass to her lips and supped. 'Ahhh, that's good. Let's sit down.'

Sadie looked around. Every table was full. 'Where?'

Bronagh led the way to a table where several men crowded, talking loudly over the music, and tapped a burly man on the shoulder. 'Excuse me, son.'

'What's happening?' The man looked up. He was balding, with a cheery face and ruddy cheeks.

'I don't suppose there's room for two wee ones?' Bronagh rubbed her spine. 'My bad back aches and this place is jammers – there's nowhere to sit.'

'You don't have a bad back,' Sadie whispered.

Bronagh muttered, 'I do now.'

The man stood up. 'You can have my seat, darlin'. I'll get a couple more.'

'You're so kind.' Bronagh fluttered her eyelashes and took his chair. The man disappeared for a moment and came back with a stool for himself and one for Sadie. 'Here y'are. Move up, fellas.'

Everyone at the table budged along and Sadie squeezed in. Bronagh was all smiles.

'Hello. We're staying at the Citi. We're from Ballycotton.'

'Oh, are you?' The man scratched his head. 'You're what we locals call culchies.' He turned to his mates and they joked. 'We're Dubliners. You're bumpkins.'

'I'll have you know we came here in our Ferrari,' Bronagh said airily. 'We're ladies of leisure.'

'You'll be buying the next round, then,' one of the men said. He was wearing a flat cap.

Sadie was worried they'd end up buying drinks for everyone

in the bar, but Bronagh replied, 'I was hoping you nice chaps would get them in. We're widows.'

'What'll you have, darlin'?' The man in the cap stood up. 'Whiskey?'

'Now you're talking.' Bronagh lifted her glass in thanks. 'I love Dublin, Sadie.'

'I'm Jim – and Pete's buying,' the balding man said by way of introduction. 'We always come for the live music.'

'I'm Sadie,' Sadie began and Bronagh took over.

'I'm Bronagh. We're sisters. Our surname is Corr. You've probably heard about my grandchildren, what with you being music lovers.'

Sadie felt the familiar shiver of horror go through her.

'The Corrs?' Jim was impressed. 'The band that did "Breathless"? I love them. They were from Dundalk, weren't they? Good-looking family.'

'We always have been,' Bronagh agreed. 'I helped them get started, you know. I wrote one of their songs.'

'Which one?' Jim asked.

Sadie jolted Bronagh, raised a warning eyebrow to suggest she quit while she was ahead and whispered, '"Runaway".'

'"Runaway",' Bronagh said, full of herself.

'My favourite,' Jim said.

Pete arrived with a tray of whiskies. 'Here y'are.'

'Did you know, lads, yer wan here is The Corrs' grandma.' Jim reached for a whiskey. 'She wrote one of their songs.'

'I did. "Runaway".' Bronagh was quick to catch on.

Sadie tried to change the subject. 'I love this music – I like a bit of violin.'

'And which of your grandchildren was it who played the violin in The Corrs?' Pete asked, just to check.

Bronagh nudged Sadie, who whispered, 'Sharon.' She put her lips against Bronagh's ear. 'Alfie loved them.'

'Sharon – oh, she's such a nice girl. Married now, with six kiddies,' Bronagh said with full confidence.

'Here's to you, ladies. Welcome to Dublin.' Jim held up a glass.

'Sláinte,' Pete chimed.

Bronagh grabbed a whiskey. *'Sláinte.'*

There was a chorus of *'Sláinte'* around the table.

Sadie sipped quietly and decided she'd keep an eye on Bronagh, who appeared to be accelerating out of control.

An hour and two more drinks later, Sadie was amazed that Bronagh's speech was perfect and she could remember the name of everyone at the table. Furthermore, she was chattering to Jim, Pete, Ally, Darren, Bill, Beaky and Connor as if she'd known them for years.

Sadie sat patiently as Bronagh related stories about The Corrs, her grandchildren, all wonderful kiddies who loved her baking and came to tea on Sundays. Bronagh paused every so often to allow Sadie to insert their names: she hadn't a clue.

Sadie closed her eyes, allowing the thrum of the music to fill her ears. It was wonderful, the uplifting whoop of the violin, the comforting thrum of the guitar, gentle voices lifted in song. It was as familiar as the blood in her own veins. She was tired, but she told herself that she needed this break. It was doing her good. There'd be a hearty breakfast tomorrow, one she didn't have to make herself, with hot black coffee. It might be fun to go shopping, and she reminded herself to send postcards to Sean, Nora and Niall. She'd send Biddy one too, even though she was in Spain.

The musicians began to sing 'Whiskey in the Jar'. Sadie

remembered dancing to the song with Alfie all the time years ago, the good old times. Then she opened her eyes.

Bronagh was up, enjoying herself, lifting the skirt of her dress and doing the Riverdance. The men around the table cheered and clapped.

At a nearby table, two men were arguing. Voices were raised, insults flying. A glass tipped over, full to the brim. Sadie stared in dismay. The argument was becoming heated. One man stood up and shouted something in fury, then the other took to his feet. Another glass toppled. Beer splashed and dripped.

Bronagh threw her arms in the air and began to sing the chorus.

There was a clattering noise, a loud tinkle. Chairs were overturned as the fight broke out. Someone picked one up to fend off his opponent and Pete jumped up to avoid the brawl. As he stepped back, he cannoned into a man carrying a tray of beers, which fell from his hands with a crash. The man turned angrily.

More roars went up. Another punch was thrown, then another. Someone shrieked and a full-scale fight broke out.

Bronagh reached for Sadie with a squeal. She grabbed her wrist and whispered, 'Run!'

Heart pounding, Sadie ran for all she was worth. She was glad to.

6

'Run, Sadie.'

Bronagh gripped Sadie's arm like a vice and tugged her forward. Sadie was panting, hobbling, glancing nervously over her shoulder. The fight was in full swing. Punches were being thrown nineteen to the dozen, more glasses smashed. Tables tumbled, chairs crashed. The shouting and cursing was almost as loud as the music.

'Quick.' Bronagh hauled Sadie towards the door and out into the cold night air, hurrying her down the street. Finally, they slowed down.

Bronagh groaned, breathing hard. 'I bet that never happened to Michael Flatley.'

'What shall we do now?'

'We'll go back to the hotel, have a cuppa and an early night,' Bronagh said. 'I've had enough of the high life.'

'So have I,' Sadie wheezed. 'My hips are killing me. I need a sleep.'

'I need a holiday.'

'This is a holiday.'

'I mean a proper one,' Bronagh said. 'We can go wherever we want. We have the Ferrari.'

'A holiday where?' Sadie was confused. Perhaps it was time to call it quits. 'Rory will want his car back. We could just go home.'

'No, Rory'll be fine about it.' The hotel was in sight. Bronagh beamed. 'Let's go to England.'

'England? Why would anyone want to go there?'

'We can visit Bunty's brother. The sexy one who makes all the cakes.'

'Why?'

'He's a sex symbol. Don't you remember Bunty saying to Rory's Lola that they'd be made welcome there if they went to Cornwall? And he said it would only take a day or two. We should go.'

'Why?'

'Devon's in the middle of nowhere. It's probably warm and summery there. They have a riviera climate. It's freezing here in Ireland.'

'How long would we stay?'

'Just a few days. Then we'd come back home. Ooh, let's go, Sadie. Think about it. England, where they make the best cakes and it'll be all Christmassy. Bunty's brother's hospitable. And her sister's nice.'

'But how will we get the ferry?'

'From the ferry port.'

'But how will we get tickets?' Sadie leaned against Bronagh as they staggered through the grand entrance to the Citi.

'Leave it to me.' Bronagh breathed into her face deliberately. 'Do I smell of alcohol?'

'Not as much as the Irish Whiskey Museum in Grafton Street.'

'Good. Right, back me up.'

'What?' Sadie felt the familiar sinking feeling.

'Back me up, Sadie.' Bronagh waltzed up to the reception with the mahogany desk. Sadie was impressed by her get-up-and-go. She felt exhausted and ready for bed.

Bronagh spoke sweetly at the woman on Reception, who had dark glossy hair tied back. 'Good evening.'

'How may I help you?' the woman asked.

'I'm Bronagh Doyle. Sorcha O' Connor and I are in room six. I wonder, could you book a ferry for me?'

The woman hesitated. 'You can do it online.'

'I don't have the online.'

'A phone?'

'No, I don't have one of those either. I'm on holiday,' Bronagh said by way of explanation. 'I need to get to England tomorrow.' She put on a tragic expression. 'My brother in Devon's taking his last breath as we speak.'

'Brother?' Sadie groaned; she wasn't enjoying Bronagh's performance at all. She was amazed how she got away with it every time.

'Oh, I'm sorry.' The receptionist looked shocked.

'It's a matter of life and death. I won't make it in time to say my goodbyes unless we get a wiggle on,' Bronagh said melodramatically.

'I'll see what I can do.' The receptionist tapped a keyboard. Bronagh and Sadie exchanged glances. 'There's one leaving at eight-fifteen tomorrow that gets you into Holyhead at eleven-fifty.'

'Grand. Can you book it for both of us?'

'One way? With a car?'

'One way for now.' Bronagh nudged Sadie. 'We'll be in the Ferrari. Shall I give you all the details? I've my insurance documents with me and we've got our Public Services Cards that we use for the bus.'

'Do we?' Sadie was amazed how Bronagh had thought of everything. In truth, she'd rather have gone home.

'Rory put me on his insurance. He's done that for Niall too, and Erin, and Pat, and Nora and Maeve. All the documents live in the glovebox.'

Sadie groaned again. Things were moving too quickly. 'What about breakfast? We'll have to leave early.'

'We will.' Bronagh's eyes gleamed behind her spectacles. 'Could you get us both on that ferry, please?' She turned to Sadie and whispered, 'Sadie, we're going to England. It'll be a riot.'

'That's what I'm afraid of,' Sadie said and groaned for a third time.

* * *

The wind blasted in their faces as they stood on the deck of the *Stena Adventurer*. Sadie and Bronagh had tied their headscarves tightly beneath their chins and pulled the collars of their coats up. They still shivered.

Sadie said, 'It's Baltic and I'm hungry. Let's go below and get hot coffee and some beans on toast.'

'Good idea,' Bronagh said. 'If we get to Holyhead by lunchtime, we'll have a break. Is Holyhead in Wales?'

'It is.'

'How will we get lunch, Sadie?'

'We go into a café.'

'But they speak Welsh.'

'We'll speak slowly.'

'So, Sadie, it's about seven hours to Devon. That's ten hours with your toilet stops.'

'Maybe we should stop overnight somewhere.'

'Yes, we'll do that.'

'How do you know how far it is?'

'I got the woman on reception at the Citi to go on the line for me. And I got a road map and marked it with a pen.'

'When did you do that?'

'While you were in the loo at the ferry port. We drive through Wales on the A470 and that way we miss the spaghetti place in Birmingham. We go through lots of villages that start with two Ls. Like Llandrindod Wells.' Bronagh wiped her mouth. 'Llanelly, Llantrisant – and a place called Three Cocks.'

'Is that a pub?' Sadie was shocked.

'I think it's a village, but we'll be in the red man magnet, so it'll be fun finding out if there really are three cocks—'

'Bronagh!' Sadie shot her a look that was pure disapproval. 'Maybe we should've gone home?'

'Ah, you'll feel better once we're in sunny Devon, dipping our feet in the sea. They all drink cider there.'

'Why?'

'It's a local speciality,' Bronagh said. 'We'll have a lovely time.'

'I hope you're right.' Sadie imagined sitting in her terraced house in Kildare Avenue by the fire, eating buttery potato cakes. Bronagh tucked an arm through hers.

'What if we stay the week and come back next Sunday? We'll be home well in time for Christmas. And Robert can phone Bunty later today and tell her where we are.' She gave Sadie an encouraging pat. 'Everything'll be dandy.'

Sadie didn't really want to. 'All right.'

'We'll enjoy it.'

'I hope so.'

'We will. Now let's get a coffee. It'll keep us awake for the drive through Wales.'

'We'll stop overnight somewhere though?'

'We will.'

'Bronagh.' Sadie hung back. 'Promise me one thing.'

'If I can.'

'Don't tell people we meet that you're The Corrs' gran or Bono's auntie.'

'Why ever not?'

'It's lies.'

'It's not, not really. It's just a bit of blarney. Imagine how pleased they'll be, thinking they'd met a celebrity.' Bronagh took in Sadie's frown. 'Right. So, what you're really saying, Sadie, is try not to make a show of myself. Is that it?'

'Yes. And don't get us into any trouble.'

'Me?' Bronagh gave the innocent look of an angel in a headscarf. 'I'll do my best, Sadie. Come on, let's grab something to eat. I'm ravenous.'

* * *

It was after midday as Bronagh and Sadie drove along the A55 from Holyhead. The rain was coming down in sheets. Bronagh peered through the whooshing windscreen wipers at the road ahead, driving slowly. Sadie said, 'This will take all day and half the night.' She wiped the passenger window with her hand and stared through. 'Look at the coast. And the lovely scenery. So green.'

'It's all this rain,' Bronagh grumbled.

'And the mountains in the distance. It's pretty.'

'So's County Clare. The grass is emeralds and the seas are sapphires. Ireland's like a jewellery box.'

'That's poetic,' Sadie sighed. 'Lovely words. Are you feeling a bit down, Bronagh?'

'A bit. Ireland's where my heart is.'

'Do you wish we hadn't come?' Sadie was thinking the same thing. They could always turn round...

'No, I'm glad we did. Only – Sadie – I love Ireland. It's the place I grew up in. Where Alfie and I were kids. I met Michael. We had Kathleen. We were happy.'

'Aren't you happy now?'

'I am, I am. But you know...'

'Not unless you tell me.'

'I'm getting on a bit.'

'And?'

'And, well, I can't have much longer. And I regret things.'

'What things do you regret?'

'My bosoms.'

'Bronagh, how can you regret your bosoms?'

'They're too flat.'

'No, they're not. They're just right.'

'I always wished I had the buxom ones like you have, Sadie.'

'Believe you me, they aren't all they're cracked up to be.'

'What aren't?'

'The big bosoms. I know the men like them but really it's none of their business what we have on our fronts.'

'They do make a lot of fuss.'

'You can't run fast with big bosoms,' Sadie said truthfully. 'It's harder to squeeze through gaps. And some men want to have a conversation with them, rather than your face.'

'They do anyway, even if they're small,' Bronagh said sadly, turning the Ferrari down a narrow road lined with sweeping trees.

'I always wanted the smaller ones.'

'And I always wished mine were bigger.'

'No, you be happy with what you've got. Your bosoms are lovely as they are.'

'You're the best friend in the world.' Bronagh smiled. 'And Michael liked them. But we won't go on about that now.'

'No, best not to.'

'I'm just low on confidence, that's all.'

'The woman who danced in a Dublin bar wearing red shoes is low on confidence?' Sadie said affectionately. 'I don't believe it.'

'I'm masking.'

'What's that when it's at home?'

'Pretending to be something I'm not.'

'Well, you're fine as you are, Bronagh, so don't pretend any more.' Sadie patted her arm gently. 'Look how amazing you are. Driving a Ferrari through Wales, taking us to Devon where we'll have a grand old time.'

'Are you looking forward to it?' Bronagh asked. They passed a pretty signpost, surrounded by flowers, proclaiming the name of a village she couldn't pronounce.

'I am,' Sadie replied. 'I'm starting to see the opportunities.'

'What opportunities?'

'It'd be nice to meet Bunty's family, Robert and – Hattie, that's her sister's name. She's divorced now, you know.'

'Hattie?'

'She married a man called Geoffrey. He was an arse so she kicked him into touch.'

'What did he do?'

'He bullied her, Bunty says.'

'I can't abide a man who's a bully.' Bronagh sighed. 'You and I were so lucky with Michael and Alfie.'

'We were.'

'There would never be anyone like those two wonderful men.'

'No, you're right.'

'Ah.'

'Yes.'

Both women were lost in thought for the next fifty miles, each thinking back to happy times, remembering sweet golden years filled with the best memories.

As they drove into Maentwrog, the rain stopped. Bronagh said, 'Will we get a coffee and a sandwich?'

'Yes. We can stretch our legs, have something to eat and a pee.'

The Ferrari rumbled slowly through the village, Sadie and Bronagh peering through the windows.

'There's a hotel,' Sadie said. 'Do you think they'll have sandwiches?'

'It looks a bit posh.' Bronagh pointed into the distance. 'This is the Snowdonia National Park. Isn't it beautiful?'

'Look at the little cottages and the huge hills in the distance. You can imagine men working in the mines and coming home for a Welsh rarebit.'

'That's cheese on toast. I'd want more than that to fill me up if I was down the pit. Oh.' Bronagh gasped. 'What a beautiful little church. And look, there's a sign to visit alpacas.'

'I need a sandwich,' Sadie insisted. 'Where's the café?'

'I'll drive on a bit and ask someone,' Bronagh said, accelerating past a man who stood with his hands in his pockets, staring. Bronagh poked her head out of the window and shouted, 'Afternoon, sailor.'

'You could have asked him,' Sadie grumbled.

'He looked scary,' Bronagh cackled. She drove along a dusty road marked A470. 'There must be a café around here.'

'There's nothing, just houses.' Sadie's stomach growled. 'Maybe there's a supermarket.'

'This is the middle of nowhere. Hang on, what did that sign say?'

'Penny Brian?' Sadie misread. 'Look, a little shop. A post office. They might have a sandwich and a drink.'

Bronagh slowed down. 'Right, Sadie, off you go.'

'Me?'

'I'll wait in the car, just in case.'

'In case of what?' Sadie felt suddenly anxious.

'In case they speak Welsh.'

Sadie shook her head. Bronagh was making no sense. She slipped out of the Ferrari and said, 'Do you mind what you get?'

'I'll eat anything,' Bronagh said and as an afterthought she called, 'Tell them you're Brenda Fricker and you're here rehearsing for a big film.'

'I will not,' Sadie said, then she disappeared.

After what seemed like an age, Sadie appeared with an armful of groceries. She tugged the door and almost fell into the seat.

'Where've you been?'

'The kind man let me use his toilet out the back. He had a lovely soft accent. I bought sandwiches and some drinks.'

'Good. Right. Let's drive to somewhere quiet and we can eat and have a snooze. I'm tired out.'

'We don't want to be late getting off to Devon, Bronagh.'

'Ah, we'll be fine.'

Bronagh drove for a few miles through sweet-scented countryside and stopped by a five-bar gate leading to a field of long grass and a farm. She opened a window and said, 'Fresh air. That's lovely.'

'Can't you smell the animals?' Sadie made a disgusted face. 'The air's full of manure.'

'Country smells.' Bronagh didn't care. 'What's in my sandwich?'

'Ham or egg mayo?'

'I'll have the ham. Any crisps?'

Sadie passed her a bag. 'Salt and vinegar. Keogh's.'

'That's perfect. And what's to drink?'

'Lemonade or Coke.'

'Coke.'

'It's not the healthiest lunch.'

'No, but we'll be dining with Robert soon. He's a great baker. We'll pay him properly for the B & B.'

'We might be too late getting there tomorrow. He might be in bed.'

Bronagh laughed. 'This is a Ferrari. We can make time.'

'You can't break the speed limit. The police in this country are fierce.'

'Can you imagine it? Them waving down the Ferrari doing 110 miles an hour, making us get out and there we are, two older ladies with attitude.'

'You're not to speed, Bronagh.'

'I won't.'

'I mean it.'

'I won't,' Bronagh said through a mouthful of crisps. She tipped the packet upside down, allowing the last crumbs to tumble into her mouth, and screwed up the paper with a crackle. There was a soft fizz as she opened the tin of cola, a quiet glugging. Then she said, 'I might have forty winks.'

'Twenty. Then we'll get going.' Sadie inspected her coat. 'I've crumbs everywhere. I don't want them to go all over Rory's Ferrari, not with the posh seats.'

'It'll be fine,' Bronagh said, closing her eyes. 'I'll get it valeted before I give it back.'

'Valeted?' Sadie asked.

'I'll whip round with the hand-held vacuum,' Bronagh replied.

'Right.' Sadie closed her eyes and exhaled. 'That's good.'

Ten minutes later, the rain started again, pounding on the windscreen like a soothing drumbeat. Sadie and Bronagh didn't hear it. They were fast asleep, their heads on each other's shoulders.

7

The thudding of the rain had stopped. Someone was rapping hard on the car. Sadie opened her eyes with a jolt. Loud noises always made her jumpy. A big hairy hand with pale knuckles was banging on Bronagh's window.

Sadie yelled, terrified. 'Bronagh! Wake up.'

Bronagh sat bolt upright. 'Jaysus. I mean – I thought I was dreaming.'

'Who's that?' Sadie hissed, cowering from the hulking shape that loomed outside. 'He looks like a serial killer.'

Bronagh wound the window down, all formal. 'Hello. Can I help you?'

A large ruddy face with big whiskers poked through the window. 'What's going on?' He was middle-aged with a thatch of greying hair and a well-worn coat. 'What are you doing in front of my gate?'

'We were sleeping,' Bronagh said, as if it were the most normal thing in the world.

'Sleeping, is it?'

Bronagh made a 'duh' face. 'I'm tired from the driving.'

'Are you Irish?'

'Of course.' Bronagh was on the defensive. 'And you're Welsh. There's no law against it.'

'But there's a law against people parking in front of my gate,' the farmer snapped.

'We're sorry, we'll go,' Sadie offered sweetly.

'Is this your car?' the farmer asked suspiciously.

'Why wouldn't it be?' Bronagh retorted.

'Two old biddies in a Ferrari? I've never seen that before.'

Bronagh made her voice light. 'I don't suppose you have, but we're rich. We're film stars.'

Sadie groaned and gave the 'here we go' expression.

'Film stars?' The farmer's heavy brows came together with suspicion. 'What film stars?'

Sadie touched Bronagh's arm. 'Please don't.'

'I'm Bridget Bardo,' Bronagh spluttered. 'And this is – Raquel Welsh.'

The farmer's knitted brows furrowed even more. 'Brigitte Bardot wasn't Irish.'

'Don't be silly,' Bronagh said dismissively. 'Bridget's an Irish name. Of course I'm Irish.'

'And you're Raquel Welch, are you?' The farmer peered in to look at Sadie. He gazed at her chest, where her coat was pulled tight. 'I liked Raquel.'

'She's still the woman she was. She's got the body of Venus,' Bronagh boasted. 'Of course, I'm not as hot as I used to be – too much champagne and sunshine and sex in the nineteen sixties.'

The farmer looked confused. 'You're not Brigitte Bardot.'

'Look, I'm sorry we parked in front of your gate,' Sadie soothed gently. 'We were just going.'

'It's all right, Raquel,' the farmer said humbly. 'I've always been a fan. It's just that your friend's a bit—'

'Bridget's a brilliant driver. We'll be off in our little red car right now and we won't disturb you ever again.' Sadie spoke quickly. 'Thank you so much.'

Bronagh revved the engine. 'Yes, thanks for letting us park here, *monsieur*,' she cooed. *'Au revoir. Bon voyage. Ooooh là-là.'* She pressed the accelerator again, causing the farmer to jump back, then the car took off with a roar down the narrow road.

'What are you like, Bronagh?' Sadie grumbled reproachfully.

'I feel loads better now I've had forty winks. What time is it?'

'It's almost five. We overslept.'

'Well, let's find a hotel, somewhere to stop for the night. Tomorrow morning, we'll be bright and breezy. We can drive to Devon like the clappers. Once we get to Bristol, it's M5 all the way, so we'll be dandy.'

'Right. I'm worn out, Bronagh. I can't feel my hips. Or my bum.'

'Don't worry, Sadie. We'll be in sunny Devon before you know it.' She tugged out the map from the glovebox. 'Look, there's a nice pub in Pandy Bach, about ten miles away. Let's stop there, get supper, sleep on mattresses of goose feathers and we'll be grand tomorrow morning.'

'Do you think so?'

'Trust me.' Bronagh winked. 'I'm a French actress.'

They both burst out laughing. Bronagh turned back onto the A470 and pressed her foot down.

* * *

The next day, they got up late and enjoyed a lovely Welsh breakfast of laverbread, cockles, Welsh bacon, sausages and eggs. The B & B was idyllic, a picture-postcard thatched cottage nestled between two hills. Bronagh declared she could eat laverbread every day, it was so delicious. Sadie secretly thought it tasted nice but it looked a bit strange.

They thanked Cerys and Gareth, the hosts, and were on their way by half past ten.

At Abergavenny, they made a wrong turn and got lost.

They did the same at Newport. So they paused for lunch.

At Weston-super-Mare, they stopped for a toilet break and a rest, and fell asleep for two hours.

By seven o'clock, the sky was velvet dark and the lights from vehicles on the carriageway going north glared blindingly. Bronagh was starving and Sadie's legs ached.

Sadie groaned. 'Are we there yet?'

'Not far.' Bronagh yawned. 'We're just about to turn onto the back roads to Dawlish.'

'So – ten more minutes?'

'Yes. Half an hour tops.'

'I'm exhausted.'

'Me too,' Bronagh admitted, checking for road signs. 'You've been a good navigator though.'

'I haven't.' Sadie inspected the crumbs on her knee, the bag of rubbish at her feet. 'It's a good job we picked up some snacks.'

'It is. Ah, this is the turn-off, the B3192.' Bronagh glanced at the road map on Sadie's knee and took a left turn onto a narrow road flanked by trees.

'I wish it was light. It would be nice to see the forests and the ocean.' Sadie wriggled uncomfortably. 'Maybe we can come back.'

'There'll be so many things to see and do,' Bronagh said. 'I asked the receptionist in the Citi to show me some pictures of Dawlish on the line. It looks very quaint. It has a sandy beach and a railway going through it, and they have black swans there.'

'I can't wait to get to Robert's.' Sadie was suddenly anxious. 'Do you think he'll be awake? He won't mind us calling in?'

'Oh, Bunty says he's very nice. I wish we could've let him know though. It would've been polite.'

'We'd have had to have asked Bunty for his number.'

'I know. We'll have to send everyone more postcards from Dawlish. Do you think they'll have got the ones from Dublin yet?'

'Oh, they will.'

'Robert will be fine with us calling on him,' Bronagh said decidedly. 'The English are just like the Irish, they welcome family into their homes at all hours.'

'I hope you're right.'

'I am, I am.'

'Robert lives in a little village just like Ballycotton.'

'Smaller, though.'

'Bunty says it's a friendly village with a church and a pub.'

'An English pub. They're to die for. People buy you drinks all the time.' Bronagh turned down another dark road. There were no lights other than the headlight beam from the Ferrari. She said, 'It's eerie down here. A deer might jump out, or a badger. Or a sheep.'

'Do sheep wander wild here?'

'Everything wanders wild here.'

'You'd better slow down.'

'I'm creeping along, Sadie.'

'We don't want to hit a deer.' Sadie peered through the window. 'I can't see a thing.'

'I saw a sign to Millbrook. It's not far.'

'Good. Bunty says they have a gardening club that meets in the pub. Lots of people go and they eat scones and drink gin.'

'It sounds like my kind of club.'

'And when they had the baking competition, the whole village turned out. Sean said they had a great day. And it was televised.'

'Perhaps we'll be on TV?' Bronagh noticed a sign. 'This is the village. Right. How will we know it's Robert's house?'

'He has animals and a big patio.'

Bronagh slowed the Ferrari to a crawl. 'There aren't many lights. What time do the English go to bed?'

'I've no idea.' Sadie shrugged. 'There's a place on the right with a bit of land to it. Do you think that's Robert's?'

'It might be. There are no lights on though. Look, we're in the village properly – there are lots of little cottages.'

'And a village green, and there's the pub.' Sadie leaned over Bronagh's shoulder. 'It's called The Pig and Pickle.'

'Is it open?'

'Keep driving, Bronagh.'

'I just thought we could ask someone.'

'Look at that beautiful church.' Sadie pointed.

'Well,' Bronagh huffed. 'There's the post office, there's the school and now we're at the other end of Millbrook. Look. There's the sign. "Thank you for driving safely".'

'It's not a very big place.' Sadie was confused. 'Should we go back?'

'There's nowhere to turn round. I'll keep driving for a bit. Maybe Robert lives just outside the village.'

'Why would he do that?'

'I don't know, Sadie. Because he's got animals.'

'You're tired. You're getting crotchety.'

'I'm not crotchety.'

'You are.'

'I'm fine.' Bronagh stared through the windscreen.

'You always get crotchety at the end of the day.'

'I've been driving for hundreds of miles.'

'You've done well. That's not the point. I just said you get crotchety – oh. What's that? It's black as hell out here. Not a single house about. Stop, Bronagh. This must be it.'

'It's a turning to a house. There's a white sign.' Bronagh slowed down and read out loud. '"Tails of Hope Farm."'

'It's an animal sanctuary,' Sadie said. 'I bet this is where Robert lives. Sean said he has animals, goats and hens and all.'

'Look,' Bronagh added excitedly. 'He runs a B & B too. It says on the sign. Bed and Breakfast.'

'That's music to my ears.' Sadie was worn out and her hip was giving her a hard time. 'A bed.'

'And breakfast.' Bronagh turned the steering wheel, driving slowly up the gravel drive that crunched beneath the tyres.

'I can't see any animals.' Sadie stared into blackness. 'I think there are some fields though.'

'The animals are all tucked up – and that's where I want to be. There's the house. And there's a little light on.'

The Ferrari came to a stop outside a tall white building, a security light gleaming outside. There was a glimmering lamp at one of the bedroom windows. Sadie and Bronagh clambered out, their limbs aching and stiff. The air smelled sweet, of honeysuckle and damp grass.

'Robert will be glad to have customers. We'll pay him for the B & B, of course. But we'll tell him who we are.'

'Who are we?' Sadie was so tired she was confused.

'Well, you're his brother-in-law's mammy and I'm his brother-in-law's auntie.'

'Right.' Sadie watched as Bronagh rapped the brass door knocker that was shaped like a horse's head. There was no response.

'Perhaps Robert's asleep,' Sadie said nervously.

'He has a partner now, doesn't he? The Cornish woman who bakes.'

'She's called Tressy,' Sadie said. 'We haven't met her.'

'We haven't met any of them since Sean's wedding and that was years ago,' Bronagh said. 'Maybe Tressy's up, making the sourdough for the breakfast.'

'Oh, the smell of fresh bread.' Sadie drooled, imagining the aroma.

A light illuminated the hall behind the door glass. Sadie and Bronagh exchanged glances. 'We're on,' Bronagh said, a look of relief flooding her face.

The door opened to reveal a short woman in a dressing gown, her unruly hair pinned up. She might have been in her fifties or sixties. Her face took on a suspicious expression. 'Hello?'

'It's us, your Irish family. You must be Tressy.' Bronagh enveloped the woman in an enthusiastic hug. 'We're Sean's mammy and auntie.'

The woman pulled back. 'Who?'

'Hello.' Bronagh was delighted. 'We've come to stop for a few days.'

'Who are you?' the woman asked again. She didn't look pleased.

'Sean and Bunty's family. From Ballycotton,' Bronagh enthused. 'We're absolutely knackered. I don't suppose you've got a bed ready. We'll pay the going rate.'

The woman's frown deepened. 'Who did you say you were?'

'Bronagh and Sadie,' Bronagh said patiently.

Sadie felt the penny drop with a thud. 'Bronagh, this isn't Robert's house at all. We're at the wrong place.'

'Oh, no.' Bronagh's face crumpled as if she would cry. 'I thought we were here.'

'No, we're not here.' Sadie put an arm around Bronagh's

shoulder as she spoke to the woman. 'I'm sorry. We thought this was our relative's house. We just came over from Ireland. We've been driving for two days. We're exhausted.' She felt Bronagh collapse against her. 'I don't suppose you could put us up for the night? Bed and breakfast?'

'Oh. I see.' The woman peered over her shoulder to the car. 'It's a bit late. Is that your car?'

'It is,' Sadie began. She saw Bronagh open her mouth and feared the worst.

'We're on holiday, living it up. We're film stars—'

'No, it's my grandson's,' Sadie interrupted, taking charge. 'But we'd really love it if you had a spare room for us to get our heads down.'

'Oh.' The woman stared at her for a moment. Sadie offered her widest, most winning smile and the woman almost smiled back. 'Right. Of course. Well – I have a double room already made up. A double bed. Would that be OK?'

'I'd sleep in the cowshed, I'm so bushed,' Bronagh whispered, her head against Sadie's shoulder.

'Come inside,' the woman said kindly. Now she was properly smiling, she looked much more hospitable. 'I'm Hazel Barton,' she said. 'Welcome to Tails of Hope.'

'You're a sanctuary,' Sadie said gratefully.

'We are. I'll tell you all about it in the morning. In fact, you can have the tour after breakfast,' Hazel said.

'Breakfast,' Bronagh moaned.

Hazel led them up a short flight of steps, opened a white wooden door and flicked on a light switch. A cosy room was illuminated, a big brass bed, a chair with cushions, pretty floral curtains, a light wardrobe, an en suite bathroom.

'Heaven.' Sadie sighed with relief at the sight of it. 'I'm so tired.'

'Why don't you settle in?' Hazel said. 'You've had a long day. If you like, I'll bring you a hot drink up. How does milky cocoa sound?'

'I could kiss you.' Bronagh sank onto the bed, her eyes closing.

'Would a biscuit or two be welcome?'

'Thanks, Hazel, it would.' Sadie gave her a look of gratitude. She watched as the door closed and turned to Bronagh.

'Well, this is more like it.' Sadie collapsed next to her and breathed out in relief. It wasn't her own bed, but it was a bed. And right now that was all she wanted.

'It's luxury.' Bronagh spoke her thoughts aloud. 'I'm going to love staying in England. I've just decided, Sadie: the meaning of life is an Englishwoman in a dressing gown bringing milky cocoa.'

Sadie closed her eyes and smiled. Bronagh was right.

8

Back in Ballycotton, Bunty and Sean sat in front of the television, a hot cup of cocoa burning the skin of their palms. The log fire was dying down; Bunty yawned, resting her head against Sean's shoulder.

'I think it's bedtime.'

'Let's just have five minutes, then we'll go up.' Sean slurped cocoa.

'All right.' Bunty glanced around the room. They'd tidy up tomorrow. There was a packet of biscuits, half eaten, on the coffee table, a newspaper, sweet wrappings and the day's layer of new dust. Her eyes moved to the picture on the mantelpiece, a young Sean and Bunty holding a little bundle wrapped in a shawl, baby Daniel. Danny boy. It was the only picture she had of him. And the photo was the one thing she enjoyed dusting. Sean had put it there after they came back from visiting Hattie and Robert in Devon, and placed a little candle next to it. He wanted to keep their baby's memory alive from now on. It felt better to talk about it than to hide the hurt away, as they'd done for years and years.

The television rattled. Sean wrapped an arm round Bunty. 'Mammy's in Dublin, then.'

'That's what the postcard said.'

'And she'll come back with Auntie Bronagh in a day or two.'

'Rory's fine about them borrowing the car.'

'He's good as gold.' Sean gave a short laugh. 'Maybe we can borrow it when they're back and I'll take you out somewhere swanky.'

Bunty grinned. 'Pat said the same thing to Nora.' She closed her eyes. Then something vibrated against her shoulder. 'Your phone's going off, Sean.'

'At this time of night?' His face was momentarily worried. 'I hope it's not Mammy.'

'She hasn't got a mobile.'

'I mean bad news.' Sean held the phone to his ear. 'Oh, Niall, hello. What?' A frown deepened between his eyes. 'Rory's heard from them? When? Oh? Where?' He began to laugh. 'She hasn't? In the Ferrari? They're a right pair. What? Yes, right, we will.'

'What's happened?' Bunty eased herself upright from the sofa.

'That was Niall. They've been in contact with Rory. And Rory's told his da.'

'From Dublin?'

'Well, this is the thing.' Sean was dumbfounded. 'Auntie Bronagh rang Rory from the reception desk of the Citi Hotel in Dublin about the car insurance documents. They used them so they could get on the boat.'

'What boat?' Bunty made a shocked face. 'Where on earth have they gone?'

'You'll never believe it. Rory thought it was hilarious.' Sean put his phone down. 'They've gone to England. The receptionist booked them a ferry crossing. They've gone to stay with your brother. In Devon.'

'Oh, no.' Bunty put both hands to her mouth. 'To Robert's?'

'We should ring him.'

'We can't.' Bunty was suddenly anxious. 'Robert and Tressy are in Cornwall. He said so when we spoke on the phone on Friday night. They won't be back until midweek.'

'Ah.' Sean scratched his head. 'So where are Mammy and Auntie Bronagh staying?' He exhaled slowly. 'Neither of those two has a mobile between them. What'll we do?'

'I've no idea,' Bunty said.

Sean's phone rang again and he picked it up. 'Nora? Yes, Niall just rang and told us. So you know they've gone to England in the Ferrari. But Bunty says Robert's away until midweek. I know. I wonder where they're staying. Yes, we will, tomorrow. See you.'

'What did Nora say?' Bunty asked.

'She's coming round tomorrow, first thing. Niall and Maeve too. We'll talk about it all then.'

'I'll make breakfast,' Bunty said. 'What do you think we should do?'

'Can you imagine it? Trouble follows Auntie Bronagh like a shadow and Mammy's not much better. They're a bad influence on each other,' Sean muttered. 'We'll talk about it as a family.'

'It's a worry, Sean.'

'It is.'

'Do you think they drove all that way in the Ferrari?'

'It's a long distance for two old ladies.'

'Your mammy's all right, she's sensible,' Bunty began.

Sean looked at her as if she had said something ridiculous. He opened his mouth to reply; his phone rang again. He snatched it up.

'Ah, Rory. Yes, Your da rang me too. And Robert's away from

home, so we don't know if they'll have anywhere to stay. You did what? Oh, that was nice of you. Yes, right, we will. We'll see you first thing tomorrow. Bunty and I will make everyone breakfast. Yes, we definitely need to do something. Well, I'll see you and Lola then. Goodnight.'

He put his phone down and met Bunty's anxious expression. 'That was Rory. He wanted to let me know that Mammy has got the insurance documents, and she and Auntie Bronagh got on the boat to Holyhead. They'll be in England by now. And he spoke to the receptionist at the Citi, to check they'd got off all right and he sent her a bouquet of roses to thank her for her trouble. He's a nice lad. We'll all meet up here first thing.' He exhaled slowly. 'Well, Bunts, something has to be done before they get into any more trouble. Robert's away – they've got nowhere to stay. We can't let them roam around Devon causing havoc, and that's for sure.'

* * *

Sadie opened her eyes to the sound of hammering rain. She waited a moment and realised slowly that it was spattering inside the room, not far away, and that she was in England. There was an empty body-shaped space in the bed next to her. Bronagh was in the shower. She eased herself up gently. Her body ached; her muscles throbbed. Her joints were stiff and she needed her meds. Yesterday and the day before had taken it out of her. She wasn't thirty any more. She groaned. 'Can I get in the shower after you, Bronagh?'

'I'll leave it on,' a chirpy voice came back to her. 'Ooooh, it's hot. And yer Hazel wan has left some shower gel in here. It's grapefruit and orange. I smell like a Spanish orchard.'

Sadie glanced at the clock. 'It's eight o'clock. I'm ready for breakfast.'

'So am I.'

Sadie eased herself out of bed and moved stiffly to the window, tugging back the floral curtains. Outside, she saw open fields, several horses grazing, some donkeys. She stared harder. 'They've got alpacas here.'

'It's an animal sanctuary,' Bronagh's voice echoed from the shower.

'And there's a young woman down there with horses – she's got a jacket on and wellingtons.'

'I hope that's not all she's got on.'

'She looks about twenty-something. Perhaps she's Hazel's daughter. Or she might be a farm worker.'

'Who knows?' Bronagh emerged from the shower wrapped in a fluffy towel, her purple and grey hair dripping. 'Jump in. Enjoy.'

'I will.' Sadie filled a glass with tap water and swallowed her pills.

'I left you one towel.'

'Good.'

Sadie peeled off her old pyjamas and edged precariously beneath the hot drops. Her skin burned and tingled; it felt delicious. She called, 'You're right, it's lovely. I'm going in for the bodywash.'

'I wonder what's for breakfast?'

'I don't care. I'm starved,' Sadie shouted. 'All we ate was rubbish yesterday. It makes me sluggish.'

'The drive made me sluggish,' Bronagh called back. 'Ooh, look at all those fields. And they *are* alpacas. Hazel promised us a tour.'

'She did.' Sadie rubbed a citrus-smelling gel onto her skin and inhaled deeply. 'Do you think she knows Robert?'

'It's an English village – everyone knows everyone.' Bronagh made the muffled sound of someone struggling into a jumper. 'I thought Devon was supposed to be sunny.'

'It's winter.'

'There's a wind,' Bronagh answered. 'I can see the young woman's ponytail blowing everywhere. I bet it's cold out.'

'It will be.'

'We might need to buy some more clothes, Sadie. We could get wellies and those waxy coats. We'd look like gentry. Like Camilla.'

'Who's Camilla?'

'Charles's wife, the queen wan. She's our age.'

'Is she?' Sadie turned the shower off and stepped out. 'No, I've nearly ten years on her.' She patted herself with a towel. 'But we'd look nice in those tweedy jackets and the flat caps and wellies. Like they wear at the races.'

'Don't talk about races. Michael used to drive me mad with the horses. It was the only thing I disapproved of, Sadie.'

'Sean and Niall like a flutter.' Sadie remembered sadly that Alfie had been just as bad as she emerged from the en suite wrapped in a towel. 'Do you think they have retired racing horses here?'

'I suppose all animals are welcome. I admire people who look after the old nags and clapped-out donkeys that no one else wants.' Bronagh thought for a minute. 'They're past it, just like us.'

'We're not past it,' Sadie insisted. 'We might be old, but we still cook, wash, go shopping.'

'We don't shop. We get the grocery delivery on Monday nights.'

'Do you think we're like the animals here, Bronagh? Bone-tired and useless?' Sadie certainly felt it and the thought made her heart sink.

'Not at all, but I'm just saying, Sadie. Some people would think that. Some societies respect their old people, they think they're wise and special. But we just get ignored or treated like a stereotype, young ones calling us fogeys. Yet some people at forty are finished. We're not bad, considering.'

'We're doing all right.' Sadie struggled into her clothes; her skin was still damp. 'And this old lady needs a cup of coffee and some toast.'

'Or an English breakfast.'

'Is that the same as an Irish one?'

'Ah, no.' Bronagh thought for a moment. 'Ours is better. We have the black pudding. Or the white pudding. And lots of fried potatoes,' she said. 'I don't care what the difference is. Let's go and get breakfast.'

* * *

In the spacious farmhouse kitchen Hazel presented them with plates of sausages, eggs, bacon, mushrooms and tomatoes.

Bronagh's face shone. 'This looks lovely.'

Hazel poured coffee into china cups. 'Did you both sleep well?'

'Like tops,' Bronagh said, with a mouthful of sausage.

'Like logs,' Sadie said at the same time.

'You both looked exhausted when you arrived. It must have been a long drive.'

'I was an eejit to think I could do it in two days. It nearly killed me,' Bronagh admitted. 'But now we're here.'

'The sanctuary looks lovely,' Sadie added, by way of conversation. 'What animals do you have?'

'All sorts. We never turn an animal away.' Hazel's face was filled with kindness. 'We have horses, alpacas, donkeys, chickens. We also have feral cats in the barn to keep the rats away, an owl or two and a few hedgehogs.'

'That's impressive,' Bronagh said. 'It must be a long day, working with that little lot, keeping them all fed.'

'My daughter does a lot of the work. We have volunteers too, but we're always on the lookout for more. And fundraising's a big part of what we do.' Hazel refilled Bronagh's cup. 'My parents started it up. It was my mum's big project.'

'Where are they now?' Sadie held out her cup for more coffee.

'My mother passed away a few years ago. Tails of Hope was her passion. Dad lives here. He loves the place.'

Bronagh scrutinised Hazel's face. If she was in her fifties, her father could be a similar age to herself. She was suddenly interested. 'Does your da still work here?'

'He tends to do accounts mostly, although he loves to be outside feeding the animals.'

Bronagh patted her hair. 'I can't wait to meet him.'

'Are you sisters?' Hazel asked.

'Sisters-in-law. Sadie married my brother, Alfie,' Bronagh said.

'And you're here for a holiday or to stay with family?' Hazel seemed to be remembering. 'You said last night that you're visiting relatives.'

'Robert and his partner, Tressy. And Robert's sister Hattie,' Sadie explained. 'My son's married to Robert's other sister, Bunty.'

'Robert Parkin. I know him, to say hello to. He's the man who bakes the cakes. And he has goats.' Hazel's face clouded. 'I don't think he's at home at the moment.'

'Oh?'

'I was standing behind him last weekend in the post office and he said something to Debbie behind the counter that he was going to Cornwall for a few days. His partner's Cornish. She's meeting old friends in Padstow.'

'You heard all that in the post office?' Sadie asked.

Bronagh's face fell. 'When will they be back?'

'Later this week. I'm sure that's what he said,' Hazel said.

Bronagh looked at Sadie. 'What'll we do?'

'Wait for him?' Sadie's mind was racing. She'd been feeling a little homesick. But – shouldn't she be more adventurous, like Bronagh? Didn't she deserve a holiday in sunny Devon? As soon as she got back to the Baltic cold of Ballycotton, the routine would kick in again. No, she needed a break. 'Yes, let's wait until he's back.'

Bronagh stared at her almost empty plate. The breakfast had been delicious. 'Hazel, would it be all right if we stayed on?'

'You could,' Hazel replied. 'To be honest, we don't have many guests this time of year, so I'd be glad of it.'

'That's perfect.' Sadie stood up, ready to go. 'And is your offer of a tour of the sanctuary still on?'

'I'd be delighted,' Hazel said.

'But first, is there any more toast and coffee?' Bronagh waved Sadie down again. 'And peanut butter? Yesterday really took it out of me.'

9

In Ballycotton, Rory watched thoughtfully as the O'Connor family attempted to make a decision around the circular breakfast table with the shamrock-embroidered linen cloth.

'What do you think we should do?' Niall asked, munching toast. Sean lifted his coffee cup and gazed at each face for answers. Besides himself and Bunty, there were Niall and Maeve, Nora and Pat and Rory, who'd been working from Niall's extension all week, and Lola.

'Well, I'm not worried about the car,' Rory said casually. 'It's funny to think of Grandmammy and Great-Auntie Bronagh tearing up the tarmac in England.'

Lola shot him a look. 'What if they've scraped your paintwork?'

'Ah, it's only paintwork, Lola.'

Nora laughed. 'The pair of them can't be trusted.'

'Because they're old?' Lola wondered.

'No, because they're Sadie and Bronagh.' Pat spluttered. 'They're hellraisers.'

'It'd be different if we knew they were at Robert's,' Sean said anxiously.

'I'll phone him and ask him when he's back.' Bunty offered more toast. Pat took two pieces.

'Yes, but we don't want to spoil his holiday, Bunts. He might think he has to come home for Mammy's sake,' Sean said. 'Let's leave him a few days.'

'It would be different if Mammy had a phone,' Niall said.

'Everybody has a phone.' Lola rolled her eyes. 'Perhaps they can't see the screen.'

Rory wasn't listening. 'Just let them enjoy themselves. I'm sure Auntie Bunty's brother will be back in a day or two and we can ring him then.'

'Mammy's not young any more.' Sean wiped his furrowed brow. 'Or Auntie Bronagh.'

'They're full of beans, though,' Bunty said loyally.

'Maybe, but we can't just leave them to run riot.' Sean sipped coffee.

'I agree with you, Sean.' Niall was buttering more toast. 'Mammy's our responsibility since Da died. They both are. Uncle Michael's not around now either. It's expected that we look out for them.'

'Then we have to find them.' Niall's face was thoughtful.

'We should.' That was Nora's thought too. 'And there's only one way we can do it.'

'There is.' Rory folded his arms. He'd made his mind up.

'Oh, no. It'll be Christmas in a few weeks,' Maeve groaned.

'I might have a model shoot in Dublin this weekend – ski wear.' Lola looked unhappy.

'We haven't decided what to do yet,' Sean said. 'But we should put it to the vote. Right. Who thinks we should go to

Devon and bring Auntie Bronagh and Mammy back? Hands up those of us who think it's a good idea.'

Rory grinned and stuck up his hand.

* * *

Sadie and Bronagh, in headscarves, coats and borrowed boots, followed Hazel across the frosty field. The west wind was raw and made their fingers red and stiff with cold. Hazel was wearing a woollen hat, a wax coat and a scarf. She moved briskly. 'Shall we see the horses first?'

'We're fond of horses.' Bronagh smirked. 'My husband, God rest his soul, invested a lot of money in them.'

Hazel gazed towards a field stretching beyond. Five horses grazed happily. She said, 'We're fond of them too. The grey mare has been with us for eight years. Her owner couldn't afford to keep her.'

'Why do you take them in?' Sadie asked.

'They're neglected, lost or abandoned.' Hazel leaned against the gate. 'The chestnut one there was an ex-racehorse. Of course, he's old. His racing days are over.'

'What's his name?' Bronagh was all interest.

'He was once called Prince Pirate. We just call him Pi now.'

Bronagh leaned over and held out a hand. 'Pi, come to Bronagh.' The chestnut horse looked up, sniffing. 'He's very bright.'

'He is,' Hazel agreed. 'He's an intelligent boy.'

'How old is he?' Sadie asked, thinking he looked a little melancholy.

'Eighteen. He retired ten years ago. He damaged a leg in a fall.'

Bronagh's hand was still out. Pi walked amiably towards her, his front leg still a little wobbly. 'He's lovely.'

Pi paused by the gate, close enough to allow Bronagh to rub the blaze on his nose. His eyes were trusting as he breathed into her palm.

'Can I feed him?' Bronagh asked.

'We wouldn't mind helping out a bit.' Sadie felt energised this morning. Devon was bright and cold, but the salt-from-the-sea air was refreshing.

'Of course. You'll meet Poppy later. That's my daughter. She'd be delighted with any help. She'll introduce you to them all.' Hazel paused. 'I wonder, would you like to have dinner with us tonight? I'd be happy to do dinner, for just a little bit more, and you could meet my father.'

'We'd love that, wouldn't we, Sadie?' Bronagh said as Pi nuzzled her hand.

'Definitely. I thought we might drive into Dawlish this afternoon and take a look around,' Sadie suggested.

'That's a good idea. All the Christmas lights will be on,' Hazel said. 'Shall we walk on and meet the donkeys? Then we can say hello to the alpacas.'

Bronagh seemed unwilling to leave Pi, but she gave the chestnut horse a final pat. 'How many donkeys do you have?'

'Three. Diana, Mary and Florence.'

'The Supremes.' Sadie smiled. 'Am I right?'

'You are. Well done.' Hazel led them down a stony path towards another field. 'It's nippy in the air. We had a sharp frost this morning.'

'Just a few weeks until Christmas.' Sadie was thinking of home again, her own things, the familiar scents of the past.

'When do you get the decorations up, Hazel?' Bronagh asked, her hands deep in her pockets.

'We started in the snug and the living room. We'll finish doing it this weekend.' Hazel gave a sigh. 'I love Christmas.'

'So do I,' Bronagh said brightly. 'Imagine spending Christmas in an animal sanctuary. It must be wonderful.'

'It is,' Hazel said. 'We've just put our Tails of Hope Christmas cards online, and a scheme for sponsoring an animal as a gift.'

'Don't you get financial backing?' Sadie asked.

'Yes, Paul found sponsors who give regular donations, and we hold a few fundraising events. The B & B does well in the summer. And we get lots of visitors then. Poppy runs stalls at local fetes. We break even.'

'You're doing a wonderful job.' Sadie was full of admiration.

'It's what we love,' Hazel said with a smile. They had reached a field with three old donkeys. A young woman with a long ponytail emerged from the barn and waved. Hazel waved back. 'That's Poppy. She sees to the donkeys every day.'

'That looks like hard work,' Bronagh grunted.

The young woman strode over to them and held out a hand. 'Hello. These three are The Supremes. Come and meet them.'

'I think that's a lovely name for the donkeys.' Sadie walked through as Poppy held the gate open. 'Do they mind being petted?'

'They love it,' Poppy said.

Hazel smiled. 'I'd better get back to the house, Poppy. I promised your grandad I'd catch up with him.' She paused. 'Do say if there's anything you need. I'm always around the house. You say you're staying tonight and tomorrow?'

'Can we stay until Wednesday night and take it from there?' Sadie asked. 'It depends if Robert's back.'

'I'm happy for you to stay as long as you like.' Hazel beamed. 'If I don't catch up with you before, I'll see you for dinner at seven. It'll be in our family kitchen.'

'That's lovely,' Bronagh said. 'Thanks, Hazel.'

They watched her walk away back to the house across the

glistening frosty field. Sadie had to ask. 'Does your dad live here, Poppy?'

'Not now,' Poppy murmured. The wind blew strands of fair hair across her face. 'He left when I was nine. There's just me, Mum and Grandad.'

'Is this your full-time job?' Bronagh asked.

'It is. I'm really lucky.' Poppy smiled. 'I took some courses at college. Animal Care. Animal Management. Grandad was an accountant before he took this place on. We love all animals here. We never turn a needy animal away.'

'That's great,' Bronagh said. They had reached a vast open barn that housed the donkeys, and she selected the tallest one, fondling its ears. 'Who's this?'

'Diana.'

Sadie began to pat another donkey, who eyed her gently. 'And this one?'

'This is Mary, and her sister's Florence,' Poppy said. 'Did you know that donkeys' brays can carry up to sixty miles in the desert?'

'Are they desert animals?' Bronagh asked.

'They derive from the African wild ass,' Poppy explained.

'I've met a few wild asses in my time,' Bronagh chuckled, rubbing Diana's nose. 'Are they as stubborn as people think, donkeys?'

'Not at all. They are sociable and loyal.' Poppy put her hands on her hips. 'Would you like to meet the alpacas? You can help me feed them.'

'What do they eat?' Sadie asked.

'Plants, roughage. Ours are going to get carrots and a few oranges this morning.' Poppy pointed towards a diamond-frosted field. 'It's a bit of a walk away. Is that all right?'

'I'll do my best.' Sadie was already tired. 'I'll get my steps in this morning. Bronagh and I are off out for lunch.'

'Mum says you can put your car in the garage overnight. I've never been in a Ferrari.'

'It's my grandson's. He lent it to us,' Sadie said, and was immediately embarrassed that she wasn't entirely telling the truth.

'He sounds nice,' Poppy said.

'Rory's wonderful. My whole family are.' Sadie realised again how much she was missing them. That was her problem. She was a mammy. And a Grandmammy. It had been a long time since she'd just been Sadie. But she knew the next few days were an opportunity to find that part of herself again. The part that wasn't always thinking of someone else.

Bronagh was striding ahead. 'How many alpacas are there?'

'Four. All males. Juan, Carlos, Angel and Jose. Angel is the argumentative one. He often spits at the others.'

'I've met men like that,' Bronagh spluttered. 'Poppy, do you have a boyfriend?'

'No. I did have one, but we fell out.'

'Might you fall back in again?' Bronagh asked, and Sadie nudged her gently. Bronagh could be inquisitive to the point of insensitivity.

'No.' Poppy looked unhappy. 'I'm only twenty-five. There's plenty of time for finding "the one" and anyway, most of the men I meet aren't a patch on my animals. Look.' She pointed to a field where four alpacas were watching them with interest. Her face shone as she said, 'Come and meet the boys. They'll melt your hearts.'

'They look so cuddly,' Bronagh said. 'Yes, and I've met men like that too.'

10

As the sun was setting, Sadie and Bronagh walked arm in arm through Dawlish, hanging onto each other for warmth and to ease their aching legs. The car journey from Holyhead had really taken it out of them. They were licking ice creams, swirly cones with a chocolate flake and sprinkles. Bronagh had a smudge of cream on her nose.

They paused to stare up at Christmas lights, strings of tiny gold beads with dangling baubles of sparkling bronze. The shops on the parade were a swirl of red and green stars. A café that looked out onto the sea sported twinkling lights and, outside, a fir tree glowed with silver decorations.

Across the road, signs with the words 'Merry Christmas' fizzed from red to gold and back to red. Bronagh slurped ice cream. 'Is it Christmassy enough for you, Sadie?'

'It's hard to ignore, for sure,' Sadie muttered quietly. 'I wonder if Sean and Bunty have their deckies up yet.'

'I like Dawlish. All the Christmas lights must be for the visitors, because it's a seaside place. But in Ballycotton, we just have a few baubles in the baker's. Oh, will you look at him?' Bronagh pointed at a gigantic Santa in a shop window, laughing so hard that his scarlet belly vibrated. 'Look at all the presents in that sack.'

'If I was a three-year-old, he'd scare me to death.'

'I never believed in him when I was three,' Bronagh said. 'I knew it was my da who put my present under the tree. I watched him do it.' Her face was soft in the flashing lights. 'Once he'd had a few whiskeys on a Christmas Eve. It's a wonder he didn't knock the tree over.'

'You had a tree? You must have been rich.'

'We used the same one every year. My da dug it up in December and planted it back in the garden in January. That's proper recycling.'

'Mammy used to make paper chains with us. We covered the whole room with them. And she'd make toffee twists and biscuits as treats.' Sadie was reminiscing again and the soft emotions returned to her like an ache. 'I remember my da sold his bike one year to buy us presents. He walked to work for the next three months in the bitter cold.'

'They were good times. And did you have an old paraffin heater?'

'We did – they were smelly but the fuel was cheap and they belted out the heat. You'd scorch your legs if you stood too close.' Sadie pointed to the sea. 'What about a little walk on the beach? Can we manage it?'

'Just a few paces. Then we'll go back. What do you think Hazel's making for dinner?'

'I've no idea but I'm starving.'

'And we'll meet Hazel's da. What do you think he's like?'

'Our age. A bit doddery on his pins, like me. No, I expect he's very kind,' Sadie said.

'What makes you say that?'

'Because he loves animals. He's saving God's creatures.'

Bronagh chuckled. 'Well, we'll liven him up a bit.'

'I bet Hazel's a great cook.'

'She has the smile of an angel. But I think she's frazzled.'

'Frazzled.' Sadie understood only too well.

'Overworked. Like all women. Poppy's nice. I don't expect she gets out much, living in a village. There's not much to do.'

'Same as Ballycotton,' Sadie agreed. 'Just listen to the sea shushing and whooshing.'

Sadie and Bronagh stood on the beach together, their eyes closed, filling their ears with the sea's whispers. Bronagh smiled. 'It's just like a secret lover, murmuring sweet nothings.'

'Or the comforting voice of God.' Sadie opened her eyes and stared into the ocean, dark as obsidian. Beyond, little lights twinkled from distant houses. The waves rushing onto pebbles was the only sound. She felt her body relax.

Bronagh said, 'I'm glad we came here.'

'Me too,' Sadie agreed. She inhaled fresh air and felt immediately calm.

'It's good to listen to the sea. It stops me worrying about unimportant things.'

'What unimportant things do you worry about, Bronagh?'

'My nose.'

'What about your nose?'

'It's squidgy.'

Sadie frowned. 'No, you've a lovely nose.'

'I always wanted fine features like yours. A straight nose, a chiselled one. Mine's like a button. You can squash it.'

'Lots of beautiful women have button noses, Bronagh.'

'Like who?'

'The Mona Lisa. She has a squidgy nose. And Elizabeth Taylor. And Audrey Hepburn. And Snow White.'

'Oh?'

'Button noses are cute.'

'I always thought my nose was wrong for me. I wanted your nose.'

'Your nose is adorable. You're adorable.' Sadie gave Bronagh a hug. 'Mine's too big. It takes up too much of my face.'

'Don't be daft. You've a nice nose,' Bronagh said. 'Shall we get back?'

'We'd better.'

They walked along to where they had left the Ferrari, in a car park. As they approached it, Sadie said, 'What's going on there?'

Bronagh squinted through her glasses and shouted, 'Hey. Get off.'

Two boys, probably ten or eleven years old, were leaning against the bumper. One of them was taking photos of the car on his phone. The other started to kick the tyres. Bronagh increased her speed as best as she could. 'Go on, clear off. That's my car.'

'No, it's not,' one of the boys snickered. 'This is a Ferrari. Old bags don't own Ferraris.'

'And what would you know, you little muppet?' Bronagh lifted her handbag as if she would bash the boys with it. 'Now clear off.'

'It's not your car,' the other boy spat. He had cropped hair and small eyes. 'It's ours.'

'Are you Irish?' the first boy asked. 'Are you in the IRA?'

The boy with small eyes took a threatening pace forward. 'Prove it's your car. Go on. I bet you can't.'

'Look, be good lads and move on, please,' Sadie said reasonably, but her pulse had started to twitch. 'We want to go home.'

'To Belfast?' The first boy gave a derisory snort. 'Did you steal this car? It can't be yours. You're skanks.'

Sadie had no idea what he meant, but an alarm bell was ring-ing. She could handle her own children, but these two had no respect. 'Excuse me, would you please just—?'

'We'll move if you pay us.' The boy with the small eyes made his eyes even smaller. 'What's it worth, this car? Thousands? We'll move if you give us a hundred quid.'

'Each,' said the other boy as he plonked himself on the bonnet.

Bronagh put her hands on her hips. 'Look, will you move on? Or I'll get the police.'

'Oh, yeah?' The second boy made a face. 'The pigs are all too busy waving speed guns about. They won't give a toss about two old grannies.'

'Just go home to your mammy,' Bronagh said carefully.

'Why don't you piss off?' The small-eyed boy spat on the ground. He eased himself off the bonnet and took a step towards Bronagh. 'You're just a skanky old crone. Piss off back to Ireland and live in the bogs.'

'Look.' Sadie grabbed Bronagh's arm nervously. She felt something shift. The boys had been toying with them; now there was the sense of threat. 'We need to go home.'

'Give us two hundred,' the first boy said with a scowl that clearly meant business.

'Just give it a rest, lads.' A clear, strong voice came from behind Sadie. A young man wearing a baseball cap and a heavy coat took a pace forwards. His hand held the small fingers of a little boy in an anorak with the fluffy hood up. He whisked the child up into his arms. His face was placid, unfazed. 'Go on, let these ladies drive home.'

'It's not their car.' One of the boys glared.

'Just go home, eh?' the man said again. 'You're better than this, terrorising old ladies.'

The boys looked at each other. Suddenly, faced with a

square-set man who was probably in his thirties, their arrogance seemed to diminish. They looked at each other for a moment, making their minds up. They seemed smaller, younger.

'Get on,' the man said kindly. 'Off home.'

'Whatever,' one of the boys muttered, turning away.

'Skanks,' the other grunted as he followed the first one through the lines of parked cars.

Bronagh looked at the young man in the cap as if he were a superhero. 'Thank you.'

'I was just on the way home. We've been on the beach. I work shifts, so it's nice to do the school run.' The young man spoke to his son. 'It's time we were getting back. Mum'll have our tea ready.'

Bronagh flourished her keys and opened the car. 'We're really grateful.'

'The kids were trying it on,' the young man said. He was wearing an Iron Maiden shirt beneath his anorak. 'Most of them are no trouble. I'd hate you to think we didn't offer a warm welcome round these parts.' He kissed his son's cheek. 'Are you on holiday?'

'We are.' Sadie felt a rush of gratitude. Her pulse was still pumping too hard. 'We're stopping at the animal sanctuary in Millbrook.'

'I know it. I've driven past.' The young man smiled. 'We've been meaning to go there but we never get round to it.'

'It's lovely,' Bronagh said. 'The alpacas and the donkeys. And the horses.'

'Can we go to see the horses, Daddy?' Beneath his hood the little boy had adorable curls.

'Are they doing any Christmas events?' the young man asked.

'I don't know.' Sadie was already thinking about the missed opportunity.

The man said, 'I'll take a look online. Have they got a website?'

'Of course. They have a really good one,' Bronagh gushed. In truth, she had no idea.

'Right – thanks.' The young man adjusted his child's position, hugging him closer against the slicing sea breeze, and was on his way towards the shadowy cars parked beneath a street lamp.

'No, thank *you*,' Bronagh called after him. 'Happy Christmas.'

'And to you too,' the voice came back.

As they wriggled into the car, Bronagh flopped into the seat, emotionally exhausted. 'I don't suppose it was wise leaving the car there. It attracts attention.'

'We could have left it at the B & B and taken the bus.' Sadie agreed. Her heart was still walloping beneath her coat.

'Let's get back.' Bronagh felt relief rush through her. 'I thought those boys might take us on. And us just being helpless old ladies. You don't suppose Hazel's da has some brandy? I need a drink.'

'Go on with you.' Sadie grinned, but she had the sinking feeling that they'd got away with it by the skin of their teeth. 'Thank goodness for the nice young man. Let's just get back. We've time for a shower before dinner time.'

'All right.' Bronagh started the engine and the lights illuminated the dark road home.

11

Hazel's kitchen was warm and welcoming, heat belting out from a shiny aubergine-coloured Aga. There were strings of twinkling Christmas lights in each corner, a few cards festooning the Welsh dresser, and everywhere smelled of delicious cooking. A square table in the middle of the room was already set for five people and, as Sadie and Bronagh tiptoed in politely, Hazel and Poppy were bustling around, ladling soup, filling wine glasses.

Poppy looked up. 'Would you like some Merlot?'

'Well, it's a weeknight but—' Bronagh met Sadie's eyes '—I suppose I can force myself to have a glass or three.'

'Thanks,' Sadie said, hovering near a chair. She still felt shaky after the car-park ordeal.

'Sit anywhere,' Hazel said. 'Help yourself to bread and soup.'

Sadie sat down gladly. 'Is your father joining us, Hazel?'

'He's on his way.' Hazel glanced towards the door. 'Dad'll be here as soon as he smells the food.'

'Grandad's a law unto himself.' Poppy smiled. 'I expect he's heard we have lady guests and he's making himself smell nice.'

'Oh, really?' Bronagh patted her hair. She'd taken extra trouble with it, spraying a liberal amount of floral perfume everywhere. Sadie had just worn her spare clothes. She wished she'd packed more.

'The soup smells divine.' Bronagh lifted her spoon.

'My mum makes great French onion,' Poppy said, taking a seat. 'Then we've got chicken and rice, and brownies with ice cream.'

'Lovely. We'll wait for your father though.' Sadie flashed Bronagh a look that told her not to dunk the huge piece of bread she'd just grabbed.

On cue, the door opened and a distinguished-looking man with thick white hair walked in. He was freshly shaven, wearing a crisp shirt and a charming smile. He gave a small nod towards Bronagh and Sadie. 'I heard we had guests. And you're from Ireland? Welcome.'

'It's good of you to invite us to dinner,' Sadie said.

'I'm Bronagh and this is my sister-in-law, Sadie. We're widows,' Bronagh explained by way of introduction.

'Paul Sullivan.' The man held out a hand. 'Pleased to meet you both.'

'Sullivan's an Irish name.' Bronagh was delighted.

'My grandfather was from Donegal,' Paul explained.

'We're from Ballycotton, County Clare.' Sadie couldn't help smiling too.

'Western Ireland, all rolling countryside and the craggy Atlantic coastline,' Paul began.

'You sound like a holiday brochure,' Bronagh chortled. 'And Donegal, the romantic northwest coast of Ireland, all castles, coastlines and majestic mountains.'

'I've never been. I really ought to.' Paul took a seat opposite Bronagh.

'Never been to Ireland?' Bronagh was appalled. 'But we're only just across the water.'

'I've been to Dublin,' Paul said smoothly. 'But you're right, I should visit Donegal.'

'It's not far from us. We'll put you up in Ballycotton,' Bronagh offered. Sadie nudged her gently as a reminder to wind her neck in.

'This is lovely soup, Hazel.'

'Hazel's a great cook.' Paul smiled fondly. 'She's great at everything – both my girls are. I don't know what I'd do without them.'

'We do our best,' Hazel muttered.

'You haven't always lived here?' Bronagh asked.

'No. Dad was an accountant. I grew up in Westonzoyland,' Hazel explained. 'Dad bought this place when he retired fifteen years ago.'

'I remember Poppy telling us. We were talking to someone about Tails of Hope in Dawlish, and they'd never visited,' Bronagh said.

'We have a website, but it needs updating,' Poppy sighed. 'My job. But I'm so busy with the animals, I never get time.'

'The winter months are quiet, though,' Hazel explained. 'We really ought to update our website and plan for the summer. I'd love to come up with more fundraising ideas. We do events when we can. But animals always need cleaning and feeding.'

'We make most of our money in the summer,' Poppy added. 'But we're always looking for new ideas and volunteers.'

Hazel passed a basket full of rolls of bread. 'It's nice to have you to stay.'

'You're related to Robert Parkin?' Paul recalled. 'Is that right?'

'He's my son's wife's brother,' Sadie explained with a grin.

'But he's not back until tomorrow at the earliest.' Bronagh looked at Paul hopefully. 'So we might be here a bit longer.'

'Stay as long as you like,' Hazel offered.

'We've no other guests,' Poppy added. 'Have dinner too, if you like.'

'That'd be lovely.' Bronagh glanced at Paul again.

'I know Robert Parkin a little bit,' Paul said. 'He runs the local garden club. Isn't he a bit of a celebrity baker?'

'He is.' Sadie felt a flush of pride. 'Bunty, that's my daughter-in-law and Robert's sister, was telling us about the big bake off they had.'

'We should have got involved with that, held it here,' Poppy said ruefully. 'It would have been great publicity.'

'A huge opportunity missed,' Paul admitted.

'Hindsight's a wonderful thing.' Hazel collected the soup bowls. 'We have themed days and school visits. The animals are our priority.'

'As they should be,' Bronagh agreed.

'But we're looking for new ideas all the time.' Poppy leaned forward.

'Well, that little boy we met in the car park would love to pet animals,' Bronagh said.

'And the two little thugs who were sitting on our Ferrari would understand a bit more about kindness,' Sadie added thoughtfully. 'Learning to be compassionate would do them the world of good.'

'I'd love the animals to help needy children more. Mum always said we should.' Hazel was on her feet. 'Who's for stroganoff and rice?'

'I am,' Sadie and Bronagh said together.

'The sea air gives you an appetite.' Bronagh held out her glass. 'And a small top-up would be very welcome, if it's all right with you, Hazel.'

* * *

After dinner, Paul invited Sadie and Bronagh to accompany him for a glass of warmed brandy while Poppy and Hazel stacked the dishwasher. Bronagh moved like greased lightning. Within moments, the three of them were sitting in a small snug, enjoying a log fire and twinkling lights from a real pine tree, cradling glasses of cognac.

Paul sat back, the firelight illuminating his face. He crossed his legs, relaxing. Sadie closed her eyes, feeling warm and well fed.

'So, Paul—' Bronagh was keen to chatter '—Sadie and I had the grand tour this morning.'

'Oh?' Paul raised an eyebrow. 'Did Poppy take you round?'

'Yes, and I met Pi. He was a lovely fella. And The Supremes.'

'Ah, the donkeys,' Paul said. 'I've always had a soft spot for Diana.'

'And we made friends with the alpacas. They're funny.'

'They are. They always end up arguing, with Angel spitting at the others.' The ready smile on Paul's face disappeared. 'We rescued them from someone north of Bridgwater who'd treated them quite badly. They were thin and neglected when we took them in.'

'You wouldn't think so to look at them now.' Bronagh was impressed. 'They're the picture of health. Fat as butter.'

'I always wanted to help animals in difficult circumstances. It started off as a mission of mercy. When I retired, I had a big property to sell and Hazel had just been through a messy divorce. Wendy and I bought this place as a project for the whole family. But Wendy was the ideas person. She had all sorts of plans.'

'Did she?' Bronagh asked.

'She wanted to open up a tearoom, create a play area for kids, an area for parents to relax. She even thought about giving riding lessons to needy children. She'd been reading about sensory play for toddlers. We intended to do all that and more.' He passed a hand over his face. 'It's such a shame.'

'What happened to Wendy, Paul?' Sadie asked gently, sitting up in the armchair.

Paul stared into the firelight. A sigh shuddered through his tall frame. 'It took three months. From diagnosis to the day she passed. I nursed her here the whole while.'

'I'm sorry,' Sadie said quietly, understanding how he felt. 'These things are tough, Paul.'

'We know. I lost Michael and Sadie lost Alfie,' Bronagh muttered. 'It's hard to believe it. One moment, the person you love most in the world is there in your arms and you're thinking, oh, where shall we go next weekend? Shall we shop in the Co-op tomorrow? Just taking everything in life for granted. Then suddenly, your whole world's upside down and nothing will be the same again.' She turned to Sadie. 'At least Sadie and I have each other. We have our family.'

'We do.' Sadie's eyes shone. She pushed the sad feeling away.

'Family's important.' Paul sipped from his glass. 'Hazel and Poppy work hard. But one day we'll have this place just as Wendy hoped it would be.'

'What would your dream be, Paul?' Bronagh asked.

'I want to give a home to more needy animals. There are so many out there.'

'Aren't you a charity?' Sadie asked, her mind already searching for fundraising ideas. 'Can't you get donations?'

'We get money from gifts, yes, and we raise as much as we can ourselves. I'm always on the lookout for new ideas and money-spinners.'

'You aren't losing money, are you?' Bronagh was horrified.

'No, we break even. We make sure all our animals have a secure future. But Wendy had big, big dreams. I'd so love to make Tails of Hope everything she hoped for. A hive of activity all year round. More animals. More learning centres. Better publicity. A teashop, even.' Paul sighed. 'Ah, I've gone on and on. Let's change the subject. Tell me about your family in Ireland. I've seen the Ferrari you drive too. It's a beautiful car.'

'The Ferrari's my grandson's,' Sadie explained. 'He's into property in Dublin with my son, Niall.'

'Rory lent it to us to drive here in,' Bronagh added and Sadie wondered if she had forgotten about Partlan Brown and the cake and doing the Riverdance in the bar in Dublin.

'We've such a grand family back home,' Sadie told him. 'But we're visiting Robert for a few days.'

'I've heard he's a wonderful baker.' Paul leaned back in his seat, stretching his legs. 'I bet he makes mince pies and Christmas cakes. Are you staying on for Christmas?'

'Oh, no, just for a day or so, then we're off back to Ballycotton.' Sadie closed her eyes. The heat from the fire was making her sleepy.

'Christmas is quite special in Millbrook,' Paul murmured. 'There's a wonderful carol service at the church, two days before Christmas.'

'And do you get much snow?' Bronagh wanted to know.

'Not often – down here the weather's mild, but I remember years ago, when Wendy was alive, we had a real flurry of it.' Paul gazed at the brandy in his glass. The liquid shone like amber. 'We worked flat out to keep the animals fed and warm but, you know, I enjoyed it so much. It felt like being part of the Nativity, surrounded by them amid the falling snow, and the cosy nights by the fireside.'

'It must've been magical.' Bronagh finished the drink in her glass and glanced at Sadie, who was breathing deeply, her eyes closed. 'Well, Paul, it's been nice meeting you. But I better get Sadie up to our room. The heat's got to her and the sea air. She's sound asleep. I don't want to leave her here dozing for long. Unless you've another small glass of that delicious brandy?'

12

After breakfast the next day, Sadie and Bronagh wrapped up warmly in coats and headscarves and made for the front door. Hazel was in the hall cleaning the stairs, the vacuum cleaner whirring noisily. She looked up and switched it off. 'Are you going somewhere nice? The weather's picked up, lovely winter sunshine. There's a hard frost on the ground, mind.'

'We're used to a bit of frost, Hazel.' Sadie smiled. 'Bronagh and I wanted to say good morning to the animals.'

'We'll stroll into Millbrook,' Bronagh said. 'It's only a few minutes' walk. I think we can manage that.'

'We need to stretch our legs. We can have a doze this afternoon, Bronagh.'

'I'll see you later.' Hazel smiled at them cheerily. 'I suppose you'll call in to see if Robert's back home?'

Sadie exchanged looks with Bronagh. 'He'll need to rest after his journey. We'll pop in tomorrow and introduce ourselves.'

'Tomorrow's Thursday,' Bronagh added. 'We were thinking we might go home on Saturday.'

Sadie tugged her arm. 'Let's go and see the animals, will we? Horses first.'

'Poppy's with them now – and I think Dad's helping her.'

'That's nice.' Bronagh seemed suddenly more eager to go. 'Come on, Sadie, we're keeping a gentleman waiting.'

'Paul?'

'Pi, the racehorse. He's my favourite.' Bronagh winked. 'We'll catch up later, Hazel.'

As they closed the door, the vacuum cleaner started to whirr again. Bronagh leaned closer to Sadie. 'I was thinking, perhaps we should stay here at the farm. I mean, we hardly know Robert. I know he's family, but we can't impose. Besides, it might be nice to stop with Hazel, and we can call on Robert during the day.'

'It'll be expensive. Bed, breakfast, evening meal.'

'But you heard Paul last night, Sadie, they need the guests. It's for the animals.'

'I've only got one change of clothes and they're in need of a wash.'

'Right, so, here's the plan. This morning we'll walk into the village and have a look around. This afternoon we'll go back to Dawlish. I saw some nice charity shops yesterday. We'll get ourselves kitted out.'

'Perhaps they'll have some wellington boots.' Sadie hugged Bronagh's arm as they walked over crisp white-tipped grass. 'On Saturday we'll go home. Will we ask Hazel to book the ferry for us on the line?'

'We might. Look, there's Pi.' Bronagh pointed. 'And Poppy's with him. And Paul. Good morning, Paul.' She waved frantically, dragging Sadie towards the field. Sadie was conscious of an ache in both her legs and her hips. She'd take things easy today.

'Slow down, Bronagh.'

They arrived at the gate and Sadie slumped against it gratefully. 'Well, it's a cold one this morning.'

'It is. How are you, Paul?' Bronagh's eyes sparkled. 'And Poppy. How's it going? How's Pi?'

'He's fine. I'm just checking the horses' coats for rubbing because they wear rugs.' Poppy patted Pi's neck. 'Pi's doing great.'

Bronagh lifted a hand and the chestnut horse ambled across, nuzzling her palm. 'He knows me.' She was delighted. 'We're friends already, aren't we, Pi?'

Paul came over to join them, lean in a wax coat, jeans and wellingtons. Bronagh noticed his brightly striped scarf. 'Don't we all need the woollies in this weather?'

'We have gloves and hats you can borrow,' Paul offered.

'That's kind,' Sadie replied. 'We're off shopping this afternoon, so we'll be all right.'

'And I suppose Robert's back later,' Paul said. 'Have you arranged to see him?'

'No, we were thinking...' Sadie noticed her breath made a mist on the air. 'We'd like to stay here with you until Saturday morning, if that's all right. We'll catch up with Robert tomorrow, and it'll be good to spend time with him, but—'

Bronagh rested her face against Pi's white blaze nose. 'I'm becoming fond of this one. We like it here, Paul. We don't want to impose on Robert. It's not as if he knows us well.'

'I'll ask Hazel to book it.' Paul looked genuinely pleased. 'So, will you be staying to dinner tonight?'

'We'd love to.' Sadie grinned.

'Or we could...' Paul paused. A thought had come to him.

'We could what, Paul?' Bronagh asked, interested.

'We could go into Dawlish for something to eat. A night out. Do you like curry?'

'I love a good biryani. And the Peshwari nans.' Bronagh was

full of enthusiasm. 'But we won't let you treat us. You've all those animals to think of.'

'We'll split it, then.' Paul's eyes shone. 'I'll ask Poppy and Hazel if they want to come.'

'Mum and I are binge-watching TV tonight.' Poppy stopped brushing one of the horses. 'You go, Grandad. It would do you good to go out for once.'

'You'll have such a good time with us, Paul.' Bronagh was visibly excited. 'I can't wait to tell you about the scrapes we got into in Dublin. Wherever we go, Sadie and I, we have such larks.'

'Behave yourself, Bronagh Doyle,' Sadie said firmly. 'But thanks for asking us, Paul. We'd love a night out. After all, we're on our holidays. Right. Curry tonight. Meet Robert tomorrow, stay here on Friday night, then on Saturday, we'll go home.'

'We will.' Bronagh leaned forward to kiss Pi's nose. 'I'm beginning to get fond of this one. I might want to take him home with me. What do you think of that, Pi?'

* * *

There was a cold wind whistling through the streets of Ballycotton and the sky was dark with rainclouds. Three cars were parked outside Sean's house: his Peugeot estate, Niall's Range Rover and Pat and Nora's silver DeLorean. Niall scratched his head worriedly.

'Are you sure that thing will last the journey, Pat?'

'You're joking me. This is a supreme model.' Pat was clad in a woollen hat and a red puffer jacket. 'This car was driven through time in that film and it stood up to all sorts. I'm sure it'll get us to England.'

'It didn't really go back to the future, Uncle Pat,' Rory explained gently.

'I don't like the idea of sharing your da's big car with all your family,' Lola said beneath her breath as she clung to his arm. 'It'll be nice to have your Ferrari back, Rory.'

'I'm in no rush. We're on holiday, Lola. From today.' Rory looked at each face, delighted.

'The ferry tickets are booked, we're all packed,' Sean said cheerily. 'I think we're just about ready to go. Bunty's texted her sister. Hattie's just got back to Millbrook, but she says she's not seen hide nor hair of either of them.'

'That's a worry, Sean.' Niall scratched his head. 'Where do you think Mammy and Auntie Bronagh have got to?'

'Perhaps they've been arrested.' Maeve's voice came anxiously from the passenger seat of the Range Rover.

'No, they'll be having a whale of a time,' Sean said. 'But I think we've made the right decision to fetch them home.'

'And we can have a look at the seaside while we're there,' Rory added.

'And try some of Robert's famous cakes.' Niall licked his lips.

The door to Sean's house opened and Bunty and Nora emerged, carrying several heavy bags. Pat said, 'What do you have there, Nora? The kitchen sink?'

'Or a spare engine for the DeLorean?' Niall quipped.

'It's just luggage,' Nora puffed. 'Can we put it all in your car, Niall? Ours won't have the space.'

'I'll be amazed if that old banger makes it to Dublin,' Rory teased, his eyes full of mischief. 'Tenner on it, Da?'

'Go on.' Niall grinned. 'I bet Pat's car makes it to the ferry port. I reckon it'll pack up in Wales.'

'I'll have you know I service this car myself,' Pat spluttered.

'That's what I'm betting on, Uncle Pat,' Rory said with a wink.

Bunty handed two of the bags to Sean. 'I made sandwiches and flasks of tea and coffee and there's some biscuits.'

'We'll be all right.' Pat adjusted his woollen hat. 'Shall we make a move? It's a cold day to be standing about.'

'It is,' Sean agreed. 'So, by my reckoning, we'll get the ferry over to Holyhead, spend the night in a B & B somewhere in Wales and catch up with Mammy and Auntie Bronagh by close of play tomorrow.'

'If we take it steadily.' Niall was hopeful.

'I get travel sick,' Maeve groaned.

'We'll look after you, Mammy,' Rory said kindly. He wrapped an arm around her and kissed her cheek. His poor mother deserved a break. His da was a good fella but, Rory thought, he had no clue how to treat women. 'I think it will be good craic, going to England. We should stay for a few days.'

Lola looked bored. 'It's a good job my photo shoot was cancelled. I'd have missed some important work.'

'Ah, it's Christmas, near enough.' Rory shrugged. 'Don't we all deserve a bit of a holiday?'

'Let's make tracks.' Sean jingled his car keys. 'We'll try to stay close together on the roads. I know the way.'

'I'll bring up the rear. I'm your wingman,' Niall said. 'You never know what might happen to Pat's rickety old car.'

'The DeLorean's a classic,' Pat protested. 'It'll beat the lot of you.'

'It's reliable too,' Nora agreed. 'It's hasn't broken down since—'

'Since last time you took it out, Auntie Nora,' Rory recalled with a smile. He decided it was up to him to hurry everyone along. 'Right. Let's get going.'

Lola looked at her delicate shoes. 'Do they wear normal clothes in Devon? Isn't it all rubber boots and mackintoshes?'

'Ah, you'll be fine.' Rory helped her gallantly into the Range Rover.

Niall clambered into the driving seat. 'Right, we're off. This is it – the O'Connors' England road trip.'

'I just hope Mammy's all right.' Sean scrambled into the Peugeot. He turned to Bunty. 'I can't say I'm not a bit worried, Bunts.'

Bunty squeezed his hand. 'Don't fret, love. I bet when we get to Robert's, your mum and Auntie Bronagh will be sitting at the kitchen table with Hattie, Robert and Tressy diving into a cream tea, arguing about which comes first, the jam or cream.'

'I hope you're right.' Sean started the engine. 'So why do I have that feeling in my stomach that it's all going to be an unholy riot when we get there?'

'That's what I'm looking forward to.' Rory grinned. 'And couldn't we all do with a holiday in Devon?'

* * *

Sadie and Bronagh hesitated outside The Pig and Pickle.

'Shall we go in?' Bronagh suggested.

'Why do we need a drink?' Sadie asked. 'My waterworks have been shot since Dublin.'

'But it's cold.'

'Alcohol lowers your blood temperature.'

'But maybe they do hot chocolate. Come on, Sadie,' Bronagh insisted.

'We'll be drinking tonight with the curry. I don't want to overdo it.'

'You won't. We can have lemonade tonight. Let's go in.'

Sadie hesitated. 'You won't do the Riverdance? Or pretend to be Brigitte Bardot?'

'No. Come on,' Bronagh coaxed. 'It's where all the locals hang out. They'll tell us where Robert is – and which house he lives in

– and when he's coming back. They'll all know everybody else's business. It's an English village.'

'All right,' Sadie agreed reluctantly. 'Just one drink. But behave yourself, will you?'

'Me?' Bronagh did her best impression of an angel. 'When have I ever done anything else?'

Sadie led the way into the bar that smelled of strong hops. Inside, the room was dark but Christmas lights twinkled from each corner. There was a log fire roaring in the hearth and Sadie tugged Bronagh over towards the armchairs next to it. 'I'm shattered. I need to sit down. The walk from the farm took longer than I thought.'

'You kept stopping for a rest.' Bronagh looked around. Two men in caps were hunched over pints in the corner, their backs turned. She slumped into a chair and extended her hands. 'This is nice though. I love it when a fire's so hot it scorches your flesh. It reminds me of being a kiddie and the old paraffin fires.'

A woman with a ponytail and faded jeans appeared behind the bar. She called, 'Hello. What can I get you?'

Bronagh was as quick as a flash. 'Do you have the Christmas drinks?'

'We have spiced mulled wine, gingerbread gin, mulled cider, snowballs and an alcohol-free cocktail called cranberry kiss.'

'Any hot chocolate?' Sadie needed something warm and comforting.

'I have some sachets of mince pie hot chocolate out the back,' the barmaid said. 'I can do you one of those with a swirl of cream.'

'That'd be grand. Yes, please.'

'Make that two,' Bronagh added. 'That's very kind of you.'

'While you're at it, Shelley,' one of the men piped up, 'we'll have one of those hot chocolates. They sound nice. And two more pints, please.'

'Coming up, Colin,' Shelley said, and then she was gone.

'This is lovely.' Bronagh snuggled close to the fire. 'I could do with a warm-up.'

'So, you're a long way from home, ladies.' One of the men in caps swung round, still clutching his pint. 'What brings you to Millbrook?'

'Oh, the craic.' Bronagh patted her hair. 'It's a lovely place you have here.'

'It is,' the other man in the cap spoke up. 'We're a friendly community. Are you staying long or passing through?'

'We're staying at Tails of Hope Farm,' Sadie explained. 'It's a gorgeous place.'

'Animal sanctuary,' one of the men said.

'Paul Sullivan still owns it, doesn't he, Dennis?'

'I think so. They had a lot of visitors in the summer. I remember seeing cars queueing. But there hasn't been much recently.'

'It's the cold weather,' the first man explained.

'We're visitors though,' Bronagh said loyally. 'It's a lovely little farm. And if you're all so friendly here, why aren't you sponsoring an alpaca for Christmas?'

'It's too bloody cold to go down there,' the one called Dennis grunted.

'Nobody's interested in a herd of old nags in the winter. Animals are a fair-weather industry,' the one called Colin moaned. 'So, what did you say brings you to Millbrook?'

'We're visiting,' Sadie began. 'My son's wife's brother lives—'

'We're on the run. From an obsessed fan,' Bronagh took over. 'He's mad for us both. Because of who we are. Because we're famous. He can't leave us alone. So we're trying to escape.'

'Obsessed fan,' Dennis said. 'What fan?'

'One who follows us wherever we go, even into pubs, so you'd better watch your back.' Bronagh was on a roll. She looked round nervously and shivered with fear. 'Because we were so popular in the sixties. We haven't changed that much and the crazed fan follows us all over the country because he's obsessed. So we have to keep moving, to be safe. The police advised it. The CID.'

'The CID?' Colin puzzled. 'Really?'

'Oh, no,' Sadie muttered.

'Oh, yes,' Bronagh said as if it were nothing. Sadie shook her head in disbelief.

'So who are you?' Dennis supped his pint.

'Don't you recognise us? I'm sure you're both old enough to remember us in our heyday.' Bronagh pretended to be amazed. She turned to Sadie. 'They don't know who we are, Jean.'

'They don't,' Sadie said nervously, her voice a whimper. There was no point trying to stop Bronagh now.

'Well, put us out of our misery,' Dennis said, mouth open. 'Who *are* you?'

'My friend here's Jean Shrimpton, the supermodel from the nineteen sixties, and I'm her best friend, Twiggy.' Bronagh folded her arms crossly. 'I'm surprised you even had to ask.'

Shelley appeared with the hot chocolate and Sadie breathed a sigh of relief. She'd never be as wicked as Bronagh, not ever. But Bronagh was her best, best friend and Sadie loved her unconditionally.

13

Sadie linked arms with Bronagh as they left The Pig and Pickle, her heart brimming with affection. 'They didn't believe you though.'

'They did, they did,' Bronagh insisted. 'The Dennis wan called me Twiggy when we left.'

'Twiggy wasn't Irish.' Sadie laughed. 'Everyone knows that.'

'I was Twiggy from County Clare. I told them my accent used to be Cockney, but since I moved into hiding I had to change it, for safety.'

'The Colin wan didn't fall for it.'

'He did, Sadie. And the mince pie chocolate drink with the blob of cream floating in it was lovely. Where will we go now?' They were walking along the pavement on the road that led to the edge of Millbrook and on to Tails of Hope Farm. 'We forgot to ask those men where Robert lived.'

'Well, I couldn't, Bronagh, not after all that stuff about us being sixties supermodels.'

'We'll ask Paul. He'll know. There will be a little smallholding in the village full of goats and it'll be Robert's place, and he'll be at home and everything will be grand. Oh, will you look at the school over there? There's a big sign, advertising a Nativity. I wonder when it is.'

'Since when have you liked Nativity plays?'

'Don't you remember when our kids were little? It was hilarious. So much goes wrong in a Nativity. Kids forget their words. Someone stands on someone else's costume and it rips and there are fisticuffs. Joseph and the first shepherd had a proper barney when Kathleen played Mary. No wonder she became a nun.'

'I remember going to the Nativity in Ballycotton, oh, it must have been in the early sixties. Sean was an ox. Nora and Biddy were shepherds. Niall was a king. And Nora's Pat was an ass.' Sadie shrugged. 'Nothing's changed.'

'But a Nativity's a wonderful thing. All those pure voices singing "Away in a Manger". When's this one happening?'

'It says it's next Wednesday.'

'Oh, yes. I can see it now. Look at the lovely church.'

'St Jude's. It's so beautiful.' Sadie gazed at the tall spire.

'The patron saint of lost causes.' Bronagh shook her head. 'Like the poor animals up at Tails of Hope. It's such a lovely place. But that Colin said it didn't get much business in the winter.'

'Oh, Paul's heart's set on taking in more animals. I suppose it'll all bounce back in the summer, queues of traffic, busloads of kids.'

'They're a bit short-staffed though. Just the three of them, working all the hours.'

'Hazel said the volunteers only come in the summer. But they care so much for those animals.'

'We should go in and offer a prayer,' Sadie suggested.

'For the animals?' Bronagh asked.

'No, for forgiveness, after you telling all those lies.' Sadie squeezed her arm affectionately. 'Let's have a look around, will we?'

'It looks a welcoming place,' Bronagh agreed. 'Paul said they do a carol service.'

'I like a good Christmas carol. Lifting our hearts and our voices up. It's lovely.'

'It is.'

Sadie opened the wooden door to the church, twisting the antique handle, and they stepped inside. The air was chilly; something fluttered high in the rafters and she shivered, feeling the chill of reverence she'd always felt in a holy building since her own mammy sent her to Sunday school as a kiddie. They moved slowly towards the enclosed wooden pews, each with hassocks to kneel on and a knotty wooden shelf holding small Bibles. The silence was shattered as loud, resounding music belted out.

'What the—?' Bronagh nearly jumped out of her skin. 'I thought we'd stepped into a horror film.'

Sadie met Bronagh's horrified expression. 'It's all right, it's just the organ.'

'I expected Quasimodo to swing past on a bell rope.'

'No, it's church music. It's beautiful. Listen.'

Sadie and Bronagh clung to each other in the draughty church as the melodies lifted on the air, first 'O Little Town of Bethlehem', then 'God Rest Ye Merry, Gentlemen', 'O Come, All Ye Faithful' and finally 'In the Bleak Midwinter'. Sadie closed her eyes and was lifted to a place of calm and peace. Each note of the music was warm, sweet and filled with expectation. When she opened them again, her eyes were filled with tears.

Bronagh clapped. 'That was just incredible. Well done, the church organist. What a talent.'

A woman climbed down from where the organ was. She was

small, with a silver pixie haircut, a warm jacket, jeans tucked into boots. 'Oh, hello – I didn't realise I had an audience.'

'You have such a gift for music,' Bronagh said.

'I was just practising for the carol service.' The woman held out a hand to shake. 'Are you visiting?'

'Well, we're musical. We're Bono's—' Bronagh began but Sadie took over. She thought it might be wise.

'We're staying at the B & B down the road for a few days. We came on the off chance to visit my son's wife's brother, but I think he's in Cornwall.'

The woman was staring. 'You don't mean Robert Parkin?'

'We do,' Sadie answered.

'You must be Sean's mother?' The woman looked from Bronagh to Sadie. 'From Ballycotton?'

'That's right. I'm Sadie O'Connor and this is my sister-in-law, Bronagh Doyle.' Sadie was relieved that they had told the truth. The village community was so warm and friendly: everyone knew about everyone else, even their relatives.

'I'm Hattie,' the woman told them. 'Robert will be back this evening. He and Tressy don't know you're coming but they'll be thrilled. Bunty texted me and asked me if I'd seen you. Sean's a bit worried.'

'Is he?' Sadie was confused. 'Hattie? Oh, you're Bunty and Robert's sister?'

'I am,' Hattie said.

'But you're not in Cornwall.' Bronagh was puzzled.

'I've been to Oxfordshire for a few days to clear out my old bungalow. The sale's finalised and I had to arrange for my piano to be put in storage. My ex-husband—' A look of something between unhappiness and relief crossed Hattie's brow. 'We've sold the house and now we can finally go our separate ways.'

'Good riddance to bad rubbish, then?' Bronagh suggested.

'Exactly. I'm looking for a small place of my own.' Hattie smiled. 'Very small, given house prices here. But it'll be my own space.'

'Well, that's nice,' Sadie said encouragingly. 'So how about we all meet up tomorrow?'

'Come to lunch with us, please.' Hattie's voice was filled with enthusiasm. 'I'll pick you up from – where are you staying?'

'Tails of Hope,' Sadie and Bronagh said together.

'I know it. I'll collect you at midday,' Hattie decided. 'Shall I message Bunty and tell her you're both OK?'

'You'd better.' Sadie felt a wave of relief. 'And can you mention that the car's fine too?'

'The car?' Hattie was mystified.

'We borrowed my grandson's car to drive down,' Sadie explained.

'It's a Ferrari,' Bronagh added.

Hattie was impressed. 'You both drove all the way from Ballycotton in a Ferrari? Well.'

'Well, that's us.' Bronagh shot her nose in the air proudly. 'We came on holiday on the spur of the moment and we're having a grand time. We're off shopping this afternoon, and we have a hot date this evening.'

'A hot date?' Hattie asked. 'Already?'

'We're only going for a curry,' Sadie said quickly. She wasn't sure why, but perhaps it was better if Hattie didn't know they were going out with Paul. If Hattie passed it on to Sean, goodness knew what he'd think. And Sadie had just met Hattie – she didn't want her to think she and Bronagh were man-eating tearaways. She'd find that out from Niall soon enough.

'Well, I'll see you tomorrow. Robert will be so pleased.' Hattie shook their hands again. 'And it's good to meet you both. I'll look forward to lunch.'

'We will too,' Bronagh said. 'Especially if Robert makes some of his famous cakes.'

'There will definitely be cake,' Hattie called as she disappeared through the door.

'She's a nice person.' Bronagh turned to Sadie. 'It gets better and better. A hot date with Paul and lunch with Robert and the relatives tomorrow. Bunty said he's a bit of a babe magnet.'

'No, she didn't. She said that some women are attracted to him because of his baking.'

'That's the same thing.'

'The problem is, Bronagh...' Sadie took her friend's arm and led her towards the church door '...Sean knows where we are now, and that we came all this way in Rory's car. You don't think he'll be cross because we disappeared? And what about Partlan and the Guinness cake?'

'He'll be champion. Sean, I mean, not Partlan. Partlan will have forgotten all about the cake. Don't look so glum, Sadie.' Bronagh's laughter tinkled, an echo that rose to the roof. 'Sean won't worry now he knows we're here, and we can tell Hattie we'll be back in Ballycotton on Sunday evening, and everything will be fine and dandy.'

'I hope you're right,' Sadie said as they opened the door and stepped out into the white winter sunshine. The world opened up to her, like a wide embrace, and she felt her heart expand. 'Well, the afternoon beckons. We're off shopping for some new outfits.'

* * *

Rory watched thoughtfully: the three cars were parked in a line in a lay-by on the R109, near Phoenix Park in Dublin. Seven other passengers stood in a circle, looking confused.

'We can't miss the ferry,' Sean said. 'Do you think we ought to go on without you, Niall?'

'It's never done that before.' Niall groaned. 'A Range Rover's the most reliable car.'

'You thought my DeLorean would be the one to break down,' Pat cackled. 'I told you it wouldn't. I told you.'

'I'm so glad to stop for a break. I feel travel sick.' Maeve turned to Rory. 'I think your girlfriend's perfume upsets my stomach.'

'My perfume's Dior,' Lola grumbled.

'What exactly is wrong with the Range Rover?' Bunty asked.

'It's all the modern computers these things have,' Sean explained. 'There's so much to go wrong.'

'It just flashed up, the "check engine" light.' Niall scratched his head. 'It's never done that before. It could mean anything – up to and including a faulty catalytic converter. It could even be a sign of internal engine failure.' He groaned. 'I can't drive it with the computer like this. And I only filled it up twenty minutes ago.'

'What will we do?' Maeve asked.

Nora folded her arms. 'We can't miss the ferry.'

'You'll have to go on without me,' Niall said sadly. 'I'll have to stay here, find a garage and get it sorted out. It's too risky to drive it like this.'

'Well, Rory, you can come with me in the DeLorean,' Pat said expansively.

'Or you can come with us in the Peugeot,' Sean said.

Lola pulled a face. 'I wish we had the Ferrari.'

'We're going to England to get it,' Maeve said. 'Or we were, before my husband's precious car failed.'

'Hang on, Da.' Rory's eyes lit up. Suddenly, he knew what the problem was. A grin spread across his face. 'When you were in the garage filling up, did you put the cap back on properly? Only – ah, I thought so. Look.' He pointed to the petrol cap, which had been screwed back on askew. 'There's your problem. The computer will flash up to tell you to check the engine if the cap isn't properly on.'

'Oh, Rory, well done.' Maeve breathed out in relief.

'I was rushing to fill it up,' Niall said by way of explanation. 'I couldn't have put it back on properly.'

Pat put his hands on his hips. 'So, you thought my DeLorean was unreliable, Niall, but you've so many tricks and gizmos on that thing to go wrong.'

'My computer's very reliable, I'll have you know,' Niall insisted. 'It knew the cap was off.'

'But you didn't. You thought the whole engine had failed,' Pat cackled.

'We should just get going,' Sean suggested. 'We don't want to lose any more time.'

'We'll be fine if we go now,' Bunty added reassuringly.

'Are you sure you don't want to come with us in our car, Maeve?' Nora joked. 'Ours doesn't have all the weird gizmos.'

'But it's a smooth ride and I have aircon,' Niall argued.

'Please don't bicker, I feel sick enough as it is,' Maeve protested.

'I'll get you something on the ferry to settle your stomach, Mammy,' Rory said gently. 'They'll have sparkling water.'

'Let's hope it's not a bad crossing.' Lola put a hand to her hair, where the wind had blown it across her face. 'Bad crossings make me boke.'

'I think it might be a bit choppy,' Pat said. 'I'll be glad when we're in England.'

'I wish we weren't going at all,' Maeve grumbled.

'It'll be great fun,' Rory said. 'We can have a beer on the boat, watch sport on the big-screen TV. Mammy, I've booked dinner. And cabins for us all. You can sleep as long as you need to. We'll be ready for anything when we get off in Wales. We can really start to enjoy ourselves.'

'Speak for yourself.' Lola crept back to the Range Rover and clambered in.

'Thanks, Rory,' Niall whispered discreetly. 'I thought we were banjaxed there.'

'Not at all.' Rory wrapped an arm around his father. He knew he was feeling a bit of an eejit and he wanted to cheer him up. 'We'll have a grand time in England, Da, don't you worry.'

Sean watched as Maeve slunk around to the passenger seat. Pat and Nora slid into the DeLorean, lowering the gull-wing door flamboyantly, starting the engine.

He took Bunty's hand. 'It'll be great to see Robert and Hattie and Tressy again, Bunts. Then we'll be home for Christmas.'

'We will,' Bunty said. 'But I can't imagine what Millbrook will make of it when we come motoring through their quiet village in all these cars. It'll look like the Clampetts have arrived. I can hardly wait to see everyone's face in The Pig and Pickle.'

Rory grinned. A few days away, with his entire family. He was looking forward to it so much.

14

The Korma Kitchen in Dawlish was busy for a Wednesday evening. Paul led the way, shaking hands with the owner, Jaithra, who showed him, Sadie and Bronagh to a table by the window. Paul looked very smart in a jacket, shirt and chinos. Sadie had bought herself a bohemian maxi dress from a charity shop, but Bronagh had really pushed the boat out. She was wearing a sparkling silver dress and a fake fur stole, her pale purple and silver hair swept up in a tiara. She looked the epitome of glam.

Bronagh thought Paul was a true gentleman. He was very complimentary. 'You both look like Hollywood film stars.'

Sadie was about to tell him that they'd bought up half the stock of the Dawlish charity shops that afternoon, but Bronagh beat her to it. 'That's very gallant.' She patted her upswept hair. 'It's often been said that I look like Brigitte Bardot. Or Twiggy.'

Sadie flashed her a 'don't you dare' look as she picked up a menu. She changed the subject. 'Will we have starters?'

'I'll have everything,' Bronagh said. 'I love papadums. We sometimes go to the Masala Chowk in Ballycotton, but this place is nicer.' She closed her eyes for a moment, moving rhythmically to the music that filtered from speakers, the gentle sound of a woman's voice, a sitar and a tabla.

'I haven't been here since the summer.' Paul picked up the menu. 'I'll have a soft drink, because I'm driving, but can I get you a bottle of wine?'

'I might have lemonade,' Sadie said.

'I'll have a whole bottle to myself, then.' Bronagh was still jigging to the music, holding up stage hands, the fingernails painted a vibrant green. 'I'm loving this holiday. Your farm's wonderful, Paul. All the animals.'

'Tomorrow we're having lunch with Robert,' Sadie said. 'It'll be nice to spend time with him. I've never met Tressy, and I don't think I've seen Robert or Hattie since Sean and Bunty's wedding.'

'It's a pleasure to have you to stay.' Paul smiled. 'You certainly brighten the farm up.'

'We're like sparkling Christmas fairies.' Bronagh was as excited as a child. 'I can't wait for Christmas. So much goodwill and kissing under the mistletoe. It's a shame it can't last all year. What do your family do at Christmas, Paul? Do you have the big traditional dinner?'

'It's just me, Hazel and Poppy now,' Paul sighed. 'This year we're thinking of going veggie. Hazel wants to make a nut roast. It's Poppy's idea; she thinks an animal sanctuary should take a stand against animal cruelty.'

'How do you feel about that?' Sadie asked, interested.

'Good wine, good company, Christmas pudding. I'll be happy.'

'In Ballycotton we usually go to Niall's or Sean's, the whole family round one table, and we each take a dish. We have turkey and roasties and I make the best gravy in County Clare, everyone says so.' Bronagh clapped her hands. 'Sadie makes the pudding. It's full of dried fruit and gallons of brandy.'

'I've made it already; it's in the larder,' Sadie remembered.

'Perhaps we should all come up to Ireland?' Paul joked. 'It sounds lovely.'

'You'd be very welcome,' Bronagh began. A waiter arrived at the table. 'What red wine would you recommend?'

The waiter was about to reply, but there was a loud banging at the window and everyone looked at a man who was standing outside, grinning and waving.

Paul was astonished. 'Well, if it isn't—' he waved a hand '—Solly! Goodness me. Come in. Come on in and say hello.' He turned to the waiter quickly. 'Can you just give us five minutes?'

The waiter nodded politely and stood back as a man in a smart overcoat came in. He wore a thick scarf and a cap, which he took off to reveal a smooth head. Paul looked delighted to see him. 'Sadie, Bronagh, this is Solly. Solomon Duke. He used to be a client of mine when I was an accountant.' He shook the man's hand warmly. 'What are you doing here? It's been a long time. Good to see you.'

'I was just about to call in for a takeaway.' Solly had a rich voice, a slight lilting accent. 'Supper for one.'

'Can you stay? Have dinner with us?' Paul asked. 'I haven't seen you in years.'

Solly looked at Sadie, then at Bronagh's glamorous outfit. 'Oh, no, I don't want to interrupt. You have company, Paul. You're celebrating.'

'Not at all,' Bronagh said enthusiastically, giving the man the once-over. 'Stay. Make it a foursome.'

'There's certainly room for one more,' Sadie agreed.

'Are you sure?' Solly hesitated.

'Of course. Bronagh, Sadie, this is Solly. He and I go back years.' Paul seemed truly pleased to see his old friend.

'I knew Paul for about twenty years. We lost contact when he retired. I had a plumber's shop, just a small concern, me and my wife. Paul did our accounts. He retired and I got a new accountant and I branched out into storage and warehouses.' Solly removed his coat; he was wearing a cashmere jumper and jeans. 'But thanks. I'd love to join you.'

He sat opposite Bronagh and she beamed in welcome. 'I have to ask. You've a bit of an accent. Where are you from?'

Solly laughed, showing a perfect smile. 'You have an accent too. I'm guessing you're from Ireland.'

'We are, we're on holiday at Paul's farm,' Bronagh said.

'We're from County Clare,' Sadie explained.

'I thought my accent had gone.' Solly shrugged. 'Windrush generation. I came here with my parents in 1948 from Trinidad. I was four years old.'

'You're not still working, Solly?' Paul asked.

'I have the warehouses, but nowadays I get someone to manage them. I've got a boat. I like to spend my retirement days at sea.'

'A boat,' Bronagh said, fascinated. 'What sort of boat?'

'Just a little cabin cruiser.' Solly picked up the menu.

'I have a Ferrari,' Bronagh began and Sadie interrupted.

'It's my grandson's. He lent it to us.'

'I love Ferraris. Cars are a passion of mine. I collect classics.' Solly noticed the waiter hovering nearby and said, 'May I have a sparkling water, please?'

'I'll have sparkling water too,' Paul said.

'So will I.' Sadie glanced at Solly and felt instinctively that it was the right thing to do.

'Just me for the wine, then?' Bronagh made a mock-sad face. 'Ah, no, I'll have a Coke, please.' She beamed at the waiter. 'And a stack of those lovely papadums. Eight, please, and all the chutneys.'

'Well, this is really nice.' Solly turned to Bronagh. 'So you're on holiday?'

'Just for a few days, visiting relatives, before Christmas.' She indicated Paul. 'It's lovely at the farm.'

'I heard you'd taken on a new business?' Solly asked Paul.

'Hazel, Poppy and I run an animal sanctuary. It was really Wendy's project. She died a few years back.' Paul's voice cracked slightly.

'I'm sorry to hear that. I liked Wendy,' Solly said kindly. He paused. 'You know Marina left me?'

'No.' Paul shook his head. 'I didn't.'

'My own fault.' Solly met Sadie's eyes then Bronagh's. 'I could've been a better husband. But now I'm married to my boat. Mind you, it's cold out on the sea at the moment. I prefer it in here in the warm, with spicy food and sparkling company.'

'Yes, it's lovely.' Bronagh's eyes lit up as the papadums arrived. She met Solly's eyes. 'I'm starting to really enjoy myself now.'

* * *

Bronagh was amazed how quickly the next two hours passed, and she hadn't even thought about wine. The conversation bubbled. Solly was an entrepreneur, a risk-taker. He'd made money and lost it so many times; now it appeared he was a successful businessman, but his life had taken a downward turn. Her spoon was poised over a dish of rasgulla, a squishy white dumpling cooked in sugar syrup. But she was taking in every word.

'So what happened next, Solly? When it was your wedding anniversary, and you were in the posh restaurant?'

'I'd bought Marina an emerald ring. She liked jewellery. I had it in my pocket. I was going to present it to her at the end of the meal as a sort of apology.'

'Why did you need to apologise?' Sadie asked.

'I'd been working away. And I hadn't covered myself in glory. I'd come home late a few times.' Solly gave a shrug. 'Having a bit of money meant I could gamble, and I loved the thrill of it.'

Paul chuckled. 'I remember it well, as your accountant. You either made loads of money or you lost it all.'

'I lost the emerald ring too.' Solly shook his head at his own stupidity. 'It must have fallen out of my pocket when I paid the waiter. Of course, I'd drunk far too much. Marina and I got into an argument in the taxi on the way home and I said a few things I didn't mean. So she said something she definitely meant.'

'What did she say?' Bronagh asked, intrigued.

'It was an ultimatum. I had to choose the drink and the gambling, or her.'

'Which did you choose?' Bronagh's mouth was open.

'The drink chose for me. I couldn't stop. I got drunk and lost money, then I won a lot more and tried to buy Marina off with presents and promises, but it didn't work. She packed her bags.' He gave a deep sigh. 'I haven't touched a drop of alcohol or gambled since that night.'

'Can't you go after her?' Sadie asked.

'It was four years ago,' Solly said. 'She's with someone else now. She's happier. He's a better man.'

'Don't say that, Solly – you're a lovely fella,' Bronagh blurted without thinking. 'Everyone makes mistakes. I do, all the time. I mean, the other night, I did the Riverdance in a bar in Dublin.'

'You didn't?' Solly couldn't help laughing.

'She did,' Sadie spluttered. 'And back in Ballycotton, we accidentally shoved a Guinness cake in an officer's face when he was judging the bake off in the pub.'

'He wasn't pleased.' Bronagh covered a snigger.

'You're both such a breath of fresh air,' Paul said. 'You can see why I invited them, Solly.'

'I certainly can.'

'Shall we have coffees?'

'I'd love one.' Bronagh didn't want the evening to end.

'Me too,' Sadie agreed.

'Then we will,' Solly announced. 'On one condition though.'

'What's that?' Paul asked.

'You let me pick up the bill,' Solly offered.

'Oh, no, we couldn't,' Bronagh began, but Solly lifted a hand insistently.

'I came here this evening to get a butter chicken takeaway for one. I was going to drive back to my house on the cliff, which is far too big for me, and eat it all by myself while I watched some predictable sport on TV. But I bumped into you, and I've had a whale of a time. Seriously...' Solly's eyes gleamed. 'You've been a tonic.' He took Bronagh's hand and brushed his lips against it. 'It's not every night that a man can eat out with a woman in a sparkling dress and a tiara, so, please indulge me. It would be my pleasure.'

'Mine too.' Bronagh clapped her hands. She glanced furtively at Solly. He was handsome. He reminded her of Errol Brown in Hot Chocolate. She'd always had a thing for Errol in the seventies. His eyes had always glimmered when he'd sung 'You Sexy Thing' and Bronagh had imagined it was just for her.

'If you're sure,' Paul began.

'Definitely. And, Paul—' Solly seemed genuinely happy '—I'll visit you at the sanctuary.'

'Please do.'

'You must have a scheme for sponsoring. I'd be glad to oblige.'

'We do a scheme all year round,' Paul said. 'Thanks, Solly.'

'I'm going to sponsor Pi before I go home,' Bronagh added.

'You're just outside Millbrook?' Solly asked.

'You can't miss it,' Bronagh enthused. 'It's a beautiful place. You should come over. There's a racehorse called Prince Pirate. We call him Pi.'

'And there are alpacas and donkeys, owls too,' Sadie added.

Solly sat back in his seat, looking relaxed. 'I'd love to drive over and say hello some time.' He waved a hand and called, 'Four coffees, please.'

'Well, it's been lovely catching up, Solly.' Paul stretched his legs. 'We must do this again. Next time, dinner's on me.'

'We'll keep in touch,' Solly said. His fingers moved to a gold chain around his neck and he met Bronagh's gaze. 'It's just a shame you both have to go back to Ireland. I can't remember when I had such a good time. Thank you, Bronagh and Sadie. It's been wonderful. Perhaps we can meet up again.'

'Perhaps.' Sadie glanced at Bronagh, who was gazing at Solly, all eyes, and hoped she wasn't giving her heart away. She knew how impetuous Bronagh could be.

'We have a very busy schedule.' Bronagh lifted an eyebrow coyly, thinking that Solly had a bit of Samuel L. Jackson in him too. 'But we might just be able to squeeze you in.'

15

The sky was pitch dark in the lay-by not far from Shrewsbury, where three cars were abandoned in a line. The back of the DeLorean was open and Pat scratched his head while Rory and Niall stared at the engine. Pat said, 'The DMC-12 DeLorean was designed in Northern Ireland. It should be sound as a pound.'

'Why's it not going, then?' Niall asked.

'I've no idea.' Pat sounded astonished. 'It just seemed to fade out.'

'I win.' Niall held out a hand triumphantly and Rory placed a ten euro note in his palm.

A few yards away, Bunty was pouring coffee from a flask, handing cups to Maeve, Nora, Lola and Sean. She said, 'Where are we staying tonight? Perhaps we should ring the B & B and tell them we're late.'

'Aren't we booked into that hotel in Telford?' Nora looked at Maeve. 'What's the phone number?'

'How should I know?' Maeve shivered as she sipped coffee.

'Because you booked it on the ferry,' Nora retorted.

'I thought you'd booked it on the ferry?'

'No, Maeve, we all agreed you'd do it.'

'We did,' Bunty said gently.

'But I suggested you, Bunty.' Maeve looked as if she'd cry. 'Why does no one ever listen to me?'

'So we've nowhere to stop tonight?' Nora asked.

'Are we sleeping in the cars?' Lola looked disgusted. 'That can't happen. I need a hot shower and an electric plug for my heated tongs.'

'Leave it with me. It's only after eight. We'll find somewhere for tonight, and we'll be off to Devon as easy as clockwork.' Bunty pulled out her phone. 'Oh, look. There's a message from Hattie – they're all having lunch tomorrow. We might be there in time to join them. I'll send a smiley emoji and a thumbs up. There. Now – let's find some hotels in Telford and pick a nice one.'

'That's assuming we ever get moving,' Nora snorted.

'It's your car that's broken down,' Maeve replied, annoyed.

The men pored over the DeLorean's engine, puzzled. Rory knew it was up to him to sort things out. He said, 'Did you notice anything unusual, Uncle Pat, while you were driving? Before the car stopped? Any signs of something going on that wasn't quite right?'

'Yes, I did. The car's performance was a bit weak. The power seemed to go and the engine sputtered a bit. It felt like the brakes were on the blink too.'

'So have you run out of petrol?' Rory asked.

'The fuel gauge said I had a quarter of a tank,' Pat insisted.

'But you told me the gauge was unreliable,' Niall said.

'So I did,' Pat remembered. 'Well, perhaps that's it. Perhaps the tank's empty.'

'Let's check,' Rory said hopefully.

Bunty was busy talking into the phone, surrounded by a

group who were listening to her every word. 'Can you do four rooms? All doubles? No, it doesn't matter that they aren't all on the same floor – in fact it might be better if – all right, yes, I'll book those please. The name's O'Connor. No, I expect we'll be with you within the hour even if we have to abandon the DeLorean. What? That's good to know – I'm sure we'd all be glad of a drink and something to eat in the bar before we turn in. Yes, that's lovely. Thank you.'

'Do we have rooms?' Nora asked.

'Yes, we're all booked in,' Bunty said. 'It sounds like a lovely place too. They have four floors and a bar and a restaurant.'

'A bar.' Pat's eyes lit up.

'All I want is a room with a shower,' Lola said, relieved.

'Thank you, Bunty.' Maeve seemed grateful. 'Now we need to get that heap of junk fixed.'

'The DeLorean's not a heap of—' Nora began but Niall was hurrying over, waving happily.

'No worries. Everything's fine. Pat just ran out of fuel. Rory and I'll drive into Shrewsbury and fill up a can. We'll all get off to the hotel.'

'Good. It's all booked.' Bunty winked at Maeve.

'I'll go ahead with Bunty, Maeve and Lola if you like,' Sean offered gallantly. 'They can settle in.'

'We could,' Bunty said. 'It'll be nice to have a warm meal and a good night's sleep before we set off to Devon tomorrow. We should be there by lunchtime.'

'There's no need to rush, is there?' Pat joined them. 'I've heard they have the British Motor Museum near Leamington Spa. That's on the way. I'm sure we could all stop off for an hour or two...'

'I'm not stopping at any motor museum,' Maeve grumbled.

'Well, I'd love to, while we are here,' Nora added.

'Why don't we just get the Ferrari and go straight back to Ireland?' Lola said sulkily.

'It'll be nice to see Devon though.' Rory was doing his best to raise the mood.

'And sample Robert's cakes,' Bunty added. 'I'd really love to catch up with Hattie.'

'I'd like to see the seaside,' Rory said. 'And they do a nice cider in Devon.' He was looking forward to new places, meeting new people. It bothered him a little that Lola didn't share his enthusiasm for adventure. He hoped the trip would help her to chill out and enjoy herself. She hadn't looked happy since they'd left Ballycotton.

'Cider,' Pat laughed. 'That's a ladies' drink.'

'It certainly is not,' Maeve replied. 'I won't drink fizzy apple juice. It'll give me the guts ache.'

'I think we should get Pat's fuel and be on our way,' Sean suggested diplomatically. 'After a nice meal and a few beers, we'll all be feeling top of the world.'

'Speak for yourself,' Maeve said, eyeing the DeLorean. 'If you ask me, the whole journey's been a farce.'

'Perhaps we should start enjoying it?' Nora proposed.

'I agree,' Bunty said. 'Come one, everyone, chin up.'

'Let's get this party started, Mammy.' Rory beamed in Lola's direction and was met with a weak smile. It would have to do, he told himself. 'When we get to the hotel, the first round's on me. And dinner.'

* * *

The following morning, Sadie and Bronagh enjoyed a lovely breakfast before wrapping up warmly, on their way to visit the animals. It was almost eleven o'clock. Sadie pushed her arm through Bronagh's, snuggling closer for warmth as they stepped out into the sharp, cold air. Today they were both shod in wellingtons and wrapped in woollen coats. Sadie said, 'Hattie's picking us up for lunch so we can spend the morning here on the farm. The mist is everywhere though; you can hardly see your own hand.'

Bronagh looked down at her wellies. 'I feel like the proper English lady.' She winked. 'So, all I need now is a proper English gentleman to keep me happy.'

'You need no such thing, Bronagh Doyle,' Sadie said quickly. 'You're all right as you are.'

'I've always liked men, though,' Bronagh said as they crunched through white-tipped grass towards the horses' field. 'It's nice to have someone to banter with.'

'You can banter with me,' Sadie replied.

'Well, to flirt with. Flirting's fun.' Bronagh's eyes twinkled. 'It makes me feel a desirable lady, to have a man to flirt with.'

'It does not.' Sadie disagreed. 'Flirting's just game-playing.'

'How do you mean?'

'Flirting's silly. It's promising one thing and doing another.'

'Not at all, not at all,' Bronagh argued. 'Flirting's chemistry between an alpha male and female. It's been that way since cave dwellers' times. A man shows he's got something a woman wants and she teases him a bit to get it.'

'Such as?'

'Money. A nice car.' Bronagh thought about it. 'Sex.'

'That's rubbish,' Sadie said. 'A man and a woman should be nice and respectful together. Courting's the best thing. And being romantic. That's what makes the world go round.'

'You mean like he gives her a box of chocolates to soften her up a bit before he has a ride?'

'No, Bronagh, I do not.' Sadie was appalled. 'I'm talking about that lovely time in a relationship where a man calls at the door and speaks politely to your da, then he takes you out somewhere special and he behaves like a gentleman.'

'Before you get married and you have to wash his stinky socks and he forgets to flush the lavvy?' Bronagh laughed.

They were approaching the fence. Pi and the other horses raised their heads, noticing them. Sadie felt the pang of sadness return. 'My days of having a man in my bed are well gone now. I miss Alfie every day.'

'I miss my dear Michael.' Bronagh agreed. 'But we don't have to give up. Plenty of women get married again, even at our age.'

'Like who?' Sadie asked in disbelief.

'Joan Collins. She's loads older than we are – in her nineties and her husband's thirty years younger than she is. She has style, Joan. And the right attitude.'

'And she's stinking rich,' Sadie snorted. 'No, it wouldn't be for me.'

'But just think about it.' Bronagh leaned against the fence, her face dreamy. 'If you had to choose one of them, which would it be?'

'One of whom?'

'Paul or Solly. They're both handsome and rich and good fun. Paul's not exactly rich, but he has a farm. That's a different sort of rich.'

'And all those animals.'

'Paul's a proper gentleman. Solly's a bit more edgy; he's had a hard time and worked his way up, and he has a boat. And a house on the cliff that overlooks the sea.'

'Did he say that?'

'Weren't you listening, Sadie? A girl needs to know these things.'

'I wouldn't pick either of them.'

'But if you had to. If you absolutely had to. You know, if someone said they'd cut your throat if you didn't pick one...'

Pi trotted over and Sadie patted his nose. 'I'd pick this one. The old racehorse.'

'Then I get to have them both.' Bronagh laughed. 'Paul's more of a Steve McQueen type. Or Paul Newman. Gentlemanly, reserved but kind. Whereas Solly's more of a gritty he-man, a Samuel L. Jackson.'

'He's nothing like Samuel L.'

'Or Errol Brown. Off Hot Chocolate. He's zany and good fun. He has the chat-up lines, and there's a rugged side. And he's good company. Not that Paul isn't... I bet they're both romantic, though. They know how to flatter a girl. And it would be nice to double-date on Solly's boat.'

'You're talking rubbish with your double-dating.' Sadie tutted, an attempt to warn Bronagh not to throw her heart away, especially for a holiday romance. 'That's enough of you. Let's just pet these horses before we go to Robert's.'

'But if you had to pick one and give the other one to me, Sadie? You have to say.'

'No more nonsense, Bronagh Doyle. Oh.' Sadie turned abruptly as a Land Rover came rumbling through the gate. 'Is that Paul?'

'It is, and Poppy's with him,' Bronagh said as the Land Rover pulled up and Poppy leaped out.

'Guess where we've been?'

'You look pleased.' Bronagh took in her shining face. 'Have you won the lottery?'

Paul stepped from the driver's side. 'We've just rescued another donkey.'

'He's at a house in Lustleigh, on the moors. The owners can't keep him because they're moving away. So we'll bring him here.'

Paul blew on his hands and rubbed them together. 'They called him Sandy but we'll give him another name.'

'Will he go in with The Supremes?' Bronagh asked. 'That'll be nice for him.'

'He will eventually, but Dad wants our vet to give him the once-over. He'll have to spend some time by himself at first,' Poppy explained. 'He'll be in the new arrivals' area, so that we can keep an eye on him. We have to prevent the potential spread of any diseases.'

'I see,' Bronagh said, but she didn't. 'So what will you call him?'

'Sandy's not right for him now – it's a fresh start,' Poppy decided.

'Let's ask our guests to choose,' Paul offered.

'He needs a pop-star name if he's to live with The Supremes,' Sadie suggested.

'One from the nineteen sixties, to match the girls.' Bronagh was thoughtful. 'What about Bob Dylan? Or Mick Jagger?'

'He's a gentle soul,' Paul explained. 'Quiet and dignified.'

'It has to be Buddy Holly, then,' Sadie said.

'Who?' Poppy asked.

'Buddy Holly. My mum loved him.' Bronagh placed a hand over her heart. 'He sang romantic ballads about Peggy Sue and true love ways.'

'Buddy Holly was in the fifties,' Sadie said. 'Will that be all right?'

'Definitely,' Paul said. 'Buddy Holly it is.'

'Where is he now?' Bronagh wanted to know. 'The donkey, I mean. Not Buddy.'

'We went to see him early this morning. He's a bit lonely by himself. We couldn't turn him away.' Poppy stamped her feet to warm up. Her breath was mist on the air. 'We'll get his home ready and go back for him this afternoon.'

'We'll get the vet to look him over too.' Paul seemed pleased, despite the added cost. 'You'll be able to meet Buddy later.'

'That's lovely. After lunch with Robert.' Bronagh reached out and patted Pi's nose. 'You'll have another friend here at Tails of Hope.'

'We should go inside. I'm getting cold,' Sadie said. 'I'm looking forward to spending time with Bunty's family.'

'I wonder what's for lunch,' Bronagh said. 'After all, Robert's a prize-winning baker. We can expect something delicious and hot.' Bronagh rolled her eyes flirtatiously. 'Just how we like our men.'

'Speak for yourself,' Sadie muttered to herself. 'Nowadays I'm happier with a half of stout and a plate of Irish stew.'

16

'I'm off to pick them up.' Hattie was ready to leave, the car keys in her hand.

Robert was still fretting. 'What if they're vegetarian? Vegan, even?'

'They won't be, Robert.' Tressy squeezed his arm affectionately. 'Bunty would've said.'

'But that's the problem.' Robert was flustered. 'Bunty hasn't said anything at all since you messaged that Sadie and Bronagh were here, that you'd met them in the church and invited them to lunch. I thought she might've asked when they were going home or made some comment about the fact that they brought the Ferrari. I mean, we don't even know why they're here in the first place. It seems a strange time to have a holiday, in December.'

'You've just got back from Cornwall. Rest. Anyway, they seem all very laid-back in Ballycotton,' Hattie soothed. 'I expect they wanted a break.'

'And everything's ready for lunch.' Tressy kissed Robert's cheek. 'The casserole and dumplings are perfect, and there are extra potatoes, and cake and scones. They'll have a wonderful time, and so will we.'

'Beef casserole's not very Irish.' Robert was doubtful.

'They won't want Irish food, they're in Devon. They'll want to sample local produce,' Hattie said.

'I haven't met them since Bunty's wedding. They struck me as a bit wild.' Robert's frown deepened. 'There was a lot of dancing, as I remember.'

'That was years ago,' Hattie said. 'They've quietened down.'

'You should've seen them at Bunty's reception.' Robert shuddered. 'I don't think I'd ever seen anyone dance after a few drinks like Sean's Aunt Bronagh. She was quite frightening.'

'She was just having a good time,' Hattie remembered.

'She kicked her legs and clapped and sang. She told me I should let my hair down.' Robert seemed still traumatised. 'Do you think they'll be all right staying at the sanctuary? I mean, ought I to put them up here? They are family.'

'Let's play it by ear,' Hattie advised. 'We'll show them round. They can meet the goats and the chickens. Afterwards, I'll text Bunty, and we'll sort arrangements out.'

'I'll get one room ready just in case – they'd have to share a double.' Tressy was her usual easy-going self. 'They'd be welcome.'

'But we have the gardening-group meeting this evening.' Robert was still fretting. 'Well, it's officially the Millbrook Gardening and Baking Group.'

'I'll take them back to the farm before then,' Hattie said gently. 'And you can concentrate on your talk.'

'Everything's ready,' Tressy reminded him. 'We've made sponge cakes and a few mince pies and a pavlova.'

'Susan Joyce brought the agenda round yesterday.' Robert

shuddered. 'I'm supposed to be talking to the group about icing Christmas cakes.'

'I always find brushing the top of the cake with a bit of vodka helps.' Tressy hugged him. 'Now let me get you a hot drink, Robert, while Hattie collects our visitors. I don't want you stressing. Just enjoy yourself. The two Irish aunties will be delighted, the amount of bother you've been to, making them such a nice meal.'

'Have I overdone it?'

'Not at all, my lover.' Tressy ruffled his hair. 'You take it easy. Go to the conservatory and put "Clair de Lune" on. A bit of Debussy always calms you down.'

'I think I will,' Robert said. 'And Isaac Mewton's asleep in there. I'll pop her on my knee and have a few minutes to myself. Thanks, Tressy. You're right. I'm getting stressed over nothing. I'm sure Sadie and Bronagh will be the perfect guests.'

Robert took himself off to the conservatory. Lights twinkled from all corners. A real fir tree in a colourful pot created a festive glow. Beethoven was playing through the smart speaker. Two dozen Christmas cards were looped on bright string across the wall: he had so many friends in the village.

He stared through the window towards the fields. Beyond the patio, the chickens were huddled in their coops keeping warm, and, further away, the goats were in the field, chewing at a hedge. He looked up at the sky; it was blank as paper, a pale winter sun gleaming weakly. The grass was brittle with frost but, inside the conservatory, the heating was on full and the room was cosy. Robert, still in his slippers, slumped on the sofa next to Isaac Mewton, who opened one eye and began purring. He stroked the black fur down to the white socks and repeated the action, feeling soothed already.

Robert told the smart speaker to play Claude Debussy's Clair de Lune and closed his eyes, allowing the delicate piano notes to soak into his skin like massaging fingertips. He felt Isaac clamber on his knee and he rested a hand on her back, rubbing the softness between his fingertips. He exhaled slowly. The music drifted through the air and he was already feeling calm.

Light notes trilled around him and Robert felt the tension soak away. He was soothed by the magic of the music. His anxieties soaked into the sofa, where he was held safely. He felt himself relax as the notes rippled around him like a cascade of water, and he began to drift.

In a warm place, subliminal, between sleep and wakefulness, Robert felt contented. He breathed out in satisfaction. His home was filled with the comforting aromas of baking. He had Tressy in his life now; wonderful, big-hearted, beautiful Tressy, whom he loved to distraction. Hattie was staying with them and it was always wonderful to wake up each morning to the joyful sound of her laughter. She planned to move to a place of her own in the new year, the house would be his and Tressy's, the two of them. Christmas would come soon and, with it, the magic of togetherness.

He was fast asleep, snorting softly, Isaac on his knee making snuffling sounds of contentment. His body was relaxed, almost numb.

A witch's cackle made him leap a mile. Robert sat up, his eyes still closed, his hands out in front of him, and shrieked. Isaac leaped from his knee.

Bronagh said, her hands on her hips, 'You were well out of it there, Robert, snoring like a steamroller.'

Robert blinked, opening his eyes. Two women stood in front of him, both smiling. The one with silver and purple hair, who was wrapped in an oversized woollen coat to her ankles, had taken off her shoes. A toe wiggled through a hole in the sock. She wore glasses and was short and lean. The other woman was taller and rounder, with a huge coat and a headscarf, a kind face, twinkling eyes. Robert placed a palm over his heart to encourage it back to normality.

Sadie held out a hand. 'Pleased to meet you again, Robert. It's been far too long.'

'It has.' Robert shook it lightly. 'Sadie. Good to see you.'

'Is it a cheeky sleep you were having, Robert? Have you been on the wine this morning while you were cooking? I know I like a tipple when I'm in the kitchen, hard at it.' Bronagh held out a hand in greeting, not wishing to be left out. She didn't wait for him to reply. 'What a lovely house you have. It's very warm. Hattie picked us up in her Nissan Micra. It's a comfy car. We came down in a Ferrari.' Bronagh chuckled. 'Lunch smells good. I'm starving.'

Sadie was still smiling. 'It's kind of you to invite us, Robert. We're staying at the Tails of Hope Farm. It's nice there.'

'I know it fairly well. Paul, who owns it, comes to the church sometimes. Not that I go often. But Hattie plays the organ nowadays.'

'I know, we heard her at it,' Bronagh said. 'She has a lovely touch. All the carols. Puts you right in the mood.'

'Thank you.' Hattie was waiting politely in the doorway with Tressy. 'I'm practising for the Christmas service.'

Tressy held out a hand. 'I'm Tressy Carew, Robert's partner. From Cornwall.' She shook both women's hands. 'But I live here now. And in Cornwall. Robert and I have a home each. That's why we missed you the other day. We were in Padstow with friends.' She looked from one face to the other. 'Lunch is ready. Is beef casserole all right? With dumplings. And we have potatoes, new ones from Robert's garden. He grows them all year round.'

'My stomach's eating itself,' Bronagh said. 'That sounds lovely.'

'Shall we go in?' Tressy led the way. 'I have wine or sparkling elderflower or water, whichever you prefer.'

'The elderflower sounds grand,' Sadie began, but Bronagh's voice carried from the back of the line.

'I don't suppose you have any stout or ale? I'm partial to a bit of ale with beef. It brings out the flavour. My taste buds are going a bit nowadays.'

Two hours later, the meal was mostly over. The remains of the raspberry meringue were still heaped on a dish on the table. Bronagh couldn't help reaching out a finger and picking out a couple more raspberries, the cream clinging to them. Three empty bottles of stout and three bottles of elderflower pressé stood amid the empty glasses and plates.

Sadie sighed with contentment. The break was doing her the world of good. 'That was so delicious. I don't think I've eaten so much in an age.'

'Do you always eat like this, Robert? There's not a pick on you,' Bronagh observed.

'I'm often busy in the garden; it keeps me fit,' Robert said by way of explanation. 'If you like, I can take you for a tour of the smallholding later on, and introduce you to Vincent Van Goat and the Great Goatsby, and the hens.'

'That would be lovely. We love animals.' Bronagh grabbed his arm. 'Up at Tails of Hope they've got The Supremes – they're the donkeys – and the horses – Pi's my favourite – and the alpacas with the Mexican names and a few others – and a new donkey.'

'We like it there. The owners are friendly. And besides...' Sadie looked longingly at the meringue but she was too full to eat any more '...I think they need all the help they can get. There don't seem to be many visitors.'

'Oh? I didn't know,' Robert said.

'So how long are you staying?' Hattie asked tactfully.

'Just until the weekend. We ought to take Rory's Ferrari back.' Sadie exchanged looks with Bronagh.

'Doesn't he know you've got it?' Tressy joked and was quick to notice a look of guilt cross Sadie's face.

'Oh, yes, we left a note. And we phoned up. He's no bother, Rory. Heart of gold.' Bronagh took a breath, ready to explain. 'So, The Hole in the Wall was having a bake off for charity – just like you did, Robert – and the judge put his face in the cake and blamed us. Well, he only turned out to be a sergeant in the gardai.' She began to laugh. 'So Sadie and I borrowed her grandson's car and took off to Dublin.'

'To Dublin?' Hattie was mystified.

'Like Thelma and Louise,' Bronagh added mischievously. 'On the run.'

'It's a long story.' Sadie was hoping to avoid saying any more. But Bronagh was keen to tell.

'We were drinking whiskey and dancing in a bar in Dublin and a fight broke out. So we made ourselves scarce. Then we had an idea, to go on holiday. We knew Bunty's family lived here, so we took off.'

'You don't think the police will follow you here?' Robert asked, worriedly.

'Oh, not at all. It was only Partlan. It was something and nothing.' Bronagh laughed. 'We'll just drive back at the weekend and it'll be fine. Rory's a nice lad. He won't mind that we have the car.'

'Everyone will be warming up for Christmas,' Sadie explained.

'Well.' Robert looked from Bronagh to Sadie. 'Can I make anyone coffee?'

'I'd murder a cup of tea,' Sadie said, and she meant it.

'Me too – and perhaps a scone.' Bronagh's eyes were larger than her stomach. 'We can walk it off by visiting your animals. What did you say your hens were called again?'

'Princess Lay-a,' Robert began.

'Jabba the Cluck,' Hattie added.

'Obi Wan Henobi.' Tressy smiled.

'After all the wans in *Game of Thrones*,' Bronagh guessed wrongly, and Sadie's heart expanded with affection. 'Well, I'd love to meet them all.' She stretched her arms above her head. 'Maybe you can play some of that tinkly-winkly music you had on when we came in and we can all have a doze. It sent you right off.'

'I'm shattered,' Sadie agreed. 'It's all this Devon air.'

'Ah, but—' Robert looked suddenly alarmed. 'We have a baking and gardening club meeting at five.'

'What, here, in your house?' Bronagh asked. 'Bunty said you were a bit of a sex magnet because of all the baking. Will the ladies all be round after your recipes?'

'The meeting's held in The Pig and Pickle,' Tressy explained kindly.

'In the *pub*.' Bronagh was suddenly wide awake. 'Well, I'm very interested in baking and – what's the other thing you do?'

'Gardening,' Sadie whispered.

'I love a spot of gardening. We'll come to your meeting with you.' Bronagh swiped a nearby ginger biscuit through the cream on the meringue and ate it. 'Well. That's grand. It's decided.' She turned to Sadie. 'I love it here in Devon. It has everything, doesn't it? Cute animals, handsome men, fabulous food and a pub. I think we just might have to stay on.'

17

Christmas lights shimmered in the snug of The Pig and Pickle, hired for one and a half hours by Susan Joyce. Tables had been pushed together so that people could sit facing one another: there were more attendees than usual and not enough seats.

Susan sat at the head of the table, demanding that Robert sit next to her. Tressy was on the other side of him, then Hattie, with her friend Barry Butler, who looked contented, smiling in round glasses. According to half of Millbrook, Barry was Hattie's secret lover. Next to Barry was ex-police officer, Eric Mallory; his wife, Edie; then Angie Pollock and Jill Davies, both great fans of Robert's. Jill had taken the bus from Dawlish in the hope of sampling some of Robert's baking, asking for copies of the recipes for his masterpieces.

Sadie and Bronagh examined each face. Hattie had offered to drive them back to the farm, but the pub was much more interesting.

'I declare the meeting open,' Susan said smartly. 'So, introductions first. Welcome to Bronagh and Sadie, from Ireland.

Could I ask everyone to give our visitors a huge Millbrook welcome?'

The locals mumbled, 'Hello.'

'Bronagh and Sadie are Robert's relatives from Ireland,' Susan added smoothly. 'So could I ask each of you to say who you are briefly?'

A man in a trilby coughed profusely by way of introduction. 'I'm George Tenby, pensioner.' He indicated the woman next to him in a shaggy coat, who looked too hot, given the pub's log fire. 'Mary, wife.'

'Hello,' Mary said curtly. She looked quite capable of introducing herself.

'I'm Francis Baxter, vicar of St Jude's,' said a slim man in an ill-fitting suit. The woman next to him gave a light cough.

'Sally Baxter. Francis's wife. I teach at the primary school in Millbrook. Pleased to meet you.' Sally folded her arms neatly and blushed.

The next woman pushed back her hair before flourishing a notepad. 'Rosie Eagle. Journalist for *The Chronicle*.' She paused. 'I haven't been to a meeting in ages. Too busy. But we have precious little going on this time of year. It's all "will it be a white Christmas?" and storms unleashing strong tides on the beaches. I need something local I can get my teeth into.'

'I can't wait to get my teeth into Robert's sponge cake,' Angie said, a bit too enthusiastically. Everyone eyed the spread at the bar. Robert had brought a Victoria sponge, a passion-fruit pavlova and a batch of savoury scones. Tressy had brought a batch of bite-sized pasties.

'Colin Bennett.' One of the men in a cap looked at Bronagh. 'I didn't think you were Twiggy.'

'Pardon, Colin?' Susan folded her arms crossly.

'I struggle to buy myself a pint on the pension this government gives me, so if anyone wants to take pity, mine's best bitter,' he said instead.

'He's richer than he makes out. He's got thousands in Premium Bonds. Whereas I—' a chuckle came from the window seat '—Dennis Lyons, local grumpy git – I won't sit with you all. I've got a stinking cold for Christmas, and I don't want to pass it on.'

'Thank you, Dennis,' Francis said graciously. 'Well, it's a pleasure tonight to welcome you both, Sadie and Brenda.'

'Bronagh,' Bronagh interrupted.

'Bronagh,' Francis spluttered in apology. 'And they are Robert's sister Bunty's—' He looked puzzled. 'What are you again?'

'I'm Bunty's mother-in-law and Bronagh's my sister-in-law,' Sadie explained.

'We're from Ballycotton,' Bronagh continued. 'We're here on holiday. We're staying at Tails of Hope Farm.'

'You're definitely not Twiggy, then. I remember you had hot chocolate,' Colin said.

'I remember Bunty,' Dennis said unwisely. 'She came down last summer. She has a nice figure, good legs.' He began to cough and wheeze loudly, although it was more down to indiscretion than his cold.

'I wouldn't let my nephew Sean hear you say that,' Bronagh warned.

'Although Bunty's a good-looking woman,' Sadie said loyally.

'If we might proceed,' Francis said quietly. 'Robert, you were going to advise us on the icing of the Christmas cake. A very important activity at this time of year, and one fraught with potential for error.'

'I haven't iced mine yet,' Sally told everyone. 'The one I made last year went wrong and the cake got all mixed up with the icing. It looked like slurry.'

'I've been waiting for Robert to instruct us.' Susan was preening. 'I was hoping he might offer classes. One to one is nicest.'

'Well...' Robert stood up and unfolded a piece of paper shakily. 'So, my speech. Icing the cake. Right, well. Tressy brushes hers with vodka to make the icing stick.'

'I do,' Tressy said.

'Big boozers, the Cornish, all of them.' Dennis reached for his pint.

'Are we?' Tressy smiled sweetly. 'Is that pop you're drinking, Dennis?' She raised her glass of lemonade. 'Cheers.'

'So, I cover my fruit cake with marzipan before the fondant or royal icing to keep moisture in and stop oils from seeping through and causing discolouration,' Robert continued.

'I've never liked marzipan, but I'd try yours, Robert. It might change my mind,' Angie purred.

'I agree,' said a mouse-like Jill.

'Traditionally, the white layer would be royal icing, although you could use shop-bought fondant icing. For a really flat surface, I use two very thin layers of the fondant,' Robert said. Rosie appeared to be scribbling it all down.

'I like a Dundee cake myself,' Sadie said.

'I had a malted-milk snowman cake once. I ate the lot.' Bronagh grinned.

'I like a madeira,' George Tenby mumbled. 'But Mary doesn't know how to bake them.'

Mary threw him an evil look. 'Supermarkets sell them. Buy one.'

'I can't be dealing with all that cake,' Eric Mallory said. 'I mean, it's roast dinner and all the trimmings and there's the pud and brandy sauce and mince pies. It's too much in one day.'

'People overeat in the western world. Privilege of the rich,' Colin told everyone.

'Don't be so daft. It's only a blow-out once a year,' Bronagh retorted. 'We can all go back to eating bread and jam after.'

'So...' Robert took a patient breath. 'Start by laying the icing at the back of the cake and lower it down to the front. You can use the flat of your hands to smooth it. And neatly trim away any excess icing.'

'I'd just buy one from the shop,' Mary said. 'To save all that palaver.'

'But the point is to learn how to ice your own, Mary,' Angie said hotly.

'I'm just saying,' Mary replied. 'It's a lot of unnecessary fuss.'

'It's art,' Barry said gently.

'If you want the season of goodwill, you won't find it in our house if Mary's in the kitchen,' George joked and Mary's eyes were daggers.

'I like a Guinness cake. You can get them from Doughty's Delights, in Ballycotton. They're twenty euros.' Bronagh raised a glass of stout. 'Sadie's son Niall's wife gets hers there. And Partlan Brown loves them.' She burst out laughing.

'Am I missing something?' Francis asked.

'That was the bake off that went wrong,' Sadie explained.

'Go on, Robert,' Hattie coaxed gently. 'Tell us all how to ice the cake. It *is* Christmas.'

'Well...' Robert glanced around until all eyes were back on him. 'I'm rather partial to finishing a cake with a ribbon. You can use any leftover icing to make a pretty snowy Christmas scene – Santas and fir trees, sleighs and reindeers.'

'Bloody hell, I don't believe it.' Dennis gasped and everyone turned to look.

'What is it?' Susan asked anxiously.

'What's happened?' Francis asked.

'A car's just pulled up outside – you know the flashy one with the flux capacitor in *Back to the Future*. Now a man's getting out. He's got a ponytail – and there's a woman all dressed in denim. I think it's *him*.'

'Oh, no.' Bronagh grasped Sadie's hand. 'Do you think this is who I think it is?'

'It definitely surely is.' Sadie felt her heart rate double. Her face held a caught-in-the-act look. 'What'll we do?'

'They've come to take us back, Sadie.'

'Who?' Eric almost shouted. 'Where?'

Dennis pointed, open-mouthed. 'Dr Emmett Brown – *Back to the Future*. He's the man with the white hair who drives the car – and he's with Marty McFly's mother. She's straight out of the nineteen fifties too.'

'Is it the DeLorean time machine?' Eric said, in awe.

Colin pushed back his chair and scurried over, staring through the window into the darkness, not thinking about catching Dennis's cold. He gasped. 'You're right. It's them, in the film. The doctor.'

'Dr who?' Mary shrieked.

'No – not Doctor Who, the one in *Back to the Future*,' Dennis said. 'It's his car, the one with those gull-wing doors – and here's another car just arrived, a big Range Rover, and lots more people are getting out and now they are talking to the doctor, the one who travels through time in his plutonium-powered car.'

'No,' Bronagh said grimly. 'It's our Pat.'

Sadie stood up abruptly. 'It is. And Niall. Oh, dammit.'

'What on earth are you talking about?' Rosie held her notepad up. 'What's happening?' She rushed over to the window. 'Look – another car has arrived now, an old banger, and two more people are getting out. Now they're coming in.'

'Sean?' Bronagh and Sadie exchanged looks. 'That's torn it.'

'I hope they buy some drinks.' Shelley's voice came from behind the bar.

'Can you get me another pint, please, before they do?' Colin shouted.

'Me too,' Dennis asked.

'Mine's a Bloody Mary,' Mary called out.

'I'll have one too, with a double vodka,' Bronagh shouted. 'It's our Niall. And Nora. And Sean. And Rory.'

The door opened with a bang and eight figures straggled inside, four men and four women. Sean put his hands on his hips and said, 'Hello, Mammy.'

Sadie stood up, ready to take charge. 'Sean – Niall – what are you all doing here?'

'Don't tell me,' Bronagh gasped. 'Rory's come for his car back.'

'You haven't broken it, have you, Auntie Bronagh?' Niall asked.

'No, it's safe in a garage.'

'We went to Robert's place, and no one was in, so we came here,' Sean said by way of explanation.

'So what about I buy us all a drink?' Rory beamed. 'What will you be having, everyone?'

Dennis snarled, 'This is a private meeting and you've interrupted it.'

'Indeed you have,' Colin agreed. 'It's the Millbrook Gardening and Baking Group. Robert was just instructing us on icing a cake.'

'It looks like he's finished, to me,' Pat said. 'And we've come to stay with Robert. He's our relative. Well, he's Bunty's.'

Robert looked anxious. 'You've all come to stay? With me?'

'You're looking well, Bunty.' Colin stared at Bunty's chest.

'Hello, Colin, hello, Dennis.' Bunty folded her arms and glared.

'So, now we're here – let's get some drinks in.' Pat smiled at Shelley. 'Hello there. We'll have whatever the ladies are having, and pints of the black stuff, please. We've done driving. It's been a long day.'

'We'd just finished the meeting,' Barry said quickly.

'We haven't,' Susan insisted. 'I need to do AOB.'

'Any other business. It's time for a pint. There. You're done.' Pat cackled good-humouredly.

Dennis got up slowly. 'I think you've missed the point, mate. We've hired this room. For an hour and a half. For our meeting.'

'I'm not your mate,' Pat began. There was a sudden silence that felt awkward.

'And you're not welcome at the gardening and baking group meeting. Go in the other bar.' Dennis looked around to gauge the others' reaction. 'Coming here in a ridiculous car, interrupting our meeting, shouting the odds.'

'Ridiculous car?' Pat repeated. His eyes narrowed, like Clint Eastwood in a western film shoot-out.

Rory took a deep breath; it was absolutely the wrong move to slander Pat's car. He said, 'Now, Uncle Pat—'

'Don't you dare call my car ridiculous,' Nora said quickly.

'Why don't you tell your pet dog to stop yapping?' Dennis told Pat, and the silence that followed was filled with tension.

Pat's voice was low, furious. 'No one speaks to my wife like that. Or insults my car.'

'Uncle Pat...' Rory repeated, a calm warning. Pat was the salt of the earth, but everyone in Ballycotton knew you never said a bad word about his car. Or his family.

'Nobody insulted your silly car.' Dennis took a step back.

'Why don't you go back to Ireland or whatever stone it was you crawled from?'

'Now, there's no need for that.' Niall put a hand on Pat's shoulder.

Pat shrugged it off and shook with anger. 'No one bad-mouths my wife.'

'Why don't we have a drink?' Rory suggested affably, making sure that Lola was standing behind him, just in case.

'I'm telling you you're not wanted here.' Dennis sniffed self-righteously. 'We hired this room. Go to the public bar.' He wiped his nose nervously.

Pat took a pace forward and Dennis took one back, in synchronisation. Then Pat moved back and Dennis shuffled forward, like a dance. Shelley called from the bar.

'Stop it, Dennis. Of course they're welcome. Your meeting time's up anyway. What can I get you all?'

Pat glared, his eyes glinting. 'Apologise, you eejit.'

'I won't apologise to a leprechaun,' Dennis said somewhat foolishly, his face showing straight away that he'd realised his mistake.

'Right.' Pat put his knuckles up, a bantam ready for action. 'You asked for it. Do you want to step outside?'

'If I have to.' Dennis showed his fists reluctantly.

'Now, now.' Francis looked terrified. There was a tension-filled pause where everyone held their breath.

Tressy stood up. 'Don't you dare.'

'Behave yourselves, all of you,' Bunty added.

Robert took a step, putting himself between Pat and Dennis. He breathed in deeply. 'Look, I'm sorry about what Dennis said. Any relative of my sister's is welcome here.' He turned to Dennis. 'Please sit down; you're spreading germs.'

'Sit down, Dennis, like you've been told.' Sadie's voice was a thunderbolt. She put her hands on her hips. It was like the old times, when her kids were little, squabbling. She'd tell them what was what. 'You too, Pat Healy. You're making the place look untidy.' Her eyes blazed. 'Alfie would be ashamed of you all, coming to England and acting like hooligans. Now, behave yourselves and buy everyone drinks in a civilised manner. This is our Robert's village. Don't you dare make a holy show of him and Bunty.' She glared at Dennis. 'Now – you can apologise for what you said about my daughter, or it'll be me landing a punch on your nose.'

Dennis's mouth was open. 'I'm – I'm sorry.' He turned to Nora. 'Sorry.'

'And you can apologise to Dennis for being an eejit,' Sadie said to Pat.

'Sorry,' Pat muttered.

'Right. Now we can be friends. We'll buy you all a drink, in the best Ballycotton tradition,' Sadie insisted, folding her arms.

'And we can share cake,' Hattie suggested calmly.

'I'll get the drinks in.' Rory stepped forward, taking his chance. He didn't like arguments. Peace was definitely the way forward. And didn't a round of drinks always encourage peace talks? 'What are you all having?' He looked at Shelley. 'Drinks all around, please, miss. And a double of whatever you want for yourself, to say sorry for the disturbance.'

18

By half past ten, the snug of The Pig and Pickle hummed with loud chatter and happy laughter. As Shelley collected empty glasses and replaced them with full ones, the villagers of Millbrook mingled with the O'Connor family. Nora turned to Shelley. 'Can you give me your recipe for the mulled cider? It was very nice.'

'I will. Would you like another?' Shelley was delighted.

'I'd love one too.' Maeve grinned, a rare sight. 'Put them on my husband's bar tab.'

Shelley hurried back to the bar, her ponytail swinging. Business was booming.

Pat clapped Dennis on the back. 'I've always wanted a DeLorean, so I saved up for years and I had to go up to Castlebar in County Mayo to get it. I bought it from a man with a barn full of classics and I fell in love with it as soon as I laid eyes on it. DeLoreans have such style.'

'I think I'd look good in one.' Dennis coughed into his elbow. 'I loved that film, *Back to the Future*. I always fancied myself as Marty McFly.'

'I'll take you for a spin around the village,' Pat offered magnanimously.

Lola was regaling Mary and Edie with her troubles. 'The thing is, I'm a professional model. I do swimwear. Anyway, on one shoot they wanted me to wear this frumpy grey apron and stand in the kitchen like a housewife. I said to the photographer, "Do I even look like a housewife?"'

Edie agreed. 'Being a housewife is overrated. Eric expects everything to be perfect and now he's retired, I see less of him than ever.'

'I'm not keen on housework,' Mary said. 'I shove something in the oven and take it out once a day. That's as much as I'll cook. And as for vacuuming – it hurts my back.'

Lola looked disgusted. 'I've never cooked anything from scratch in my life. I mean, what are restaurants for?'

'The thing about Millbrook is—' Colin was chatting to Bunty '—there's no life in the place. The Pig and Pickle's never this much fun. I blame the government. They've systematically squeezed the soul from pensioners. I can hardly afford the price of a pint. But you all come down from Ireland and immediately there's a party.'

'But Millbrook's so calm,' Bunty insisted. 'It's nice and sleepy.'

'That's not good, believe me – it's only one step from being dead,' Colin grunted. 'But it's better now you're here.'

Hattie flourished her phone. 'I've just spoken to Paul up at the farm and he'll be down here soon with the Land Rover and drive all Bunty's family in relays back to his place. So no worries about the beer you've drunk. Paul can't believe his luck – all his rooms are full.'

'It's worked out well.' Barry glanced at the clock. 'Closing time soon. Do you fancy coming back to my cottage for a nightcap?'

'It's only across the road.' Hattie reached for her bag. 'Why not?' Barry took her hand and they moved towards the door unnoticed.

'The problem is, there aren't nearly enough newsworthy events in Devon,' Rosie Eagle complained to Bronagh. 'The bake off in summer was such a success. We got the TV involved. It was a community event and everyone loved the Cornwall versus Devon thing. We need something like that again.'

'A good murder perhaps?' Bronagh suggested.

Rosie frowned. 'I was thinking of something more local interest.'

Bronagh patted her hair. 'I'd be on the TV. I could do an interview. I can share my beauty tips about how to stay young. I could tell everyone how Sadie and I escaped to Devon, chased by the Ballycotton garda.'

Sadie was sandwiched between Francis and Sally Baxter. It felt nice to be in a new place, listening to new people. It was refreshingly different from The Hole in the Wall. And Sadie was enjoying the craic. Besides, now she had her family around her, it was like being enveloped in a warm hug.

Sally said, 'I loved the way you spoke to your family just before, like the matriarch. No one listens to me. I can't do anything with my daughter, Tilda. She's in London at the moment with her boyfriend. They have a few bookings in a jazz club. She won't even tell us if she's coming back for Christmas.'

'Isn't that what a mammy's for, laying down the law?' Sadie felt a warm glow of pride, but she was sorry for Sally, who looked tired out. 'I expect you'll hear from your daughter soon.'

'Christmas is a busy time for us here,' Francis said. 'What with the church services, then school end-of-term events: Sally's head of Key Stage Two at the primary school. It's all concerts and Nativity plays and making paper decorations.'

'The Nativity's going so badly,' Sally said.

'Can you not give some of the work to someone else? Bring in a few elves to play with the kiddies? Oh but...' Sadie paused, her eyes gleaming. She'd had an idea and it filled her with a new energy.

'The rehearsals aren't going well for the Nativity. I'm helping Adam Thompson to put it on – he's our year five teacher – and the performance is next week. But three of the lambs have got tonsilitis and the child who plays the angel Gabriel keeps fighting with the Virgin Mary.' Sally groaned. 'It'll be a disaster.'

'I'm sure Francis will put a word in with the good Lord.' Sadie winked. The spark of a plan ignited – a proper Nativity! – and she was suddenly lost in thought.

'So how long are you staying in Millbrook?' Robert asked Sean, Niall and Rory. 'We weren't expecting you at all.'

'Total cock-up on our part,' Sean said. 'It was all a bit of a rushed job. Maeve forgot to book the hotel last night. Bunty thought she'd replied to Hattie's text, but she'd just sent an emoji. It's nice to be here though. And I'm glad we're staying with yer man on the farm. So, we'd only planned to pick up the Ferrari, have a quick look round and go back to Ireland. But Rory here's dead keen to stay.'

'I am. I'm winding down for Christmas, and I have my laptop, so I can work remotely.' Rory looked around cheerily. 'It's so nice here. I want to do some walking, see the seaside and the moor.'

'In the Ferrari?' Robert imagined the engine roaring around the peaceful Devon countryside.

'It'll be good craic, having a break here. I think we should stay into next week, Da.' Rory gave his cheeky grin and wrapped an arm round Niall. 'What do you say?'

Niall was ambivalent. 'I don't see why not. But what about your girlfriend, Rory? She doesn't look happy.'

'Ah, we've only just met. It's not serious.' Rory glanced towards Lola, who had folded her arms and was sulking. In truth, his father was probably right.

'Does Lola know that?' Sean asked.

'It's the car she likes, not myself.' Rory winked. 'She keeps asking me for a big Christmas present, but I haven't really thought about it. I can't imagine we'll be together long after Boxing Day.'

'Doesn't that bother you?' Robert asked, appalled.

'I'll live.' Rory was still wondering what to buy her. 'I don't think I'm *the one* for her...'

'The little Cornish pasties are so easy to make,' Tressy was telling Angie, Jill and Susan. 'And they're just a mouthful, not the whole thing, so they're better for the waistline.'

'Tressy, I have to ask...' Susan took a deep breath. 'Were you attracted to Robert because of his baking? Did he fall for you because of your perfect scones?'

'I've always wanted to ask that,' Angie said.

'It's so romantic,' Jill cooed.

'Well, I'd say it was more a meeting of minds,' Tressy explained.

'And bodies,' Angie said with a twinkle.

'And souls,' Jill sighed.

'You're both in your seventies,' Susan observed in her businesslike way. 'I'm still in my sixties. Would you say that love at an older age was better now than when you're young?'

'More fulfilling?' Angie asked.

'Dreamier?' Jill cooed again.

'I'd say it's about finding someone who's a soulmate. And we fell in love at first sight.' Tressy folded her arms. 'Robert and I have so much in common. Our baking, our philosophy on life, our sense of humour.'

'If only there were more Roberts in the world,' Susan said sadly. 'Every woman needs a Robert.'

'He's the ideal man, isn't he?' Angie agreed.

'Well, why don't you go online dating and see what's out there?' Tressy advised. 'There must be lots of older men who'd be delighted to meet you. You've so much to offer.'

'Have we?' Susan asked.

'Of course,' Tressy asserted. 'Good-looking, strong women, capable. What's stopping you?'

'Perhaps we should give it a whirl,' Angie murmured.

'We could,' Jill echoed.

'The three of us might just make a joint venture – the Millbrook Misses...'

'The Millbrook Mistresses.' Angie gave a mischievous wink.

'The Millbrook Maids,' Jill tried.

'You speak for yourself,' Susan said as she nudged Angie and the three of them burst into an evil cackle.

Shelley rang the bell and called, 'Last orders, please.'

Colin and Dennis hurried to the bar to buy one last pint and Sadie called, 'There's a Land Rover outside. It's Paul. He'll take us all back to the farm. Come on, everyone. Shelley says your cars will be safe here overnight. It's time for bed...'

* * *

Sadie lay in bed, staring through the open curtains. The moon was high, a silver disc that slid behind a cobweb cloud and emerged slowly as if it had all the time in the world.

She was thinking. She'd believed she was going back to Ballycotton in two days' time. But Niall and Sean had been talking in the Land Rover about staying on a bit longer. Sadie liked the idea.

Conversations buzzed in her head: words she'd heard Paul speak about the farm, about Buddy the new donkey, the rising vet's bills, the much-needed updating of the website. He was talking excitedly of his wife's dream of opening a teashop, accommodating so many more needy animals.

She felt sorry for Francis and Sally, who didn't know if their daughter was coming home for Christmas, who were working far too hard. And Robert had told her how much he'd enjoyed the evening in the pub, how nice it was to feel sociable nowadays. He'd once thought himself a bit of a fuddy-duddy, but he'd had such a good time in The Pig and Pickle. It had been his first Christmas celebration.

Sadie wanted to help them all. That was her nature, to help everybody. A plan began to form, little bits of a jigsaw moving together, snapping into place. Tomorrow was Friday. Perhaps they could stay for a few more days, until next Wednesday or Thursday. It would be good for the farm too, to have more paying guests. She breathed out deeply, her mind buzzing with a new idea. Children, animals. It was an exciting one...

'I had a good time tonight,' a voice from the darkness said. 'I never really thought people liked me much, but they all seemed to.'

'Bronagh?' Sadie rolled over and stared at the bed next to her, the mound in the darkness. She'd thought Bronagh was asleep. 'What did you just say?'

'That's why I'm always a little bit zany and over the top. I want people to like me.'

'Where's this come from?' Sadie could hear from her empty tone that Bronagh's confidence had drained away.

'From all my life. When we were at school, you were always the popular one.'

'I was not.'

'You were, you were.' Something in Bronagh's voice cracked. 'I was just the skinny kid nobody could be bothered with. Everyone liked you. You were clever and pretty.'

'That's rubbish.' Sadie's maternal and protective streak were in overdrive.

'That's how I remember it, Sadie. That's why I was your friend at first. So some of it might rub off.'

'Thanks very much.' Sadie felt so sorry for Bronagh.

'No, I mean it. I always loved the way you were so calm and sure of yourself. That's what my brother saw in you too. Alfie loved you.'

'And I loved him back.' Sadie sighed. 'Bronagh, you're beautiful. You're funny and smart and witty. Everyone admires you for it.'

'But I'm a bit too wild. I drink too much at times and show off. It's to get attention. It's because I think nobody will notice me if I don't. That's why I put the purple streaks in my hair.' Bronagh took a deep breath of despair.

'Bronagh, it's *your* hair, you do what you like with it and, to be honest, when you get to our age, people expect us to be eccentric.' Sadie was clenching her fists beneath the duvet. In her heart she was fighting Bronagh's battles, against all the invisible people who might make her feel less than the wonderful soul she was.

'You don't think I'm – OTT?'

'Over the top?' Sadie asked, furious. 'You just be who you are, Bronagh Doyle. Everyone loves you for it.'

'Even Michael used to say I made a holy show of myself at times.'

'Michael was proud of you. Now let me tell you something.' Sadie raised her voice. She rolled over again, making the bed creak, then she was ready with her opinion. 'There are plenty of women out there who are shadows. Their husbands' shadows. Shadows of themselves. Women who don't say boo to a goose. I've always admired your pluck, your sense of justice, your fun. I've always marvelled when you climb up on the tables to dance and sing a song until you've sung your lungs out.'

'*You* admire *me*?' Bronagh's voice was tiny.

'I do.' Sadie meant it. 'You're strong and brave and feisty, and you don't give a shite what anyone else thinks. You say what's in your mind and what's in your heart, and there's plenty in that heart, Bronagh. You're generous and sweet and you look good whatever you wear and you're the nicest, funniest friend anyone could have. Not a day goes by that I don't thank God for a friend such as yourself.'

There was a long silence, then Bronagh said, 'Do you mean that? All of it?'

'I do.'

There was the small sound of a hiccup that might have been a sob. Bronagh said, 'I love you, Sadie.'

'I love you back.' Sadie smiled. Bronagh was almost convinced. And Sadie loved her for her cockiness and her vulnerability. She rolled over again. 'Now get some sleep and stop acting the maggot, or we'll both look a sight at breakfast. Paul might be there. You don't want to be smiling at him with eyes like pee holes in the snow, do you?'

'Paul?' Bronagh was silent for a while. 'Or Solly?' she said softly. 'So many men to choose from. I wonder which one I'll pick.'

'Pick them both.' Sadie closed her eyes. She'd finalise her planning tomorrow. In moments she was asleep.

19

There were ten people around the breakfast table at Tails of Hope the following day. Hazel was delighted when Sean and Niall greeted her lightly fried eggs and toast with uproarious applause.

Pat smacked his lips. 'These are the best baked beans I ever had.'

'You must tell me what you put in them,' Nora gushed. 'I'll cook them like that at home.'

'It's nice not to have to make my own breakfast for once,' Maeve added.

'More coffee, please.' Niall raised his cup. 'We should come on holiday more often.'

'I soak my own beans and bake them.' Hazel beamed. 'I add a bit of black pepper.' She hesitated. 'Will you all stay for dinner tonight? I always do fish and chips on Friday. With mushy peas.'

'Mushy peas? Count me in.' Sean rubbed his hands. 'We can hit the town tomorrow for a family meal.'

'Tressy said we should keep tomorrow free. She has something planned,' Bunty added. 'But yes, please, Hazel.'

'Can't we go out somewhere, just the two of us, Rory?' Lola said sulkily.

'Home-cooked fish and chips though.' Rory noticed her pouting in his direction, eyes of a baby doll, but he knew his priorities. 'I'll take you out soon, Lola – somewhere really swanky. That's a promise. But I think we should spend the first day with the family.'

'I've spent the last two days with your family,' Lola said beneath her breath. 'That's enough for any sane person.'

'We need to discuss how long we're staying.' Sadie made a mental note of the conversation. She'd ask Rory later where his relationship with Lola was going. 'So we can tell Hazel up front.'

'She'll have to get the extra groceries in,' Bronagh added.

'Perhaps we should be back in Ballycotton in time for Christmas,' Sean said. 'So how about we stay into next week? Maybe go back next Thursday.'

'Shall I organise ferry tickets? The crossing might be busy close to Christmas,' Bunty said.

'Let's leave it a day or two,' Niall suggested. 'We might want to change our plans and go back earlier.'

'Or later.' Rory was developing a soft spot for the sanctuary. It was a lovely, warm, friendly place. He wanted to stay on.

'It'll be good to catch up with Hattie, and spend time. We're very close.' Bunty turned to Nora and Maeve. 'We could have a girls' day out Christmas shopping in Exeter.'

'I'd love that.' Nora clapped her hands.

'And Tressy promised to show me how she makes her scones so crumbly,' Maeve said. 'She's very nice, Tressy. I think she'd be a really good cookery teacher.'

'Robert's meringue was to die for,' Nora added. 'I'd love a tour of his little smallholding, with all the chickens and the goats.'

'But this farm is just like home,' Bronagh said. 'After breakfast I want to see the horses and introduce you to Pi, and The Supremes, and Buddy. Oh, and the alpacas.'

'What's an alpaca?' Lola frowned. 'Are they the furry things people make jumpers out of?' She pushed her food away uneaten and Pat speared the fried egg.

'Waste not, want not.' He lifted his fork. 'I'm going to check over the DeLorean this morning, make sure she's running smoothly after the last two days. And I promised Dennis and Colin a spin in her later on.'

'Let's spend the day at leisure,' Bronagh said. 'We'll all take it easy. It's been a long two days' travelling. Everyone can get their bearings. We'll meet up at dinner and discuss the rest of our stay.'

'I'll take you out, Lola,' Rory said gallantly, doing his best to make her feel happy. 'We can go to the seaside.'

'Whatever,' Lola replied half-heartedly, and Sadie was quick to notice it.

'I want to look round that pretty church in the village,' Maeve said.

'Hattie plays the organ there,' Bunty remembered.

'And I have someone I need to talk to today.' Sadie dabbed her mouth with a napkin. 'But first, Bronagh, we'll go and introduce everyone to the animals, and I want to have a little word with Paul. After that, you and I have a message to run.'

'Where are we going?'

'Top secret.' Sadie's eyes sparkled with the new plan that had been a spark in The Pig and Pickle. It was all she could do to keep her lips sealed. 'But I have to tell you, it doesn't involve any men.'

'That's a shame,' Bronagh grumbled. 'I won't dress up, then.'

* * *

The O'Connor family congregated outside the donkeys' field while Poppy spoke about the resident animals, answering a flurry of questions. Rory wanted to help feed the horses and seemed oblivious that he had mud on his designer trainers. Pat took to the alpacas immediately and Sean and Bunty developed a soft spot for Pi. Buddy was in the new arrivals' area, looking completely uninterested.

Paul and Sadie had their heads together in a long conversation, then she returned to Bronagh and hooked an arm through hers.

'We're taking that walk now. Put your best coat on.'

'Are we meeting a man?' Bronagh was full of interest.

'No,' Sadie said firmly. 'We need to make a good impression. Go on. And make sure you've got walking shoes. Where we're going's ten minutes from here.'

'Is it Millbrook?' Bronagh asked. 'Are we meeting Dennis and Colin in the pub?' She pulled a face. 'I don't think they'll stand us a pint.'

'Enough of you.' Sadie was in charge. 'We're on business. I've a plan I want to share. And you're my assistant.'

'Assistant? I'm no assistant.' Bronagh pulled a mock-sulky face. 'We're partners in crime. Thelma and Louise.'

It was almost twelve o'clock as Sadie and Bronagh strolled down the winding road towards Millbrook. It was a cold, sharp day, the pale winter sun high in a mackerel sky. They paused outside the primary school. Loud shrieks from in the playground met their ears and Sadie said, 'Here we are.'

'The school? Whatever for?'

'It's lunchtime. The kiddies are all outside. I hoped Sally would have a few minutes for us.'

'Oh – what's on your mind?'

'Let's go in and you'll see.'

Sadie and Bronagh paused at the reception desk where a dark-haired woman in a navy suit looked up. Her lanyard said her name was Mrs Julie Page. She said, 'Can I help you?'

'We'd like to see Sally, you know, Mrs Whatsername... the vicar's wife,' Sadie said.

'Do you have an appointment?'

'No, we don't. But it's lunchtime, so she'll be free,' Sadie persisted.

'Teachers seldom have free time, even at lunchtimes,' Julie said. 'I can't let you see Mrs Baxter unless you have an appointment.'

Sadie ignored her. 'Give her a ring and tell her we're here. She asked us to pop in. And we have something special for her.'

Julie eyed them suspiciously. 'What is it?'

'Pardon?'

'What do you have for her?'

'An opportunity, one she can't afford to turn down.' Sadie's eyes gleamed. 'Go on, call her.'

Julie seemed unsure. 'I'll just try the staffroom. Who shall I say it is?'

'Bronagh and Sadie,' Bronagh said quickly.

Julie picked up the phone and pressed a button. 'Hello, is Sally there? Can you ask her to come to the phone?' She looked up, meeting Sadie and Bronagh's twin positive faces. 'Ah, Sally, there are a couple of Irish ladies here for you. What? All right. I'll tell them. In a few minutes.' She put the phone down crisply. 'She's on her way.'

'That's good.' Sadie rubbed her hands together. 'It's nice and warm in here. It's Baltic outdoors. You'd think it would be warm in Devon, but it's definitely not.'

'Are you from the north or the south of Ireland?' Julie asked, looking at her computer screen.

'County Clare.' Bronagh grinned. 'We're here on holiday. By accident.'

Julie looked confused. 'Where are you staying?'

'At Tails of Hope,' Sadie explained.

'I'm from Exeter.' Julie had clearly never heard of it.

'We're Robert Parkin's relations,' Bronagh said proudly and Julie gave a smile of recognition.

'I know of Robert. He's the man who did the bake off. I've heard his cakes are amazing. And his scones. Isn't he the best baker in Devon?'

'And beyond.' Sadie was glad that Julie had at least heard of him. 'We need to put Tails of Hope on the map.'

There was a clacking of heels and Sally arrived, looking a little anxious. 'Hello. I wasn't expecting to see you.' She glanced at the clock on the wall. 'The bell goes in eleven minutes.'

'We'll be quick. Is there somewhere we can talk?'

'You can come up to the staffroom. Julie, I'll sign them in – can you give them visitor lanyards?' Sally turned back to Sadie, looking flustered. 'Where was I? Yes. I was just having a meeting with a colleague about the Nativity play.'

'Oh?' Bronagh was immediately interested. 'How's it going?'

'We rehearsed this morning. It's not going well at all. Poor Joseph suffered from a bout of vomiting and diarrhoea and one of the shepherds had a nosebleed...'

Sadie wrapped the lanyard around her neck. She and Bronagh followed Sally up a flight of steps to a door that opened into a cosy little room crammed with books on shelves, files, laptops and desks. It reminded Sadie of a hobbit's home. In the corner was a kettle and a tray of cups. Sally said, 'Do you have time for a cuppa?'

'I'd bite your hand off for one,' Bronagh said.

'Shall I make it?' A blonde, handsome young man who couldn't have been thirty made his way to the kettle. 'Coffee?'

'Tea if you have it, with milk.' Sadie was already in efficient mode.

'This is Adam Thompson, my colleague,' Sally explained.

'It's my class who are doing the Nativity.' Adam shrugged as if he was resigned to failure. Bronagh nudged Sadie and gave her a 'wish I were sixty years younger' look.

'My class aren't very good at acting,' Adam apologised.

'I expect their mammies will love them anyway,' Bronagh said.

'So, I've a proposal,' Sadie began. 'I just spoke to Paul up at Tails of Hope and we suggest you do the Nativity up at the farm. It's authentic. It's only a short walk from here and I'm sure the kiddies in the play will raise their game once they are surrounded by real donkeys.'

'Oh, yes.' Bronagh's eyes gleamed. 'Just imagine how nice it will be – fairy lights in the barn, straw, a proper manger, benches for the audience.'

'And donkeys – four of them,' Sadie said emphatically.

'It might work.' Sally looked at Adam. 'What do you think?'

'It's a brilliant idea.' Adam handed over two piping-hot mugs. One of them had 'Student Tears' written on the side and the other read 'I Survived Another Meeting that Should Have Been an Email'.

Sadie said kindly, 'It must be tough being a teacher.'

'It has its moments,' Adam agreed, and Bronagh thought again how devastatingly good-looking he was.

She said, 'So – to be or not to be – the Nativity in the barn. That's the question.'

'I think we're missing a trick if we don't. The place is on our doorstep,' Adam said.

'But what made you think of it?' Sally wondered.

'Julie on Reception had never heard of Tails of Hope. We need to spread the good news. It's great publicity for them at this time of year. We'll get Rosie Eagle the reporter up there and maybe all the parents can get an invite in the new year to do the tour of the farm with their kiddies...' Sadie was amazed how easily the words tumbled out of her mouth. She hadn't planned any of it.

Bronagh wasn't far behind with the sales pitch. 'Paul's organising a really big publicity campaign leading up to Christmas. He wants to put the place right up there.' Bronagh raised a hand in the air to show how high 'there' was. 'They have donkeys and alpacas and horses and owls.'

'Do you think they'd let us borrow the alpacas for the Nativity too?' Adam's face filled with enthusiasm.

'There weren't any alpacas in Bethlehem,' Sally said.

'I know, but the more animals, the better, and the kids would love it. Go on, Sally; it'll be so Christmassy.' Adam gave a pleading look Bronagh would never have refused. 'We should have thought of it earlier.'

'You should.' Bronagh agreed with him.

Sally hesitated. 'I could use the minibus to get the instruments and the Clavinova up there. Then we could run the children up. I'll ask Barbara what she thinks. She's our head.'

'She'll be well up for it,' Adam said. 'As long as we do a health and safety form and let the parents know.'

'So, what about we rehearse here in school on Monday and Tuesday, then on Wednesday we come up to the farm to practise?' Sally was thinking on her feet. 'I'll be able to get parental permission letters out by then, and we can do dress rehearsal on Wednesday afternoon.'

'What about the refreshments?' Adam asked. 'We usually do a cup of tea and a biscuit.'

'I'm sure we can do better than that. Leave it to me.' Bronagh lowered her voice. 'Sadie, do you think Robert and Tressy will do mince pies, mulled wine and squash?'

'I'm sure we could persuade him. We can all help,' Sadie told her, as if she planned projects every day of her life. She was starting to enjoy herself.

'I think we're onto a winner,' Adam said. 'The farm won't expect half the ticket prices or anything like that?'

'Not at all. I already asked Paul. The publicity's the main thing,' Sadie insisted. 'And the craic.'

A bell clanged loudly and Sadie noticed both teachers stiffen. Sally said, 'That's it. We'll have to go.'

Adam held a hand out and shook Bronagh's then Sadie's. 'You might just have saved the world's worst Nativity. And I can't wait to tell my class.'

'I'll speak to Barbara this afternoon, but I'm sure she'll love the idea,' Sally said. 'Right, come on, Adam. It's money, measurement and 2D & 3D shapes for class 5AT this afternoon.'

Adam groaned. 'Maths isn't my best subject. But thanks so much for saving our play. It's lovely to have met you.'

'You too.' Bronagh was still gawping.

'I'll phone Robert tonight,' Sally promised.

'And I'll look forward to seeing you on Wednesday,' Adam said.

Sally opened the door. 'I'll have to usher you both out. But thank you both so much. I'm looking forward to the Nativity now and I certainly wasn't before.' Sally lowered her voice. 'Perhaps we can catch up again in The Pig and Pickle over the weekend? Last night was really fun. I drank two G & Ts, which is an awful lot for a school night.'

Then she was gone.

Five minutes later, Sadie and Bronagh stood outside the school hugging themselves against the sharp blast of wind that funnelled around the corner.

Sadie stared up the road towards Tails of Hope, feeling warm and fuzzy. She'd never been a project manager before. And it felt strangely different, more important, somehow, than just being someone's mammy. 'Right, we'd better head back to the farm and tell everyone the good news. We can get Bunty to ask Robert if he and Tressy can help us do refreshments for a hundred doting parents.'

20

That evening, the O'Connor family sat around the huge wooden farmhouse table eating fish and chips. The kitchen was warm, the shiny aubergine Aga was belting out heat, and everyone's cheeks were rosy. Paul was squashed between Sadie and Bronagh, Hazel sat next to Niall and Maeve, and Poppy was perched at the end with Lola and Rory, Pat and Nora.

Sadie was still animated about the Nativity play. It occurred to her that she was much more focused on herself than she'd been at Ballycotton. Yes, she felt like an organiser, and it felt good. Powerful. 'It's a grand idea to have it here,' she enthused. 'The kids'll adore it. And the publicity will be huge.'

'I asked Robert,' Bunty announced. 'He'll make mince pies and iced cakes. We'll all help. Tressy suggested Robert wears a reindeer costume and we'll dress as elves, but Robert isn't keen. Hattie said she'd work on him.'

'I was thinking,' Paul said, 'we'll deck the barn out with fairy lights and put in a little manger. The Supremes will feel right at home.'

'What about the alpacas?' Bronagh asked. 'I think they'll add to the ambience.' She had no idea what she meant.

'We can place lots of animals on the stage,' Hazel said.

'Well, haven't we all had a grand day?' Pat shoved two chips into his mouth, sticking out like Dracula fangs. 'I took yer man Dennis out in the DeLorean and nearly blew his head off round the tight corners. I offered Colin a ride in the car but he was scared stiff.'

'Afterwards they bought us a drink in The Pig and Pickle,' Nora added.

'Wonders never cease,' Bunty said.

'Rory took me to Haytor,' Lola mumbled. 'It was cold and windy.'

'I wanted to climb the big rock, but Lola couldn't do it in the dagger heels.' Rory grinned. He'd done his best to encourage her, but in the end he'd stood patiently next to her while the others clambered to the top. Lola had stood bored at the bottom as he'd imagined the panoramic view. He'd felt more space open up between them, the chasm of incompatibility.

'It's a great view up there,' Poppy explained. 'You can see for miles, right out to the ocean.'

'I'd have loved that.' Rory raised both eyebrows, wishing he'd been there, and Lola gave Poppy a glare that could kill.

'Robert's invited us round on Sunday night for a buffet and drinks,' Sean told them. 'Niall and I were saying, we could go out on Saturday night, somewhere local. And, Paul, Hazel, Poppy, we'd like you to come too.'

'I'd love to.' Hazel's face shone.

'There's a pub not far away, The Highwayman's Roost. They do great food,' Poppy said.

'I wish I could but—' Paul couldn't help smiling '—I've got a dinner invitation for tomorrow night.' He turned to Bronagh and Sadie. 'So have you both. Solly's invited us.'

'Can we go?' Bronagh's face lit up. 'Is it on his boat?'

'It is.' Paul seemed excited.

'We'll do the family meal and you can double-date on the boat, Mammy,' Sean said.

'It's not a double date,' Sadie began frostily.

Bronagh nudged her and whispered, 'Well, it might be.'

Niall shrugged. 'No worries. You enjoy your boat trip. But don't come back complaining you've hurled up your dinner because the sea was so choppy.'

'Niall,' Sadie said abruptly, ever his mother, despite her son being in his sixties. 'Not at the dinner table.'

'Sorry, Mammy.'

'I'm looking forward to the Nativity,' Maeve said. 'I remember when you and Erin were young, Rory. She was so good at acting. She played the Virgin Mary because her face was sweet and her hair was the longest in the class.'

'And I played the ass.' Rory wrapped an arm around his mother. 'Or was it the goat?'

Maeve seemed sad. 'I miss those days.'

'All those children in costume, singing carols and hymns.' Bunty had a faraway look in her eyes. 'I wish.'

Sean squeezed her hand beneath the table. 'We'll enjoy the Nativity, Bunts. It's festive. And it'll be good publicity for the animals.'

'It will raise a few pounds,' Sadie said quickly. 'I was thinking – can we get a festive sponsorship scheme off the ground in time for Christmas? We might persuade the parents to sponsor Pi and Buddy and The Supremes and the alpacas.'

'I'll ask Hattie to contact Rosie Eagle. Perhaps she can put something in the paper,' Bunty said. 'She can do a report on the Nativity too.'

'Great idea. I need to work on our website,' Poppy said. 'It's not really my thing though. I just don't have the imagination.'

'I do,' Rory said gallantly. 'I'm a whizz with websites. I'll give you a hand, and we'll get a festive sponsorship up.' He turned to Lola. 'We can do that, can't we?'

Lola looked unhappy. 'I was hoping we'd go to the seaside.'

'We can do both.' Rory smiled at Poppy and he felt a new warmth envelop him. There was so much about her he was beginning to admire. 'I'll take a look tomorrow, Poppy, if you like.'

Poppy blushed slightly. 'Thanks, Rory.'

'No problem.'

Sadie made a mental note of the chemistry between them.

'So that sorts out the Nativity and the website and maybe sponsoring.' Bronagh frowned. 'But there must be more ideas.'

'Do you need more schemes?' Niall asked.

'We always wanted to do a shop for teas and gifts.'

'Leave that one with me. Making money's my thing.' Niall rubbed his hands together.

'It's not the best time of year,' Paul added. 'We do well in the summer. But what we really need is something that pulls in the crowds all year long.'

'Christmas is an opportunity to get the ball rolling,' Nora insisted.

'How can we build on the Nativity's success?' Sadie was thinking hard, her head buzzing.

'The O'Connors will come up with something,' Pat said. 'That's what families do.'

'Let's not worry about it now. We're on holiday,' Sean said. 'On Sunday evening, when we meet at Robert's, we'll do what they do at the Millbrook Gardening Group and have a big talk about it. By then—' he pushed the final piece of battered fish into his mouth '—we'll be having such a wonderful time, the ideas will flow like mulled wine.'

* * *

Robert sat in his armchair in the conservatory, his eyes closed, listening to Puccini, Isaac Mewton purring on his knee. The goats had been fed, the chickens were safely in the coops and he'd just cooked a wonderful seafood paella for four. He'd never been happier.

Tressy was snuggled on another armchair, browsing through recipe books. Hattie and Barry were sitting on the sofa, their shoulders touching, gazing at something on Hattie's tablet. She was frowning, clearly uninspired.

Tressy said, 'I thought we could make chicken skewers, goat's cheese and cranberry tartlets, mini kebabs, blue cheese and chive scones, halloumi dippers, pitta breads.'

'That sounds lovely,' Robert said quietly. He might have been talking about the food, the music or the rich resonance of Tressy's voice.

'And to follow, espresso martini chocolate pots, white chocolate and passion-fruit mousses.'

'Delicious.' Robert gazed at Tressy's sweet face, her apple cheeks.

'I like Bunty's family, Robert.' Tressy turned to Hattie. 'I liked Bunty and Sean immediately when I met them last summer, but Sadie and Bronagh are down to earth. And everyone's so friendly.'

'Mmm,' Robert agreed.

'Easy to spend time with.' Hattie was still engrossed.

Barry looked up. 'I like Niall. And Rory's a lovely lad.'

'It was Maeve I took to,' Tressy said thoughtfully. 'She's a bit – I don't know – in need of a friend. She seems a bit left out.'

'I think Niall's away from home a lot. He has properties he manages in Dublin. Rory too,' Hattie observed. 'And Erin, Rory's sister, and her husband are often abroad. She and Maeve are close. She's a bit of a hippy, Erin. They have a camper van.' Hattie put the tablet down. 'Which is about all I can afford, Barry.'

Robert sat up, hearing the edge to her voice. 'What is it, Hat?'

'I'm looking for somewhere to buy.' Hattie made a sad sound. 'Now the bungalow's sold, I thought it might be easy to find a little cottage, a couple of bedrooms, somewhere to put my piano. But everything's so expensive or so small. Or both.'

Robert nodded. 'It's because we're close to the sea.'

'I found this one. Marina Terrace.' Hattie began to read. '"A cosy, two-bedroom cottage, oozing with character, in a tucked-away position with a manageable garden. In need of modernisation."'

'It sounds all right,' Tressy said.

'Modernisation though.' Barry looked worried.

'Cosy? It's the size of an egg box. And yes, it's practically falling down,' Hattie sighed. 'Here's another. "Mews-style cottage in the heart of the town centre with galley kitchen and bijou bathroom." But when you look closely, it's awful.'

'What's wrong with it?' Robert said, his eyes still closed.

Hattie huffed. 'It's tiny. And you can smell the damp from just looking at the photo.'

'It doesn't look good,' Barry agreed. 'All right for youngsters. A doer-upper.'

'I'd like to stay in Millbrook, but there's nothing I can afford,' Hattie said. 'It's hopeless.'

Barry looked at her with puppy-dog eyes. 'There's no rush. More houses might come up in the new year.'

'They might.' Hattie squeezed his hand.

'You can stay here as long as you like,' Robert said.

'We like your company,' Tressy agreed.

'But you need your own space. You're a couple,' Hattie groaned. 'I've no idea what to do. I'm sure Geoffrey could have got more for the bungalow if he'd held out.'

'Do you think he accepted the lower offer on purpose?' Robert asked.

'No, I accepted it too,' Hattie said. 'I'm ready for my own place. Barry, we could take a drive and look at a few of them from the outside. If they pass the test, I could book a visit.'

'That makes sense. But don't worry, Hattie. Things'll be right as rain, you'll see,' Barry said kindly.

'Anyone for a cuppa?' Tressy asked.

'I'll make it.' Hattie didn't move. 'I had a message from Bunty. The family want to support the animal sanctuary to expand. Paul Sullivan says they want to take in more animals.'

'And so they should,' Tressy said firmly. 'We're making a start with the Nativity play. I might make us all some green elf costumes.'

'Please don't ask me to dress up.' Robert felt panic seize him. 'I'd look silly.'

'You'd look gorgeous,' Tressy told him. 'And we need all the attention we can get. Maybe I'll just get us reindeer antlers, red noses.'

'I'd probably be all right with that.' Robert smiled. 'It wouldn't be too embarrassing. Those ones that flash.'

'I think it's lovely for the community to come together at Tails of Hope,' Barry said. 'I wonder – I could paint pictures of the animals.'

'Why would you do that?' Robert asked. 'Other than you'd do a great job.'

'The farm could sell them as a new range of Christmas cards,' Barry said. 'I could get them ready for next year.'

'Good idea,' Hattie said. 'But we need to help them now.'

'We know what we're good at, and that's baking,' Tressy explained. 'We should stick to that. Maybe we could do the occasional market stall.'

'I'd be happy to do that,' Robert agreed. 'But a few sponge cakes won't save all those donkeys and horses.'

'We'll think of something,' Hattie said.

'It's a little bit like your house-hunting. Like buses that never come, then two come at the same time.' Barry's eyes twinkled behind the round glasses.

'What do you mean?' Hattie squeezed his hand.

'Things that seem difficult later become easy. The answers fall into place when we least expect them.' Barry's smile was one of pure contentment. 'Just keep the faith, Hattie. Things'll work out. They always do...' He stood up slowly. 'Now, how about you and I go to the kitchen and make that pot of tea?'

21

The next morning after breakfast at Tails of Hope, everyone disappeared to do their own thing. Niall took Maeve and Nora into Exeter shopping and Bronagh invited herself along. She was keen to find something in the charity shops to wear that evening. She intended to dazzle on Solly's boat.

Paul was busy in his office. The vet arrived to check Buddy over, and Hazel took her to the new arrivals' field. Pat was meeting Dennis and Colin in the village. He left early in the DeLorean, whistling happily. Sean and Bunty had gone to Robert's house: Robert, Hattie and Tressy had invited them to lunch in Dawlish.

Sadie found herself alone, but she was glad of the peace and quiet. Her knee joints ached. She'd overdone things a bit lately and she needed to relax.

She lay on the bed in her room, the curtains closed, thinking. In truth, she was enjoying being in England, but she missed Kildare Avenue. Home wasn't much, three bedrooms, a small kitchen, a cosy lounge. But it was the silly things that mattered: the cushion covers with 'Crappy Diem' embroidered on them.

Nora had taken great pains over them as a young teenager at school, misspelling Carpe, and Alfie had found it so funny. Nora had always hated needlework with a passion.

Sadie recalled the framed artwork in the hall, the pictures her kiddies had drawn at school, and the memory hugged her. Sean was a particularly good portrait artist and she'd framed the one he'd done, aged seven, labelling it 'My Mammy and Da'. She and Alfie were potato-shaped, with curved crimson lips and sticking-up hair, but they were holding hands, just as they always had. That picture meant so much to Sadie.

The house was her own museum of memories, her refuge. It breathed when she breathed, and she missed it. She was looking forward to going home.

But she was on holiday, and she intended to enjoy it. Carpe diem, as the cushion covers almost proclaimed. She was looking forward to the meal on the boat with Solly and Paul, the Nativity play, then she'd go back to Ballycotton in time for Christmas and enjoy it with her family. That was what she wanted most.

Sadie eased herself upright and decided to go for a stroll. She wanted to watch the vet at work with Buddy. She tugged on her coat, wrapped a scarf around her head – she hated having cold ears – and pushed her feet into newly cleaned wellingtons. Once her woolly gloves were on, she was ready for the cold weather. She closed the door and wandered downstairs.

Voices came from the breakfast room. As she passed, Sadie waited for a moment, listening. She could hear Rory's light cheery tone.

'The home page looks good now. We can add some more photos of the animals, and their names. We can take a few now.'

'That'd be great.' Poppy's voice was filled with gratitude.

Rory continued, 'We'll update the sponsor page. People can commit money to an animal of their choice, and they'll get photos and stuff. We'll do an events page, advertising what's coming up – like the Nativity play. And what about a Visit Us page and a Support Tails of Hope page with info about the work that's done here, and a map? No, we'll put the map on the home page with the opening hours.'

'Can you do all that?' Poppy asked.

'It's a doddle,' Rory replied. 'Maybe later we could talk about creating a teashop.'

'That was Grandma's greatest wish,' Poppy sighed. 'But we couldn't afford to build it. Or staff it.'

'There's plenty of space near the old barn though,' Rory said.

Sadie's heart expanded with admiration for her grandson. She heard Lola whine, 'I thought we were going shopping, Rory.'

'Ah, just a bit longer, Lola. Then we'll get off.'

'I'm sorry.' Poppy sounded apologetic. 'I don't want to keep you. You're on holiday.'

Lola said, 'This is boring.'

'Well, I'll just finish this page and take a few photos.' Rory was ever the peacemaker.

'For goodness' sake,' Lola said. 'I'm going to my room.'

Rory watched her stand up, in a huff, and it was all he could do not to shrug his shoulders. In truth, Lola could do what she wanted. It might give her a chance to calm down. Besides, he wanted to finish helping Poppy.

Then the door opened and she stood facing Sadie, her arms folded. Lola sniffed, 'I've had enough of this. I want to go home.'

'It's a long walk,' Sadie said. Lola walked off in a strop towards the stairs, ignoring Rory's mystified expression. Sadie wondered if she should have been kinder and asked Lola to go with her to see the animals, but she didn't want to interfere. It was better to leave her and Rory to sort themselves out.

She pushed the front door open and the cold air hit her in

the face. It was a bright day, a cotton-wool pleated sky overhead, but a raw wind drifted from the farm, bending the trees and flattening grass. Sadie shivered, pushing her hands in her pockets, leaning into the breeze, head down, as she plodded towards the fields.

She passed the horses, snug beneath their blankets. Pi watched her, nodding his head, and she called out, 'How are you doing this morning, Pi?'

She passed The Supremes – Diana, Mary and Florence – and wondered when Buddy would join them. It made her smile, to think of them all braying in harmony. The alpacas were in their enclosure, leaning over the fence like spectators, as if waiting for treats. Sadie wondered what alpacas ate. She paused to look at their furry faces, the long necks, shiny eyes and pointed ears. She said, 'Now which of you is which?' She tried to remember. 'Carlos and Juan are dark brown, Jose is a fawny colour and Angel is white with the fluffy mop of hair. Isn't that right?'

Three alpacas seemed to be gurning, their bodies relaxed. Carlos and Juan were munching grass. Jose was watching, immobile. But the white one, Angel, flattened his ears and puffed air from his nostrils. His lips slackened and Sadie saw the warning signs.

'Now, don't you spit at me, you little horror,' she said.

Without further ado, she was on her way towards the new arrivals' enclosure with a barn at the back. She could hear voices. Hazel and Paul were staring at Buddy, who stood placidly while a woman in a wax coat and wellington boots examined him. Paul called a friendly greeting. 'Hi, Sadie. Buddy's just having the once over.'

'It seems he's a she,' Hazel said, looking nonplussed. 'The owner must have been wrong.'

'I'd assumed she was a gelding.' Paul frowned. 'The paperwork said so too. I'm beginning to think the last owner wasn't very reliable.'

Sadie pushed open the little wooden gate and approached the group. 'Hello.'

'This is Zoe Fenton, our vet,' Paul said.

'Hello.' Zoe stood up. 'I won't shake hands.' She was wearing plastic gloves. She had a pleasant, weather-worn face, as if being outside was the most natural place to be. Sadie was freezing cold.

Paul said, 'I'm glad you came, Zoe.' He turned to Sadie. 'We have a few problems with Buddy.'

'But we can't call her Buddy now. What about Holly?' Sadie joked.

'Yes, it's Christmas.' Paul smiled weakly.

'Holly it is, then,' Hazel agreed.

'I'm afraid Holly's not very well.' Zoe's tone was serious. 'I think she might have hyperlipaemia.'

'What's that?' Sadie asked nervously. 'Can you cure it?' She reached out instinctively and stroked Holly's neck. The donkey didn't move. 'Is it bad?'

'It's a disease caused by too much fat in the blood,' Zoe explained. She looked worried. 'It can be brought on by stress, loss of a companion, all sorts of factors.'

'The last owner said he used to have two donkeys and one died,' Paul explained. 'He seemed very keen to move this one on.'

'Will she be all right?' Hazel's voice quavered.

'I'd have to monitor her. She can't be introduced to the other donkeys yet. The worst-case scenario is that the liver and kidneys degenerate and eventually all the organs in the body fail.'

Sadie left her hand resting against the donkey's neck, filled with sadness. The poor creature seemed so resigned She moved her fingers to scratch the long ears, but Holly didn't respond.

'Can you help her?' Paul asked.

'She looks underweight, she has bad breath. They aren't good signs.' Zoe laid her hand on Paul's arm. 'Keep her warm and covered, encourage her to eat.'

'She's had next to nothing since she's been here,' Paul said.

'Check she can chew and swallow. Watch carefully for sham eating.' Zoe met Paul's eyes. 'I'll come back on Monday. Call me if you need me before then.'

'I will,' Paul said quietly. 'Thanks, Zoe.' He glanced at Sadie. 'It's freezing out here. Let's get Holly into the warm shelter; we'll go back to the house and have something to warm us up.'

'There's a pan of soup on the Aga.' Hazel's face was strained as she and Paul exchanged looks. Sadie knew that they were worried about the donkey. She was worried too: she felt instinctively that Holly had given up.

* * *

Back in the kitchen, Poppy was serving butternut soup into bowls.

'The website's looking brilliant,' she enthused. 'Rory's taken some pictures and it's perfect.'

Hazel sat down. 'Are you confident you can keep it up?'

'Oh, yes. Rory has new ideas about sponsorship and people bequeathing money. Everyone who sponsors an animal will get a keepsake: gifts, soft toys, nothing too expensive, but the same sort of animals we have here…' Poppy's cheeks glowed. 'And Rory thinks a teashop might work.'

'How could we staff it though?' Hazel wondered.

'Where's Rory now?' Sadie asked.

Poppy glanced away. 'He's taken Lola for lunch in Dawlish. I hope I haven't upset her.'

'No, she'll be fine.' Sadie kept her voice light. 'She and Rory aren't serious.'

'Oh?' Poppy said and Sadie noticed her reaction. She liked Rory more than she'd admit.

'No, she's just here for the holiday,' Sadie said mischievously. 'It's not like they're serious.'

'Ah,' Poppy said. 'I see.'

'Buddy might have a disease. We're calling her Holly now,' Paul muttered.

'She's a girl?' Poppy asked.

'She is. I think her previous owner may have been a little less than honest,' Paul told them.

'Will she be all right?' Poppy was anxious.

'We'll keep an eye on her,' Paul promised. 'Zoe's coming back on Monday.'

'Oh, dear,' Hazel sighed. 'Poor thing.'

Paul seemed to sag in his chair. 'I hate to lose an animal.'

Hazel glanced towards Sadie. 'You don't mind us talking shop?'

'Not at all.' Sadie was poised, spoon in the air, listening, concerned.

'Vet bills mount up. We're breaking even, we're doing fine. But we'll have to pull all the stops out next summer. I was hoping to take in more rescued animals.'

'We're working on it.' Poppy's expression was full of optimism 'We won't let the animals down. The new website will do the trick and we'll get wider advertising. Rory's all over it.'

'Will the Nativity help?' Sadie asked hopefully.

'It'll certainly bring in new interest,' Hazel said.

'So you can build on it.' Sadie slurped soup. 'Lots of new events.'

'Events tend to start in the spring,' Paul explained. 'People don't like to be out in the cold.'

'I see.' Sadie chewed her lip, thinking hard. 'But now's Christmas. A time for families, for giving.'

'It's something I've thought about doing for a long time,' Paul admitted. 'It's an opportunity we shouldn't miss.'

'I'm here.' There was a whoop of joy and Bronagh came hurtling through the door with an armful of bags. She stopped and noticed the food on the table, inhaling the rich aroma like the Bisto kids. 'Aah, soup. I don't suppose there's a bowl going spare? I'm starving.'

'Of course there is.' Hazel scraped back her chair. 'Take a seat.'

'How was Exeter?' Paul asked.

'You should see the cathedral – it's so pretty – and the little avenues of shops. I went into the charity shops and I bought—' She rummaged through one of her bags. 'Look.' She held up a silver-sequined evening dress against her. It dragged on the floor. 'This is so nice. And...' She tugged out a pink fascinator in the shape of a top hat, with a pink feather and a decoration of net. 'And these – oh, I'll look the dog's bollix—' She stopped herself and held up two long evening gloves in emerald-green silk. She noticed Paul looking at her. 'You're not supposed to see these. I was going to stun everyone. But it doesn't matter. And, Sadie, I got you this... what do you think? It's lovely.' Bronagh was back in the bag again. She tugged out a burgundy velvet dress, holding it up, proud of herself. 'Isn't it sophisticated?'

'It's nice.' Sadie liked it instantly. 'Thanks, Bronagh. I love velvet. But—' She frowned. 'We'll be on a boat. Won't we freeze to death?'

'We'll eat below deck,' Paul said. 'If I know anything about

Solly, he'll dress for the occasion. He likes putting on the Ritz.' He thought for a moment. 'I better dig my best jacket out.'

'I can't wait.' Bronagh sat down with a bump. Hazel put a bowl of soup in front of her, and she dug in, dipping a hunk of bread.

'Solly said something about cooking steaks.'

'Double, triple heaven,' Bronagh sighed, her mouth full. 'And afterwards, perhaps we can wrap up and go on deck and drink brandy and look at all the little boats in the bay. I'll feel just like Elizabeth Taylor. Or Princess Grace in Monte Carlo.'

Sadie finished her bowl of soup, thinking about dinner on the boat, the sparkling conversation, fine wine, and the burgundy velvet dress she would wear. She was looking forward to it too.

But Bronagh had that gleam in her eye that meant romance. Sadie admired Bronagh's optimism, the way she wore her heart on her sleeve. As far as Sadie was concerned, though, there'd only ever been one man for her. Paul was a lovely person, but he'd never replace Alfie.

No one could.

22

'The house is so quiet.' Sadie put the finishing touches to her make-up.

'Everyone's gone to The Highwayman's Roost.' Bronagh was clipping large earrings to her lobes. 'Hazel looked lovely in her pretty blue dress.'

'And Poppy was gorgeous in the sparkly top. I'm sure she has an eye for Rory. What do you think?'

'I've no idea.' Sadie pressed her lips together. She knew all right. She'd recognised the telltale signs when she'd seen Lola walk out in a huff. And she'd seen Rory's reaction, the way he'd glanced at Poppy. She promised herself she'd make sure her grandson was all right. 'Romance is the last thing on my mind.'

'And it's the first thing on mine. So – Solly or Paul?' Bronagh asked again.

'Don't you dare,' Sadie joked. In truth, she felt a little nervous about the so-called double date. Paul was nice, but she just wanted to be friends. Worse still, she had no idea what Bronagh was throwing herself into. Anything could happen.

The taxi called at Tails of Hope Farm at half seven. Paul had insisted on booking one. He sat quietly between Sadie and Bronagh in a smart white jacket and chinos, Bronagh wearing her silver dress and the fascinator. She had borrowed a faux-fur coat from somewhere – Hazel perhaps – and was feeling glamorous, crossing her legs and uncrossing them just to hear the swish of her dress. Sadie was huddled in a coat, the burgundy velvet dress beneath. She loved the way it fitted her snugly on top, then hung loose from the hips. It was perfect.

The taxi was filled with the smell of a perfume called Sex Cougar, which Bronagh had insisted on buying on the ferry. Sadie thought it smelled like rose petals, tarmac and chips, but Bronagh loved it. Paul smelled of an aftershave that suggested nutmeg or cinnamon. Sadie had simply put on a subtle scent, but now the taxi was filled with a mixture of overpowering aromas that made her eyes water. Paul appeared not to notice.

Sadie stared out of the window, alone with her thoughts. The taxi drove through the countryside, trees swaying overhead in the breeze, a full moon like a copper coin high in the darkness. She wondered if there was music playing in The Hole tonight. It would be festive there, full of cheer.

The taxi began to climb a hill, and little lights appeared on both sides of the road. A tall house loomed to the left, festooned with Christmas decorations. Another house had a projector in the garden that threw images of huge whirling snowflakes onto the front.

A sign told them that they were in Dawlish. The sky was crammed with stars and Sadie thought there would be an overnight frost. She was worried about Holly: the little donkey had looked miserable. She might have imagined it – all donkeys had sad expressions. But Holly's eyes had held an inevitability that made Sadie feel melancholy.

The taxi weaved on, round bends, up hills and down, accelerating towards a shadowy marina with bobbing boats, lights twinkling against a velvet sky, the town tiny in the distance.

'There's some money moored here – ordinary Dawlish people don't own boats,' the driver mused as he changed gear.

'My friend owns one,' Paul said. 'It's the blue-and-white cabin cruiser.'

'Lucky beggar,' the taxi driver replied. 'I'd love a boat. I like fishing, the peace and quiet.'

Bronagh took in the clusters of boats, the inky water, the distant lights, and said, 'It's dreamy.'

The taxi slowed and Paul said, 'That's the boat over there, *The Old Man*.'

'Why's he called it that?' Bronagh asked.

'After the Ernest Hemingway book, when the old fisherman tries to catch a giant marlin,' the taxi driver called back. 'There are mackerel to be had round here.' He revved the engine. 'I'll pick you up at midnight, as arranged, Mr Sullivan.'

Sadie and Bronagh scrambled out, followed by Paul. The taxi rumbled away, and Sadie inspected the shiny exterior of a smart cabin cruiser. A man was waving to them from up on deck and Bronagh called out, 'Solly, we're bang on time.'

Solly helped them on board, sophisticated as James Bond, and led them below, where there was a kitchen full of light, a stainless-steel cooker and a table set for four with crystal glasses and napkins.

'Welcome.'

He was immaculate in a dark suit, white shirt and bow tie. He pressed a button on a remote and jazz music began to play through a speaker. The music lilted gently, a saxophone, a sultry voice.

Bronagh nudged Sadie. 'This is the life.'

'Please sit down.' Solly poured sparkling wine. 'I hope you like champagne. If not, I've got sparkling elderflower.'

'I'll have the champagne,' Bronagh blurted.

'I must say, you look especially lovely this evening, ladies.'

'So do you, Solly.' Bronagh was already sipping her drink.

Solly beamed. 'I hope you like steaks. I've made a peppercorn sauce with red wine and double cream.'

'It smells delicious.' Bronagh was wide-eyed. 'Will there be potatoes?'

'I've done sautéed potatoes, kale, carrots and peas.' Solly looked pleased with himself. 'To be honest, I've been busy all day. I don't usually cook.'

'You call in for takeaways.' Sadie smiled.

'I don't enjoy cooking just for myself. It's been a while since I invited guests on the boat. I even gave the place the once-over this morning.' For a moment, Solly looked anxious. 'But you're here, I can relax a bit. Let's do a toast. Paul, would you like to...?'

Paul lifted his glass. 'To a wonderful evening.'

Bronagh lifted her glass. 'To our host. To Christmas.'

'To my first meal at sea,' Sadie muttered nervously as she felt the boat lurch beneath them. 'And thank you, Solly.'

'To new friends.' Solly's eyes shone. 'And good times.'

The glasses clinked. Paul and Solly said 'Cheers.'

'*Sláinte,*' Bronagh and Sadie chorused together, and Sadie felt the glowing warmth of friendship, old and new.

* * *

It was past eleven. The meal was eaten, plates empty, two bottles of champagne consumed, but the conversation hadn't stopped bubbling. Everyone was drinking coffee and putting the world to rights.

'I always say,' Sadie said firmly, 'your health is the most important thing in the world.'

'It is,' Paul agreed.

'My back plays me up,' Bronagh groaned. 'I have sciatica sometimes when I wake up and it's murder. But if that's all I have to complain about, then what do I have to complain about?'

'My arthritis drives me mad,' Sadie admitted. 'Thank goodness for my meds.'

'When I was drinking heavily, I was so unfit,' Solly confided. 'My blood pressure rocketed. Giving up alcohol saved my life.'

'A drink from time to time is nice.' Bronagh met Solly's gaze and tried again. 'But I admire you for taking control, Solly. It takes guts to give it up.'

'It certainly does,' Paul agreed. 'I was unwell a few years ago.'

'I didn't know.' Solly was surprised.

'I was stressed from work, all the extra hours. I had severe chest pains. The doctor sorted me out, put a couple of stents in. I'm a different man now.'

'You're looking well on it.' Bronagh patted his arm. 'Just don't go stressing over those animals.'

Paul's face clouded. 'I'll try.'

'But times like this help – a shared meal, friends,' Solly said. 'I'm healthier now, but if I spend too long by myself, the anxieties flood in.'

'Loneliness is a terrible thing,' Bronagh agreed. 'I have my family and friends.'

'I like quiet time by myself in my own house,' Sadie said thoughtfully. 'But it's important to choose when you want to be alone and when you don't.' She turned to Solly. 'That was lovely. I really enjoyed it.'

'Me too.' Bronagh wasn't to be outdone. 'The tiramisu was to die for. I bet Robert makes the tiramisu.'

'Robert?' Solly asked. 'Oh, the man in Millbrook who bakes.'

'My daughter-in-law's brother,' Sadie reminded him.

'I must try one of his creations.' Solly smiled.

'I'm doing my best to eat less cake,' Sadie admitted.

'You look very healthy, Sadie.' Paul was paying her a compliment. 'I was thinking this morning when you came over to look at the donkey how radiant you look.'

'Oh, no. My joints ache. And my bladder plays me up.' Sadie put a hand over her mouth and chuckled. 'I got married at sixteen and had four children quickly. Childbirth takes its toll on the waterworks.'

Bronagh's brow clouded. 'I just had the one child, Kathleen. She's a servant of the Lord now.'

Solly looked puzzled. 'Has she died?'

'She's a blessed nun.' Bronagh sighed. 'It was hard to come to terms with it at first. I respect her decision, of course, but I don't get to see her much.' Tears filled her eyes. 'And I miss Michael. They've all gone. Thank goodness for Sadie.'

'Good company, good friends.' Solly understood. 'Bronagh – Sadie. We've had a lovely evening. How would you like to go up on deck with a glass of something warming and look at the Exe estuary?'

'I'd love that, Solly.' Bronagh was on her feet, a little unsteady. Solly picked up a tray: glasses, brandy, apple juice. Bronagh clutched his elbow.

Paul offered his arm to Sadie. 'Shall we go up?'

'We certainly should,' Sadie said. 'I want to see the world from the sea.'

* * *

On deck, they stared into the depths of the black water. Waves lapped against the side of the boat, a comforting whisper. The harbour lights twinkled, making little zigzag patterns on the inky sea. In the distance, Dawlish town was silent, the coastal houses and restaurants glowing yellow, making the sky an indigo colour.

'Ah, yes,' Bronagh said softly. 'Health's everything. I always think it's important to cope with stress by staying cheerful.'

'You're right, Bronagh. I found retirement a chance to reset.' Solly's arm rested against hers. 'I try to focus on being at one with the world.'

'I wish,' Paul murmured. 'Tomorrow I've still got a sick donkey to deal with.' He was clearly worried. 'We want to help all the animals we can. There are so many more like Holly, in need of rescuing and rehoming. Wendy's last wish was to offer them sanctuary.'

'You're doing a grand job.' Sadie felt a burst of warmth and affection for Paul. 'The Nativity play will cheer us all up.' She turned to Solly. 'Will you come?'

'You must,' Bronagh insisted. 'You can meet our family, and Robert and Tressy will be there. And his mince pies.'

'I'd love to.' Solly was delighted.

'The thing is,' Sadie began slowly, 'I've been thinking...'

'Always dangerous, Sadie,' Bronagh said with a grin.

'About what you said, Paul. About your Wendy's wish to save as many animals as she could. Winter's a quiet time but – I've come up with a Christmas idea to promote your business. It's only small, but it'll be fun. It might mean us staying on just a few more days. I'd have to speak to the others, of course.'

'Do tell.' Bronagh was all ears.

'What are you thinking?' Paul asked.

'Well, it involves the O'Connors and Robert and Tressy. And all the animals. And definitely Pat's car. And a wee bit of organisation up front. That's Rory. And the reporter, Rosie Eagle, too – we'll need her on board.'

'I love a project,' Solly said eagerly. 'Go on, Sadie. I'm in.'

'We'll put our heads together before the taxi comes.' Sadie's pulse quickened. She was organising again. It was a talent she hadn't known she had, but it filled her with a new energy. 'It's a chance to make some money for the animals and bring the real spirit of Christmas to Millbrook.'

23

On Sunday morning, Sadie eased herself out of bed. Surprisingly, she felt good, given the champagne and the steak and the tiramisu she'd stuffed down the night before. She peered through the window at three figures in the fields below tending to the animals. She placed her cheek against the windowpane. The glass was cold. But it looked colder outside, the grass white with frost, the sky bleak, the sun pale.

Lola was shivering inside her coat while Rory and Poppy larked about, feeding the horses. They both looked warm, lifting forkfuls of hay. Rory said something cheery to Lola and she glanced away. Sadie felt sorry for her – she felt left out, although Rory was doing his best. Last night, she'd mentioned again about going back to Ireland. Sadie hoped she'd go soon.

She remembered the plans she'd made with Bronagh, Solly and Paul last night. Her big festive idea. It would make some money and raise awareness. Best of all, there would be a lot of dressing up. It was a good thing they hadn't bought ferry tickets yet – they could go back to Ballycotton on Sunday, in plenty of time to get Christmas celebrations under way.

The project filled Sadie with a warm, fuzzy hopefulness as she gazed at the animals. It had to be said, even though her children were grown, she was still a mammy. Which meant that she was caring and full of love, and in Sadie's mind that extended to the animals.

She watched Rory and Poppy petting the horses. Rory definitely had a way with them. Sadie thought with a smile: didn't all the O'Connor men have a knack with the horses, one way or another? Sean, Niall and Pat had certainly wasted enough money on them over the years and Alfie had been no better. Sadie had bickered with him on many a Saturday night when he'd come home, his pockets empty, because a dead cert had come fourth. She regretted that now. She'd tell him to go and enjoy himself.

Lola turned away, and Rory went over, wrapped an arm around her and she seemed momentarily appeased. Sadie assumed Rory had offered to take her out in the car. Poppy said something, a friendly word, but Lola took no notice. Sadie was immediately on her grandson's side – perhaps he should take Poppy out instead.

There was a sudden groan from the bed across the room, the wail of the living dead. Sadie had forgotten about Bronagh. She sat up, her silver and purple hair over her face, her eyes glinting like those of a creature from the deep. She moaned, 'I feel deadly this morning.'

Sadie hadn't the heart to tell her that she looked the worse for wear. Instead, she said, 'It was probably the second brandy you had on the deck.'

'O-o-oh.' Bronagh blinked hard. 'I need a cup of tea. And breakfast. Mind you, that steak was good. And the peppercorn sauce was to die for.'

'It was,' Sadie said. 'Do you recall the plans we made? Were you sober enough to remember what we committed to?'

A grin spread across Bronagh's face. 'I do. And Solly said he'd get the costumes and presents and stuff. We'll borrow Pat's car.'

'We'll talk about it with the family and decide who's doing what.'

'It'll definitely get the Christmas spirit going.' Bronagh clapped her hands. 'I feel festive already!'

* * *

Sean and Bunty were feeling festive too as they drove down a narrow street in Dawlish. Christmas lights gleamed in every window. Bunty exclaimed, 'Don't you just love Christmas?'

Hattie sighed from the back seat. 'I'm just imagining spending it in a little place of my own next year. My own decorations, my space.'

'Strings of shiny robins,' Sean said.

'Or a silver waterfall, like rain, dripping from an oak tree in the garden,' Barry added.

They turned a corner and Bunty murmured, 'I think we're here. Millennium Avenue. What number is it?'

Hattie called from the back. 'Seventeen.'

Barry pointed. 'It's that one there. I recognise it from the photo. The one with the green door and the holly wreath.'

'Oh, no.' Hattie was disappointed. 'It's even tinier than in the picture. No, that's not for me. I won't be asking the estate agent to view it. Which one's next, Barry?'

'Number seven, Heron Close.'

'The one with the pocket-handkerchief garden,' Hattie sighed. 'Well, let's go and check that one out. It can't be more than a few minutes away.'

'Dawlish is such a welcoming place,' Bunty said cheerily as

the car moved off. 'Some of these houses are really pretty. I bet you can see the sea from the upstairs rooms.'

'But it's not Millbrook,' Sean observed. 'That's the problem, isn't it, Hattie?'

'It is,' Hattie groaned. 'I'm spoiled at Robert's. What with the garden and the patio, and the church just up the road where I can practise playing the organ.' She turned to Barry. 'Your cottage on the green.'

Barry took her hand. 'Living in Millbrook suits you.'

'Can't you stay on at Robert's?' Bunty suggested as the car turned a corner.

'Robert and Tressy don't want me under their feet.'

'Robert said he loves having you around, Hattie,' Bunty said.

'Robert's a darling, Tressy too, but they're a couple – they need privacy to wander round the house in their underwear.' Hattie smiled at the thought as she peered through the window. 'This is it – Heron Close. Number seven.'

The engine idled as four pairs of eyes stared at a small house with cracked rendering, dingy curtains and dirty windows. Barry said quietly, 'It's empty, I think.'

'I can't imagine anyone living in there,' Sean added.

'I won't be viewing this one either,' Hattie decided.

'What's next on the list?' Bunty asked.

'The last one is – The Retreat, a tiny cottage on Chapel Lane, Starcross. It sounds really nice. Two bedrooms, a little garden.' Hattie closed her eyes. 'Imagine – my own little kitchen, herbs and flowers growing in a window box, the bedroom looking out over the Exe. Shall we drive past that one now?'

'Starcross is a bit of a distance from Millbrook,' Barry said slowly.

'Help me choose somewhere.' Hattie turned to him with a smile. 'I value what you think.'

'I'd like that.' Barry squeezed her hand. 'If you're going to live away from Millbrook and me, it has to be the right place.'

* * *

Tressy and Robert strolled towards the hens' field. She reached for his hand. 'Are you looking forward to the buffet?'

'I am.' Robert pushed the gate open. 'If you'd told me last week that the entire Irish contingent from County Clare were coming to stay, I'd have been terrified. But it's nice they're here.'

'You're becoming a social animal,' Tressy said. 'You'll be out dancing and drinking cider next.'

'You're wonderful.' Robert took her hand. 'I can't thank you enough.'

'For what?' Tressy met his eyes.

'You've been good for me.'

'And you for me too.' Tressy was all apple cheeks and sweetness, and Robert felt his heart lurch. 'Before I met you, all I did was work in the tearooms every day, put my feet up at night and listen to classical music. It was a routine and I thought it was good enough. Now...'

'Now?' Robert asked hopefully.

'You've made my life complete. You've given me something to wake up for each morning. A hand to hold. Lips to kiss.'

Robert felt himself becoming emotional. 'Tressy, that's the nicest thing...' He looked down as Isaac Mewton rubbed against his legs. 'I'm blessed.'

'Now we'll use our happiness to help other people,' Tressy said. 'That's what we were put on earth for. To love somebody and to reach out to others.'

Robert blinked. 'By baking cakes?'

'Perhaps,' Tressy said and Robert was reminded again how

much he loved the soft sound of her Cornish accent. 'But I've been thinking about what Sadie's been saying about Tails of Hope. How come the Millbrook people haven't been doing much to support the animals?'

'I suppose we weren't really aware of them,' Robert muttered. 'I know Paul Sullivan a bit – but I had no idea the place had financial difficulties.'

'They're hanging in there. But we need to reach out,' Tressy said. 'The whole of Millbrook does. I mean, what's the real meaning of Christmas?'

'Family?' Robert guessed. Seeing Tressy wasn't reacting, he tried again. 'Jesus's birth?'

Tressy stood in the middle of the field. The hens had congregated around her feet. She threw some corn down and Princess Lay-a scuttled forward, clucking loudly, followed by Jabba the Cluck and Obi Wan Henobi. Several others followed, their necks forward. Tressy sprinkled more corn. Robert thought she looked like a goddess.

'Love,' Tressy said simply. 'That's the meaning of Christmas, Robert. Love.'

Robert looked at her, the chickens bunched at her feet, her cloud of hair illuminated by pale sunshine, corn falling from her fingers like golden rain, and he knew for certain that he was in love for ever.

He was right. Tressy was a goddess.

* * *

'Is it about how I look?' Lola asked sulkily as she stood in the bedroom. 'Am I not pretty enough for you?'

'You look like a goddess,' Rory said kindly. Lola always looked good. But some things were more important than looks, Rory thought.

'Then what's wrong between us?'

'Nothing's wrong.' Rory sat on the bed. 'Well, I can see you're not happy.'

'I'm not. I hate England. It's horrible.'

'Is it?' Rory looked baffled. 'I'm loving it here.'

'That's not all you're loving.'

'What do you mean?'

'You've got eyes for that Poppy wan.'

'I have not.' Rory stopped himself and thought for a moment. He wanted to be honest, but he didn't want to hurt her feelings. 'I just like her, Lola. She's fun to be with. And she cares about the animals. And it was a blast doing the website.'

'The animals smell.' Lola folded her arms. 'I want to go home, Rory.'

'Are you sure?' Rory looked up from the bed sharply. He saw it as an opportunity, if he was honest. 'Is that what you want?'

She nodded. 'I want to go right now.'

Rory walked over to her, his hands on her shoulders. 'I'm sorry, Lola.'

'I thought you liked me.'

'I do. But we agreed it wasn't serious,' Rory said. 'Didn't you have fun?'

Lola shook her head. 'I pretended I did.'

'Like I said, I'm sorry.' Rory gave her a hug. And he meant it.

Lola tugged away. 'It was nice at first, all the dressing up and going out in the car in Dublin. But then we went to Ballycotton and – I hate your family, the way they all joke around and hug each other like—'

'Like a family?' Rory said. He couldn't understand why Lola hadn't taken to them all.

'I suppose so.' Lola's lower lip drooped. 'I want to go back.'

'I'll sort a ticket out, and drive you to the airport.' Rory felt both regretful and relieved at the same time. 'And until you go, I'll sleep in the armchair.'

'When I've gone, I suppose you'll be chasing after *her*?'

'I'm not thinking of it. Why would I?' Rory shook his head. He tried not to think of Poppy, her smile, her prettily blushing face, the way she was just so nice and kind and funny. 'I just want to make sure you're all right.'

'I'll be all right,' Lola said grimly, 'once I'm back in Dublin.'

24

That evening, Robert's kitchen was filled with the warm aroma of spiced wine and a jewelled spread of buffet treats. The chatter sparkled like glitter. The visitors weaved in and out to fill their plates and glasses, then back to the living room and the conservatory to mingle. Robert and Hattie were in the living room talking to Sean and Bunty.

'We're staying on,' Bunty explained. 'The Nativity play's on Wednesday. After that, we'll be on our way.'

'I phoned Rosie,' Hattie said. 'She wants more Christmas events in *The Chronicle*. She'll come to the Nativity to take some photos – the school will advise her on which children she can photograph, but I imagine Mary, Joseph and all the animals up at the farm would be great publicity for the farm.'

'And your food's a big draw.' Sean was munching a mini quiche. 'Refreshments are a crowd-pleaser.'

'I can't say I like the idea of dressing up as a reindeer to serve them though,' Robert groaned.

Sean shoved a small Cornish-pasty bite into his mouth. 'Ah, we have no choice, Robert. Mammy said the Nativity's a special time for the kiddies.' He glanced over to where Sadie and Bronagh were talking with Tressy and Maeve. 'We're all being reindeers. She said so.'

Robert looked worried. 'I'd better polish my antlers.'

Pat came blustering in from the kitchen, a glass of mulled wine in one hand and a wedge of cake in the other. He nudged Robert affectionately as he passed. 'I can see why all the women in the village have the hots for you, Robert.'

Robert put a hand up in protest. 'Oh, no, no.'

'I'd have the hots for you myself if you made this sort of food for me every day. I'll have to take you for a spin in the DeLorean.'

'There's really no need,' Robert protested, but Pat was off back to the kitchen for a top-up.

A few paces away, Maeve was hanging on Tressy's every word. 'So you put the jam on the scone first, but doesn't the cream fall off?'

'Not at all,' Tressy said. 'The clotted cream sits perfectly. I mean, if you do it the Devon way, you have to balance the jam on the bleddy cream. That's bonkers, if you ask me.'

'No, it's not,' Robert called cheerily from a distance. 'It's the Devon way every time.'

'It's the only thing we disagree on.' Tressy's eyes sparkled.

'You're both wonderful bakers,' Sadie said diplomatically.

Bronagh was nibbling quiche. 'I'm moving in with you both.'

'Well, it's funny you should say that.' Tressy lowered her voice. 'I was discussing the meaning of Christmas with Robert earlier. When did you say you were going back?'

'After the Nativity,' Maeve replied.

'Mmm.' Tressy was thoughtful. 'I don't suppose you'd hang on a bit longer? I've got the beginning of an idea.'

'Does it involve costumes?' Bronagh asked. 'I'm always happy to glam up.'

'More to the point, will it help the farm?' Sadie wanted to know.

'Definitely yes to the second. And I'll need you two on board.' Tressy turned to Maeve. 'You said something to me earlier about wanting to bake.'

'What I said was...' Maeve looked suddenly nervous, 'I'm useless at baking. I cheated at the bake off at The Hole in the Wall. I still feel awful about it but I so wanted to do well, so I bought one and I pretended it was my own.'

'And I accidentally stuffed Partlan Brown's face in it,' Bronagh added proudly.

'Which, I suppose, is the short version of why we're here,' Sadie explained.

'Right. Maeve, what would you like to make?' Tressy asked.

'All sorts. Meringues, sponges. A real Guinness cake would be too hard though,' Maeve admitted. 'I'd so love it if Niall said to me, "Maeve, my darlin', you bake the best Guinness cake in Ballycotton."'

'What does he say to you at the moment?' Tressy asked kindly.

'Normally he says, "I can't eat this, Maeve – it'll break my teeth."'

'Well, that won't do, will it?' Tressy patted her shoulder affectionately. 'Ladies, let's go to the kitchen and get another refill, and I'll share my little plan. Then you can tell me if we can make it work or not.'

As they hurried into the kitchen, Nora rushed past them in the other direction, holding a glass in one hand and a slice of quiche in the other. She said, 'Have you seen Niall?'

'I think he's in the conservatory,' Maeve said. 'Why?'

'Oh, nothing.' Nora was being mysterious and took off, increasing her pace. She found Niall sitting in Robert's armchair,

Isaac Mewton on his knee, his eyes closed, listening to Puccini. She said, 'What on earth are you doing?'

Niall smiled angelically. 'I've eaten good food, drunk a bellyful, and now I'm listening to grand music with a grand cat for company.' He opened one eye. 'I spent my whole life working hard and making money, Nora. But all that's behind me. I'm chilling out now and feeling grand.'

Nora put her hands on her hips. 'Then I suggest you get your grand arse out into the front garden. There's an unholy row going on out there.'

'Why? What's happening? Has Pat overdone the mulled wine?' Niall eased Isaac onto the chair arm.

'It's your son. And it's not good. Follow me,' Nora ordered, and Niall was on his feet.

The row could be heard in the front garden as soon as the front door opened. Lola was uncontrollable, waving her arms and shrieking. 'I just want to go home, Rory. I hate it here.'

Rory's voice was soothing. 'I'll get you that ticket. Next Wednesday. Or maybe afterwards.'

'I want to go,' Lola sobbed. She was drunk, slurring her words, finding it difficult to stand. Rory had his arms around her for support. 'I hate this stinky English village that smells of cow shite. I hate it.'

'But it's a fine place,' Rory argued. 'I promised I'd get you back home and I will.'

'I hate you, Rory O'Connor,' Lola shrieked like a banshee. 'I never wanted to come here.'

Rory was surprised she was so angry. He thought he'd explained. 'I took you out to lunch earlier and we agreed I'd get you a plane ticket after the Nativity.'

'I hate everything.' Lola threw herself against Rory and began to pummel his chest. 'I hate you. I hate you.'

'But—' Rory attempted to catch her wrists and a flailing fist caught his cheek '—we agreed we'd just be friends until I could get you back to Dublin.'

'I know what you're up to behind my back. You're after chatting *her* up.' Lola's hands thrashed again and Rory wrapped his arms around her tightly to stop her hitting him.

He spoke gently. 'Calm down, Lola.'

'I will not calm down.'

Niall thought it was time to intervene. 'What's going on?'

'This isn't the way we behave at someone's house,' Nora scolded.

'Lola's upset. She's had a few wines,' Rory began apologetically. He couldn't blame her entirely.

'She's making a holy show of herself,' Nora said quietly.

'Come inside – or take her back to the B & B,' Niall advised.

'I won't go back to that smelly farm, never, never,' Lola said, swaying, her face tight with anger. 'He and that Poppy wan are thick as thieves.'

'Poppy's a nice girl,' Rory began, feeling defensive.

'Is she now, Rory? Is that what she is? I've seen how she looks at you. You're both making eyes at each other the whole time.'

'We are not,' Rory said hotly. 'Behave yourself, Lola. I wouldn't do that. I'll book you that ticket tonight and you can go back to Dublin and forget about me.'

'You broke my heart—'

'But we agreed—'

'I hate you.' Lola tried to slap him again and Nora intervened, tugging her away, glaring at Rory to tell him to take a step back. She wrapped an arm around Lola.

'You're coming inside with me. I'm making you a strong coffee and you're going to drink every drop and calm down.'

'I hate you all.' Lola burst into tears.

'There'll be no argument.' Nora dragged Lola into the house.

Niall inspected his son's face. 'Are you all right, Rory?'

'I'm fine.'

Niall took a deep breath. 'Lola's a bit jealous?'

'No. We talked, Da. We're over. She's going home soon.' Rory hated upsetting people. He'd tried his best to make everything better. 'She just wants to leave. I've no idea why she got so mad with me. The drink, I suppose.'

'What about what she said? About Poppy? Do you like her?'

'I don't know, Da.' Rory realised he had a new, warm glow beneath his chest, strange feelings of protectiveness and happiness and something else he couldn't explain. 'She's nice. I've never met anyone like her. We – get on. But I didn't mean to upset Lola. I mean, she knew the score between me and her.'

'And what is the score?' Niall asked calmly.

'It was just a bit of fun. She's going home as soon as I can get her a ticket. I'll sort one out for her tonight. She's trying to be a model in Dublin. She had a job, being the "before" in a "before and after" make-up shoot. She's a nice enough girl. She only liked me because I've a smart flat and a fast car and I took her to swanky places.'

'And how do you feel?'

'I was all right with it.' Rory decided it was his own fault. Lola had pursued him and he'd just rolled with it. Ever the peacemaker. 'But we've moved on. We're done.'

'Rory, I'm glad to talk things through, man to man. You're twenty-six now.'

'I am, Da,' Rory said.

'And you aren't thinking of settling down?'

'Maybe one day.' Rory's mind filled with thoughts he didn't want to have, at least until after Lola had gone.

A figure stepped from the shadows. Sadie approached them and her voice was low. 'What's happening here?'

'We're just talking, Mammy,' Niall said.

'Then why's Nora inside with Lola bawling her eyes out?' Sadie put her hands on her hips. It was time to tell the men what was what. Sadie had a lifetime of practice. 'We're Robert and Tressy's guests. We're having a lovely time. I won't have it spoiled.'

'I'm sorry, Grandmammy,' Rory said softly.

Sadie approached him. 'Is that a bruise on your cheek?'

'Ah, it's nothing. Lola's a bit disappointed with me.'

'They've split up.' Niall took a breath. 'She drank a bit much. She accused Rory of playing around with Poppy from the farm.'

'And is he?' Sadie made her eyes small, suddenly protective, the matriarch.

'No, of course not, honest,' Rory said. 'I wouldn't do that.'

Sadie took a breath. 'Lola's your guest, Rory. If you've split up, you put her on a plane home.'

'I've said I will. Tomorrow, Grandmammy.'

'And, Rory, you'll sort things out in your own backyard. I don't want the whole of Millbrook to think that we're a bunch of muppets.'

'Last night, when we all went to The Highwayman's Roost, Poppy and I were larking around,' Rory told them. 'I sat between Lola and Poppy. And Poppy was chatting away, but Lola whinged all the time about all the carbs in the food.'

'Were you rude to Lola?'

Rory didn't pause. 'No, the opposite. I was trying to get her to talk. Poppy was too. But I couldn't help noticing. Poppy's so nice to be around. She makes me laugh. I never had a girlfriend who did that. And when she smiles, her nose does this crinkly thing and it's pretty. Usually with girlfriends, it's all about the car and going places and they don't like it when I joke and act the maggot. But Poppy's different.'

Niall raised an eyebrow. 'Do you know, Rory, I felt that way when I met Maeve. She bowled me over. I'd no idea what had hit me. She was cute and funny and I just fell for her.'

'Is that so?' Sadie shot him a fierce look. She'd let him have it with both barrels now. 'Perhaps you should tell Maeve that more often, son. From the look on her face most of the time, I think she's forgotten you ever loved her.'

Niall looked as if he'd been slapped. 'Do you think so, Mammy?'

'As plain as the nose on your face. You need to give that some thought, and make her feel like a special woman again. And as for you, Rory...' Sadie turned to her grandson. Her voice was gentle. 'I know you and Lola have broken up, but she's still here. And she has feelings.'

'I'll buy her ticket tonight,' Rory said honestly. 'I didn't mean to hurt her.'

'I know that,' Sadie replied. 'But she needs to be gone. You and Poppy. There's a magnetism.'

'Is there?' Rory asked. 'Really?'

'I hadn't noticed either,' Niall protested.

'You're a pair of planks.' Sadie pressed her lips together. 'Rory, I want you to go away and think about how you really feel about Poppy. And get Lola on the next available plane.'

'I will, Grandmammy.'

'And, Niall.'

'Yes, Mammy?'

'I noticed Maeve's glass was in need of a refill before I came out. I'm just saying. That poor woman has been starved of affection for too long now.' She took a step forward. 'Do you both hear me?'

'We do.' Niall scuttled into the house.

Rory kissed Sadie's cheek. 'Love you, Grandmammy. You're the best. And thanks for the words of wisdom. You might even be right.'

Sadie watched them go back into the house. She said, 'Men can be so thick.'

She realised she had no coat on. She was shivering cold. She hugged herself and hurried back towards the door. She was still a mammy; her family needed her, and it filled her with happiness. She deserved a pat on the back.

But there was a glass of spiced wine in the kitchen with her name on it.

25

Monday morning came, bringing a harsh wind and cold rain. Sadie and Bronagh huddled in coats and headscarves, watching Paul and Zoe examine Holly in the barn. Poppy hovered behind them anxiously.

Zoe asked, 'Has Holly eaten anything?'

'No,' Paul said sadly. 'I've been keeping a close eye on her. So has Poppy.'

'She hasn't got an appetite.' Poppy looked distraught. 'I've been trying to tempt her, but nothing's working.'

Bronagh asked, 'Can you help her, Zoe?'

'I can try.' Zoe didn't sound convinced. 'She badly needs fluids to correct electrolyte imbalances. I can give her some non-steroidal anti-inflammatory drugs.'

Bronagh shook her head. 'Will she be all right?'

'I've done my best.' Zoe turned to Paul. 'I'll drop by tomorrow.'

Paul looked forlorn. 'I was hoping to introduce her to the other donkeys. We have children coming down for a Nativity play.'

'Keep Holly separate and don't let her be disturbed,' Zoe advised.

'Is she in pain?' Sadie asked. 'She's so quiet.' She ruffled Holly's ears, but the donkey just stared ahead.

'Donkeys are very stoical,' Zoe explained. 'They hide their pain symptoms much more than – say – horses. Some people interpret that as them having no feelings. Donkeys suffer in silence.'

'I'd love to home more donkeys. Any animal that needs refuge.' Paul shook his head. 'I'll keep Holly inside and keep her warm.'

'Good.' Zoe pushed her hand in her pocket for her car keys. 'I've done the best I can. We just have to hope it's enough.'

'Thanks,' Paul muttered.

'Well, I have to be off. There's a farmer in Sidmouth with calf scour. More dehydration problems to fix,' she said encouragingly. 'Give me a ring if there's any change.'

Sadie watched her walk away, feeling a sense of helplessness. 'What do you think, Paul? Will Holly pull through?'

'The vet didn't sound hopeful,' Paul replied.

'I'd hate to be a vet,' Bronagh admitted. 'All those sick animals. It'd break my heart.'

Poppy turned away, visibly upset. 'I'd better feed the alpacas. You know how grumpy Angel gets if he doesn't have carrots by elevenses.' She turned to Sadie and Bronagh. 'Thanks for everything.'

'We just want to help,' Bronagh said.

'Thank you, both.' Paul tried to look positive. 'What are your plans for today?'

'I think we'll have a rest day.' Sadie felt exhausted already. 'Tomorrow and Wednesday, we'll be getting ready for the Nativity. So Bronagh and I will take it steady, perhaps have a drink in

The Pig and Pickle over lunch, take forty winks this afternoon. The others are all going out to the moors, clambering on rocks.' She shook her head. 'That might have been for me thirty years ago.'

'I'll buy you both a drink at lunchtime,' Paul offered. 'Yes, a lazy day's a good idea. Tomorrow we'll have to get the barn ready for the Nativity. And I think the reporter's coming round.'

'Rosie Eagle?' Bronagh was suddenly interested. 'I'll need to look my best if I'm getting my photo in the paper...'

* * *

Rory walked towards where his Ferrari was parked in the drive of Tails of Hope, next to a DeLorean and a Range Rover. Niall and Pat were inspecting their cars, kicking the tyres to check for air. Rory said, 'Hello, Da, Uncle Pat.'

'Where are you going?' Niall asked.

'For a drive. I'm after getting Christmas presents.'

'Oh?' Niall asked. 'Where's Lola?'

'Asleep. With a hangover. She's keen to stay out of my way. I've got her a ticket to fly back to Dublin from Bristol. There wasn't much available though.'

'Oh? That'll be the Christmas rush,' Niall said.

'Probably. I couldn't get her one until after the Nativity, and that's a first-class one, so I'll buy her a big present to take back with her. After the kiddies' play, I'll drive her to Bristol and wish her the best. Then we'll say our goodbyes.'

'She was never the one for you,' Pat told him.

'Ah, I know.' Rory shoved his hands into jeans pockets. He'd lived and learned; he'd chalk it up to experience. 'That doesn't mean to say that I won't see her right.'

'You're a good lad,' Niall said.

'Well, I fell on my feet, working for you, Da,' Rory said, his face gentle with gratitude. 'Life's good. I want to give a little back.'

'So you're buying Christmas presents?' Pat looked hopeful.

'I am.' Rory grinned. 'I was thinking I might get something for Poppy too.' He met Niall's eyes, his own thoughtful. 'You know you were saying last night about that father and son talk?'

'I was.' Niall shifted in his feet uneasily. 'What do you need?'

'Some advice. About women. I mean – about how you felt when you met Mammy. You were telling me last night and it was good to hear.' Rory raised an eyebrow. An idea had come to him. An opportunity to bond. 'Why don't you come with me and we'll get a drink? And you can tell me more.'

'I will. And if you're buying presents, perhaps you can help me pick a good one?' Niall looked troubled. 'I should buy something special for your mammy, and I've no idea what to get.'

'I'm your man.' Rory wrapped an arm around him, suddenly filled to the brim with the Christmas spirit. 'Do you want to come along, Uncle Pat? Auntie Nora might like a gift. I'm sure the three of us could help each other out.'

* * *

On Tuesday evening, they shared another noisy family dinner at the farm, with thirteen people round the table. Sadie needed to wind down. They'd spent the whole day with the animals, feeding them, tidying the barn. Bronagh was exhausted too – she was having a shower and an early night. Tomorrow was Wednesday, the day of the Nativity dress rehearsal, and she intended to sparkle. Hazel and Poppy had gone down to the new arrivals' barn carrying a torch in the dark to see if they could tempt Holly to eat. She hadn't had a bite all day, although she had pretended to nibble. Zoe had called it sham eating.

Lola was upstairs in her room on her phone while Rory sat in the living room, scribbling café design ideas in a notepad. Bunty and Sean, Nora and Pat and Niall and Maeve were at The Pig and Pickle. Hattie and Barry were there too. Hattie had been looking at houses all day and had drawn a blank again. She needed cheering up. The O'Connor clan were welcomed as regulars in the pub now, enjoying banter with the village crowd. Shelley was delighted with the extra business. Sean and Bunty were drumming up support for the Nativity play.

Sadie wandered around the farmhouse by herself. She passed the lounge, where the television was, and wondered whether to go in and watch the soaps. She decided against it and wandered off, around a corner, down a corridor, pausing at a room marked 'Private'. Inside she could hear music: 'Born to Be Wild' by Steppenwolf. She knocked lightly. It could only be one person. A low voice murmured, 'Come in.'

Sadie opened the door and hesitated. Paul was seated at a desk, in front of a laptop. There was a spreadsheet on the screen, lots of numbers. Paul smiled. 'Sadie. I was just thinking of you.'

'Oh?'

'I'm looking at some of the ideas Niall and Rory have come up with.' He raised an eyebrow. 'It looks like the Irish fairies have sprinkled magic dust over Tails of Hope.'

'Tell me more.'

'Niall's a whizz with figures. He's been looking at what I might invest to extend the place. And Rory's a real design ideas kid. I'm just so touched by how your family want to help the farm.'

'That's what the O'Connors do.' Sadie grinned.

Paul indicated a bottle of brandy on the desk. 'Will you have a cognac?'

'That might be nice.' Sadie nodded. It was just a drink. Between friends.

'No Bronagh tonight?'

'She wants her beauty sleep.'

'And you don't need it,' Paul replied.

Sadie wasn't sure if he'd paid her a compliment. 'I'd rather have a nightcap.'

Paul poured two brandies, handing a glass to Sadie, indicating an armchair in the corner. 'Take a seat.'

Sadie settled herself and sipped warming brandy. She decided to take the bull by the horns. 'So, you've been making plans?'

'It could be really good,' Paul said. 'I'm desperate to make this place the sanctuary Wendy dreamed of.'

'More animals?'

'Lots more. We'd never turn a needy animal away.'

'So – you need to think bigger.'

'That's what Niall said. And Rory.'

'Paul.' Sadie leaned forwards. 'I know we won't make much money from the Nativity. It's just there to let the locals know you're here. And on Saturday, the Santa event I'm working on is the same. You need a long-term plan.'

'Are all the O'Connors business geniuses?' Paul looked astonished. 'You're so kind.'

'Bronagh and I've had a lovely time here. You've been a good friend,' she said. 'Have you never heard the old rhyme, "There are good ships and there are wood ships, ships that sail the sea, but the best ships are friendships, may they always be"?'

'I haven't.'

Sadie's face took on a faraway look. 'Not long after we started dating each other, Alfie bought me a little gold claddagh ring.'

'What's that?'

'It's a special symbol. The heart represents love, the crown represents loyalty and the hands represent friendship. Those things are really important to Irish people.'

'To all people,' Paul said.

'"From Dublin's fair city to Galway's rugged coast, friendship's spirit spreads to those who seek it most",' Sadie quoted.

'A poem?'

'One I was taught at my mother's knee.' Sadie met his eyes. 'Paul, the sanctuary is important. So we all want to help. You've opened up your home to my family. We'll open up our hearts in return.'

'You have more plans?' Paul asked. 'I'm touched.'

'I'm on it. I'll let you know when I know.' Sadie drained the brandy from her glass and stood up. She walked over and pecked Paul's cheek. 'For now, I'm going to sleep on it. Tomorrow it'll be clear as daylight. After all, each sunrise brings a new day with new hope.'

She was gone, leaving Paul staring after her, mouth open. She'd given him plenty to think about.

26

Early on Wednesday, Bronagh was scuttling excitedly around the main barn like a clucking hen, piling up bales of hay and placing old carpets across the earth to form a stage area for the children, adjusting one of Poppy's old dolls in the trough they'd adapted as a manger. Paul, Niall and Sean arranged wooden benches in front of the impromptu stage, and trestle tables down the side for refreshments. There was a huffle when a minibus arrived with the Clavinova piano, Rory and Pat plugging in extension leads and making a space for the orchestra, which involved a lot of percussion instruments and a few recorders.

Hazel arrived mid-morning with refreshments, flasks of tea and coffee, and Sadie helped her dole out hot drinks to everyone who was busy hanging decorations.

Rory came up to Sadie, wrapping his arm around her affectionately. 'We've got the performance area looking good, Grandmammy.'

'You have.' She met his gaze, assessing his expression. 'How's Lola?'

Rory glanced at his ex-girlfriend, filing her nails, standing with Bronagh, who was forcing a packet of biscuits on her as if it would cure all ills. 'She's ready to go home tomorrow.'

Sadie frowned. 'She's had enough of country life?'

'And she's had enough of me. But we've moved on. And we've wished each other well.' Rory was already looking forward. 'I love it here. It's so calm – the seaside down the road, the animals. It's a lovely break from the city. Mind you, I'm worried about the donkey.' He was concerned. 'Poppy says poor Holly's still not out of the woods.'

'The vet's coming again soon.' Sadie felt the familiar sadness clutch at her heart. 'I hate to see an animal suffer.'

'We're all hoping for the best.' Rory offered an optimistic grin. 'The barn's looking good for the kiddies' play though.'

'Definitely,' Sadie said, wearing her organising hat. 'Hattie's already briefed Rosie Eagle, and she's put something about it in *The Chronicle*. We'll have lots of people on the door.'

'I'm looking forward to being a reindeer – or an elf. Whatever you want me to be.' Rory shuffled his feet in the straw.

Sadie decided now was the time to ask. She was concerned about her grandson. 'Are you sure you'll be all right? Now you and Lola have parted ways?'

'Oh, I'm grand.' Rory brightened. 'We were never right for each other.'

'Mmm.' Sadie watched Rory's eyes flicker to Poppy, who was busy helping Hazel to collect cups. Poppy smiled back and blushed. Sadie understood completely.

An hour later, excited voices rang from outside the barn and the children were shepherded in by Sally Baxter, Adam Thompson and three classroom assistants. They were already in full Nativity costume. Their eyes widened when they saw straw bales, twinkling lights, a manger with the baby, tinsel around its head for a halo.

Sadie felt Bronagh arrive at her side; she heard her cackle. 'Oh, look. Joseph's a handsome lad. I bet his mammy spent hours making that costume. And there's Mary in the blue robe. She reminds me of Kathleen.' Bronagh moved closer. 'And the angels, all the gauzy material – and all the cute shepherds. Look at the tiny one at the end with the curly hair. He's a proper little chancer.'

'I like the kings best.' Sadie smiled. 'The shiny crowns and the velvet cloaks.'

The children were gazing around, some awestruck, some less interested. A shepherd sat nonchalantly on a bale of hay, put his feet up and pulled out a mobile phone.

Bronagh linked her arm through Sadie's. 'When I was at school, I always wanted to be the one that brought the myrrh. Balthasar, he was called. I whinged about it and our teacher, Miss O'Casey, said, "Kings are men, Bronagh, not girls". The boys got all the good parts. I had to play a sparrow because of my spindly legs. She told me that, Miss O'Casey, that I had spindly sparrow legs.'

'I remember Miss O'Casey. I was an ox in her play. She told me I was the right shape for an ox. Bovine, she said I was. These three kings are girls and boys now,' Sadie said. 'Thank goodness that's changed. It used to be that Mary was only there to hold the baby and be meek and mild. Now she gets to sing a lovely song.'

'Hello. We're all here,' Sally called, looking around. 'It's such a good idea to stage it in a real stable. We're fully sold out, thanks to the change of venue. I don't know if it's the atmosphere or if it's Robert's refreshments.' Her attention was taken up by a little blonde boy who was in tears. She knelt down. 'What's the problem, Noah?'

'It smells horrible. I'll get asthma.'

Bronagh was outraged. 'I swept the place from top to bottom. You could eat your dinner off this floor.'

Another child approached, a bold-faced girl. 'I thought we were having animals on stage with us, Mrs Baxter. You said there would be donkeys and alpacas. Where are they?'

'They're resting now so they're full of energy tonight,' Sadie soothed.

'It's you who need rehearsing, not them,' Bronagh added. 'They're good at their roles already.'

The girl pulled a sulky face, as if she'd been fobbed off. Sally clapped her hands. 'Right, class 5AT. Go to your places, please. We're ready for our first run-through. Mr. Thompson.' Sally waved to Adam, who was deep in conversation with Lola. 'Shall we start?'

'Ready when you are, Mrs Baxter.' Adam said something to Lola and her face lit up. She had never looked so interested. The children scurried to their places. Someone next to Sadie and Bronagh blew a large toot-toot on a recorder. Sally played a clanging chord on the Clavinova and thirty voices launched into 'Away in a Manger'.

Bronagh turned to Sadie, rolled her eyes, gave her a 'here we go' look and covered her ears with both hands.

* * *

It was almost seven-thirty. Strings of festive lights flashed and twinkled in the barn as parents huddled on benches, chatting expectantly. Sadie and Bronagh were checking tickets on the door, which meant they stood in the full force of the breeze, wrapped in warm hats and headscarves, directing fretting parents to their seats. The children were already in costume, ready to start, eyes huge with anticipation. Sally signalled with one finger over her lips that they weren't to make a sound.

One small girl in a woolly sheep costume ignored her and waved to her mother, who was sitting in the second row, pointing her phone. Adam was chatting with Lola again, their heads close, then a small child prodded his arm and he adjusted the shepherd's dressing gown.

There was a flurry of activity behind the trestle tables, people arranging cups, plates of cakes and scones, turning down bubbling urns. Sean, Pat, Rory and Niall were strutting around in flashing reindeer antlers and red noses, butting each other. Robert looked less comfortable in his headgear, his shoulders hunched. Hattie, Bunty, Tressy and Nora were laying out mince pies, dressed as fairies with leafy crowns, starry circlets and, in Tressy's case, a headband of twinkling stars.

Hazel was talking animatedly to a woman clutching a bouquet, dressed elegantly in a cream suit. It was Barbara Webster, the head teacher.

Sally stood up and gave a small cough. 'Ladies and gentlemen. Beloved parents,' she began nervously. 'Well, this is it. The evening you've all been waiting for. And I'd like to say thanks in advance for all the costumes you've made, pouring your heart and soul into every stitch; for the evenings you've tirelessly rehearsed lines with your children, for making the journey here in the bitter cold. And,' she added hurriedly, 'Mr Thompson and I are grateful to Tails of Hope for allowing us to use this wonderful venue for our performance. It reminds us so much of the first stable in Bethlehem, the holy manger.' She indicated the children who were staring, open-mouthed, and there was a gasp from the audience, an 'Aww,' right on cue, as the first donkey, Diana, poked her head into the barn.

Sally added, 'So let's welcome the other stars of our show tonight. The Tails of Hope animal residents.'

Poppy, Hattie and Barry led The Supremes into the barn. They stood placidly, uninterested. Paul was organising Juan, Carlos, Jose and Angel to stand together at the back where they'd cause least trouble. The alpacas looked, bemused. Angel was looking for mischief. He shifted, turned the wrong way, showing his backside, and Paul urged him back into position. The children laughed and Angel looked pleased with himself.

Paul and Poppy stayed in position behind the alpacas, out of sight but ready to pounce, in case they were needed. Rosie Eagle leaped up from somewhere on the front bench and began taking photos of the donkeys and the alpacas. Some of the parents pointed at the animals, cooing, 'How cute.' Sadie winked at Bronagh. The sponsorship plan was working well.

The audience's chatter subsided. Adam moved to the front of the stage and raised a finger, a sign for the performance to begin. Sally banged out a chord on the Clavinova, the recorders whistled, the percussionists rattled tambourines, maracas, seed shakers and wooden scrapers and the cast launched into 'Away in a Manger'.

After the last chords faded, a confident girl in a brown dressing gown took a step forward and spoke in a clear voice. 'I'm just a poor shepherd, but tonight I have witnessed the greatest of wonders. A mother and her newborn baby are here in the stable. He is the Messiah, as was foretold by the prophets of old. Come with me now and we'll meet him together.'

'I'm Joseph, a carpenter,' said Joseph, standing tall. 'Mary, my wife, and I travelled for days. Mary rode on a donkey – we're humble folk, no money for anything fancier. And then she had to give birth to her son here in the barn because all the rooms were full. But now we have a beautiful baby.'

Mary looked at him fiercely. She had no words to speak in reply, but if looks could kill, Joseph would have fallen dead on the floor. There was no love lost between this holy couple.

A girl in a gauze costume pushed her way forward, almost falling over a hay bale. Her voice was loud as she shouted, 'I am Gabriel, an archangel. I have come to deliver a message from God, and it's this: today, the Son of God has been born on earth to save mankind.' She began to sing, and the audience took one breath of amazement; she certainly had the pure voice of an angel.

The orchestra inhaled loudly, instruments at the ready.

Bronagh turned to Sadie, covering her ears. 'Oh, no, it's the recorders again.'

On cue, a chorus of wind instruments whistled and shrieked as five girls hurried downstage in haloes and long frocks, moving in a synchronised dance, singing 'Unto Us a Boy Is Born'.

Carlos and Angel edged forward, very interested in the gauze material of their costumes. The curly-haired boy in front of them wearing an ox mask pushed the alpacas back, frowning furiously. They ignored him and stepped forward. Jose tried to eat the child's hair. The little boy's face was panic-stricken. Diana and Florence began to munch some of the residual hay bales and the bold-faced girl who had asked about the animals earlier turned furiously and said, 'Shhh.'

Another confident child moved downstage, a girl in a white angel costume. Her face was sweet and composed. She clasped her hands as if she were about to perform. She said, 'I'm archangel Michael, lead singer in a heavenly choir. We sing for joy to celebrate the birth of Jesus, the saviour who brought a new joy to the world.'

The Clavinova banged out a chord in introduction and the girl started to sing 'Joy to the World' in a sweet tone. She was another gifted performer. As the song developed, she opened her arms to encompass The Supremes, singing 'Joy to the World' to each of them. The audience muttered 'Aww' again as the singer raised her voice for the final verse.

Diana raised her voice too, not wanting to be outdone. A loud braying filled the air. Florence and Mary joined in with an emphatic hee-haw, the deafening donkey chorus drowning out the angel's solo. The child did her utmost to get to the end of her performance and stomped off back in line.

On cue, a confident voice shouted from stage left, 'This must be the place, Melchior. We've travelled for so long, in our quest to find the child who will be king, and to greet him.'

Another child roared, 'I'm weary, Caspar. The camels are weary too.'

At this point, Angel and Jose began to snort.

A third, a tall girl, called out, 'For we have followed the star for hundreds of miles.'

'Let's go in, Balthasar, and meet this wonderful child,' the first boy boomed and three children walked on, a perfect line of velvet cloaks, gold-crowned heads held high.

'I bring gold, for a king,' the first king intoned as he knelt down.

'I bring frankincense, for one who is divine,' the second added, kneeling.

'And I bring myrrh, for sorrow and death,' said the third. 'Gifts fit for a child who will be loved for ever after. We are here to honour and worship the new king.'

Before Balthasar could present her gift, a pushy alpaca stepped forward, sniffing the myrrh. Then Angel stuck his nose it, wrestling it away from the little king who yelled, 'That's my myrrh. Get off.'

Angel was not deterred. He pulled the pot away, pushed his nose in deeper and began snuffling. It stuck on his face.

'Praises to the heavens,' the first king shouted and Diana brayed three times in agreement. She shuffled round in the hay to make herself comfortable and a tiny voice shouted, 'Ew. What's that horrible smell?' Several children groaned, waved hands in front of their noses and stood back, horrified.

Sally quickly began to crash out chords on the Clavinova and the children in the orchestra joined in with shrieking recorders and rattling percussion instruments. Right on cue, the cast sang, 'Ding, Dong! Merrily on High'.

The alpacas surged forward, determined to be the stars of the show. Carlos ran into the audience, snaffling the bouquet that Barbara Webster intended to present to Sally at the end of the performance. His mouth was stuffed with flower heads. Jose had taken a liking to Rosie Eagle's digital camera and was trying to eat it. He turned his attention to her woolly scarf, tugging the tasselled end.

Juan pushed in front of Mary and sniffed the manger, pushing the doll onto the floor. The baby Jesus rolled away into the audience. Angel sat among the orchestra, a recorder in his mouth, wheezing. He dropped it in disgust, raised his chin, flattened his ears and spat at the electric piano. A child laughed. Several more began to giggle.

The Nativity cast reached the end of the song and bowed in unison as they had been drilled. The alpacas took to their heels and galloped into the audience, who clapped and cheered as if it was the funniest thing they'd ever seen. Barbara was on her feet, holding the remains of the bouquet above her head.

'Delightful, wonderful. A performance we'll remember for years to come. Thank you to the teachers for their patience and dedication. And now, perhaps, it's time for refreshments.'

Sadie and Bronagh exchanged satisfied glances as the audience mobbed the trestle tables, everyone desperate for Robert's cakes. Robert found himself swarmed by several women who patted his shoulder and asked for recipes. The alpacas surged towards the food, followed by The Supremes, who were braying excitedly.

Robert looked around anxiously. 'Don't let them eat the mince pies.'

'If you'll form an orderly queue, please. Alpacas at the back.' Sean tried to take control, his antlers winking.

Niall added, 'You'll all be served in good time.'

'You will,' Pat agreed. 'Just tell me or one of my reindeers what you want. We're Dancer, Prancer and – Chancer. Here to serve up Christmas in a glass. Now, who's for some spicy punch?'

27

The next morning, Hazel poured extra coffee into each cup. Everyone looked tired. Pat slumped over the breakfast table and groaned, 'I don't know how Robert does it, coping with all that attention. Being a babe magnet is tough. I'm shattered.'

'Those women were all over me for the cakes.' Sean was impressed. 'Some woman kissed me and said they were the best mince pies ever.' He thought for a minute. 'I wonder if I should learn to bake.'

'No, Sean.' Bunty shot him a warning look.

'Robert's mince pies were incredible.' Hazel placed toast on the table.

'He puts calvados in.' Sadie reached for her cup. 'Lots of it.'

Bronagh said, 'Those poor teachers. How do they manage those kids day in, day out?'

'It was the alpacas that wore me out,' Nora groaned. 'They should come with a health warning, especially the one that spits.'

'And the donkeys. That braying noise is seriously loud,' Bunty added.

'So where's everyone else this morning?' Maeve asked.

Hazel was filling coffee cups. 'Poppy and Paul are up in the barns,' she explained. 'Feeding. Doing checks.'

'Rory's outside, talking to Lola,' Nora added. 'I saw she'd packed her bags. She's flying back to Dublin today.'

'She hasn't enjoyed herself,' Pat said. 'It's a shame. We're having a riot here.'

'We are. So, go on, Mammy.' Niall reached for toast. 'Tell us your plans. What's happening next?'

'Did I see you, Tressy and Hattie telling Rosie Eagle yesterday?' Bunty asked.

'No, Hattie was talking to Rosie about the carol service. She's playing the hymns. Tressy has an idea of her own. But—' Sadie flourished an arm, feeling pleased with herself '—ta-da! On Saturday afternoon, we're holding a Big Santa Extravaganza up in the barn. It's a proper fundraiser. We're dressing up as Santa's little helpers, giving presents to kiddies.'

'Do we have to dress up again?' Maeve asked, unenthusiastic.

'I liked being a reindeer.' Pat beamed. 'I thought I looked very butch.'

'Butch wasn't the word I'd have chosen,' Nora muttered.

'You don't need a red nose, Pat,' Sean teased. 'You're there already.'

'That's me.' Pat cackled. 'So, tell us what's happening.'

'It was our idea, mine and Sadie's. And Solly's. Solly's an entrepreneur.' Bronagh was pleased with herself. 'Rosie's advertising it in the paper. Tickets will be on the door. Father Christmas will arrive on Saturday to greet all the little children. And the farm animals will be there, so everyone will see how cute they are and want to sponsor them.'

'Let's hope they behave this time,' Hazel said under her breath. 'The animals, I mean.'

'Solly's providing presents, toys and treats. Robert and Tressy will do refreshments and Robert's raffling his Christmas cake.' Sadie was enjoying the important feeling of being a project manager again. It wasn't a big stretch, she decided, from handling an unruly family to organising a new promotional idea.

'He and Tressy made one each,' Bronagh added. 'They don't need two.'

'And I had this great idea.' Sadie's face shone with enthusiasm. 'We'll invite the kids to bring a toy they've outgrown and wrap it up, so it can be given to a charity for kiddies with no presents. We can organise that under the umbrella of Tails of Hope.'

'Brilliant.' Hazel was delighted. 'That's just the ethos we want for the sanctuary. Caring for others. Being thoughtful. Sharing.'

'So, we'll do the barn up as a grotto.' Bronagh clapped her hands.

'And Santa will make a grand entrance in your DeLorean, Pat,' Sadie added excitedly.

'I'll get to be Santa, will I?' Pat insisted. 'I'll get a fluffy white beard.'

'I'd be the best Santa,' Niall retorted. 'You can be my chauffeur, Pat.'

'I should be Santa, I'm oldest,' Sean argued. 'You tell them who's Santa, Mammy. Can I do it?'

'I thought Paul might want to – it's his farm,' Sadie suggested tentatively.

'Or Solly – he's providing the presents,' Bronagh said loyally.

'Robert might make a nice Santa,' Hazel offered as she refilled cups.

'Why can't one of the women do it?' Nora asked.

'I will,' Bunty volunteered. 'I'll be Ms Claus.'

'That's silly,' Niall said. 'Santa's a man.'

'Said who?' Maeve shouted. 'A man?'

'The kids expect a man,' Pat explained.

'Only because men have got away with it so long,' Nora retorted.

'Well, perhaps I should do it.' Bronagh's eyes took on a dreamy look. 'I could pull it off.'

'I'll decide,' Sadie said firmly. She was in charge now, well and truly. 'And I think it ought to be—'

The door opened and Paul and Poppy came in hurriedly, looking exhausted. All eyes were on them as Poppy said, 'Sorry we're late for breakfast. We've just come from the barn. Zoe the vet's just left.'

'Why?' Sadie asked. 'What's the news?'

They all knew from his expression before Paul said it.

'We've lost her, I'm afraid.' He was out of breath. 'Holly's dead.'

* * *

The rest of the day was quiet. Everyone disappeared to do their own thing. Rory and Lola were missing; Sadie assumed he'd taken her to Bristol airport.

Pat, Niall and Sean went into Teignmouth to find a bookmaker's. Maeve disappeared with a book. Bunty and Nora sat in the lounge to watch television. Paul and Poppy went back to work: there were other animals to tend to. Bronagh tugged at Sadie's sleeve. 'Is it all right if we go outside as well?'

'It's Baltic out there.' Sadie shivered at the thought.

'Just for a short while. Then we'll come in again and have a cup of something hot.'

'Why do you want to go out?' Sadie asked. Bronagh didn't

reply. She had tears in her eyes. Sadie wrapped her in a hug. 'Get your coat and your wellies. Go on. Let's go and see Pi.'

'Thanks, Sadie.'

Wrapped as warmly as they could, hugging each other for extra heat, Sadie and Bronagh squelched outside in wellington boots towards the field where the horses stood with their heads down. They seemed to know something had happened.

Sadie leaned against the gate and stared upwards. 'The sky's white as a folded sheet. Do you think that's snow up there?'

'It might be.' Bronagh peered up, one eye closed. 'It is. A huge chunk of it just landed in my eye.'

'That was rain.'

'It was white. Snow.' Bronagh held out a hand towards the horses and made soft clucking sounds. 'Come on, Pi. Come and say hello.'

The horse seemed to hesitate for a moment. Something about his expression was troubled. He trotted over and Bronagh held out her fingers for him to sniff. 'I love this horse to bits. He knows I need a hug.'

Sadie patted Pi's nose. 'We all do.'

Bronagh said, 'How old did Hazel say he is?'

'Pi? Eighteen.' Sadie read her thoughts. 'He won't die yet.'

'How long do horses live?'

'I don't know. Twenty. Thirty. I think some might live longer than that.'

Bronagh sniffed. 'How old do you think Holly was?'

'It's hard to tell. Maybe she had a hard life.' Sadie looked away and her eyes filled. 'She was on her last legs.'

'But Paul would never have turned her away.'

'He wouldn't. That's the whole point of this place.' Sadie sighed. 'I had a drink with him last night.'

'Oh?' Bronagh arched an eyebrow. 'Just a drink, was it?'

'More a meeting of minds.'

Bronagh leaned her face against Pi's soft nose. 'I adore this boy. It'd break my heart if anything happened to him.'

Sadie felt a jolt of warning, the need to hug her friend. Bronagh was very sensitive; she always got too involved. 'We're off home soon, Bronagh. Don't get too attached.'

'I know but – just leaning against him like this does my heart good. Skin against skin. And he's warm and breathing and huggable. It's therapy.'

'It is.' Sadie's eyes shone at the thought. She'd mention the idea of a petting area to Paul later. 'People and animals have so much to give each other.'

'They do. Paul wants to give them all a decent home. That's what we all want.' Bronagh patted Pi's neck. 'They're just like us, animals, aren't they?'

Sadie thought about it. 'They have more legs.'

'But they think, they feel love. They like attention and to be cared for,' Bronagh said.

'I suppose so.'

'Pi's been a racehorse all his young life, but he's old and knackered now. And nobody wants him. That's why I like him so much.'

'Oh?' Sadie knew what was coming.

Bronagh had tears in her eyes. 'We understand each other, me and Pi. We're the same. I feel old and knackered too. I need putting out to grass.'

'Bronagh, don't.'

'It's true. Before too long I'll need someone to take care of me. I won't be able to feed myself, or take myself to the jacks, or get dressed in the morning. Then what'll I do? I have no kiddies and grandkiddies like you do.'

'You have family. We're family.'

'But what if I'm sick?'

'There are good hospitals, nursing homes. They take care of people,' Sadie said simply.

Bronagh shuddered. 'I'd rather be in my box.'

'What's brought all this on?'

'Holly.'

'Come on. Where's my tough girl? Where's the feisty little mog that lives next door? Bronagh Doyle, come here and give us a hug.' Sadie wrapped warm arms around her friend.

'I don't feel tough.' Bronagh's body seemed to sag in Sadie's arms. 'What if I end up like Holly?'

'We all end up. But not today,' Sadie insisted firmly.

'But what will I do?'

'What about a drink down The Pig and Pickle?' Sadie was prepared to try anything. 'Or we could get a bus into Dawlish. We could shop till we drop.' The meaning of her words hit her. 'Well, not drop.'

Bronagh turned to the chestnut horse, patting his nose. 'What shall we do, Pi? Is it me and you next? Are we waiting for the Grim Reaper?' The horse stared at her as if he understood every word.

'That's nonsense and you know it, Bronagh. Let's go for a drink.'

'I don't feel like it.'

'Let's go inside. I'm cold.'

'The horses are out here. I bet they're cold too.' Bronagh turned as a large van rumbled through the gates and chugged along the path. They watched it continue past the horses' enclosure, up towards the new arrivals' field. Paul opened the gate and the driver stopped by the barn.

Bronagh said, 'Who do you think that is?' She turned to Sadie. 'The van had Forest Lawn written on the side.'

'You know what it is,' Sadie said, her voice low. She closed her eyes, waiting for Bronagh to realise, ready to hug her.

'I don't. Forest Lawn? Is it a gardening service? Maybe they are having some landscaping done for the spring.' She stopped, putting a hand to her mouth. 'Oh, no. It's the van, come for Holly.'

'We should go in,' Sadie said quickly, wanting to protect her, but Bronagh was gaping towards the barn. 'Bronagh, let's go back.'

'Oh, Sadie...'

Sadie wrapped an arm around her and ushered her firmly in the direction of the farmhouse. Bunty was waiting at the door. She said, 'Sadie, did you see the crematorium van?'

Bronagh burst into tears.

'Right, that settles it.' Sadie had made her mind up. 'We're going down the pub.'

'Or you could come with us,' Bunty suggested. 'Me, Nora and Maeve. They're upstairs putting their hats and coats on. I've invited Hazel too. She could do with being cheered up. We're off down Hattie and Robert's. Tressy's just invited us round.'

'She has?' Sadie said. 'That's kind of her.'

'I was talking about, you know, Holly, and how upset we all felt.' Bunty spoke in a low voice. Sadie glanced towards Bronagh and hugged her again. 'Tressy's wonderful, Sadie,' Bunty added. 'She said at times like this, women need the company of other women. She said to come straight over. You should both come.'

Bronagh looked up, her eyes red. 'What will we go there for?'

'Sisterhood. Solidarity.' Sadie folded her arms, in charge now. 'We need to drink tea. Put the world to rights. Come on, Bronagh.

We'll go together. That's how we move forward. We take one small step, then we take another.'

'We do,' Bunty said. 'The men will be betting on the nags, losing money like it's going out of fashion. But we'll do what women do best. We'll communicate with each other, talk sense and cheer each other up,' she said. 'Is it any wonder we women live longer than they do?'

28

That afternoon, a group of women sat in Robert and Tressy's cosy living room watching the rain drizzle rivulets down the windows. Bronagh looked disappointed. 'I hoped it would snow, but it's turned into a downpour.'

'It doesn't snow often in the south-west.' Tressy sniffed. 'It rains a lot though.'

'It's the same in Ireland,' Nora said with a shrug.

'I remember we had a big snowfall in 2010. We got snowed in for days.' Hazel glanced around. 'This is a lovely place you have here, Tressy.'

'Thanks, we like it,' Tressy said.

'Where's Robert?' Maeve asked.

'In the kitchen, making crumpets.' Tressy pointed towards the door. 'He won't be long.'

'I thought I could smell something wonderful.' Maeve inhaled the heavy scents of baking.

'We thought you needed cheering up,' Tressy said to Hazel. 'I was sorry to hear what happened to the little donkey. I thought hot crumpets with lashings of butter might help.'

'A whiskey works for me,' Bronagh said gloomily.

'Robert's very kind,' Bunty added. 'Is Hattie with him?'

'No, she's gone up to the village to see Barry,' Tressy said. 'There was something he needed to talk to her about.'

'Are they an item? I wasn't sure,' Nora mused. 'They always sit closely, like a couple. Mind you, after a while, most couples sit as far away from each other as possible.'

'They're fond of each other,' Tressy explained. 'Hattie had a bad marriage. Geoffrey Bowen was a controlling prig. She likes Barry but I can't blame her if she doesn't want to jump into another relationship like a grasshopper on heat.' Her eyes twinkled. 'Like me and Robert did. We just knew instantly.'

'It took me and Pat ages to get together. I hardly noticed him at first,' Nora said with a shrug. 'I was dating someone else. But Pat always had his eye on me.'

'It was love at first sight with Niall and me.' Maeve seemed sad. 'Now I'm just part of the furniture. But at least we had Erin and Rory. Rory works with Niall in Dublin. Money's Niall's first love now.'

'Rory's Ferrari's a fabulous car to drive,' Bronagh drooled. 'I'd love one of my own.'

'You can drive his,' Sadie retorted.

'Has Lola left?' Hazel asked. 'I thought I saw her earlier.'

'Rory's running her to the airport in Bristol,' Sadie said.

'I see.' Hazel said no more. Sadie wondered if she was thinking of Poppy.

'I thought we could talk about Saturday afternoon.' Tressy changed the subject expertly. 'So who's being Santa?'

'The lads are fighting over it,' Bronagh laughed. 'I think Solly or Paul should do it, but Niall, Sean and Pat are deadly keen.'

'Whoever does it has to be good with children,' Sadie said.

'That rules Pat out,' Nora teased. 'He just fancies himself making a grand entrance to the barn door in the DeLorean.'

'I think a woman should do it.' Bunty's expression was dreamy. 'I'd love to be Santa, surrounded by the children.'

'I'm much happier being a little helper,' Maeve said. 'We'll all be gnomes and fairies, won't we?'

'We can supervise and hand out presents at the same time.' Sadie had it all worked out. 'The men can be reindeers and serve the refreshments. Multitasking.'

'So – Santa Claus – he's patient, kind, sweet-natured,' Tressy said.

'That rules Niall out,' Maeve quipped.

'I thought Paul,' Sadie suggested gently.

'He's much better with animals,' Hazel said.

'Well, I know someone who'd be perfect.' Tressy beamed. 'Of course he'll say no, but he's the kindest man.'

The door opened and Robert appeared, holding a plate of steaming crumpets, butter melting down the sides like liquid gold. He noticed seven pairs of hungry eyes on him and he smiled shyly. 'Anyone for a crumpet?'

* * *

Meanwhile, Hattie was standing at the window in Barry's cosy living room staring at the rain. The log fire roared, a small fir tree in the corner flashed silver lights. Barry placed his hand on her shoulder.

'I always find the rain calming.'

'Do you?' Hattie murmured. 'Most people find it depressing, especially this cold winter rain.'

'When Anne died, I used to drive to Dartmoor and walk in the rain a lot. It felt strangely cleansing. Anne's passing knocked me for six. I didn't really see it coming. Five years ago she was well, then the doctor said she wasn't.' Barry was quiet for a moment. 'It happened so quickly.'

'It must have been hard.'

'It was.' Barry sighed. 'I'd go for walks on the moors, Haytor, Wistman's Wood, Fingle Gorge. Just me, with my thoughts, trying to get used to how life had changed. It would rain, and the wind would be so harsh I thought it'd slice me in half. But being battered by the elements was strangely comforting, like I was alive, still in touch with the real world. There was hope.'

'I understand.' Hattie turned to face him. 'What's on your mind?'

'You are,' Barry said enigmatically. 'I never thought I'd feel something like this, not after Anne.'

Hattie brushed his cheek with her fingers. 'We agreed we'd take things slowly.'

'What about the house you looked at yesterday in Starcross?'

'The Retreat?' Hattie shrugged. 'It's small. But it might do.'

'You were going to think about it.'

'I have thought. It might be the best I can find.'

'Do you like it?'

'Tim Evans rang me this morning trying to chivvy me along, but I won't be rushed. He said a woman had been round for a viewing.'

'Do you want to live in Starcross?'

'I might wait until the new year and see what else comes on the market.'

'There's another option.' Barry's eyes shone.

'Oh?'

He took a nervous breath. 'I can make room for a piano in here.'

Hattie reeled a little. 'You're asking me to move in?'

'We'd be together. And we're just across from the church.' Barry looked hopeful.

'But it's your house. Yours and Anne's.'

'We could make it ours,' Barry said.

'That's sweet of you.' Hattie took his hand.

'Just imagine. You playing the piano, I'd be painting. In the summer we'd sit in the garden. In the winter we'd be together by the fireside, or in the kitchen.'

'Is that what you want, Barry?'

'It's a two-person cottage, Hattie. It's just right. *We're* just right.'

Hattie gave a deep sigh. 'I hadn't seen this coming.'

'We've known each other as long as Robert and Tressy have.' Barry's face was earnest. 'They moved in together straight away. You and I get on so well.'

Hattie hesitated. 'What about love?'

'Love.' Barry squeezed her fingers. 'You know how I feel.'

'I need time,' Hattie said honestly. 'I'm fond of you, Barry. Very fond. We're good around each other. But I'm not ready to move in. Perhaps I need my own space first.'

'Whatever you think is best,' Barry said quietly. 'I've made my speech, and you know what's in my heart. If you decide it's what you want, I'd be the happiest man.'

Hattie nodded. 'I'll give it some serious thought.' She moved away, reaching for her coat. 'I'd better go. Tressy and Robert have invited a house full. I should be there.'

'All right.' Barry looked a little hurt. 'We'll see each other soon.'

'We will.' Hattie tugged on gloves, scarf and hat, and kissed his cheek. 'It'll be a quick walk back in all this rain.'

Barry saw her to the door and Hattie stepped out, hurrying towards the gate. The clock at St Jude's said it was half past three.

She looked beyond, towards the primary school, and was surprised to see a red car parked across the road. It was Rory's Ferrari. She wondered why he might be there.

Hattie turned the other way and scurried full pelt into the driving rain. Her thoughts raced and crashed. She asked herself if she loved Barry enough to move in with him and the answer came back quickly. He was a lovely man. They got on well. For many people of her age, in their seventies, that would be enough. But Hattie had lived with Geoffrey for so long.

She wanted to find who she was again. And she wasn't sure of the answer. Not yet.

* * *

Hattie dashed into the hall at Robert's house, shaking the drops from her clothing. She could hear raised voices coming from the lounge, raucous laughter, teasing. She rushed towards the sound.

Robert was in the armchair, Isaac Mewton dozing on his knee. He had the air of a king, surrounded by seven women seated around him on the floor, and as many empty plates and cups. Tressy glanced up as Hattie walked in. 'Hello. It's raining cats and dogs out there. We've just had crumpets. I saved you some.'

'Thanks.' Hattie was glad of the warm noisy room and the company. It dragged her thoughts back to normality. She took a seat as Tressy bustled about.

'We were just asking Robert,' Bronagh chuckled, 'how it feels to be the village sex symbol.'

'Oh, no, I'm not at all,' Robert said awkwardly. 'I just like baking.'

'We just had a visitor. Susan from the village,' Nora said. 'She said she wanted some jam. That's not what she was really after though. Her cheeks were like beetroots. Robert got her a pot of chilli jam from the pantry.'

'And she came over all unnecessary,' Bronagh butted in.

'She saw the crumpets,' Maeve added. 'She had to stay and have one, didn't she?'

'You know that scene in *When Harry Met Sally*?' Bunty made some ridiculous groaning noises. 'Well, that was Susan eating Robert's crumpet.'

Hazel continued. 'Then Angie Pollock came round and the same thing happened. She took Robert's recipe for crumpets.'

'She looked like she wanted to take Robert himself home,' Bronagh cackled.

'I'm proud of Robert. Baking and love come from the same place,' Tressy said simply. 'We Cornish have known that for years.'

'We Irish too,' Nora piped up. 'We do the best food, the best drink.'

'Giss on,' Tressy teased. 'We have pasties and cider.'

'Guinness and stew,' Bronagh retorted.

'But variety's everything.' Robert reached for Tressy's hand. 'I mean, in the kitchen.'

'How does it feel to be a babe magnet?' Bronagh asked.

'Oh, I'm not,' Robert said modestly.

'Everyone's noticed it,' Hattie said kindly. 'Women dream of a man who can bake like you do.'

'That's why I grabbed him,' Tressy chuckled.

'Well, I do enjoy baking. And the bake off we shared was very romantic.' Robert's eyes twinkled.

Hattie wondered if she should ask Barry to bake something. 'I suppose, in the old days, baking was a chore, something that women did for their men. Maybe that's why the women who eat your bakes feel tempted, Robert. But you've made it creative and fun. You've turned it into an art form.'

'Have I?' Robert looked to Isaac Mewton for help. Isaac rolled onto her back and put her paws in the air. It was her way of agreeing.

Bunty said, 'Our talented brother.'

'Last summer's bake off put Millbrook on the map,' Tressy mused. 'We should do it again.'

'With all the TV cameras?' Robert's hand descended to Isaac, stroking her fur. 'I'm not sure I could put myself through it.'

'Mmm.' Tressy was thinking. 'What if it wasn't you this time?'

'I can't cook for toffee,' Maeve said. 'I'd love to be a great baker.'

'Let's go.' Tressy was on her feet. 'What's it to be, Maeve?'

'I want to be a kitchen goddess.' Maeve smiled.

'I'd love to make meringues that don't collapse,' Nora said.

'Light, fluffy scones with cream,' Hazel added.

'Crumpets.' Bronagh licked her lips. 'More crumpets.'

'A Guinness cake, perhaps?' Sadie winked at Maeve.

'Right. That's what we'll do.' Tressy stood up straight. 'I have enough aprons. We're off to the kitchen dreckly to bake up a storm.'

'What about me?' Robert asked from the armchair. Isaac Mewton opened one eye suspiciously. 'Do you need me?'

'Not this time, my lover. You rest.' Tressy grinned. 'This time, sisters are doing it for themselves.'

'What shall I do, then?'

'Have forty winks,' Tressy replied. 'The sun will come out and you can go down the garden and feed the chickens and the goats. When you're back, we'll have a spread of goodies. And you can taste them all and tell us which you like best.'

29

It was an evening for announcements in the kitchen at Tails of Hope. Paul and Sadie each had something to say. But everyone wanted to eat first and discuss later. There was an empty chair next to Rory. Lola wasn't there, but nothing had been said about it. Everyone ate and chatted as usual, glad to be sharing a meal while the Aga belted out dry heat.

After dinner, Maeve clapped her hands and told everyone that she'd made her own Guinness cake and it was the best thing ever. Niall's eyes glistened with pride as his wife cut the chocolatey, fudgy sponge. Sean nudged Niall.

'You and I'll be baking next. Robert made the ladies crumpets this afternoon and he's a sex bomb all over again.'

'I want to be a sex bomb,' Pat said and Nora elbowed him so hard that his arm fell off the table.

Niall tucked into a spoonful. 'I'd marry you again for this cake, Maeve.'

'Women are worth more than the sum of their cooking ability, Niall,' Bunty reminded him.

'Yes, but this is a *Guinness* cake.' Niall licked his fingers.

'I made a little meringue this afternoon. Tressy helped me. I filled it with fruit and cream.' Bronagh grinned. 'I'd have shared it with you but we scoffed the lot.'

'Tressy's a wonderful teacher,' Maeve said. 'Before we go back to Ballycotton, there's a whole list of things I want to cook.'

Pat turned to Nora. 'Perhaps you and I can bake together, darlin'. It's very good for a marriage. We start off in the kitchen, get covered in chocolate and cake mix, eat all the goodies; afterwards we go upstairs and—'

'Nobody wants the gory details, Pat,' Nora said, cutting him off.

'I'll make everyone coffee, shall I?' Hazel asked. 'Paul, do you want to start on the announcements?'

'Thanks, Hazel, I will. So, as you know...' Paul cleared his throat '...we lost Holly today. But – there are always new animals who need a home. This afternoon, I was asked if we'd take Billy the Kid and Butthead.'

'Who are they?' Bronagh cackled. 'More donkeys?'

'They're goats,' Paul explained. 'Brothers. They're very lively, always in trouble. The owner can't keep them. Anyway, once they've been vetted, I won't turn them down.'

'That's good, isn't it?' Sadie asked. 'Troublesome goats?'

'Yes. I'd love to take even more goats.' Paul's eyes gleamed.

'Right. So tomorrow Billy the Kid and Butthead move in,' Hazel said. 'The first of all the new animals we'll welcome in over the next year. And we have so many plans to expand. As long as we can improve our fundraising.'

'And we can.' Paul gave Niall a thumbs up. 'We've had some great advice.'

'Talking of announcements, the Santa Extravaganza's on

Saturday night. We've agreed that Robert will be Santa,' Sadie explained firmly. 'The fairies will supervise and do front of house, and the reindeers will serve refreshments.'

'I'm chauffeur. I'll drive Santa to the entrance of the barn in the DeLorean,' Pat said proudly.

'And after that, you can serve refreshments,' Nora added.

'I've an announcement too.' Rory gave his usual cheery grin. 'Lola's gone.'

'I suppose it's for the best,' Bunty agreed. 'Back to Ireland?'

'No, she's gone to stay with Adam Thompson for Christmas.' Rory was delighted. 'I met him today. I took her cases over to his house. He's a nice fella.'

'Who?' Bronagh thought for a moment. 'Oh, the handsome teacher from the primary school.'

'It seems he and Lola hit it off big time at the Nativity. He invited her to stay at his house for a few days. I gave him the once-over, just to make sure he's not a serial killer or anything, and do you know, they're made for each other. It was clear as a bell. They just got on.' Rory grinned as if a satisfactory conclusion had been reached. 'He's off to his parents' place in Lincolnshire for Christmas and Lola's going with him. It'll give them time to develop – whatever it is they want to develop. I shook his hand and wished them both luck.'

'You're a gentleman, Rory.' Maeve smiled.

'Ah, no, I just wanted to see her all right,' Rory said honestly. 'I couldn't let her go without checking that she'd be fine.'

'So you'll be looking for a new girlfriend.' Niall made a mischievous face. 'Anyone in the pipeline?'

'There's no rush.' Rory winked and Poppy blushed.

'Talking of dates—' Paul was quick to change the subject '—Solly's invited us round to his house.' Paul met Sadie's eyes. 'Are you both free tomorrow night?'

'The house on the cliff,' Sadie remembered.

'I'll make sure I'm free,' Bronagh said haughtily. 'I'll just put Robert de Niro off again.'

'We'll look forward to it,' Sadie said, but she wasn't sure. The idea of a foursome made her just a little uncomfortable. As did the word *date*.

'So, tomorrow, dinner with Solly, Saturday's the Santa Extravaganza, then—' Bronagh looked suddenly unhappy. 'Then home?'

'I'll get the tickets organised,' Sean offered.

'Hang on.' Sadie held up a hand. 'I've one more announcement. Tressy and I've been talking, and Rosie Eagle's in on it now and, well, don't get the ferry tickets just yet, Sean.'

'Why?' Niall asked.

'Do tell,' Bunty added.

'We've a few more details to finalise before we're ready to tell you.' Sadie gave everyone a mischievous glance. 'You'll have to wait until Saturday, after Santa's given away his presents and the children have gone home. Then we'll do the final announcement. But I'll give you a big, big clue.' She was really pleased with herself. 'Tressy and I think we should do an enormous bake off.'

* * *

Solly's house was breathtaking. It overlooked the sea from a cliff top; one side of the building was entirely made of glass. Inside was luxurious, every detail perfect. The living room boasted a floor-to-ceiling Christmas tree with blue falling rain lights. Dozens of clusters of tiny gold stars twinkled from the ceiling. Sadie and Bronagh sat at a carved-oak table with gold candelabra. Food was served on bone china and drink in crystal goblets. In front of them was a vast view of the ocean and the night sky.

After the meal, Solly, smart in a dinner jacket, held a hand out to Bronagh, who was suitably dressed in her latest bargain from a charity shop, a long evening dress with black sequins that was two sizes too big, but she'd made it fit by cinching the waist with a huge belt.

'Please do me the honour. Shall we dance?' Solly asked as he pressed a remote. Frank Sinatra began to croon 'Strangers in the Night'. Bronagh was in his arms immediately and they began to smooch, Solly with his knees bent slightly because Bronagh was shorter.

Sadie watched Bronagh's besotted expression and reached for her goblet. Paul said, 'They look nice together.'

'Bronagh always looks nice.' Sadie smiled fondly.

'You're very close,' Paul observed.

'We are.' Sadie closed her eyes for a moment and the years flew away. 'We go back. Sadie was my best friend and now she's my sister, as good as. I don't know what I'd do without her.'

Paul watched her for a moment. 'Do you want to dance, Sadie?'

'No, let's leave them to it,' Sadie decided. 'There's only room for one couple on this dance floor.'

'Shall we take a walk?'

'Where to?'

Paul held out a hand. 'There's a room in this house where the view's spectacular.'

'Then lead on,' Sadie said.

She took his arm and they walked up a twisting flagstone staircase to the top floor. He pushed open a door to reveal a vast bedroom, an iron-framed bed, long sumptuous drapes at the window.

Sadie stopped dead. 'It's Solly's bedroom. We can't go in there.'

'Trust me, he won't mind,' Paul whispered. 'The view beyond the window is staggeringly beautiful.'

'Oh?' Sadie allowed Paul to lead her towards the drapes. He tugged a cord and the curtains opened. The entire wall was made of glass. Beyond was the ocean, little boats bobbing lights, the night sky, dark as velvet. Paul pushed open a glass door and they stepped into the fresh night air, onto a balcony. Sadie caught her breath. 'My goodness. Will you look at that?'

The breeze blew her hair gently and Paul wrapped an arm around her. Sadie registered its weight. It was strange to have another man embrace her. The bay was a shimmering semicircle below, the moonlight shading the ocean silver. Sadie whispered, 'Imagine living here.'

'Solly's house is beautiful,' Paul murmured.

'He's very rich.'

'He is,' Paul agreed. 'When I was his accountant, he only had a small plumber's shop. After I retired, he invested in storage, buying up places and renting them out. He's sold a few of them to land developers.' He gave a soft laugh. 'Solly told me earlier that the first million was the hardest to make. After that it was easy. But drink cost him his marriage. It almost cost him his health. I remember he and Marina being really good together.' Paul thought for a moment. 'He and Bronagh seem to like each other.'

'She's the kindest person, full of love. But we're going home soon.' Sadie frowned. 'I don't think you'll take the girl out of Ireland.'

'Or you?' Paul asked, his voice gentle. 'You'd never leave Ballycotton?'

'No, I couldn't,' Sadie said. 'It's too late to change.'

'Is it ever too late?' Paul replied. 'I feel fine. Especially since the heart op. I'll just keep going as I am until it stops.'

'We're lucky,' Sadie said. 'We have our families and our health. That's gold dust. That and this view.'

'I'll say.' Paul was looking directly at Sadie. 'I'm so glad we met.'

'So am I,' Sadie agreed. She liked him a lot. But – she knew the problem – he wasn't Alfie.

'Do you think after Christmas, once you've gone back to County Clare...' Paul chose his words '...could we stay in touch?'

'I don't see why not.'

'As friends?'

'I don't see why not, Paul.' Sadie met his eyes, her glance steady. 'But yes. As my mammy used to say, "May the hinges of our friendship never grow rusty."'

'That's so wise.'

'Wisdom comes with age. It usually comes a bit later than we need it.' Sadie chuckled. 'We could do with some of the wisdom we have now when we're eighteen. But there it is.'

She was smiling now; her life had been long and wonderful. She had regrets but, as the famous song said, too few to mention. She knew that however much she liked Paul, they were going to be good friends at a distance.

She took his hand. 'Shall we go downstairs and dance now? I think "Strangers in the Night" will suit me just fine.'

* * *

It was long past midnight. Sadie was in her bed back at Tails of Hope, almost asleep. Her legs ached from the dancing, standing in one position and swaying, but it had been a wonderful evening. Her body was relaxing and she was warm. Images of the view from Solly's house, the darkly gleaming bay, the shimmer of the moon on the water were still with her as her breathing became regular.

'I never thought I'd fall in love at my age,' Bronagh murmured from the bed next to her.

Sadie was still drowsy. 'What?'

'I might be in love,' Bronagh said. 'Do you think that's silly, Sadie?'

'It is what it is.' Sadie was so tired her mouth hardly moved. 'The food was good.'

'Everything was good. The house was incredible. All the big glass windows. And that view of the ocean. Imagine, Sadie, if I lived there.'

'You want to live in Dawlish? In a house on a cliff?' She snorted with admiration. 'You're something else, Bronagh Doyle.'

'Imagine if I did though. Living in a grand house like that. I'd think I was a film star.'

'You've always been a film star. Of sorts.'

'He makes me feel like Madonna, Sadie.'

'Solly makes you feel like Madonna?' Sadie tried not to laugh.

'Like I'm glamorous and young.'

'Madonna's not young.'

'Young*er*, then. And like I'm special. Like I'm a desirable, sexy woman.'

'You've always been a sexy woman.'

'I've never really felt sexy.'

Sadie chortled. 'Here we go.'

'I haven't.'

'Didn't Michael make you feel sexy?'

'Michael?' Bronagh said. 'He made me feel loved, important, and he made me feel that he couldn't live without me. But he never made me feel like I was a sex goddess.'

'But Solly does?'

'He might,' Bronagh chuckled. 'Tonight, he couldn't stop talking about the sequined dress. He offered to take me to Harrods and buy me a new wardrobe. He said I'd give Joan Collins a run for her money.'

'He said that?' Sadie was falling asleep.

'He said he'd be proud to be seen with me on his arm.'

'Bronagh.' Sadie tried her best to wake up. 'We'll be back in Ballycotton in the new year.'

'But what if I didn't go? What if I stayed in that big house? What if I lived there all the time and ate from that big table, all the china plates and crystal goblets, and looked out of that big picture window at the waves rushing in. It lifted my soul to see it.'

Sadie rolled over, opening her eyes, all patience. 'What will I do for a neighbour if you stay here?'

'Would you miss me?'

'Of course I'd miss you.'

'You could stay here. You could live in Devon. You could live with Paul in Tails of Hope.'

'Go to sleep, Bronagh.'

'I bet he's in love with you. He must be, Sadie.'

'Sleep,' Sadie said into the pillow.

'Do you think he loves you?'

'No.'

'Do you think Solly loves me?'

'I've no idea.'

'Well, am I in love with him?'

'Only you can answer that, Bronagh.'

'But what if I stayed with Solly? What if I moved into that beautiful place? What if we danced to Frank Sinatra, cheek to cheek, every night? What if? Sadie, what if? Sadie?' Bronagh rolled over, her mind filled with images. 'I mean, what if?'

Sadie had heard enough. She was snoring softly.

30

Sadie and Bronagh were exhausted all day on Friday and spent the day with their aching feet up. Sadie groaned that her gadding-about days were over, but Bronagh disagreed. 'By tomorrow, you'll be feeling like a spring chicken again.'

However, on Saturday morning, they were late for breakfast. It was past ten as they strolled into the dining room yawning, their eyes heavy, their limbs slow. Bunty was alone at the table munching a croissant. She watched as they slumped onto chairs.

'Did you ever see that film *The Return of the Living Dead*?' she joked.

'Do we look that bad?' Sadie's legs still ached. And her back. 'I'm too old to be burning the candle at both ends. I might go back to bed.'

'It was worth two days of agony though, Sadie.' Bronagh was still on cloud nine. 'I haven't had such fun since the nineteen sixties.'

Bunty and Sadie exchanged glances. Sadie asked, 'Where is everyone?'

'Down in the main barn, setting up for the extravaganza. The goats have arrived, Billy the Kid and Butthead. Sean and Niall are up there in the new arrivals' area now.' Bunty reached for the coffee pot and poured a cup each for Sadie and Bronagh. 'Rory was up at six, apparently. He and Poppy have been out feeding the animals.' Bunty lowered her voice. 'And he took her out for a drink last night.'

'So they're an item?' Sadie's face clouded; she was already anxious. 'What is it with the O'Connors?'

'What do you mean?' Bronagh asked.

'When it's time to go home to Ballycotton, there'll be a few broken hearts.'

'That's if we all go back, Sadie. We might not,' Bronagh said meaningfully.

Sadie reached for her cup. 'I'll be glad to go. This pace of life would kill me by January. All the gadding about.'

'Aren't you enjoying it?' Bunty asked.

'I am, I am,' Sadie insisted. 'We'll have a lovely time tonight and we'll make pots of money and it'll all go into the Tails of Hope coffers and we'll all be happy. Then, when we've done, we can go home.'

'What's eating you this morning?' Bronagh asked. 'You've got a proper case of the grumpies.'

'I'm still a bit tired,' Sadie mumbled.

'It's not all about Paul, then?' Bronagh nudged Sadie gently. 'I saw you smooching with him the other night.'

'I was not smooching.'

'I know what's bothering you. You're worried about leaving him,' Bronagh said, her eyes glinting. 'That's it. You're falling for him and you don't want to go home. Is that it?'

'Don't be silly.'

'It is. It is. You're having such a good time, you can't stand the thought of leaving.'

'Why don't you just shut up, Bronagh?' Sadie placed a hand over her mouth as soon as the words were out. She felt terrible. 'Oh, I'm sorry.'

'You've never told me to shut up, not in all your life, Sadie.'

'I know. I'm just exhausted. I'm sorry, really, I am.'

Bronagh's lip trembled. 'We've been best friends for ever and ever. Now you're telling me to shut up.'

'I've said I'm sorry.'

'Are you worried we'll grow apart?' A tear rolled down Bronagh's cheek. 'Is it because Solly loves me? Do you worry that he'll come between us? Because that'll never happen, Sadie – not ever.'

'I'm tired, Bronagh.' Sadie sighed, a long, drawn-out sound. 'I've just overdone it lately. Big time. Look.' She stood up, planting a kiss on Bronagh's head, and they hugged each other. 'Please, let's not row. A few weeks ago I was having a quiet life in Kildare Avenue, going to The Hole in the Wall for a half of stout at lunchtime, and now – now I'm a fundraising, life-in-the-fast-lane, entrepreneurial events organiser. It's worn me out a bit. I just need to rest.'

Bronagh's eyes met Sadie's, her own like a puppy's. 'We're still best friends?'

'We are.'

'We still love each other?'

'We do.'

'We're still Thelma and Louise?'

'For ever.' Sadie took two steps towards the door. 'But I'm shattered. I'm going back to bed to rest my aching bones, Bronagh. I'll be up and about later this afternoon and, I promise, I'll be right as ninepence. But just let me sleep, eh? Just a few hours. I'm an old lady.'

Bronagh saw the twinkle in her eye. 'Right, off you go. I'll bring you a cup of tea after lunch. By then all the hard work will be done...' As Sadie dragged herself through the door towards the steps, Bronagh called, 'I'll be here holding the fort. By myself. The grotto will look the business by the time you come down. Just leave it to us young ones.'

Bunty turned to Bronagh. 'You two are terrible,' she said. 'I just hope I have your energy when I'm your age.'

* * *

Robert gazed in the wardrobe mirror and groaned. He didn't recognise himself. He had gained several stone in weight around his middle, thanks to the padding of a feather pillow, and he'd never had a beard in his life, but the huge cotton-wool facial hair that surrounded his mouth made him feel foolish. He wondered how he would manage to speak with so much fluff in the way.

The red trousers hung from his legs, despite the belt and the sturdy boots. The hat was too big – his own hair stuck out beneath it He didn't look at all jovial. Robert thought he looked like a puny Santa. It had been a bad idea to agree to do it. Tressy had persuaded him, and Sadie.

He should have said no.

He tried a laugh. 'Ho ho ho.' It was feeble. He needed a deep belly rumble. He tried again. 'Ho ho ho.' It sounded as if he had wind.

Isaac Mewton was watching him from the bed. She had installed herself on the duvet, paws stretched out like a sphynx, and her face was a picture of disbelief. Robert turned round apologetically. 'I should have let Sean do it. Or Niall. Or Pat. I'm a terrible Santa.'

Isaac stared back as if she agreed wholeheartedly. Robert's shoulders slumped. He had no idea how he would face the rampant hordes of eager children desperate for presents. They'd be out of control in minutes, baying for Santa's blood.

Tressy bustled into the room, looking him up and down. 'Gorgeous, that's how you look.'

'I can't do it,' Robert said.

'Maybe you're right, something's missing.' Tressy looked him over again. 'I can't put my finger on what it is.'

'Please don't ask me to wear make-up,' Robert begged.

'You don't need it, my lover.' Tressy kissed his cheek. 'It feels strange, my Robert with a moustache.'

Robert said, 'Believe me, Tressy, it feels odd to *have* a moustache. And a paunch. And a huge beard.' He shrugged. 'I'm not sure I'll be a good Santa Claus.'

'Nonsense, you'll be wonderful. Right. I know what's missing. Attitude.'

'Attitude?'

'Robert.' Tressy heaved Robert's shoulders upright. 'Tell me, who's Father Christmas?'

'He's a fictitious male of uncertain age and origin, said to live in the North Pole and ride on a sleigh pulled by nine reindeers, Dasher, Dancer, Prancer. I forget the rest.'

'And what does Santa do?'

'He doesn't bake cakes.' Robert winced as he saw himself in the mirror. 'He delivers presents overnight to about two billion children, consuming sherry and a mince pie every time he goes down the chimney. He's a bit of a miracle, really.'

'And so are you.' Tressy kissed his cheek again. 'You bring happiness wherever you go. You're kind, thoughtful, talented, handsome – and you have a good heart. Now, tell me, is there really much difference between Robert Parkin and Father Christmas?'

'I suppose not.'

'So, tonight's mission, if you choose to accept it, Santa, is that you'll go to the Extravaganza with me by your side. I'm going to be your number one Cornish elf. I'm a Piskie, complete with a green suit, a red hat and false ears. I'll be beside you the whole time, and we'll make all those children happy.'

'Do you think I'll be all right?' Robert felt encouraged by her words – he might be able to do it. 'I never had any children to learn from – although I was a teacher for years, then a head teacher.'

'We've been children too. Don't forget that,' Tressy said. 'We know how it feels to be seven years old. We can remember the hope, the belief, the joy. It's up to us to make Christmas magical tonight. And you and I know all about making magic.' She took his hand. 'Remember the bake off last summer? How strong we were together? How invincible?'

'I do.' Robert's gentle eyes twinkled.

'And we made magic: scones, cakes, light as air. This is the same magic, Robert. It's just that you have different clothes on.'

Robert looked at himself in the mirror and puffed out his belly. 'Ho ho ho,' he rumbled.

'That's just perfect.' Tressy winked. 'I'd better get my Piskie costume on. Our sleigh's due to arrive at any moment.'

'The DeLorean,' Robert said, remembering. 'We'll turn up at our grotto in style.'

'We will. This is our first Christmas together.' Tressy brought his hand to her lips. 'Come on – let's go and make it the best one ever.'

* * *

The grotto looked incredible. As the sky darkened around four o'clock, Paul directed car after car to park neatly in the designated area. Excited children clambered out, holding parents' hands, skipping towards the barn that seemed to glow in the distance.

There was a huge sign that declared 'This Way To Santa's Grotto', and a pointing finger. Sadie and Bronagh, dressed as sparkling fairies, stood in the entrance, checking tickets, taking money and donated presents for charity, welcoming parents and pointing to the refreshments area.

The barn seemed to glow with magical light. The Supremes munched hay contentedly in one corner. Pi and his friends watched quietly from another. The alpacas mooched around in a small enclosure temporarily put up to enable children to pet them.

Reindeers, elves and fairies scampered around busily. Rory strutted around, handsome in reindeer costume, holding up a Polaroid camera, offering to take photos of children posing with the animals, which he would sell to their parents. Poppy and Hazel, in fairy costume, distributed information leaflets. Rory had compiled them earlier, with photos of the horses, donkeys, alpacas, chickens and the goats that had just arrived.

There were photos of the hedgehogs, who travelled the same route each night, pausing to rest in a dry area at the end of a barn, with nests of leaves and newspapers for shelter and beetles, snails and slugs to eat.

Bunty, Maeve and Nora were flitting around the barn in floaty dresses selling raffle tickets for Robert's Christmas cake. Sean and Niall were leading a team of reindeers. By some Christmas miracle, Colin and Dennis had agreed to give their time. Barry, Eric Mallory and George Tenby, wearing antlers and red noses, were selling drinks, sausage rolls and mince pies.

The children in hordes stared wide-eyed around the barn, asking to pet the animals. Poppy had set up a petting area, where

The Supremes stood quietly with tinsel around their ears. All the festive hits boomed from speakers and lights flashed and twinkled from every corner of the barn. At one end, bales of hay had been arranged in a sort of armchair, a sack of presents on either side, guarded by Solly, who appeared to be dressed as Noddy. Apparently, it had been the only costume left in the shop.

Above him was an archway of glittering lights proclaiming 'Santa Lives Here'. Solly had ordered it himself from Exeter, arranging for decorations to be delivered and put up, and presents to be wrapped and bagged. He was looking pleased with himself.

One single child's voice could be heard squealing with delight above all the music and noise. 'He's here.'

Everyone rushed for the entrance to the barn. From the distance came the throaty thrum of a sporty car engine and the strong yellow beams of headlights. Making as much noise as he could with his V6 engine, Pat roared towards the barn, turning circles, reversing, honking his horn, revving up for all he was worth. He switched off the engine by the barn door.

'Children, he's come all the way from the North Pole.' Pat, dressed as a leprechaun, was full of himself. 'And I brought him here for you on my magic sleigh.'

The children were silent. A single voice sighed. A little girl called out, 'It's Santa, Mummy – I can see him in that funny car.'

'Here he is. Father Christmas.' Pat was waving his arms, doing his best impression of a laughing gnome. The children applauded and cheered.

Robert scrambled out, followed by Tressy in a green jumper, leggings and a red hat and boots. He greeted each child as he passed, giving high fives, calling, 'It's good to meet you. Ho ho ho. Yes, you've been very good this year.'

Robert reached his throne of hay beneath the twinkling sign, and he called out, 'Right, who's first? We have everything here at Tails of Hope Farm – animals, mince pies, reindeers – and it's all about giving to others. There's something for everybody.'

There was a flash from Rosie Eagle's camera as Santa put his thumb up. The photo would make the front page of *The Chronicle*.

Sadie and Bronagh exchanged excited glances as children lined up quietly, Tressy handing the presents to the girls, Solly to the boys, Robert shaking hands and doing his best ho, ho, ho!

The two friends wrapped their arms around each other in a hug and Sadie said wistfully, 'It's lovely, isn't it, being a kiddie at Christmas?'

'It is,' Bronagh replied, squeezing her. 'But I stopped believing in Father Christmas years ago. Let's have a glass of champagne, eh? You've done a grand job, Sadie.'

31

It was ten-thirty, and Sadie felt even more exhausted. She sat at the long table in the farm kitchen, a glass of champagne in one hand, the other holding her head up. She could hardly keep her eyes open. Paul was by the Aga, speaking to the crowd of people jammed into the room, all holding up glasses. Paul wrapped one arm around Robert, the other around Solly. Niall and Sean were clapping and cheering, drowning out everyone else.

Sadie took a swig of champagne and tried to listen to Paul. Bronagh, next to her, was smiling for all she was worth.

'...a great success, and we have you all to thank for it. Robert here was a perfect Santa, and, Solly, thanks for providing the children's gifts and all the decoration.'

There was more applause, more toasting.

Hazel took over. 'Robert and Tressy and Hattie, and the Millbrook community, who provided the refreshments, I'm so grateful. People couldn't get enough of the food – we could have sold the same amount again. There were so many requests for doggy bags.'

'And so much interest in the animals.' Poppy looked almost

tearful. 'We gave away hundreds of leaflets. Everybody was asking about the website, how could they sponsor animals, and so many people asked if we had a gift shop.'

'We will, we will,' Niall said. 'I'm talking that through with Paul.'

'It might even happen next year.' Paul gave Niall a grateful look.

'Then we'll update the website tomorrow, Poppy.' Rory's gaze was soft. 'Sponsorship details, a page about the new goats, naming competitions, refreshments and gifts. And we'll put some photos up from tonight.'

Poppy mouthed, Thank you.

Rosie Eagle said, 'There will be a front-page article. And, of course, your next event, which my newspaper is sponsoring.'

'The winter bake off. You said that, Sadie.' Hazel gazed around the room. 'Sadie, Tressy, do you want to explain?'

'It's almost organised.' Sadie yawned. 'Tressy, do you want to do the big reveal?'

'I don't mind.' Tressy stood up. 'Right. I've called a meeting of the Millbrook Gardening and Baking Group for Monday night in The Pig and Pickle. We're doing a winter bake off.'

'For us?' Hazel asked.

'Yes, on behalf of Tails of Hope. We'll talk about it at the meeting.'

'But you and Robert will win everything,' Nora grunted.

'We won't be in it. But you can all enter.' Tressy smiled. 'It'll be held during the day, on Christmas Eve, in a marquee near the barn. *The Chronicle* will sponsor it. Rosie's promised there will be TV cameras and anyone local can enter.'

'Who's judging it?' Niall wanted to know.

'What's the prize?' Bunty wondered.

'What happens if nobody enters?' Nora added.

'And how will it make money for Tails of Hope?' Rory asked eagerly. 'Because that's what it's all about.'

Tressy said, 'You'll have to wait for the meeting.'

Sean squeezed next to Sadie and whispered in her ear. 'So we're not going home until after Christmas? Will I sort some ferry tickets now?'

'For Boxing Day.' Sadie groaned tiredly. In truth, she'd started to feel homesick for her own sofa, her own bed.

Bronagh waved her fingers to Solly and he blew a kiss. She put her lips close to Sadie's ear. 'Did you do this just for me, Sadie? So that my romance has the chance to blossom?'

'In your eye,' Sadie said with a single laugh.

'I think Mammy's ready to turn in. It's been a long day.' Sean looked at Sadie anxiously.

'If we're having Christmas here, we'll need pressies under the tree. We'll need to hit the shops,' Niall declared.

'And I want to see the sights,' Nora added. 'We could do a big family day out.'

Robert was still wearing his Santa Claus costume. He seemed reluctant to part with it. 'It's been a lovely evening.'

'But right now we're all asleep on our feet.' Tressy winked in Sadie's direction. 'It's time we drank up and said goodnight.'

Paul raised his glass again. 'To you all – with thanks, from my heart. You've been truly wonderful.'

* * *

The following morning, Sadie and Bronagh came down to breakfast to find Hazel clearing up plates and cups. Bronagh asked, 'Are we too late? It's only quarter to ten.'

'Everyone's gone to the barn.' Hazel looked concerned. 'I was in the kitchen half an hour ago. I heard Poppy and Rory come in

– they'd been out feeding the donkeys – and suddenly everyone was on their feet, rushing out. It seems something's happened up there.'

'Are any of the animals hurt?' Bronagh gasped.

'I don't think so,' Hazel began.

'Get your coat, Bronagh. Breakfast can wait.' Sadie was already on the move. She wanted to find out what had happened.

'Do you want eggs and coffee when you get back?' Hazel called.

'Scrambled, please.' Sadie's wellingtons, coat and scarf were on and she was already stepping out into the frost, Bronagh panting behind her.

Before they arrived at the barn where the Extravaganza had been, it was clear something was wrong. Bunty and Maeve emerged carrying armfuls of straggling fairy lights, trying to roll them up. Sean's voice was heard shouting, 'The legs are broken. But I can hammer them back on. It'll be good as new.'

Inside the barn, Sadie surveyed the mayhem, hands on her hips. Everything had been knocked over. Hay bales were broken up, fairy lights tugged down, trestle tables overturned and damaged. The last remains of the food were splattered on the ground, slices of cake, broken plates. A barrel had been knocked over and dented.

Sean and Niall were sweeping up with huge yard brooms. Rory and Poppy were raking hay. Pat and Nora were taking down strings of lights. A banner lay split and broken on the floor, proclaiming 'This Way To S-n--- --ot--'.

Paul was watching the clear-up, his arms folded. Next to him, Billy the Kid and Butthead stood innocently. They appeared to be smiling.

Bronagh asked, 'What happened here?'

'Poppy and Rory came up earlier, and these two were missing.' He trailed a hand against the goats' heads. 'They got out of their enclosure and made straight for the barn. There wasn't much food left, but they snaffled what they could. They went after the mulled cider, wrecked the hay bales, chewed the lights.'

Bronagh patted Butthead. 'They're naughty little fellas.' She gazed around. 'They've made a mess.'

'They have,' Paul said. 'It seems we have our work cut out with this pair. The last owner found them a handful.'

Sadie scratched Billy the Kid's head affectionately. 'He seems a nice little goat.'

'I don't think they are any more stubborn than any other goats. They just make mischief,' Paul explained.

'Who doesn't?' Bronagh asked, her eyes twinkling. 'We could take them back to the new arrivals' barn if you like, and give them some pellets.'

'You could,' Paul said. 'It will be easier when we get to know them. I once had a goat who'd do anything for a peanut-butter sandwich.'

'Let's get them back.' Sadie smiled. 'If I can bring up four rowdy children, I'm sure a couple of goats will be no bother.'

'I'm getting cold. There's ice in the wind.' Bronagh touched Butthead's collar with her fingers. 'Come on, sweetheart, let's go to the barn and give you some food. Afterwards, I'm off back to the farmhouse for some scrambled eggs and coffee.'

Sadie watched as Bronagh scurried away, her fingers through Butthead's collar, the little goat plodding happily next to her. She turned to Billy firmly. 'Now, come on, you. I want no trouble.' Billy stared at her for a moment, as if challenging her. She ruffled the fur between his horns and said, 'How about breakfast?' Billy almost nodded, trotting after her happily, his expression that of a goat who had never done anything wrong in his life.

* * *

That afternoon, Bunty and Hattie sat in The Brew Ha Ha café on the beachfront, staring through the window. In the distance the waves were dark and choppy. Hattie said, 'It's like a cauldron out there. I'm glad we're inside.'

Bunty tapped her hand. 'It's good to catch up though. I've missed you, Hat.'

'You too, so much.' Hattie turned to the waitress, who was hovering. 'Can we have two lattes, please?'

'And a toasted teacake. I love those.'

'Two toasted teacakes.'

'Right.' The waitress plodded away.

'She's not very busy today,' Bunty observed. 'There's no one else in here.'

Hattie stared round. A man in a tweed jacket and a cap was seated in the far corner reading a newspaper. Her eyes moved to the window. The wind whipped the sea in a swirl. 'It's nearly Christmas. I'm glad you're staying on for the big day.'

'Sean and I were talking about it. We're having a really good time. It's the break we all needed. His sister Biddy will be home for New Year's Eve – she texted him – and we'll all meet up in The Hole. So this is an adventure – Christmas in Devon. I'm loving it.'

'Sadie and Tressy are thick as thieves,' Hattie said. 'Organising the winter bake off.'

'It'll be a blast,' Bunty said. 'I might just enter.'

'Oh?'

'Perhaps Robert's skills run in the family.'

'They didn't rub off on me.' Hattie smiled. 'Tressy's been so good for Robert though. I couldn't believe how amazing he was as Santa last night.'

'She definitely suits him. The way they look at each other.'

'It's sweet.'

'And Sean and I are getting on so much better.'

'You seem closer now,' Hattie said kindly.

'We had to make ourselves talk about – you know – Danny, how we lost him all those years ago. We keep a candle next to his picture,' Bunty said. 'There were a lot of tears when we talked it through, but Sean and I are there for each other.' She glanced up as the waitress placed two long latte glasses on the table, and two plates with buttered teacakes. 'Thank you.'

Hattie couldn't help noticing that her teacake was a little charred, and the butter was claggy. Robert wouldn't have made them that way. She reached for her glass. 'This is nice though, meeting up.'

Bunty met her eyes. 'And Geoffrey's gone for ever. You must feel free as a bird, Hat.'

'I do. That man was a ball and chain. It's a pity it took me so long to realise it.'

'He wore away the person you were. But you're on top of the world. The house is sold. You have money in the bank. You have Barry...' Bunty hesitated. She was hoping Hattie would confide the secrets of her heart.

Hattie wasn't ready to share her feelings for Barry. She had to resolve them for herself first. 'The pretty house I looked at in Starcross, The Retreat, has been snapped up.'

'Oh, no.'

'Tim Evans told me someone else was interested and I put it down to tactics – him trying to get me to put in an offer. But a woman has done exactly that and it's been accepted. Apparently, she's single, just like me.' She shrugged sadly. 'Back to the drawing board.'

'But Robert's happy for you to stay on?'

'Robert and Tressy are good as gold.' Hattie pressed her lips together. 'It's Barry who's the problem.'

'Is it?' Bunty leaned forward. 'Do tell.'

Hattie took a deep breath. It wouldn't hurt to confide in Bunty. 'He's asked me to move in.'

'That's wonderful.'

'Is it?'

'Why not?' Bunty reached for her teacake and took a bite. She seemed unperturbed by the gloopy butter. 'Don't you love him?'

'I care for him...'

'Move in. Have fun. It'd be great. You'd be living in Millbrook, you could fit your piano in his house somewhere.'

'That's what he said.'

'So, why not?'

'I'm not spontaneous like you, Bunty.'

'Think things through over Christmas and move in January,' Bunty replied, as if it were that simple.

Hattie almost hugged her sister across the table. She wished she had some of her impulsiveness. But they were chalk and cheese. 'I had almost fifty years with Geoffrey. It was stifling. He was the most controlling man. I used to hear his voice in my head telling me what to do, even when he wasn't there.'

'But he's gone now.' Bunty had butter around her mouth. 'Good riddance. Bad rubbish.'

'I don't wish him any harm. But it's like I'm recovering. I can't leap into moving in with Barry.'

'Barry's not Geoffrey. He's kind and sweet and he cares for you.'

'I know. And I have deep feelings for him. Robert and Tressy met and fell in love in an instant. You and Sean are closer than ever. But I'm different. For me love is a slow-burning thing, not a hot flame to be leaped into. I want to be on my own for a while, learn who I am again, take time. Perhaps, I might move in with Barry. Or we might stay as we are.'

'But don't you get lonely at night time, in the dark by yourself?' Bunty asked. 'I love snuggling up to Sean, another warm, breathing body.'

'I like space.' Hattie sipped latte. 'I like stretching out my legs, having the whole bed to myself. Sleeping with Geoffrey was like floating in an ocean of unexploded mines. I had no idea if he'd nag or shout at me.'

'Hattie, that's awful.'

'It was. Now I'm learning about who I am, what I need.'

'I get it. Barry will have to be patient.'

'He's a good man. I've told him how I feel. The only thing is – and he has a point – I really would like to live in Millbrook. But I won't move in with him just because I love the village life. That wouldn't be fair.'

'It wouldn't. You're right. You need to wait for the answer to come – and it will.' Bunty finished her drink. 'Right. Shall we go for a walk on the seafront? I love spending time with you. That's the only problem about Ballycotton. My sister and brother are miles away.'

'Compromises, that's what life is about,' Hattie admitted. 'It's hard sometimes to make our minds up about how far we're prepared to compromise. But for now – yes, let's wrap up and go for a walk. We've a family Christmas to celebrate. And it'll be the nicest thing to spend it with you.'

32

The whole of Monday disappeared in frantic preparations for Christmas. The animal sanctuary glowed with festive promise. Solly had installed a new sign over the entrance – Welcome to Tails of Hope – and gold lights wished everyone a Merry Christmas. He had recycled all the lights from the grotto to the fences and barn entrances. The farm shone like a miracle.

The house was cosy. There were gifts wrapped in bright paper and ribbons beneath the tree; the O'Connor contingent had descended upon Exeter in several cars and bought bag loads of presents. As Niall had said, 'Let's show them all how we do Christmas in Ballycotton.'

Extra food had been ordered for Christmas dinner and, of course, extra bottles of tipple. Bronagh had put mistletoe in every corner, to encourage Poppy and Rory, or anyone else who felt the need for a festive snog.

Late in the afternoon, Sadie gazed wide-eyed at a sparkling Tails of Hope, inside and outside filled with the joy of Christmas. It was truly magical. The twenty-fifth was just days away. She was excited about the bake off, and Christmas Day, then she'd go home. She'd be back in her own house, her own bed. Surrounded by memories of Alfie and her old routine. In her beloved Ireland.

She ached for it.

You could take the girl out of Ballycotton but you couldn't take Ballycotton out of the girl.

* * *

On Monday evening, everyone trooped into The Pig and Pickle, where more Christmas lights flickered in the windows and corners. The usual members of The Millbrook Gardening and Baking Group sat around the table clutching drinks.

Rosie Eagle told everyone that she represented *The Chronicle* as a sponsor. Tressy, Robert, Paul, Hazel and Poppy sat attentively, next to Bunty and all their Irish guests.

But there were two new faces in the group. Solly, smart in a suit, sat next to Bronagh. And a confident-looking woman who might have been in her sixties, who had installed herself on the other side of Robert, crossing her legs neatly. Susan Joyce was already eyeing her suspiciously.

Susan clapped her hands for attention. 'Welcome, everyone. We're here tonight to talk about a special winter bake off. And to that end—' Susan nodded formally towards Solly '—I'd like to thank Mr Solomon Duke, a local businessman, who's stepped in as another sponsor.'

Solly glanced towards Bronagh with a smile.

'And—' Susan turned to the newcomer '—we have a new member. Welcome.' Susan sounded more suspicious than welcoming. 'We'll all introduce ourselves to you in a moment, but would you just like to tell us about yourself?'

'My name's Lydia Carrington.' The woman had a smooth-as-syrup voice. 'I've recently retired. I've just bought a little cottage in the area. I've heard good things about your group – especially about Mr Parkin.' She gave Robert a long look. 'So I'd like to be part of the baking contingent. And if there's a competition, so much the better.'

'I see.' Susan shot her a piercing look. 'Well, we need lots of entrants.'

'Of course. It's for charity,' Lydia said briskly.

Dennis guffawed. 'Well, there are about twenty of us here tonight – that's a good start.'

'But what about if we don't get many bakers?' Nora asked.

'What if we get too many?' Maeve said worriedly.

'How are we going to cook in a barn?' Bunty was puzzled.

'What if the weather's bad?' Pat wanted to know.

'Who's the judge?' Sean called out.

Rory added, 'What's the prize?'

'And how will we raise money from it?' Niall demanded.

'Nobody's baking in a barn. Shall I explain?' Tressy stood up. 'The bake off is on Christmas Eve, during the day. Solly's ordered a big open marquee to be put up outside – so we'll be fine whatever the weather – and the TV cameras will be there to record it all. Anyone who wishes to enter – entry fee is twenty pounds – can bring their cake on the morning, already baked, and the judging starts at eleven. The prize is a huge hamper, donated by Solly.'

'He's wonderful.' Bronagh patted his hand.

'What if there are a hundred cakes?' Jill asked.

'I hope there will be.' Tressy smiled. 'They'll be ranked first by appearance, then whittled down to the last eight for final judging.'

'Good,' Pat said.

'Christmas is about giving, not getting,' Sadie said earnestly.

'That's the Tails of Hope message,' Paul echoed.

'Visitors can donate. There will be leaflets and buckets to collect cash – thanks to Poppy and Rory for that. The judge won't know which cake was made by which person – and the judge will be...' Tressy turned to the reporter. 'Rosie?'

Rosie examined her notes and read aloud. '"Elspeth Croft-Sharland". That's Dame Elspeth. She lives in Budleigh Salterton. She does a column for *The Chronicle* once a month. She's a zoologist. She's written books about her conservation work abroad, helping to save endangered species. Now she's retired, she lobbies for international cooperation advocating tight border controls to stop animal trafficking.'

'She sounds perfect,' Paul said.

'But what does she know about cakes?' Bronagh asked.

Tressy ignored that and said, 'If you want to enter the bake off, you have to pay twenty pounds, tell me what cake you're baking and bring it along. After the winner's announced, slices will be sold to the public. And the huge hamper will be presented by Mr Duke.'

Solly gave a shy bow and was greeted by a round of applause.

'Robert and I will make a cake each to auction off to the highest bidder.'

Susan took over. 'The main thing is, it's all in aid of Tails of Hope, and it will be good publicity.'

'I don't know how to thank you all,' Hazel said quietly.

'We could make it an annual event,' Paul suggested. 'Once we've organised this year, it will be much easier next time.'

'Well, let's break, mingle and have a drink.' Tressy nodded to Shelley, who was ready at the bar. 'Any questions, come and talk to me, Sadie or Rosie. Or Susan,' she added, since Susan was wildly gesticulating towards herself.

'Next time we can open it up county-wide. It doesn't just have to be the people of Millbrook or the gardening club,' Rosie added.

'Your round.' Dennis turned to Colin, glancing at his empty pint glass. He lowered his voice. 'Well, what do you reckon?'

'I won't win,' Colin said. 'Women have had years of practice. And I bet all those Irish women are mustard in the kitchen.'

Bunty's ears pricked up. 'What rubbish.'

'Well, I won't be entering,' Mary Tenby said to George.

'Why ever not?' George replied. 'Can't you follow a recipe?'

'*You* follow a recipe,' Mary retorted.

'Me?' George looked astonished.

Francis was whispering to Sally. 'We could do a sponge, perhaps?'

'Not on your life. Term's finished – and so am I.' Sally held out her glass for another gin and tonic. 'And you have the church services to do.'

Bronagh tapped Sadie's arm. 'Will we do the competition?'

'No.' Sadie glanced around. She knew what was best. 'Too many cooks...' She indicated Tressy and Robert, who were in close discussion with the new woman. 'What do you suppose they're talking about?'

'Do you reckon Lydia Carrington's Delia Smith's sister? She looks like her.'

'Not at all,' Sadie whispered in her friend's ear. 'I'll buy you half of stout, Bronagh, and we can sit for a while.' She closed her eyes dreamily. 'I'm looking forward to going back to Ballycotton now. It's a lovely thing to be on your holidays. But when push comes to shove, there's no place like home.'

* * *

'Here you are, Tressy my love. Time to wind down.'

It was almost midnight. Hattie had gone up to bed. Robert brought two mugs of cocoa into the living room and sat down next to Tressy on the sofa by the log fire, stretching out his legs. Isaac Mewton immediately sprang onto his knee and began kneading the threads of his jumper. She settled down to purr.

Tressy sipped her cocoa. 'It was a good turnout.'

'It was.'

'I think we'll have a really good set of bakers.' Tressy smiled. 'But I know who's going to win already.'

'Who?'

'Lydia Carrington.'

'I didn't get the chance to speak to her. Susan and Angie buttonholed me. They wanted me to give them more jam for their sponges. But of course it wouldn't be fair to everyone else if I did that.'

Tressy murmured, 'Lydia's recently moved down from Hertfordshire. And guess what she did before she retired?'

Robert thought about Lydia for a moment. Her hair had been very neat. 'A hairdresser.'

'No.' Tressy gave him a knowing look. 'She was head of food technology at a further education college. And guess what her speciality was?'

'Teaching chefs?'

'Yes, to bake cakes.'

'If that gets out, it'll put everyone else off.'

Tressy lowered her voice. 'She asked me to keep schtum about it.'

'A food technology teacher.'

'And that's not all. She told me she's put in an offer on a house in Starcross. It's called The Retreat.'

Robert sat up stiffly. 'The one Hattie was going to buy?'

'Exactly. Not that Hattie wanted it that badly,' Tressy said. 'I don't think Hattie knows what she wants to do.'

'I've told her she's welcome to stay here,' Robert said.

'She's got big decisions to make.'

'About Barry? Do you think they'll move in together?'

'You're a wonderful man, Robert.' Tressy met his eyes. 'But sometimes I wonder how much you understand your own sister.'

'What do you mean?'

'What did you think of her husband?'

'Geoffrey Bowen?' Robert shook his head. 'He bullied Hattie. I wanted to punch him on the nose.'

'Exactly,' Tressy said. 'I only met Geoffrey once and I thought he was a miserable tuss. Hattie was married to him for a long time. He controlled her, he cheated on her. She suffered for years.'

'I should have helped her more.'

'We can help her now. I think she needs time by herself.'

'Doesn't she like Barry?'

'Of course she does. But it's not about Barry. Robert, you and I lived alone all our lives. We're independent and strong willed. But as soon as we met each other, we knew we wanted to be together. Hattie's been pinned down, like a butterfly. She wants to fly. She needs her own space.'

'How can we give that to her?'

'She'll work it out, my lover.' Tressy snuggled closer. 'In time. Hattie's a strong person. She'll decide what to do and, when she does, we'll support her. Whereas now...' She reached over and wrapped her arms around him. 'I'd say it's just about bedtime. We should finish this cocoa and go up. What do you say, Robert?'

'I think it's a wonderful idea,' Robert said, and he pulled her into a kiss.

33

'So,' Sean declared. 'We'll all be baking tomorrow. Today, let's get lost in the great outdoors.' He spooned scrambled eggs into his mouth. 'The Ballycotton invasion has arrived.'

'Rory's already gone ahead to Dartmoor,' Niall said, looking at the empty seat next to him.

'He and Poppy fed the animals, then they went out in the Ferrari,' Hazel said, pouring hot coffee. 'Rory wants to climb to the top of Haytor rock. Poppy's done it lots of times.'

'I heard there's a beautiful view from the top,' Pat said.

'We should go,' Bunty said. 'A nice walk would blow the cobwebs away.'

'It might stop me worrying about baking,' Maeve sighed. 'Tressy wants me to enter the competition, but I'll make a show of myself.'

'Not at all, you'll be grand.' Niall wrapped an arm around her. 'I'll fetch our things and wash up.'

'I'd get that in writing, Maeve,' Sadie said with a wink. 'It'd be nice to go out onto the moors though.'

'Go. You'll love it,' Hazel said. 'There are sheep, ponies, roaming free. The weather's perfect today, bright sunshine.'

'Do you want to come?' Sadie asked. 'And Paul?'

'He's having a business meeting with Solly today,' Hazel explained. 'I'll hold the fort here.'

'It's kind of you to let us borrow your kitchen to bake our cakes, Hazel.' Bunty held out her cup for more coffee. 'And I can't wait for Christmas Day. It'll be fun having Christmas here.'

'That's what I love most. A special Christmas dinner.' Sadie's eyes were misty. She had to admit she was feeling even more homesick now. 'Family and friends, gathered around the table, all the banter.'

'Can we invite Solly?' Bronagh asked. 'I don't like to think of him all alone at this time of the year.' She paused. 'At any time.'

'Great idea,' Hazel said.

Pat met her eyes. 'You do the best breakfast outside Ireland, Hazel.' He smiled as charmingly as he could. 'I couldn't have a bit more toast, could I? And if you've got a spare egg...'

'The chickens are laying well.' Hazel smiled. 'Of course.'

Nora nudged Pat affectionately. 'After Christmas, it's a diet for you. You've had far too many sweet things.'

'Eggs are protein – they're fine,' Pat protested.

'Well...' Niall stood up. 'Mammy, you and Auntie Bronagh can come in the Range Rover with us. Bring some cushions so you're comfy. We'll lead the way.'

'We know where Haytor is,' Sean said. 'We'll lead.'

'Oh no, the DeLorean should go first. We turn heads, don't we, Nora?' Pat insisted.

'We'll take turns,' Bunty said, making peace.

'It's nice to take time off.' Bronagh's eyes gleamed. 'Tomorrow will be so much fun.'

'It will,' Sadie agreed.

The whole jaunt to England had been wonderful and she'd never forget it. But right now, age and sentiment had caught up with her. Her own house in Kildare Avenue was waiting. It held the faint scent of Alfie, and all her memories. It was where her heart longed to be.

* * *

Hattie sat at the organ in St Jude's, practising for the carol service. She played all the favourites that she knew the congregation would love to sing: 'In the Bleak Midwinter', 'O Little Town of Bethlehem', 'Joy to the World'. She was note perfect. Just for the fun of it, she tried other pieces she liked: 'Jesu, Joy of Man's Desiring', Bach's *Toccata and Fugue in D minor*, 'Jerusalem'. The richness of the melodies moved something in her soul as each note resonated, drifting towards the church roof, filling the space with a feeling of hope and joyfulness.

She played on, wondering how she'd tell Barry that she didn't want to move in with him. She imagined his face, the affection, and how the hurt would fill his features. She had never met such a nice man, and she was truly fond of him. It wasn't that she didn't want to be with him, or that she'd never change her mind. But now she needed time alone. At this moment, the time she spent by herself revitalised her and made her the person she really was.

She began to play Schubert's 'Ave Maria'. As the music swelled, she felt a surge of positivity. She'd find her own place. Ideally, she wanted to stay in Millbrook. But the situation would resolve itself. She just needed to be patient.

The last few notes bubbled and rose on the air, then the church was filled with silence.

From the aisle, a beautiful voice rose, singing 'O Holy Night'.

Each note was pure, each word crystal clear, like an angel singing praises from the heart. Hattie listened. A guitar began to thrum softly. She knew exactly who it was.

She stepped down from the organ to where a young woman in a black lace dress was singing. Her hair was longer than it had been last summer, but it was still shaved at the sides, and she had a few more piercings. The man beside her was tall and skinny, in black jeans. Hattie was delighted to see them both.

'Tilda. You're back from London. Donkey! Good to see you both. How's the residence in the jazz club?'

'It's going well.' Tilda grinned. 'We're home for Christmas.'

'We've got a recording contract too, with Guy Fallon of Rhythm Café Records. He's signed us for an album.' Donkey hugged her. 'You look well, Hattie. And the music sounded great.' Hattie was reminded what a lovely young man he was.

'I bet Sally and Francis are glad to see you both,' Hattie said.

'We've only just got back. We came straight over – Dad said we had to ask you.' Tilda's words rushed out with excitement. 'Donkey and I would like to do O Holy Night as a duet tomorrow.'

Hattie was delighted. 'That's wonderful.'

'And we wrote a jazz song specially. Do you think we could do that as well?' Donkey asked. 'It's called "Kinda Christmas". It's about spreading love across the world.'

'I can't wait.' Hattie clasped her hands. 'What does Francis say?'

'He says he's put you in charge of music.' Tilda smiled.

'Let's do your own composition as the final piece, shall we?'

'That would be cool,' Donkey said.

'I'm so pleased to see you.' Tilda threw her arms around Hattie. 'It's been ages since the bake off. So much has happened.'

'Let me buy you both a drink in The Pig and Pickle,' Hattie

suggested. 'You can tell me about what you've been up to in London. And talking of bake offs, I have some news for you.'

* * *

Sadie and Bronagh were huddled in the Range Rover in the car park across the road from Haytor. They were wrapped in blankets, watching the others move like tiny flies up the mound of the hill towards the rough outcrop of rocks. The DeLorean and Sean's Peugeot were parked next to the Range Rover, and Rory's Ferrari was only a few cars away. Sadie imagined Rory and Poppy at the top of the craggy rock, their arms around each other, looking across the vale towards the sea at Torbay. She decided that it was romantic but there was no way in the world she'd ever get up there. Bronagh spoke her thoughts aloud.

'I'm not walking in the cold. I'd freeze to death in that wind.'

'So would I,' Sadie agreed. The soles of her feet ached. 'I've done nothing but walk since we've been in Devon. My ankles are like puffy balloons.'

'At our age we only go downhill.' Bronagh took a deep breath. 'Well, we're stuck in this car. What mischief can we get up to?'

'We've nowhere to go.' Sadie looked around. 'I can't see us getting into any mischief.'

'What if a couple of handsome fellas came along?'

'I thought you were all loved up with Solly.'

'I am. Well, I was. I don't know. It's a holiday romance. I can't take him back to Ballycotton in my pocket, can I?'

'You can't break his heart though.' Sadie thought how vulnerable Solly was now: he was lonely. It wouldn't be fair for Bronagh to take advantage.

'No, I won't. I'll make sure of it. He's been through plenty. But I was thinking – you and I might just share a small...' Bronagh's eyes twinkled as she tugged a bottle of Guinness from her coat pocket. 'Sean has no idea I lifted it.'

'Well done, Bronagh. Did you bring an opener?'

'Of course.' Bronagh produced one from her pocket and whipped off the crown cork. 'Did you think I'd use my teeth?' She took a deep swig and handed the bottle to Sadie. 'Ah, that's good.'

Sadie wiped the top with her hand and swallowed a mouthful. They'd done exactly the same thing at seventeen years old in short skirts and stilettos, outside The Hole in the Wall. It felt nice, sharing the bottle, as if it were a bond between them. She passed the bottle back. 'My mammy gave me a mouthful of Guinness when I was twelve years old and got my first period,' Sadie said. 'It didn't help with the pain, but it gave me a taste for the black stuff.'

'You were twelve before you had Guinness?' Bronagh marvelled. 'I was eight. My da wasn't looking and I guzzled what he'd left in his glass while he'd gone to the jacks. When he came back I was roaring laughing and I fell over. My da gave out to me for hours, but it was worth it.'

Sadie stared out of the window. It was blustery outside, but it was picture beautiful. Soft mossy green grass led uphill to a huge mountain of rough granite, smaller fragments scattered around like giant's pebbles. Beyond, the sky was azure, filled with lambs' tail clouds. 'How long do you think all these rocks have been here?'

'Hundreds of years. I heard Niall say they were walking near a quarry.'

'It's beautiful rolling countryside,' Sadie said. 'It reminds me of home. I'm a home-bird.'

'You've enjoyed being here though.'

'I have.'

'But you're ready to go home.'

'Yes. After we've done the bake off.' Sadie raised an eyebrow. 'Are you baking a cake?'

'Me? No.' Bronagh made a face. 'I'm not confident.'

'About baking.'

'About anything.'

'For the love of God, Bronagh – I've learned a few things about you that I never knew before this holiday,' Sadie joked. Then she was immediately serious. 'You keep telling me you've no confidence, but you're the bubbliest person I ever knew.'

'Am I?' Bronagh seemed surprised.

'Of course you are.'

'No, I'm not.' Bronagh sniffed. 'My mammy told me I was ugly.'

'She did what?' Sadie's voice rose indignantly.

'When I was a kiddie I was very small, with knocked knees. He was a good-looking man, my da – thick hair, a strong physique. And my mammy was bonny. She was slim and all the men had the eye for her. She used to say about Keith – he was three years older than me – "He's the good-looking one," she'd say. "Keith should've been the girl, with those curls and the long eyelashes. You'd win no prizes for that face, Bronagh."' Bronagh sniffed. 'Keith's gone now, five years ago, God rest him.'

'Your own mother said that about you?'

'She thought I was uppity and it would make me behave.'

'She didn't build your confidence.'

'She didn't.'

'She was wrong though.' Sadie wrapped a protective arm around her friend. 'You're beautiful.' She planted a kiss on her forehead. 'There. That's for you.'

Bronagh turned tear-filled eyes towards Sadie. 'You're just the best.'

'And so are you, every day of the week.' Sadie heard the noise of an engine rumbling, coming to a halt in the car park. 'Well, would you believe that? It's a burger van.'

'We'll treat ourselves to a burger,' Bronagh said. She found her handbag and began to wriggle from the car. 'Do you think they take real money here in Devon? Or is it all cards and crypto?'

'Or groats?' Sadie followed Bronagh towards the van. The wind blew her hair and wriggled inside the folds of her coat, making her shiver. Bronagh grabbed her arm. They stood by the burger van, their hands in their pockets, as they had done as children in Ballycotton.

Bronagh said, 'What'll you have?'

A young man appeared. He was blonde, blue eyed, with a charming smile. That was all Bronagh needed. She patted her hair and said, 'What have you got for two young ladies with free time on their hands?'

Sadie gently elbowed her aside. 'Do you have the burgers with onions and cheese and ketchup?'

'I do,' the young man said. 'Two, is it?'

'Yes, please.' Sadie watched him while he flipped the meat. She handed him a note. 'I'm surprised to see a burger van here in the middle of winter.'

'It's the school holidays,' the young man said. 'I'm a student at uni. It's my dad's van. I usually do a good trade with tourists.'

'We're tourists. We're from Ireland,' Bronagh said proudly and took her food eagerly. She bit into the burger, tasting the tomato sauce squelch. It was strangely comforting.

'I've never been,' the young man said.

'You should. It's full of Guinness and good-looking women,' Bronagh told him.

'I'm gay,' the young man said.

'Good-looking men too.' Bronagh had the answer ready. 'Do you sell lots of snacks this time of year?'

'I sell all sorts,' the young man said. 'Teas, coffees, crab sandwiches.'

'Ooooh, crab sandwiches?' Sadie's eyes shone at the thought. 'When did I last have a crab sandwich?'

'We'll have a picnic in the car.' Bronagh opened her handbag and brought out a purse. 'Two rounds of crab sandwiches and two scalding teas with milk and sugar.' She held out two notes. 'Hold the scalding. Make them molten. It's Baltic here.'

'Coming up,' the man said, and busied himself in the back of the van. He returned with two china mugs and plates. 'Here you are, ladies. Can you bring the crockery back, please?'

'We will, we will.' Bronagh met his eye. 'It's nice to see you serve food up properly. Not in those plastic foam cups that are bad for the planet.'

Sadie was licking her lips. 'We should have had the sandwiches first.'

'It all goes down the same hole,' Bronagh said. 'Come on, Sadie, let's get back to the car before we freeze.'

They huddled in the back seat, eating sandwiches, sipping tea. 'This is heaven,' Bronagh said. 'Sadie, I'll never forget these good times.'

'Nor will I.' Sadie let out a slow breath. She was feeling emotional. 'It's the simple things. Friends, food, being spontaneous.'

'And red-hot tea.' Bronagh smacked her lips. 'Is that our mob coming down the hill? They seem to be moving a bit quickly.'

'They do. And it is.' Sadie caught her breath. 'I think something's wrong with Pat.'

'He's limping.' Bronagh shoved the last of the sandwich in

her mouth. 'Quick – eat up. If he's hurt himself, he'll want our sandwiches.'

Bronagh's logic escaped Sadie. 'The van's still there. They can buy their own. I'm worried about Pat.'

Niall and Sean ran towards the car, their arms around Pat, who looked sorry for himself. Nora, Bunty and Maeve followed behind. They appeared to be uninterested. Sadie inspected Pat. He was shrieking and shivering, making a fuss. His clothes were wet through. She opened the door. 'What's happened?'

'We had a grand walk beyond the rock to the quarries,' Niall said.

'We picked up a railway track,' Sean added.

'It was gorgeous there,' Bunty explained.

'The Haytor quarry pond was all iced over. Pat walked on it to see if it would break.' Maeve looked unimpressed.

'And it did,' Nora said. 'We had to pull him out, the eejit.'

'I'm freezing.' Pat's teeth chattered and water dripped from his head and his clothes.

'Here, we have blankets somewhere.' Sadie was out of the car, covering Pat tightly so that just his red face stuck out, giving orders. 'Put him in the DeLorean. Nora, you can drive him back to Millbrook.'

'Can we stop in an alehouse on the way?' Pat was shaking. 'Just for a medicinal brandy?'

'We'll get you in a hot bath,' Niall said.

'I might get hypothermia,' Pat wailed.

'You'll get no sympathy from me.' Nora kissed his face. 'Come on, you muppet, let's get you back.'

'We can drop the crockery off in the burger van on the way,' Bronagh said.

'And get Pat a hot drink,' Sadie added.

'Time to go home,' Niall said. He pointed towards the Ferrari.

'I haven't seen anything of Rory. I suppose he's still at the top of the tor.'

'He's courting,' Sean spluttered.

'Best of luck to him.' Bronagh grinned. 'She's a nice girl, Poppy. They'll be all right.'

'It looks like the real thing to me,' Sadie murmured wisely. 'I wonder how on earth we'll persuade him to go home.'

34

The next day, Wednesday, there was mayhem in the farmhouse kitchen. So many people were baking, weighing ingredients, fussing with cake tins, greaseproof paper and melted chocolate. Maeve was puzzling over calculations. Bunty declared she needed more space because Pat had spread all his ingredients out. Pat was clad in a pink apron, asking everyone how to make zest of lemon. Rory was with Poppy in the corner, whispering and canoodling as if he had all the time in the world. He hadn't started baking yet. He claimed he could do it blindfold.

Sadie and Bronagh watched with amusement, then they sought refuge at Robert's house. Niall gave them a lift there – the temperature was raw outside, the coldest it had ever been, and Bronagh said they'd be like snowwomen by the time they arrived. Sadie had had enough of walking. But it was cosily warm at Robert and Tressy's, the log fire crackling in the hearth, Christmas lights winking, the scent of cinnamon and nutmeg hanging on the air from baking.

Sadie settled herself in the conservatory on Robert's

armchair and Isaac clambered on her knee. She stroked her fur and felt immediately relaxed. 'What a little sweetie.'

'Where's Hattie?' Bronagh asked.

Tressy eased herself down on the floor, a sheet of paper in front of her. 'She's gone to see Barry. She'll do one last rehearsal in the church, and they're off for lunch at The Pig and Pickle.'

'Do you need any help?' Sadie asked.

'We're just going through the list of entrants. There are so many,' Robert said, lifting a pen. 'Look at all the cakes, Tressy.'

'All these people? Who are the local ones? Ah. Dennis Lyons, triple-chocolate cake. Susan Joyce, passion fruit and pistachio – why am I not surprised?' Tressy said. 'Angie, white chocolate. Bunty, toffee apple. Pat, lemon drizzle. Rory, polenta.'

'A polenta cake's difficult,' Robert said. 'Good for him. Who else do we know?'

'Lydia Carrington's baking a chocolate chiffon cake with salted caramel buttercream. And Maeve O'Connor, chocolate Guinness cake.'

'I don't suppose any of them will win,' Robert sighed. 'There are entrants from all over – Exeter, Dawlish and Teignmouth.'

'I'm glad Maeve put an entry in.' Tressy smiled. 'I'd have invited her here to bake, but it might look like favouritism. Hazel must have a house full.'

'And the marquee's going up as we speak,' Sadie added.

'Tonight's the carol service.' Robert yawned. 'I'll be tired afterwards.'

'You can't lie in tomorrow morning,' Tressy said affectionately. 'The TV cameras will be here at seven, and so will Rosie.'

'I said I'd see Solly at nine,' Bronagh muttered from the sofa.

'I hope it all goes well for Paul's sake.' Sadie stroked Isaac again, feeling the comforting softness of her fur. 'He was a bit quiet at breakfast this morning. I think he's worried about tomorrow.'

'I get that,' Tressy murmured. 'What if the public don't turn up? I mean, at this time of year, people prefer their own homes and the TV. Tails of Hope will look proper daft if the competition doesn't have an audience.'

'Do you think that might happen?' Robert looked worried.

'It might,' Tressy said.

'But the newspaper was full of the event,' Bronagh remembered.

'People can be hard to predict,' Tressy observed. 'You might get three stragglers and a dog. And if it's cold or raining, we might not get anyone at all.'

Sadie shuddered, suddenly nervous. 'What if it's a flop?'

'We'll make it work. Proper job.' Tressy's eyes twinkled.

'I hope so,' Robert said anxiously. 'The TV cameras will draw a crowd, surely? I'll ask Francis to announce it tonight at the service.'

'The church might be empty.' Bronagh stretched in her seat. 'It's nicer by the fireside. I might just stay here and snooze until Christmas Eve pokes its head around the corner.'

'We're going to the carol service,' Sadie said determinedly. 'And we'll be there tomorrow for the bake off. We won't let anyone down. And if you're feeling tired, Bronagh, why not have forty winks now?'

'I will, I will.' Bronagh made herself comfortable, tucking her legs beneath her, and closed her eyes. 'It's so homely in here, I could just drop off.'

'How about I make cinnamon lattes? After that, we can go outside and feed the animals. Goatsby has a proper appetite on him at the moment. He'll bite your hand off for a carrot.'

'I'd like to feed him,' Bronagh offered. 'I'm getting so fond of all the animals. I've no idea how I will say goodbye to Pi.'

'Or Solly?' Sadie asked, a little surprised by Bronagh's fickleness.

'Of course, Solly too.' Bronagh's eyes began to close. 'Yes, I have some things I need to say to him before I go back to Ballycotton.'

* * *

Everyone was dressed warmly against the sharp air as they hurried into St Jude's. Francis was at the door, welcoming everyone warmly. There wasn't a single star in the sky.

Sadie and Bronagh, sharing the same hymn sheet, sang their hearts out. Behind them, Sean's deep baritone was the loudest voice in the church, Bunty and Nora warbling on either side of him, Pat singing for all he was worth, Maeve doing her best, faltering on the high notes. Rory and Poppy stood next to Hazel, singing the carols holding hands, oblivious of everyone else. Hattie belted the chords out from her lofty position on the church organ.

Bronagh turned to Sadie towards the end of the service. 'Well, I feel festive now. I hope the vicar has some mulled wine.'

'And a mince pie.' Sadie was suddenly peckish.

'He has,' Tressy said from their left. 'Robert and I brought a batch up.'

'Paul said his kitchen looked like a bomb site today,' Bronagh said. 'Pat's lemon drizzle drizzled everywhere.'

The gentle strum of a guitar sounded and a young man in black took his place at the front. A young woman stood beside him, dressed in a grey frothy dress, all tulle net. She clasped her hands and began to sing 'O Holy Night'.

'Oh.' Bronagh had tears in her eyes. 'What a voice.'

'It's from heaven, to be sure.' Sadie closed her eyes and let Tilda's voice take her somewhere beautiful. It was Christmas and she thought of all her blessings. Home. Family. Friends.

There was a pause. Donkey played a delicate chord as Tilda began another song. This time the guitar was stronger and her voice more bluesy. Sadie listened to the words, about people being kinder, about hope for the future, about treading gently on the earth. A few words lingered in her mind.

While some live on handouts, others eat caviar
the spirit of Christmas hasn't come so far.

Sadie sighed. They were the naïve words of a young singer, but there was truth in them. She had lived a long time. She'd seen many changes in her life, some wonderful, some less so. But some things were still the same. Poverty had a different face now, but people were still poor. She wondered if things would change for the better after she'd gone. Probably not.

She felt a hand reach for hers, take it in cold fingers and squeeze it. She turned to Bronagh, a tear glistening on her face. They were having the same thoughts.

At the end of the service, Francis stepped up to make a brief announcement.

'On behalf of all at St Jude's, I would like to wish you a peaceful and blessed Christmas. Let us hold a moment in our hearts for those less fortunate at this time of year...' He paused for reflection. 'I wish you all a safe return home, wherever home may be. But if you have time before you go, I'd like to invite you to join us for a glass of something and a mince pie.' He said, 'And if you have a free moment tomorrow, why not pop down to Dawlish beach for a breath of fresh air and watch the bake off, which begins at eleven o'clock? It promises to be quite an exciting event and it's all in aid of our local animal sanctuary, Tails of Hope.'

There was a ripple of applause and a rush for the refreshments, led by Pat from the pews behind Sadie. She turned to Bronagh. 'Give me a hug.'

Bronagh hugged her. 'And thank you.'

'What for?'

'For another year of being the best person in my world.'

Sadie squeezed her tightly. 'Love you.'

* * *

Hattie was sitting at the church organ, staring at her stiff fingers. Playing hymns, concentrating hard, had left her feeling tired. But she had been note-perfect. She thought about playing some background music, something fitting while everyone nibbled mince pies, but she was bushed. She clambered down from her perch to find Barry holding out a cup. She took it gratefully and sipped spicy wine. 'Thank you.'

'You were wonderful.' He pecked her cheek.

'And so are you,' Hattie said, thinking that he had the kindest face. 'We're meeting up tomorrow?'

'Yes, at the bake off. I have to dash off to my son's in Exeter for the rest of the day.' Barry examined Hattie's face. 'But you and I might be having Christmas in our own home next year.'

'We might.' Hattie felt suddenly very tired. Right now she wanted to be tucked up in bed, asleep. But Barry's hopeful smile filled her with affection. She kissed him. 'Thanks for being patient. You know – about me deciding where to live.'

'It's no hardship,' Barry said. 'You and I have each other, wherever you decide.'

A young man's voice came from behind her. 'Hattie, I just wanted to tell you. The organ playing was grand.'

Hattie turned to see Rory, his arm around Poppy.

'It was the best carol service ever,' Poppy said.

'Thanks.' Hattie put a hand to her head, as if dizzy.

'Are you all right?' Rory asked, all concern.

'Tired. Playing has taken it out of me,' Hattie said. 'I put my heart and soul into it.'

'Shall I walk you home?' Barry asked.

'I don't want to put you out. It's cold,' Hattie began.

'I'll drive you back in the Ferrari. It won't take a minute,' Rory said. 'I've a polenta cake to make when I get back.'

'Haven't you baked yet?' Hattie asked.

'I'm a night owl.' Rory shrugged as if it were nothing. 'And it'll be quiet in the kitchen. I like it there when there's just me. And Poppy. We'll have a glass of wine and I'll throw my lemon polenta together.'

Hattie glanced at Barry. 'I think it might be nice if Rory took me back. I'll see you tomorrow.'

'Right.' Barry kissed her cheek again. 'I'll look forward to it.'

'She just wants a ride in the Ferrari,' Rory joked. He embraced Poppy briefly. 'I'll pick you up back here in a few minutes.'

Hattie noticed the easiness between them, the trust. She wondered if they'd stay in touch when Rory left for home. After just a few days they seemed close. What did Shakespeare's character say in *Twelfth Night*? 'Even so quickly may one catch the plague?' It was so easy to fall in love. Hattie smiled at Barry, hugged him and set off for the door.

Hattie and Rory stood outside the church and caught their breath. The ground was covered in a blanket of glistening snow, and the skies were full of it, fat flakes twirling like fine feathers.

She lifted up her face and let the cold drops spatter on her cheeks, her lashes. The softness of it felt wonderful, tender as light fingers.

Rory put an arm around her. 'Here's our white Christmas.'

'Can you drive in this weather?'

'The Ferrari practically does it by itself.' Rory's hair was covered in soft flakes, a dusting that reminded Hattie of a halo. He led her to the Ferrari, parked across the road, and helped her inside.

They drove slowly to Robert's house, the windscreen wipers swishing, snow twizzling in the headlights beyond, gleaming against the black sky. In minutes, Rory pulled into Robert's drive. 'Here we are.'

'Thanks, Rory. I'll see you tomorrow at the bake off.'

'You will.'

'Good luck.' Hattie patted his hand. 'I hope your baking goes well tonight.'

'No worries.' Rory took a deep breath. He had something to say, but he'd take his time. 'Robert's house is lovely, isn't it? If I was going to buy somewhere in the country, it would be something like this.'

Hattie turned to him, wondering if he already had plans. 'Are you looking for property?'

'Always. I'm a property developer. That's what Da and I do in Dublin,' Rory said in his carefree way.

'Of course.'

'You're looking for somewhere though? My Grandmammy said—' Rory asked.

'I am. But there's nowhere I can afford in Millbrook.'

Rory burst out laughing. 'In your eye is there nowhere, Hattie. You're looking straight at it.'

'What do you mean?' Hattie asked. 'Robert's house?'

'Look at that wall on the side of the house. What do you see?' Rory wriggled down in the driver's seat and made his fingers into a camera lens.

'A wall.' Hattie was puzzled. 'Leading to the garden. Robert's living room's just behind it.' She tried harder. 'Snow's coming down thick and fast.'

'I see an extension.' Rory waved his arms dramatically. 'A big open-plan kitchen-diner, a garden room coming off it. And upstairs, a master bedroom with an en suite, a Victorian bath, a dressing room, French windows, even a balcony.'

Hattie put a hand to her face as if she'd been stung. 'What are you saying?'

'I'm wondering why you'd waste your money on another house when there's a perfectly good one here with lots of space for an extension of your choice.' Rory shrugged. 'You'd have your own place in Millbrook, a garden. Robert's house would increase in value. He'd have you as his neighbour to feed the goats when he and Tressy swan off to Cornwall. Everyone's happy. Bob's your uncle and Fanny's yer aunt.'

'Oh, Rory.' Hattie breathed out in excitement.

'That's my name.'

'You're a genius.'

'I am,' Rory said, feeling pleased with himself. 'Do you know any good builders locally?'

'Danut and Joey. They built the patio last summer.'

'That's good to know. Talk to Robert and Tressy, and talk to your builders. It's the perfect solution. Why not build one to your own specifications? That way, the builders get work and everyone's happy.'

Hattie's eyes shone. 'I think Robert and Tressy would love that. And so would Barry.'

'And you too?' Rory asked. 'That's what's most important.'

'It is,' Hattie said. 'When did the young get so wise?'

'We all have our moments.' Rory grinned. 'And then we go off and disappoint our parents by acting the goat.'

'Thank you,' Hattie said, kissing Rory's cheek.

'For the lift?'

'For the advice.' Hattie opened the car door. The snow was swirling outside. The lights were all on in Robert's house. It gleamed like a festive scene from a Christmas card. 'You're a star, Rory.'

'I am, I am,' he agreed. 'Now I have to go back and bake a star cake. Jack of all trades, that's me. Goodnight, now, Hattie. I'll see you tomorrow.'

35

It had snowed heavily overnight. Now, at nine o'clock on the morning of Christmas Eve, it was still snowing, thick flakes twirling fast. It had settled all over Tails of Hope, across the fields, on barn roofs, on the top of the marquee. Solly had arranged for twinkling red and green lights to be put up in the shape of the words 'Winter Bake Off in Aid of the Tails of Hope Animal Shelter'.

Snow had even settled on the peak of the cap worn by Ike, the TV cameraman who was setting up and ordering everyone around while sipping from a mug that read 'I love cakes'.

The animals were stirring in the fields and barns. They knew something was happening today. The Supremes were braying louder than ever. Pi and the other horses grouped together, swishing manes and snorting. The goats were scurrying around and alpacas had pricked up their ears. People were already arriving in small numbers and were immediately drawn to the animals. It was rumoured that the judge was here; she was going to judge the cakes on 'aesthetic merit' before picking the finalists to taste.

Sadie stood next to Paul at the entrance to the marquee, surveying an anonymous line of almost a hundred cakes, bright as jewels. She couldn't believe what had started as a small idea had actually blossomed. 'Paul, I'm gobsmacked. Look how well it's all turned out.'

'Do we know which one belongs to which baker?' Paul asked.

'It's top secret.' Sadie felt overwhelmingly pleased with herself. 'But I know which ones are ours. Come and look.'

Every cake looked impressive. Pat's lemon drizzle had white icing smoothed on top. He'd even piped two pretty green holly leaves and red berries. Sadie thought Bunty's toffee-apple cake looked inviting, with its white chocolate icing and caramel centre. Susan Joyce's passion fruit and pistachio brimmed with fruit and nuts. Angie Pollock's gateau looked spectacular. Rory's polenta cake was syrupy and tempting, and even Dennis's triple-chocolate cake was iced smoothly, crowned with walnuts.

But, Sadie thought, the two cakes that caught her eye were Maeve's dark chocolatey Guinness cake and Lydia Carrington's chocolate chiffon cake, which looked as if it had come straight from the patisserie kitchen of a top hotel. She crossed her fingers behind her back and hoped. Maeve had put her heart and soul into it.

'Lydia's cake's so light, but look at Maeve's...' Sadie wanted to stick a finger in and try a bit.

'I just met Lydia. She seems very nice.' Paul indicated Solly and Bronagh, who were currently deep in conversation with her. 'She's fitting into the community well.'

Sadie watched them for a while. Lydia was dressed in an expensive coat, a luxurious cashmere scarf tied neatly, her blonde hair smooth beneath a furry hat. She seemed to be regaling Solly and Bronagh with a fascinating story. She waved leather-clad fingers, doing all the talking; Solly and Bronagh were listening intently, their mouths open. Solly, Sadie noticed, had a different sort of smile on his face.

More people arrived, and even more. Leaflets were given out, donation buckets rattled, new volunteers signed up, and cheery music blared through speakers. The competition was about to begin and Sadie felt her pulse quicken. It was all going to go even better than she'd hoped. And the snowy setting was to die for.

'It's almost eleven. The judge is picking the finalists. I hope they'll hurry up about it – it's not warm.' Sadie glanced around the marquee. Rory and Poppy were dressed up as donkeys in brown suits and long furry ears, accosting passers-by, offering them leaflets, shaking buckets to encourage donations. A crowd had gathered despite the whirling snow, so many people huddled in warm clothes, watching the cameras, and the technicians calling out instructions.

Ike, the TV cameraman, was waving a hand at a smart man in a camel coat who held a microphone and looked important. Solly was still smiling at Lydia Carrington as Bronagh joined Sadie. She pointed down the path towards a field that was being used as a car park. It was full. More visitors were coming in droves.

'The O'Connors are doing a grand job, Sadie. Look.'

'We always do, Bronagh.' Sadie watched the Irish reindeers, out in full force. Pat, Nora, Niall, Maeve, Sean and Bunty were wearing antlers, stopping passers-by, shaking money buckets, directing them towards the marquee.

Paul looked suddenly emotional. 'I can't thank you enough, Sadie and Bronagh. You've done so much.'

'We've loved it,' Sadie said and meant it. A lump of uncontrollable emotion swelled in her throat. Alfie would be so proud of her project-management skills.

No, he'd always been proud of her, whatever she did.

'Giving is rewarded by the heaps of love and satisfaction you get back in return,' Bronagh replied. 'It's the real meaning of Christmas, giving from the heart.'

'It is,' Sadie said and a single tear fell. She didn't bother to wipe it away. She'd done more than she'd ever thought possible. Sadie O'Connor, a mammy from Ballycotton, was capable of so much...

'Excuse me.' The well-modulated voice belonged to a tall, slim lady in a belted woollen coat, her soft white hair tucked beneath a black beret. Sadie assumed she was around her age; she had the air of a well-educated spy. 'You must be Paul Sullivan?'

'I am.' Paul extended a hand politely.

'From Tails of Hope?' the woman asked.

'That's right. This is Sadie and this is Bronagh.'

'Pleased to meet you both,' the woman said. 'I hope you can assist me, Paul. I'm judging here today. I'm Elspeth Croft-Sharland.'

Sadie weighed her up. She'd be a good judge. She looked as if she'd stand for no nonsense.

'Elspeth, of course it is.' Paul was all smiles. 'How can I help?'

'I want an assistant to stand by me when I inspect the cakes, to witness that I'm doing it fairly and without any knowledge of which is which. You're perfect, as the owner of the sanctuary. It will put you in the spotlight too.' She took his arm. 'The cameras are rolling right now, recording the action, so we'll be filmed as we judge. Would you mind?' She turned to Sadie and Bronagh. 'Can I steal him from you for a moment?'

'He's all yours.' Bronagh grinned. 'Just make sure you pick the right cakes for the final.'

'I don't bake,' Elspeth said wickedly. 'I'll just pick a few out and taste the ones I like the look of, then I'll decide which is best.' She almost winked. 'It's a ludicrous idea for me to judge at all, to be honest. I'm not a great cake-eater.'

'But you know all about animals, and that's what today's about,' Sadie insisted.

'That's right.' Elspeth smiled through perfect lipstick.

Sadie watched Elspeth lead Paul towards the trestle table that contained eight cakes. The suave man in the camel coat was talking to the camera, surrounded by a fascinated crowd.

'Good morning and a very merry Christmas from a snow-covered Tails of Hope Farm.' He glanced up as the flakes continued to tumble. He brushed at his shoulders to show that it had settled thickly there. 'And I'm Simon Harmer, here to tell you all about the big bake off that's happening right now. This part of Devon is famous for its competitions. Only last summer, there was a Devon versus Cornwall cream-tea face-off here, that many of you will have seen,' he said. 'Now the Winter Bake Off is under way, judged by local celebrity and animal activist, Dame Elspeth Croft-Sharland. There are ninety-eight cakes under scrutiny, all of them looking incredibly tempting. But which of these delicious delicacies will be chosen for the final? And which one will win the day?'

Another cameraman edged forward, clearly zooming in on all the cakes. Simon paused. Ike gave him a nod and he spoke again. 'Dame Elspeth will now select the cakes she wants to taste. Then she will try a bit – she can't eat them all.' Simon gave a small chuckle. 'Afterwards, she'll retire to consider her judgement, and we'll be straight back for the announcement. The whole event is in aid of the Devon animal sanctuary, Tails of Hope. And now I'm going to meet local businessman and entrepreneur Mr Solomon Duke, who is a one of the sponsors of this event.'

Ike turned the camera on Solly, who was waiting nearby.

Sadie noticed that Lydia Carrington stood a few steps away, watching intently, her hands clasped. Elspeth was still judging, studying each entry carefully, her head close to Paul's as he pointed to each cake in turn. She selected one every so often, and it was removed and placed on another table.

After a long deliberation, she had chosen eight cakes. Paul cut small portions for her as the camera followed them, and she nibbled a morsel delicately from a fork, as if analysing.

Sadie felt a light touch on her shoulder and whirled round. Bronagh did the same. Robert, Tressy, Barry and Hattie were standing behind them, dressed warmly. Their matching Santa hats were topped with dustings of snow. Behind them, the farm was busy, visitors leaning over fences, arms stretched, to touch the animals. Others were donating money, watching the event in family groups, in pairs, with dogs on leads, many wearing Santa hats and Christmas pullovers.

'It's going better than we dared hope,' Robert said. 'I just bumped into Sean. His bucket's brimming.'

Tressy squeezed his arm. 'This takes me back to last summer, when we first got together.' Her face shone with happiness. 'It's been such a good year.'

'For us all,' Barry said with a faraway smile.

'Who do you think will win, Robert?' Hattie asked, hugging Barry's arm. 'You and Tressy are experts.'

'Once the finalists are chosen, it depends how the cakes taste,' Robert said. 'Texture's important. Flavour combinations that work. But on appearance alone, the chiffon cake Lydia made looks really professional.'

'She seems to be getting on well with Solly,' Tressy noticed.

'I introduced them.' Bronagh was pleased with herself. 'She's retired here for a fresh start after a messy divorce.' She nudged Sadie. 'I'm sure she'll get on with Solly.' She noticed Sadie staring at her, confused. 'We're going back home soon. We can't help the poor man from Ballycotton.'

'You're right – we can't.' Sadie wanted to hug Bronagh.

'So, who'll win?' Tressy asked. 'A fiver in the Tails of Hope bucket says that it's Maeve's Guinness cake.'

'I think Bunty's looks nice,' Hattie said loyally.

'Pat's lemon drizzle,' Sadie suggested.

'I'll go for Dennis's triple-chocolate cake, 100-1 outsider.' Barry looked doubtful as he added, 'It might. You never know.'

'Lydia's chiffon cake, every time.' Bronagh was sure. 'I spent half the morning talking to her. She has a good sense of humour – I like her.'

'The polenta cake's risky,' Robert said. 'It's hard to get the batter right. It can be too wet, too thick, too gritty.'

'Chocolate wins every time,' Tressy said. 'It's just human nature.'

'People eat with their eyes,' Sadie agreed.

'And their tummies,' Bronagh said.

Back inside the marquee, the judging had finished. Ike the cameraman was organising people in a line: Simon Harmer, Dame Elspeth, Paul, Solly. The crowd were closing in and the snow was tumbling even faster. The skies opened, goose feathers twizzling down from heaven.

'There's Hazel with Rory and Poppy.' Sadie waved them over.

'There's Dennis,' Barry said. 'With Colin and Eric Mallory and The Pig and Pickle crowd.'

'And Francis and Sally – and Tilda and Donkey,' Hattie called out.

People pushed closer. Susan Joyce and Angie Pollock found themselves next to Robert, taking up position on either side. Susan ignored Tressy, threading her arm through Robert's. 'Do you think I have a chance to win? What's your opinion of my passion-fruit cake...?'

'If you were judge—' Angie patted his back '—you'd pick my gateau, wouldn't you, Robert? Wouldn't it appeal to you, on a sensual level?'

'But passion fruit and cream,' Susan insisted. 'Now, that's really sexy food.'

'Well...' Robert seemed flustered for a moment '...I'm glad I'm not judging.' Tressy winked complicitly and took his spare arm.

A pack of reindeers appeared from the far field, tossing their antlers. Sean and Niall bounced towards Sadie. Sean hugged her with both arms. 'Are you warm enough, Mammy?'

'I'm grand.'

Niall grabbed Bronagh. 'All good with you, Auntie Bronagh?'

'Grand too.'

'Look.' Sadie was excited. 'It's time for the big reveal.'

Rory, Poppy and Hazel took their places next to Hattie as Simon Harmer addressed the crowd. 'Now, ladies and gentlemen – the cakes have been tasted, the judging has been done and we have a winner.'

Hattie noticed someone she knew in the crowd and waved in recognition. 'It's Danut, with his wife and family – he's our builder. I must go and have a word afterwards, and wish him a merry Christmas.'

'I'd like to meet him myself,' Niall said. 'It's always good to know a good local builder.'

Simon stared into the camera, his face serious to show that the judgement had been made. Elspeth was poised on his right, Paul beside her. Solly was positioned to his left. Ike waved a hand, a signal to begin.

'Dame Elspeth has made up her mind. We have a winner.'

Simon turned to Elspeth dramatically. 'And I believe it was a really close thing.'

'It was. The standard's very high,' Elspeth said confidentially. 'But I got it down to three cakes. All quite delicious.'

The crowd was silent, standing together, shoulder to shoulder. Some people huddled outside, beyond the marquee, where the snow continued to tumble from the pale sky as if it would never end. Simon coughed politely and said, 'So, could you give us the results of the Winter bake off, in reverse order?'

'It would be my pleasure.' Elspeth spoke into the camera. 'There are so many talented bakers in Devon. I wish I could have tasted every cake. The ones I sampled were delicious. I'd be proud to have made any of them myself. But in third place, I chose a cake that was simple, tasty, but had a perfect texture. It would be ideal for a Sunday tea, and I'm partial to lemon drizzle. Third place goes to – Mrs Margaret Smedley.'

Someone clapped politely behind Sadie and a woman gasped, 'Oh, that's me.'

Pat could be heard saying, 'Well, can you believe it? It was a lemon drizzle, just like mine.' He hugged the dazed and smiling Margaret, yelling, 'Here's to all the lemon drizzles in the world.'

Simon held up a hand. 'Now for second place. Dame Elspeth?'

'It was close. But in the end, I knew which one had to be the winner. So, in second place... well, I have to say, I've never had this cake before. But I'll certainly be having it again. It has Irish beer in it.'

Sadie heard Maeve gasp behind her. Her own heart lurched in anticipation. She crossed her fingers and held her breath. The crowd was silent.

Elspeth continued. 'And what a rich, delicious flavour all that

Guinness and chocolate bring to the mix. Second prize goes to Maeve O'Connor.'

Maeve slumped against Niall. Sadie turned to look, delighted: Maeve was in tears, her arms around Niall, who was blubbing too. Tressy kissed Robert; she grabbed Maeve, kissed her as well and they both shrieked 'Woo-hoo' and leaped up and down, Tressy yelping, 'I told you that you could bake. I told you. I told you.'

Sadie felt her throat swell with even more emotion. Everything was perfect. Cakes like studded jewels in a necklace. Maeve holding up a medal. The snow was whirling so thickly that it was hard to see the white canvas of the marquee behind Simon. He raised his voice for the finale. 'And so, we arrive at the moment of truth. The winner of the Winter Bake Off is...'

Elspeth paused for effect. She was a true professional: she turned to Paul triumphantly and back to the camera. 'Simon, I'm delighted to say that the winner is a cake so moreish that I could have eaten it all. The texture was to die for. It was sweet and yet crumbly. It tasted of home, of sunshine, of honey and lemon and, to be honest, I've never had one before, but I'll certainly ask this baker for the recipe.'

Sadie turned nervously to Bronagh, who mouthed, Lydia...

Elspeth continued, 'And it appears our winner is from a very talented baking family. His mother, Maeve, just gained second place. So – the winner of the Winter Bake Off Competition is...' Elspeth said. 'Rory O'Connor and his polenta cake.'

The crowd cheered and roared; Niall did a little dance of joy. 'That's my son. My son Rory. And that's my wife, Maeve,' he told everyone. Maeve was sobbing more than ever. Rory lifted Poppy up and kissed her. Pat, Sean and Bunty started to sing 'We are the Champions.'

Sadie swallowed the lump in her throat. She couldn't help

the tears that tumbled as Rory somehow made his way to the front of the huddled crowd and Elspeth kissed his cheek. He turned to the TV camera, waving and acting the goat, and kissed Elspeth back, then he kissed Paul, Solly and Simon. Solly gave him a sash to wear, Bake Off Champion, and Rory punched the air in delight. The O'Connor men hoisted him onto their shoulders and began to whoop.

Simon was speaking to Solly again, saying something about how nice it was for the community to come together in support of a good cause at Christmas, a time of joy and giving, how the public could sponsor an animal at Tails of Hope. Solly was explaining how he was an official sponsor, how he and Paul were going to make Tails of Hope the best sanctuary.

It was Elspeth's turn to talk to the camera about the wonderful job Paul and his family were doing, how all animals were dependent on humans to fight their corner. She was always looking for a good cause to support and she'd agreed to become a patron.

Then Ike shouted, 'Cut,' and told his crew that the recording was almost done, the programme would be edited and shown later in the week.

Sadie turned away, pushing through the crowd. Her heart was thumping too hard, her thoughts crowded. She needed space to breathe – the excitement was brimming over. Her work was done, and the relief made her legs wobble. Bronagh noticed and followed, taking her arm, hugging up. They walked across the squelchy snow-piled grass towards the fence where Pi was grazing quietly.

Sadie wiped her tears away and tried to disguise the wobble in her voice. 'Well, that worked out all right.'

'It did,' Bronagh agreed.

'It's snowing harder than ever.' Sadie looked up and was

blinded by the damp whiteness that dropped against her face and melted instantly. 'It's lovely.'

'It is, Sadie.' Bronagh snuggled closer for warmth. 'I think we should go back to Paul's for some lunch. I'm starving.'

'And we're going home on Boxing Day,' Sadie said with relief. 'I'm just about ready.'

'Me too.'

There was a shriek behind them. Sadie and Bronagh turned at the same time to see Lydia Carrington rushing towards them, her furry hat bobbing.

Bronagh put her lips next to Sadie's ear. 'Oh no. The cooking teacher didn't win. Do you think we'll get a rollocking?'

'How can we? It wasn't our fault,' Sadie said anxiously.

Lydia caught up with them, her cheeks ruddy above the cashmere scarf. She took both of their hands. 'I wanted to catch up with you again – before you went back to Ireland.'

'Oh?' Bronagh eyed her suspiciously.

'It's been so much fun to be part of this.' Lydia was breathless. 'I came to the meeting in the pub as a complete stranger.' Her grip tightened on Sadie's hand. 'But I've met so many people doing this competition. And you've really made me feel welcome. I'm moving to a sweet little house in Starcross, but I think I'll be spending a lot of time in Dawlish and Millbrook.' She gripped Bronagh's hand. 'Thank you, Bronagh, for introducing me to Solly. He's a lovely man and we get on so well. In fact, he's invited me to his house tomorrow for Christmas lunch. We're going to cook it together.'

'Has he? He was invited to the farm. He clearly has other fish to fry...' Bronagh lifted an eyebrow. She winked at Sadie and turned her full attention back to Lydia. 'You'll love his house on the cliff. All the glass windows. The view's stunning. And you'll get on lovely, the pair of you.'

'We will,' Lydia said.

'I thought you'd be grumpy because you didn't win.' Sadie was a little mystified. 'Your chiffon cake was beautiful.'

'It's not important.' Lydia was still smiling. 'At the end of the day, Elspeth was judge. It's subjective. And it was lovely to see Rory win. I know my cakes are to die for. So why would I care? Life's too short.' She looked back over her shoulder. 'I need to get back to Solly. But I just wanted to say – it's been so nice to meet you.'

'My pleasure.' Bronagh shook her hand. 'Have a grand life.'

'And when we're down again, we'll be sure to catch up with you,' Sadie said warmly. 'Or pop round with Solly tomorrow evening for drinks. I know Paul'd love to see you both.'

They watched Lydia hurry back to the crowd, and Bronagh pulled a shocked face. '"When we're down here again," Sadie? What was that about? Are you planning another visit?'

'No, I'm not. I'm looking forward to being back in my own home, with my own armchair and my own TV and my own mug.' Sadie took her arm and they began to walk back to the crowd, where the Irish reindeers seemed to be doing a lot of dancing and prancing. 'But we're welcome here. So, the next time you decide to hit Partlan Brown in the face with a shop-bought Guinness cake, and our Rory leaves his Ferrari outside the pub, well, it'll be nice to have somewhere to escape to.'

It had been a wonderful day. Sadie was proud, emotional and exhausted. She met Bronagh's mischievous glance and burst out laughing. 'What?'

36

Sadie woke late on Boxing Day. Bronagh's bed was empty, her suitcase packed, various bags containing presents she'd received, clothes from charity shops. But she was nowhere to be seen. Sadie remembered they'd stayed up until late last night, drinking, talking, the O'Connors, Paul's family, Solly, who'd arrived with Lydia, toasting the future, friendship. She'd had a few glasses of port, a few mince pies. She'd been elated, congratulated. But most importantly, she'd proved something to herself.

She eased herself out of bed, aching, and staggered towards the shower. Niall had said that the ferry had been booked for the night crossing from Holyhead. They'd leave after breakfast, take the journey slowly, stop somewhere for lunch. A nice hot shower now would get her through the day.

She tiptoed down the stairs. The house was quiet. In the kitchen, there was no evidence of the aftermath of Christmas Day. The room was spotless. Paul was sitting at the table, drinking coffee. He looked up. 'I'm on breakfast duties. Can I get you some scrambled eggs?'

Sadie patted her tummy. 'I'll just have a slice of toast, Paul. Yesterday was a busy day. But the Christmas dinner was lovely.'

'The whole day was lovely.' Paul's eyes shone as if tears glimmered.

'And the bake off was wonderful. We had such a blast.' Sadie recalled the emotions and tears pricked again.

'Solly's going to sponsor us. And Elspeth's our new patron.'

'That's wonderful.' Sadie sat down and Paul placed a mug of steaming tea in front of her.

'I have to tell you.' Paul looked momentarily uncomfortable. 'Elspeth and I get along really well. In fact, I'm meeting her this evening.'

'That's nice.'

'You don't mind?'

'Why should I mind?' Sadie was bewildered. 'I want you to be happy, Paul.'

'That's exactly what Bronagh said to Solly,' Paul said. 'She encouraged him to ask Lydia out.'

'They'll make a lovely pair.' Sadie smiled.

'You're a special lady.' Paul turned from the toaster.

'You should thank Partlan Brown,' Sadie remembered, thinking about how she and Bronagh would tease him in a few days' time in The Hole. 'We wouldn't be here if he hadn't chased us out of Ballycotton like Thelma and Louise.' She saw Paul's puzzled expression. 'No, it's been a blessing, Paul. Being here with you and the animals, meeting Solly and Hazel and Poppy.'

'You're welcome, any time.' Paul placed a rack of toast in front of Sadie. 'Niall and Rory paid me for the family's stay this morning. And Niall's been very generous with helping me cost out some developments. I don't know how to thank your family enough, Sadie.'

'We've had a grand time. It won't be the last you'll see of the

O'Connors. We're related to half of Millbrook anyway.' Sadie glanced around. 'Where is everyone?'

'Outside with the animals,' Paul said, returning to his coffee.

Sadie was suddenly filled with an overwhelming sentimental sadness, which surprised her. Didn't it always happen, when it was time to leave? She tried a joke to ease the ache just below her heart. 'Perhaps we should arrange another baking competition? The Pig and Pickle versus The Hole in the Wall.'

'That would be a fun night,' Paul agreed. 'I'd certainly be up for a visit.'

'But you have the animals to think of first.' Sadie smiled. 'They're what this was all about. And we did what we wanted to do. Yes, we did good. And now's the time to go home.'

* * *

Rory and Poppy had just fed the alpacas. Normality had almost returned to Tails of Hope. The marquee was dismantled now. The snow in the fields had turned to slush and water drip-dripped from the barn roof. People were bustling, packing equipment in vans.

Rory was still grinning over his prize-winning polenta cake. He bent down to pick up a bucket and when he stood up, Poppy's face was covered in tears.

'What is it?' he asked, pulling her into his arms.

Poppy sniffed into his shirt. 'Christmas was wonderful.'

'It was.' Rory drew her closer, feeling the cold of the tip of her nose against his neck. He kissed it. 'Do you think it'll snow again?'

Poppy shrugged. 'Will it snow in Ballycotton?'

'I doubt it,' Rory said. 'But I won't know, will I?'

Poppy looked suddenly surprised. 'Why?'

'Because I'm not going back.'

'What?'

'I'm staying on.'

'Where?'

'Here, on the farm. Or with Robert. Or in the village pub. I don't care. But I'm not going home.'

'Why?'

'All the questions, Pops.' Rory kissed her lips. He couldn't help smiling. That warm feeling engulfed his heart again. 'I can work remotely. Besides, there's the animals to think about. And the craic. And you.'

'Me?' Poppy shook her head in surprise.

'And anyway,' Rory laughed, 'I've a project I need to supervise.'

'What project?' Poppy was completely confused now. But a smile appeared on her face.

'Da and I have spoken to two local builders, Danut and Joey. They're going to build a café.'

'Where?'

'Here, by the barn. Where the marquee was.'

'Can we afford it?'

'Da and I can. We're sponsoring it. It'll be called Wendy's Café and Gift Shop.'

'After my grandma. Does Grandad know?'

'Da's telling him now.'

Poppy was still baffled. 'How will we staff it?'

'My grandmammy and Auntie Bronagh spoke to the village baking group and they're all up for volunteering. Susan, Angie, Dennis, Colin, Eric, Mary, Robert, Tressy, Hattie, They'll all bake cakes and make sandwiches and sell gifts. Tressy said she'd help manage it because she ran a teashop in Cornwall. She's grand.'

'Oh, Rory.' Poppy slumped against him. 'I can't thank you enough.'

'I did it for you,' Rory whispered into her hair. 'For us.'

Her arms tightened around his neck. She was sobbing now, but they were happy tears. 'And you're not leaving?'

'How can I leave?' Rory murmured, and the realisation hit him. 'It's you and me, Poppy. For the long run.'

* * *

Sadie wrapped warmly and ventured outside. It had stopped snowing, but the wind was raw, whipping settled flakes into the air. Bronagh was where Sadie knew she would be, by the horses' field, her arm around Pi's neck.

Pi was still and stoic as she rubbed his nose. 'I'll miss him, Sadie,' Bronagh mumbled. 'He's been my favourite.'

'He's a handsome boy.'

'He gets me. We've both lived our lives. We're both out to grass and, in our way, we've both been winners.'

'You have.' Sadie wrapped an arm around Bronagh. 'You have a lot in common with him. Strong, intelligent,' she said. 'Stubborn. Resolute.'

'It's been a good Christmas.'

'It has.'

'I spent a while talking to Solly and Lydia last night,' Bronagh said. 'Did you know they're an item?'

'They'll be good company for each other.'

'They will.' Bronagh linked an arm through Sadie's. 'I'm ready for Ballycotton.'

'Shall we go inside, in the warm?'

'We're leaving in an hour,' Bronagh said.

'What about Rory?' Sadie asked. 'It'll be hard for him to leave Poppy.'

'He's not coming.'

'He's not?'

'No. He's staying on for the New Year celebrations. I think Poppy's going to have a week off, and they'll go to Dublin for a bit.'

'I see.' Sadie stared up at the sky. She wasn't surprised. 'Do you think it'll snow again?'

'The sun's trying to come out.' Bronagh tugged Sadie's arm. 'Let's go in. It's time.'

'It is.'

* * *

An hour later, the Range Rover, the Peugeot and the DeLorean were packed, ready to go. Robert, Tressy, Hattie and Barry had arrived to wish them goodbye. They had hugged, promised to keep in touch, and now it was that awkward time between staying and leaving.

Tressy held out a container. 'There's Christmas cake, and a few scones I knocked up.'

Hattie hugged Bunty for the third time. 'We must come up and see you.'

'You must.' Bunty's eyes gleamed. 'I'll miss you, Hattie.' She turned to Robert. 'It's been so nice.'

'It has.' Robert had never been comfortable with goodbyes. 'You're always welcome.'

'And when you come next time—' Hattie clutched a paper tissue to her face '—I may be in my new home. Danut and Joey, the builders, are coming round in the new year to discuss an extension on Robert's place. I saw Danut yesterday at the beach and he was really keen.'

'And they're building a café for us too.' Paul's eyes shone. 'Wendy's.'

'It's perfect.' Barry wrapped an arm around Hattie.

There was a shout from the house as Rory and Poppy ran towards the group, hand in hand. Rory said, 'I thought we might have missed you.'

'Not at all.' Niall gripped Rory and Maeve in one bear hug, their eyes brimming with emotion.

Maeve mumbled into Rory's jacket, 'We're champion bakers, you and me. It runs in the family, son.'

'It does. I'll see you soon, Mammy.' Rory kissed her cheek. He took a step back and wrapped an arm around Poppy. 'I messaged Erin to say we'll be at The Hole in The Wall sometime in January. She's coming back for New Year.'

'It'll be nice to see her and John,' Maeve said.

'We'd better get off to the ferry soon.' Sean took Bunty's hand. 'We don't want to be rushing.'

Sadie embraced Rory and felt him plant a kiss against her hair. 'Thanks for the loan of the Ferrari,' she murmured, clinging to him one more time. He'd always been her favourite. That kind heart, that smile. Just like her Alfie. It was hard to let go...

'Any time, Grandmammy.'

'I loved driving that car.' Bronagh's eyes twinkled with mischief. 'I loved all the shenanigans. But it's time to go.'

'It is,' Sean reminded them.

'Group hug.' Tressy threw her arms round. 'Our story doesn't end here. We'll be back for second helpings.'

'We will, for sure,' Sadie said as she felt herself squeezed against the cold, an armful of warm bodies surrounding her and pressing together as one family. She took one last look back at Tails of Hope, then she clambered into Niall's car.

* * *

New Year's Eve in The Hole in the Wall was already becoming lively, and it was only nine o'clock. Bertie 'the Banjo' Boyd was playing 'Take Me Home Country Roads', and everyone in the pub was singing along, glasses held high. Partlan Brown was tapping his feet. Erin and John, back from their camper-van travels, were sitting with Niall and Maeve, drinking Guinness, their faces shining. Pat and Nora were at the bar with her sister and brother-in-law, Biddy and Bryan Hooper, who looked sun-kissed and healthy from their Spanish visit.

Bunty and Pat came back from the bar with a tray of drinks, depositing two halves of stout in front of Sadie and Bronagh, who wore a new pair of glasses with scarlet frames. She also had on her favourite black sparkly dress and red shoes. Her purple and silver hair piled, she looked the picture of glamour. Sadie told her so.

'You're on form tonight, Bronagh. Looking grand.'

'It's New Year's Eve and I'm loving it.' Bronagh glanced round the bar. 'Oh, look – there's Partlan in a green suit, like the bee's knees. Do you think I'll get a kiss off him at midnight?'

'Partlan?' Sadie had just taken a good gulp of stout. 'You're pulling my leg. You want to kiss Partlan Brown?'

Bronagh's eyes were roving round the bar again. 'What about Bertie Boyd? He's a good banjo player. What if he snogs as good as he plays?'

'He's had three wives. His track record's not great.'

Bronagh's gaze swivelled again. 'There's nobody else here for us. Everyone's with a partner or they're too young or, well, some of them you wouldn't touch with a bargepole. Look at yer man in the raincoat over there. He's a serial killer if ever I saw one.'

'Bronagh, that's evil. The poor man's just come out of hospital after a triple bypass. He has every right to look a bit the worse for wear.'

'What about Ryan the landlord? I like to watch him. He has a nice bum.'

'He's married, Bronagh. To Emma. She's lovely. And we don't look at men's bums.'

'Don't we?' Bronagh met Sadie's eyes. 'Well, look at Maeve and Niall, how happy they look now. The trip to Devon really cheered her up. Niall says she baked another cake today.'

'And it's put a glow on Bunty's cheeks too. She and Sean are all loved up tonight.'

'And Pat and Nora, at the bar. They look well. And it's good to see Erin and John back home.'

'And Biddy and Bryan,' Sadie said fondly, waving her fingers in greeting towards her daughter.

'They've got a lovely tan on them.' Bronagh made a cheeky face. 'Maybe we should go to their place in Spain next year. We could find ourselves a couple of handsome Spanish fellas. They'd be called Carlos and Angel.'

'Just like the alpacas.'

'I bet they'd snog like alpacas too. Carlos and Angel.' Bronagh raised her glass. It was almost empty. 'Pat, Nora, can you get us another one in, please?'

'I miss Rory, though,' Sadie said sadly.

'I do. It feels funny, his Ferrari not being outside.'

'He's where he should be though, Bronagh. With Poppy.'

'I know. And he can work from anywhere. As long as he has his laptop.'

'I think they're a match made in heaven, Rory and Poppy. Like me and Alfie. And you and Michael.'

'Ah, we're grand, Sadie.'

'We are.' Sadie winked. Her heart brimmed with love.

Bertie the Banjo began to play 'Whiskey in the Jar' and the voices in the pub rose in a chorus. Bronagh began to jig where she sat, her dress twinkling with every movement. She grasped Sadie's hand. 'I just want to dance wherever I hear this song. It's just one of my favourites.'

'Mine too,' Sadie said. She stood up. 'You and I are dance partners, Bronagh.'

'Dance partners, sisters-in-law, best friends for ever,' Bronagh said. 'Louise and Thelma.' She threw back her head and sang, 'Whiskey in the jar-oh.' She met Sadie's eyes. 'So, Sadie. Will we, or won't we?'

'Why not?'

'On New Year's Eve?'

'We should. Why wouldn't we?'

'Just like being teenagers.'

'We can do it, Bronagh.'

'In front of everyone? A big knees-up?'

Sadie raised an eyebrow. 'I don't see that as a problem. If you'll give me a hand to get up.'

'Well, I'll give you a hand up if you give me a leg up,' Bronagh said. 'Go on, go on.'

'I will.' Sadie wrapped her arms around Bronagh and heaved her out of her chair. As always, she was offering both love and support. And it always came back at her in double measures, she knew that.

Bronagh stretched upwards, standing tall, shaking her shoulders. 'Ah, that feels better.'

'What about me?' Sadie called, and Bronagh held out a helping hand.

'Come on up. I've got you.'

'You have.'

'My hips are a bit sore. And my leg's gone to sleep.'

'No, I've got you.'

'You have. And I've got you. Come one. Let's shake a leg.'

The music grew louder in The Hole in the Wall. The whole pub was in uproar, everyone clapping, cheering, stomping and belting out every word as Sadie and Bronagh danced and sang where they stood, waving their arms, shaking their legs and singing 'Whiskey in the Jar-ohhh' for all they were worth.

* * *

ACKNOWLEDGEMENTS

I'm forever grateful to Kiran Kataria and Emma Beswetherick, whose warmth, professionalism and kindness are second to none.

Thanks to the incredible team at Boldwood Books; to Amanda and Marcela and Wendy and Nia, to the brilliant designers, editors, technicians, voice actors.

Special thanks to the wonderful Sarah Ritherdon.

Thanks to Rachel Gilbey and Love Book Tours, to so many incredible bloggers and fellow writers. Your support is precious beyond words.

To the kind people who support what I do – to Martin, Cath, Avril, Rob, Tom, Emily, Tom's mum, Erika, Rich, Kathy N, Julie, Martin, Steve, Rose, Steve's mum, Jan, Rog, Jan M, Helen, Pat, Ken, Trish, Lexy, Rachel, John, Nik R, Pete O', Chris A, Chris's mum, Katie H, Shaz, Gracie, Mya, Frank, George, Stacy, Maggie, Fiona J and Jonno. I love you all.

To Peter and the Solitary Writers, my indispensable writing buddies. I always look forward to our precious time together.

Also, huge thanks to my neighbours and the local community, especially Jenny, Laura, Claire, Paul, Sophie, Niranjan and all at Turmeric Kitchen.

Love and huge respect to Ivor Abiks at Deep Studios and to Darren and Lyndsay at PPL.

Love and hugs to my family, to Ellen, Jo, Jan, Lou, Harry, Chris, Angela, Robin, Edward, Tess, Daniel, Catalina.

So much love to my mum – it's all because of you, Mum – and my dad. Irene and Tosh. I miss you both more than I can say.

Love to our Tony and Kim. Let's go barging again soon. And all the love in the world to my wonderful kids, Liam, Maddie, Cait, Joey.

And always, best love to my soulmate, Big G.

My warmest thanks always to you, my readers, wherever you are. You make this journey special.

ABOUT THE AUTHOR

Judy Leigh is the bestselling author of *Five French Hens, A Grand Old Time* and *The Age of Misadventure* and the doyenne of the 'it's never too late' genre of women's fiction. She has lived all over the UK from Liverpool to Cornwall, but currently resides in Somerset.

Download your exclusive bonus content from Judy Leigh here:

Visit Judy's website: www.judyleigh.com

Follow Judy on social media:

 facebook.com/judyleighuk

 x.com/judyleighwriter

 instagram.com/judyrleigh

 bookbub.com/authors/judy-leigh

ALSO BY JUDY LEIGH

Five French Hens

The Old Girls' Network

Heading Over the Hill

Chasing the Sun

Lil's Bus Trip

The Golden Girls' Getaway

A Year of Mr Maybes

The Highland Hens

The Golden Oldies' Book Club

The Silver Ladies Do Lunch

The Vintage Village Bake Off

The Golden Gals' French Adventure

The Silver-Haired Sisterhood

The Silver Ladies Seize the Day

Golden Girls on the Run

The Morwenna Mutton Mysteries Series

Foul Play at Seal Bay

Bloodshed on the Boards

The Cream Tea Killer

THE SHELF CARE CLUB

The home of Boldwood's book club reads.

Find uplifting reads, sunny escapes, cosy romances, family dramas and more!

Sign up to the newsletter
https://bit.ly/theshelfcareclub

www.ingramcontent.com/pod-product-compliance
Lightning Source LLC
La Vergne TN
LVHW030916080826
845145LV00013B/2917

* 9 7 8 1 7 8 5 1 3 2 6 1 2 *